Erica James is the author of twenty-six internationally bestselling novels, including most recently *An Ideal Husband*. Her books are loved by readers looking for beautifully drawn relationships, emotionally powerful storylines and evocative settings.

A keen gardener, Erica lives in Suffolk and has a growing obsession for doll's houses. She is also a keen follower of F1 motor racing and, when possible, loves travelling to Japan and the US to see her sons.

Also by Erica James

A Breath of Fresh Air
Time for a Change
Airs and Graces
A Sense of Belonging
Act of Faith
The Holiday
Precious Time
Hidden Talents
Paradise House
Love and Devotion
Gardens of Delight
Tell It to the Skies
It's the Little Things
The Queen of New Beginnings
Promises, Promises
The Real Katie Lavender
The Hidden Cottage
Summer at the Lake
The Dandelion Years
The Song of the Skylark
Coming Home to Island House
Swallowtail Summer
Letters from the Past
Mothers and Daughters
A Secret Garden Affair
An Ideal Husband

The FOREVER HOME

ONE PLACE. MANY STORIES

HQ
An imprint of HarperCollins*Publishers* Ltd
1 London Bridge Street
London SE1 9GF

www.harpercollins.co.uk

HarperCollins*Publishers*
Macken House, 39/40 Mayor Street Upper
Dublin 1, D01 C9W8, Ireland

This edition 2026

1
First published in Great Britain by HQ,
an imprint of HarperCollins*Publishers* Ltd 2026

Copyright © Erica James 2026

Erica James asserts the moral right to be identified as the author of this work.
A catalogue record for this book is available from the British Library.

HB ISBN: 9780008703516
TPB ISBN: 9780008703523

Set in Meridien LT Std by HarperCollins*Publishers* India

This novel is entirely a work of fiction. The names, characters and incidents portrayed in it are the work of the author's imagination. Any resemblance to actual persons, living or dead, events or localities is entirely coincidental.

All rights reserved. No part of this publication may be reproduced, stored in a retrieval system, or transmitted, in any form or by any means, electronic, mechanical, photocopying, recording or otherwise, without the prior written permission of the publishers.

Without limiting the exclusive rights of any author, contributor or the publisher of this publication, any unauthorised use of this publication to train generative artificial intelligence (AI) technologies is expressly prohibited. HarperCollins also exercise their rights under Article 4(3) of the Digital Single Market Directive 2019/790 and expressly reserve this publication from the text and data mining exception.

Printed and bound in the UK using 100% Renewable
Electricity at CPI Group (UK) Ltd

For Samuel and Edward and Ally, and my very grandest of grandchildren.

Chapter One

It was Saturday afternoon and one of those enchanting June days when the air was heavy with a languid sense of time standing still.

With what felt like a huge effort, Cassie Henshaw roused herself from the cushioned comfort of her sun lounger and reached for the tumbler at her side. Much as she would have liked it to be a glass of perfectly chilled chardonnay, it was in fact nothing more intoxicating than sparkling water with elderflower-flavoured ice cubes and a slice of lemon. Once again, she was on a mission to cleanse her treacherous body and shed some unwanted pounds. In all likelihood, it was a futile exercise but one she was duty-bound to pursue, as when the summer came to an end, so would her thirties.

Okay, it was really no big deal embarking on a new decade; forty wasn't exactly the end of the road, was it? No, far from it, it was something to be celebrated. But for some reason there was a teeny part of her that felt cheated, as though while her back had been turned and she wasn't paying proper attention, time had played a sneaky trick on her, fast-tracking her through to the next stage in her life.

But then that was her all over; she was too prone to be looking the wrong way when something important was happening, and often when it was right under her nose. Second-guessing was something else she did a lot and was subsequently too quick to jump to conclusions and miss the blindingly obvious.

It was how she'd lost her precious daughter to Drew-the-Terrible – her ex-husband – and his glossy new wife. She'd simply been looking the wrong way. But sitting up here on this spacious roof terrace, and with nothing but blue sky overhead and far-reaching views beyond the stone parapet, Drew-the-Terrible was the last thing she wanted to think about. Although come to think of it, imagining him toppling over the parapet and falling to his death had a certain appeal to it.

'A little excessive even by your standards,' she imagined Ben gently rebuking her with a subtle lifting of his mouth into a smile.

That was one of the many reasons she loved Ben, he could put her straight without ever putting her down. It was a rare talent in her experience. Some of his other talents included always being able to make her laugh when she most needed to. He could also put up with her when she was being less than rational, which recently was fast becoming her default setting.

Which was such a shame as she was so lucky to have Ben in her life. Lucky too to live here at Hope Hall in this charmingly bucolic setting of nearly a hundred acres, some of which had been given over to grazing cattle and sheep. There were idyllic woodland paths to enjoy and last month, wild garlic and swathes of shimmering bluebells had emerged from beneath the soft leafy undergrowth in the woods where rhododendrons and azaleas grew in dazzlingly colourful abundance. The River Cam meandered through part of the estate and in the early weeks of living here, when they'd strolled along it, Ben would talk about taking up paddleboarding, or maybe kayaking. Somehow it never happened, but they regularly played tennis on what had been the original court, now thoroughly revamped.

Cassie often thought that living here was like being on a film set; it sometimes felt too good to be true. Not that she ever voiced that opinion to Ben; she didn't want him to think she didn't love their new home as much as he did. She absolutely did.

It had been his idea to sell their Victorian house and live in these fabulous surroundings. The moment he'd heard that the former stately pile on the outskirts of Farleigh Fen village and just a short distance from the centre of Cambridge was in the process of being converted into luxury apartments, he'd made an appointment for them to view what was then no more than a building site. Based on what they had seen that day and the plans Ben studied at length, and the amendments he wanted made, he made an offer for the largest penthouse apartment, which was spread over two floors, and the deal was done.

The first time she and Ben had brought her parents here to see where they would be living, when it was still very much in the building-site stage, her mother had laughed out loud when the extravagantly turreted building had come into view. 'You're going to live in Downton Abbey!' she'd gasped.

'It's not all going to be ours,' Cassie had said, 'we'll have to share it with others.'

'Oh, that's a shame,' her mother had said, sounding disappointed. 'How many others?'

'It's been divided up into twenty apartments,' Ben had explained, 'and of various sizes.' Later, he'd unrolled the plans of the lower and upper floors of the apartment they were buying and had described all his ideas for the internal modifications from what the developer had originally had in mind.

Cassie couldn't recall ever seeing him as excited as he was at the prospect of them living here. She had been worried how much it would cost, but he had assured her that they could easily afford it. The small biotech company he had started up ten years ago had gone from strength to strength and he saw no reason why he shouldn't now reap the rewards of his hard work and success. In the early days it had been tough going, he'd taken a massive risk in resigning from the biotech company he already worked for to go his own way and specialise in providing a service for forensic investigations. His background was biology and chemistry and there wasn't anything he didn't know about DNA, and she was immensely proud of him. A little in awe, too.

Someone else she was in awe of was Nina Lavelle, who lived in the apartment at the opposite turreted corner of the Hall to Cassie and Ben. She had a roof terrace like they did but one bedroom fewer. She was the sort of woman Cassie could never be. For starters, she was unfailingly rational and wonderfully composed, and to top it all she was just about the most exquisitely beautiful woman Cassie knew. Whereas Cassie dressed to emphasise her curves and wore heels to make up for her lack of height, Nina was as tall and willowy as a model. She was effortlessly eye-catching, but without appearing to realise it.

Ice-cool and with a protective force shield in place was how Ben described Nina. He didn't mean it unkindly, he was extremely fond of her, but widowhood, he believed, had caused Nina partially to withdraw.

But then who wouldn't withdraw when the man they loved had died? Cassie certainly would if she lost Ben.

The three of them had become firm friends the day they'd met as neighbours just over a year ago when, and with their keys in hand which they'd collected from the selling agent as soon as completion had taken place, they'd both been anxiously awaiting the arrival of their removal vans. To their combined relief the two large vehicles had trundled up the long winding driveway at the same time in a slow-moving convoy. Nina's van had come from the centre of Cambridge and Cassie and Ben's from Great Shelford.

The first to move in, they'd had the vast, eerily quiet building entirely to themselves and that evening Cassie had invited their new neighbour to join them for a supper of bits and pieces which she'd had the foresight to put in a cool box and ensure would be easy to locate. Wine and glasses had been found and introductory stories shared. That was when they learnt that Nina ran a prestigious fine art gallery in Cambridge and that moving to Hope Hall represented a new start for her, following the death of her husband. Apparently, an athletic and fit man in his early forties, he'd been diagnosed with an inoperable brain tumour and in no time he was dead.

In bed that night in their new home, and after hearing Nina's heartbreaking story, Cassie had held Ben extra tight and told him she loved him. An intuitive man, he hadn't said anything silly like, *'What's brought this on?'*; he'd known, and had hugged her back and told her how much he loved her and then they'd fallen asleep wrapped in each other's arms.

She knew she was so very lucky to have Ben as her forever partner, because unlike her ex-husband he was a good and caring man and had the skills to figure out how she ticked. She'd be the first to acknowledge that there were moments when she could resemble a ticking time bomb. Of late, those moments were all Drew-related.

It infuriated her that he had managed to worm his way back into their daughter's life after years of barely any contact, other than the occasional remembered birthday or last-minute Christmas present. If he were to be believed, he was now a changed man and wanted to be the father to Emily he'd never previously shown the slightest indication of wanting to be.

When Emily, now twenty, informed Cassie that she had been secretly in contact with her father for the last year and was going to drop out of university and go and stay with him in Dubai, where he was now living with his second wife and their young son, it felt like the worst betrayal.

How could her daughter do that, when she knew that Cassie had literally been left holding the baby when Drew had done a vanishing act within two months of Emily's birth? He wasn't ready for fatherhood, he'd claimed, he was too young.

'I'll tell you who else isn't ready for this, and that's me!' Cassie had shouted at him.

Before all that had happened, when she had first discovered she was pregnant, and knowing that she wanted to keep the baby, she had given up her place at Nottingham University and had gone home to her parents to tell them her news. As shocked and disappointed as they were, they had fully supported her. Just as they had when she and Drew had hastily married in a registry office and found a place of their own, a dismal ground-floor flat in Watford where he had just started working.

It had all been such a mess and yet somehow, at that ridiculously young age Cassie had believed she was doing entirely the right thing. She had fallen for Drew because, being older than her by four years, he had been like some darkly forbidden fruit, full of temptation and an excess of allure. He used to joke that he was John Travolta to her Olivia Newton-John, playing Danny and Sandy in *Grease*. He even had a cute little dimple in his chin. After he'd left her, she could never watch *Grease* again. She still couldn't. But maybe that was out of habit now.

Ben Pearson had come into Cassie's life a few years after she'd moved back to be near her parents in the village of Linton ten miles from Cambridge. Emily was ten at the time and Ben had taken to the role of stepfather brilliantly. Emily had eagerly accepted him as a permanent presence, proudly boasting to her friends that she now had a proper daddy.

If Ben felt slighted by Emily now apparently switching her allegiance from him to a man who had abandoned her as a baby, he never showed it. Instead, he did his best to convince Cassie that they weren't losing Emily, that this was simply something the girl had to do, and they had to respect her decision.

He made it sound so easy, but then he hadn't been the one who'd been hurt all those years ago and carried the pain and resentment ever since. It was a long time to carry a grudge, but she had, and she didn't care if that made her seem petty.

She didn't help herself, of course, because while Drew was vying for the role of Husband of the Year and Superdad, Cassie tortured herself by scrolling through his wife's frequent postings on Instagram and TikTok showing off their perfect life. It had to be fake, no one really lived such a fantasy life, but it was hard to resist the queasy lure of the photos, especially those of Rosalyn herself. Fifteen years younger than Cassie, the girl's pouting lips were filled, her boobs perkier than nature ever intended them to be, her waist unfeasibly small and her nails and eyelashes absurdly long. Even when Rosalyn posted a photo of herself lounging by a swimming pool along with her son and captioned it with the comment, *Here's me make-up free and looking an absolute mess!* she looked anything *but* a mess.

What pained Cassie most was that Emily had been sucked into the vacuous stream of photos and reels, proudly touted by Rosalyn as *My perfect stepdaughter!* Or: *I've never had a sister, now I feel like I do! I'm truly blessed!*

Suddenly filled with a fierce blaze of emotions towards her ex-husband, as well as disappointment that Emily could have done something that she had to have known would cut deep with her, Cassie put down her drink, stood up and went over to the stone parapet. Resting her elbows on it, she gazed out at the beautiful view, and reminded herself just how good life was for her and that she shouldn't let the past and all its resentment tarnish her present or her future.

In the distance, she watched a heron appear from the branches of a towering oak tree as, lazily flapping its wide span of wings, it tracked a path along the river before swooping down low and onto the bank. She waited for it to move, but it stayed very still.

She could do with learning to be more still, Cassie thought, mentally as well as physically. Particularly when it came to Emily. She had to let her daughter make her own decisions and accept the consequences. But she missed Emily so much.

She missed all the silly times they'd shared, like when they watched *Married at First Sight* together – the Australian version was their favourite – and played gaslighting bingo, shrieking so loudly at the worst offenders that Ben would poke his head through the doorway and ask them what was going on.

She particularly missed their regular catch-up chats when she still felt she could guide and advise Emily and in return be mocked for being so mortifyingly out of touch.

Cassie would give anything to have that time back with her daughter, because ever since she and Ben had waved Emily off at Heathrow six weeks ago, all she had now was a skimpy ration of texts or FaceTime calls which were abruptly short and told her nothing of any real worth. They served only to leave her going quietly mad as she filled in the blanks and convinced herself that she had lost her daughter forever to Drew.

Chapter Two

Generally, Saturdays were not when Nina's serious clients came into the gallery, they preferred to visit during the week when it was quiet and they could spend more one-to-one time with Nina and invariably enjoy an exchange of gossip over a glass of champagne.

Today, and amongst the tourists who came in to browse, a Canadian couple had fallen in love with the beautiful Dorothea Sharp painting of a vase of flowers at an open window, which Nina had only recently acquired. She would have liked to have it hanging in the gallery for longer because it gave her so much pleasure every time she looked at it. That was the trouble with some paintings: she made an emotional connection to them, and it was a wrench to let them go.

Soon after the transaction had been completed and all the shipping details filled out, another couple came in. They were from Boston and on a tour around the UK, as so many were who came to Cambridge. Their taste ran more to pastoral landscapes of the nineteenth century and when they spotted the Henry Hillingford Parker haymaking scene, they were delighted as they already had a painting by the artist back at home. 'It was meant to be,' the woman had said happily while her husband handed over his American Express card to Nina.

Once all the paperwork was in order and the couple had gone, Nina decided to close. It was almost four o'clock and she felt she had a good day's work behind her. Activating the complex security system, she locked up and set off for her car, a short walk away in a private car park.

The Lavelle Fine Art Gallery in St Anne's Court had been a family-run business since the 1950s, when it was established by Nina's grandfather, Jerome Lavelle. It then passed down to her father, David Lavelle, in the late 1970s and it was now Nina's responsibility to carry the torch. Her brother had made it clear that art wasn't his field of expertise, despite having grown up surrounded by it, and he'd hightailed it off to the States to work in the tech industry. He now lived in San Francisco and was married with two young children, which was why Mum and Dad had decided to retire early and divide their time between Cambridge and the US – they wanted to see their grandchildren growing up and help as much as they could.

Nina had always believed it was her destiny to run the gallery. She'd been obsessed with her parents' world since she was a small child, marvelling at the beauty and variety of paintings on the gallery walls and the fascinating people who came and went. As soon as she was old enough, she was allowed to help in the gallery, especially when her parents held an exhibition. Inevitably she went on to study fine art and did several internships at Christie's in London before returning home to Cambridge to work alongside her parents. Her brother liked to tease her that she was the anointed one, their parents' protégée, and he was their shamefully philistine son who didn't appreciate the first thing about fine art.

'But you're the special one they want to go and live near,' she'd countered, knowing full well that Guy didn't have a jealous bone in his body and that he was far from the philistine he made himself out to be.

'There's no one I'd sooner see taking on the mantle than you,' Dad had said to Nina when the i's and t's were legally dotted and crossed, and she was officially the new owner of the business.

They'd organised a party in the gallery for all their loyal clients and friends to mark the occasion of their retirement and to celebrate the continuation of the family business, declaring it to be in safe hands for the next generation.

That had been four years ago when Hugh was very much alive, and he and Nina had believed they had a lifetime of happiness to look forward to. A future that had included children. Hugh had been so eager to be a father. When their friends and his cousins to whom he was very close had started producing offspring, he had confessed to feeling broody himself.

'I know that's the prerogative of a woman, but I can't help it,' he'd said. 'I want a child. I think we'd make great parents.'

Nina hadn't been quite ready to take that step, wanting first to establish herself fully in the gallery, but she had relented when her mother had reminded her that the clock was ticking, and that it was a well-known fact that it became increasingly more difficult to conceive the older a woman was. She was thirty-seven at that point and so she agreed to dispense with using any contraception, but on the understanding that they would have help at home when the time came so Nina could juggle the gallery with being a mother.

Hugh had had no problem with this, and joked that they should get to work straight away on filling the house with as many children as possible.

'Before we get ahead of ourselves, let's see how we manage with the one small baby,' Nina had said, ever the voice of restraint and in marked contrast to Hugh who could never do anything by halves; he was a great believer in all or nothing.

But creating that one small baby proved harder than they'd anticipated, and they soon accepted that they needed to seek professional help. The problem proved to be a shared one in as much as Hugh had a low sperm count and her eggs were failing to mature properly.

Hugh was devastated. It pained her to see him so upset and she knew then that she had to do everything in her power to create a child with him. So together they began an expensive course of fertility treatment. Which from the very first visit to the clinic opened Nina's eyes to how big the fertility industry was. She was shocked at what she discovered once the process was underway and was met with nigh on incredulity from the doctor that she hadn't already put away a stash of healthy eggs for safekeeping. Apparently young women in their twenties were being encouraged to store their eggs well in advance of wanting to be pregnant, or even having a partner. It was an insurance policy; an expensive one at that.

Hugh decided to let his parents know what they were doing, as his mother had started dropping clanging hints that it was surely time they provided her with a grandchild. Nina confided in her parents and brother, but it wasn't something she wanted to keep bringing up in conversation, and they had the good sense to realise that.

As time went on, Hugh's mother, who couldn't accept for one minute her only son could in any way be at fault, preferred to believe that the fault lay entirely at Nina's door.

'It's because you're too thin,' Hilary once said. 'If you'd eat more, you'd be pregnant in a flash.'

On one occasion she had almost inferred that Nina must in some way not be conducting herself in a proper manner in bed with Hugh, that she had to be holding back. When Nina had told Hugh this, he had laughed out loud, but then it had sunk in what his mother had really been saying and he'd been furious and threatened to give his mother an explicit rundown on their sex life, he'd spare her nothing! Thankfully he didn't, and they were all spared that embarrassment.

They'd had three attempts at embryos being transplanted into her womb, all of which had failed, when Hugh started to suffer a series of debilitating headaches. Initially he'd put it down to overdoing it at the law firm where he worked – he'd been in the office all hours and poring over documents at home until the early hours – but then he'd collapsed in the office and an ambulance had been sent for and a call put through to her at the gallery.

After a series of tests and MRI scans were carried out, the words *brain tumour* were uttered. Quickly followed by *inoperable*.

They had tried to cling to the only thing they could: denial. The experts were wrong. The tests were inaccurate. The scans were mixed up with those of another patient. This couldn't be happening to them. How could a man as vital as Hugh – as invulnerable as Hugh – be felled by something like this? Only a few weeks ago he'd been skiing with friends in Val D'Isere, returning home boasting about the black runs and off-*piste* skiing he'd done. This was a man who played squash and tennis as often as he could. A man who was looking forward to being a father and who was prepared to do whatever it took to do that. Only for a brain tumour to shatter every one of their dreams.

By the time Nina had driven out of Cambridge and had passed through Grantchester and the village of Farleigh Fen, she realised she had been driving on autopilot and was now just minutes away from Hope Hall.

Her new home.

Her home without Hugh and where she'd hoped to turn the page and start a new life.

It was the name of Hope Hall that had initially caught her attention and prompted her to contact the selling agent. By the time she had arranged an appointment to meet with the developer on-site she had convinced herself that an apartment here, by virtue of its name, could be a place of hope for her, somewhere that would help her to move on.

Driving between the majestic stone pillars either side of the entrance to Hope Hall, Nina recalled that first visit here and the mix of emotions she'd experienced. She'd felt a glimmer of excitement, something she hadn't felt in a while, but also apprehension. Could she really leave the home she and Hugh had created together in Cambridge, and which was packed full of memories of him?

The counter-argument was that a new home would give her something to think about other than her grief and how much she missed Hugh. And there was something tempting about living somewhere that had been saved by a developer from falling into total disrepair.

Could Hope Hall save her, she'd wondered as she'd driven towards the stately building that was cradled in scaffolding while work was being carried out to return it to its former glory? And could she really see herself living here, in what the sales brochure referred to as *an unrivalled idyll of luxury*? Of waking early to go jogging around the grounds and along the river. Of going for woodland walks and breathing in the fresh country air.

'I think you'd like it,' Hugh's voice had whispered to her in the car that day. *'I know I would.'*

More than two years on since Hugh had died, and she still occasionally heard his voice in her head. Now and then she still found herself laughing over something and thinking, *I must tell Hugh that, he'd find it funny too*. Then she'd remember and feel the weight of her grief all over again.

Then there were those times when she realised she had gone a whole day without thinking about him. It felt such a betrayal.

Her parents told her she was still in the early stages of grief, but was she? Shouldn't she have found a way to be free of her grief by now?

'But it takes time,' her mother told her. 'You're doing wonderfully well, darling.'

She didn't think that was true, not when some days she wanted to lash out and hurl blame at someone. But she never did. Instead, she internalised it.

She recognised the same symptoms in her mother-in-law. The woman was in so much pain. She had lost her only child. Her most treasured son. She never actually came right out and said it, but Nina knew that Hilary as good as blamed Nina for not preventing this awful thing from happening. Nina willingly let Hilary spray-gun her angry grief at her, because why not? It somehow made her feel better knowing that she was doing this for Hugh's mother.

Keith, her father-in-law, regularly apologised to Nina for his wife's behaviour and she always told him it was okay, she could handle it.

Her relationship with Hilary had never been what you would call close; they had each tolerated the other for Hugh's sake, a state of affairs as old as time when it came to in-laws. But Nina accepted that it wasn't personal; Hilary would have treated any daughter-in-law the same way, as not being good enough, or not caring enough.

At the funeral, Hugh's family had far outnumbered Nina's. Hugh's father had three brothers, all of whom had large families. Hilary had two sisters, and they too had produced a brace of children to add to the family tree.

'We're a wildly fecund bunch,' one of the many cousins once said to Nina. 'We breed like bloody rabbits!'

Hilary had been within earshot and had visibly winced, perhaps because she had only produced the one child and not a brood, or maybe because she found the word *fecund* distasteful.

The funeral had passed in a blur for Nina; she had nodded her head, shaken hands, and said what she was expected to say, but she had behaved robotically, just going through the motions of what was required of her. Her friends and her mother and father had been with her, along with her brother – her sister-in-law was minding their two children – and they had formed a protective shield of love and support around her.

At the end of it all, when the coffin had slid through the curtains and out of view and Hugh's beautiful body would then be turned to ash, Nina had wanted to go over to Hilary and say, 'I know how much you're hurting. I really do. It's the same for me.'

But she didn't dare, not when it might break the dam of Hilary's emotions. It might make Hilary throw it back in Nina's face, spitting out the words – *'You'll never understand how I feel! Never!'*

A few days after the funeral, Nina's brother and his family flew back to San Francisco, but Mum and Dad stayed on to be with her. Eventually the time came when Nina knew they had to go, it was time for her to stand on her own two feet and get on with life. Selfishly she wanted to be alone, or more accurately, to be alone with Hugh. She wanted to be able to talk to him, to come home from working in the gallery and tell him how her day had gone, just as she'd always done when he'd been alive. She wanted to lie in bed at night imagining him there beside her, breathing in the smell of him. Every night she took his favourite bottle of cologne and dabbed a few drops of it onto his side of the bed.

Parking her car in her allotted space in front of the garage block, she crossed the gravelled courtyard, tapped in the passcode to let herself in at the side entrance, then after collecting her post from the mailboxes in the oak-panelled entrance foyer, she climbed the thickly carpeted stairway to her apartment.

Once inside, she kicked off her shoes and went from the hallway with its white marble floor to the large open-plan kitchen, which was flooded with late afternoon sunlight pouring in through the large leaded bay windows. She put her laptop bag and handbag on the central island unit and went over to the kettle to make herself a mug of camomile tea. While she waited for it to boil, she sat on one of the window seats and flicked through the mail for anything that looked important or interesting.

A good-quality envelope with her address written by hand on it looked and felt very much like an invitation. She opened it and saw that she was right. The youngest of Hugh's cousins on his mother's side of the family, Fabian Irving, was marrying and the honour of Nina's presence was requested to join in with the service and the reception, when there would be dinner and dancing. There was no mention of a plus- one; the invitation was solely for Nina.

Part of her was grateful, it meant that the memory of Hugh was being respected. But then it would be unthinkable to the family that Hugh could be replaced in any way.

Yet hand in hand with that gratitude was a small glint of annoyance. Was she expected to remain a widow for the rest of her life, never to attend another function with somebody else at her side?

As the kettle clicked off, she rose from the window seat and went over to make her drink. She was being overly sensitive, she told herself, while filling a mug and then dunking a camomile teabag into the water. The invitation had been sent with all the right motives, because really there was no need for Hugh's family to include her in any of their big occasions, or get-togethers. It was a kindness on their part to invite her.

As kind as they were, she sometimes wished she could cut the tie. Whenever she was with his family all they wanted to do was talk about Hugh and recall the times they'd spent with him. How for the much younger ones he'd been their hero, the one they lived up to. For the older ones, they had endless stories about pranks they'd pulled off together, invariably instigated by Hugh. They didn't seem to realise how painful it was for Nina to listen to their tales.

Was she wrong to want to cut the tie? But if she didn't, how could she ever move forward when they gave the impression that they didn't want her to? Hugh's mother would be appalled at the very idea of Nina ever meeting someone new. Not that there was any danger of that happening anytime soon. Which was why she had been silly to be annoyed by the omission of the words *plus one* on the wedding invitation.

Taking her drink over to the window seat, she resumed the task of dealing with the rest of the mail. That was when she found the letter from the clinic in Cambridge where she and Hugh had been undergoing IVF. Opening the envelope, she unfolded the letter and braced herself.

She had known this day would come and that she would have to make one of the most important decisions of her life, but she still wasn't ready. It was never meant to be like this. She and Hugh were supposed to do this together and only when they were absolutely sure they were doing the right thing.

Chapter Three

'You're never going to let me win, are you?'

'You'd hate it if I did,' Cassie said as she slipped her racket into its case.

It was Sunday morning and she and Ben had just finished playing a game of tennis. Neither of them had played for some years before moving to Hope Hall, but now they tried to squeeze in a game most weekends. By her own admission, Cassie was a poor loser and probably more competitive than she ought to be, but it wasn't in her DNA to go easy on an opponent. Even if it was a game of Christmas Day charades with her family, she played to win and was not always a generous team player if she found herself on the losing side.

'You mean you'd hate to lose,' Ben said, using a small towel to wipe the sweat from his face.

Keeping her expression deadpan, she said, 'I wouldn't know, it's never happened.'

'*Hah!* Nina beat you the last time the two of you played.'

Cassie laughed. 'Only just. And anyway, she has the advantage in that her legs are twice as long as mine.'

'My legs are longer than yours, but you still thrash me.'

'*Aw* babe,' she said, leaning in to kiss him, 'are you hurting?'

'No,' he said with an exaggerated pout, 'I'm sulking.'

'You never sulk, that's much more my style. Come on, let's

go and have a shower together and I'll find a way to make you feel better.'

'That's low, trying to appease me by offering your body.'

'Was that what I was doing?' she said, pressing herself against him provocatively.

He kissed her. 'God, I certainly hope so.' Then taking her hand in his – Ben loved to hold hands with her, no matter where they were or what they were doing – he led them off the court.

They hadn't gone far when Cassie spotted two neighbours approaching. They were dressed in pristine Lululemon tennis whites with large racket bags slung over their shoulders and carrying matching drinks containers. They looked for all the world as though they were about to play on Centre Court at Wimbledon in a veterans match.

'*Uh-oh,*' Cassie said in a low voice, 'incoming Enforcers.'

'Play nicely,' Ben murmured.

'Don't I always?' she said. 'Hi there!' she called out, cranking up her inner dial to maximum cheerfulness and all too aware that Ben knew just how two-faced she was being.

She'd nicknamed Cheryl Saunders and Joanna Adams the Enforcers because, together with their husbands, they had taken on the running of the residents' committee and took it very seriously. Both couples were retired and in their late sixties and while Cassie was only too relieved she hadn't been pressganged into having to take on any of the roles, such as chairperson, secretary, or finance officer, she couldn't help but feel the two women relished their roles a little too zealously. They were constantly sending out emails reminding residents of the various rules they were all meant to abide by, like no excessive noise in the public areas after ten o'clock at night, no rubbish bags left by the wheelie bins, no taking of another resident's parking space and definitely no smoking in any of the inside communal areas. None of which Cassie would dream of doing, but these two women made her want to revert to being a bolshy adolescent and break every rule in the book.

Cheryl, the taller of the two women and with a face that was unnaturally taut and smooth, greeted Cassie and Ben with a quick *hello* before saying, 'Have you heard that the new owner of the apartment below yours will be moving in next Friday?'

'That's news to us, isn't it?' Cassie said, turning to Ben.

'Any idea who's bought the place?' he asked.

'According to the management company, it's a woman moving here from Essex.'

'She's getting on a bit, so she shouldn't be any trouble and hopefully will fit in nicely,' piped up Joanna, adding, 'unlike the previous owner who never made any effort to fit in, did he?'

'Only because he was hardly ever here,' Cassie said. Selfishly, she had enjoyed the owner travelling the world with his work and using the apartment below theirs as a base rather than a home; it meant for the most part it was quiet. There had also been the bonus of being able to use his allotted parking spaces when they had guests.

'I thought it would be a nice touch to throw a drinks party to welcome the new neighbour to our little bit of paradise,' Cheryl said. 'I'll send out an email and we can settle on a date for when everyone will be around. If the weather's as good as it is now, we can be outside.'

'Why not make it a barbecue?'

Cheryl shook her head as though Cassie had suggested they host a lap-dancing party. 'Oh, I don't think that's the sort of thing an old lady would enjoy, do you?'

'Which rather depends on what kind of old lady the new owner turns out to be,' said Cassie later that evening to Nina.

With Ben out for his regular basketball evening at the Hills Road Sports Centre in town, and which doubtless would end with him arriving home and heading straight for the shower while leaving his sports bag just where she'd trip over it, Cassie had invited Nina to join her for a drink on the roof garden and had quickly brought her up to speed on the latest from the Enforcers.

'I'm half hoping she'll turn out to be a wild rebel,' Cassie said. 'Or better still, one of those upper class born-to-rule types who will run rings around Cheryl and Joanna.'

Nina smiled. 'Be careful what you wish for; warring neighbours wouldn't be much fun.'

'I don't want an all-out war, but you have to admit, a couple of small battles just to take the Enforcers down a peg or two would be very satisfying.'

'Why don't you do that?'

'Because I'm all bluster and no substance, you know how shallow I am. I just witter on about things and never do anything about it. Look how I constantly complain about Emily's father, but what do I do about it? Nothing. Absolutely nothing.'

'That's because you know it's the right thing to do.'

'Yeah, that's what Ben says. *Keep the peace*, blah, blah, *play nicely*, blah, blah. But it's such a strain when all the time I'm longing to let rip and scream my head off with every known obscenity. Don't you ever feel like that?'

It was a few moments before Nina responded. 'Yes,' she said after taking a sip of her wine, 'about a hundred times a day.'

'Really?'

'You sound surprised.'

'I am. You always seem so measured and self-possessed.'

'And in one simple sentence you make me sound so dull.'

Cassie grimaced. 'You know I didn't mean it that way. I meant that I'm the irrational one and you're the opposite, you're totally logical and—'

'And there you go again,' Nina cut in with a small smile, 'making me sound hideously boring.'

'Okay, so tell me what makes you want to scream and shout.' As soon as the words had left Cassie's lips, she realised the insensitivity of her question.

'I'm sorry,' she said quickly, 'just ignore me and my big mouth.'

'It's okay, there's no need to apologise, but yes, Hugh's death still makes me want to scream and shout at the unfairness of life. Or more accurately, the indiscriminate taking away of a life.'

'What do you do when you feel like that?'

'In the early stages I cried a lot. Obviously. But then when I became sick of having puffy bloodshot eyes, I took up running, something Hugh was always encouraging me to do with him, but I never did. Now, not only does it act as a release when I push myself to punishing point, but I feel connected to him.'

'Maybe I should start running to sort out my mood swings as well as help me lose weight. You wouldn't believe it, but I'm supposed to be on a detox regime, and just look at me guzzling wine and scoffing salted almonds.' She slid the dish of nuts closer to Nina as though that would stop her from reaching for any more.

'You really don't need to lose weight,' Nina said, 'you're perfect as you are.'

'You say the sweetest things.'

'But seriously,' Nina went on, 'you're welcome to join me for a run some time.'

Cassie puffed out her cheeks and shook her head. 'I doubt I'd be able to keep up with you. Anyway, you run at crazy o'clock in the morning when I'm still lounging around in my PJs with my first cup of coffee of the day.'

Nina smiled. 'I've always been an early riser, even more so when I have something on my mind.'

Recalling Ben saying how early he'd seen Nina coming back from her run that morning, she said, 'Was that why you were running at the crack of dawn today?'

An eyebrow raised, Nina said, 'Keeping tabs on me?'

'Not at all, but Ben saw you.'

When Nina didn't say anything, but stared off into the distance, Cassie apologised again. 'Sorry, I'm blundering in, just tell me to mind my own business. But I'd like to think that if you ever needed someone to talk to, you'd know you could come to me.'

Turning her head to look at Cassie, a frown creasing her brow, Nina said, 'I received a letter yesterday which I knew would come one day, but I have no idea how to respond to it, and I know I must. I can't put it off forever.'

Telling herself to tread carefully, Cassie said, 'It's a long shot, but is it anything I can help you with?'

'Not really. I must make a decision which only I can do. It's a decision which depending on what I decide, will either change my life completely or be something I might always regret.'

'Well, I'm here for you if you need to talk it through. I know you have family you can turn to, and other friends you've known for a lot longer than you've known me, but sometimes it helps to talk to someone who's outside of your immediate social circle.'

'That's very true,' said Nina, 'but I don't think any amount of talking it through will help. You see, Hugh and I planned to have children, but we had problems conceiving and that led to us going down the IVF route. Then before we were successful, Hugh died, and now the clinic is asking me what I want to do with the embryos which are still being stored.'

'What are the options?'

'Do I give my permission for the embryos to be destroyed or donated to another couple, or do I give IVF another go before it's too late? As you know, I turned forty-three earlier in the year, so time is against me. Basically, it's now or never.'

Wow, thought Cassie, that really was a hell of a decision to make. 'What are you leaning towards?' she asked, reaching across the table to top up Nina's glass.

'Part of me wants to have Hugh's child, to have that ultimate connection with the man I loved, but the thought of doing it alone terrifies me. Selfishly, I want to move forward with my life, to be the old me, or even a new and improved me.'

'And a baby would stop you doing that?'

'I don't know is the honest answer. It would keep me tied to the past in so many ways, and would it be fair to a child to bring it into the world this way without a father? Wouldn't it be selfish of me to do that?'

'Most parents have children out of selfish need,' said Cassie. 'It's the most natural thing in the world.'

Nina tutted. 'I'm sorry,' she said, 'that was tactless. You brought up your daughter on your own, didn't you?'

Cassie nodded. 'Until she was ten, and then I met Ben who became a brilliant father to her. I never thought anyone would take me on with a young child, but he did. The same could happen to you.'

For the longest moment, Nina's gaze became fixed on a kite wheeling overhead in the cloudless sky, its wings outstretched. Dusk had yet to materialise, and it seemed to Cassie that it felt like one of those lovely June evenings that would never end. Then with a slight turn of her head to look at Cassie, Nina said, 'What would you do if you were in my shoes?'

Unsure how to answer such a precariously loaded question, Cassie hesitated, but before she could formulate a reply, Nina said, 'Is there a reason why you and Ben haven't had a child together?'

Of all the conversations they'd had since knowing one another, this was the most personal. She and Ben had of course discussed whether having a child was something they both desired, and wanting to be entirely honest with him, Cassie had forced herself to tell him what a terrifying time it had been for her when Emily had been a baby, especially after Drew had left them. She'd had her parents' support, but most of the time she had been so sleep-deprived she'd thought she would lose her mind. The exhaustion had been crippling, physically and mentally.

It had been the interminable feeding and rocking Emily to sleep that had nearly broken her. For hours and hours, she had stood rocking the fractious bundle in her arms, standing just inches away from the cot in the hope that any minute, Emily's relentlessly angry cries would subside, and Cassie would finally be able to lower her down, oh-so gently, and Emily would sleep. But Emily had the ability to sense the second Cassie even so much as contemplated placing her in the cot and the squalling would start all over again and with the volume increased. Added to this was the constant pain Cassie was in, with nipples cracked and sore and her breasts feeling like they were on fire.

Yes, it all passed eventually, and in the end every minute of the nightmare was worth it because she loved her daughter so much. But how could she ever let Ben see her like that, at her very worst? She'd told him everything, even crying as the memories had come flooding back, and he'd said he never wanted to make her do anything she wasn't one hundred per cent happy doing.

'I'm sorry,' said Nina when Cassie hadn't answered her question. 'I shouldn't have put you on the spot like that.'

'Oh, don't be sorry,' Cassie said more lightly than she felt. 'It's all in the past. Besides, Ben has his work cut out with me, I'm the biggest kid going; there isn't room for another one in our relationship!' She laughed, trying not to think of the occasional doubt she experienced that maybe she had selfishly denied Ben the joy of being a real father to his own child.

Chapter Four

Venetia Randall-Jones had moved house many times in her life but at the age of seventy-nine, she planned on Hope Hall being her final resting place. It gave her the greatest satisfaction, knowing that being here meant she had finally come full circle.

The precious bottle now located, but sadly not any glass tumblers, she stood in the surprising order of the spacious sitting room with a bone china mug of single malt whisky in her hand. She drank deeply from it, savouring its reviving peaty smokiness.

It had been a long day, and the removal men had only just left, each pocketing a generous tip from her by way of grateful thanks for their hard work and for going the extra mile for her. Whenever she'd attempted to lift anything the burly man in charge would say, 'That's alright, darlin', how about you tell us where it needs to go and then pop the kettle on to make us a drink?'

Under normal circumstances she would be riled by some young whippersnapper referring to her in such a manner, but she was only too grateful for the help in this instance. Of course, there was still plenty to unpack and put in place, but the heavy work had been done for her. The good thing was that she had been very thorough in streamlining her life while preparing for this move. She hadn't wanted to bring anything with her that she now deemed unnecessary. The amount of junk with which one travelled through life was absurd, so much of it completely useless and nothing but a burden. The wonder was she'd hung on to so much all these years. She had found the process of decluttering her life enormously pleasing and had been energised with a ruthless streak to see just how much she could get rid of. It had been a cathartic experience.

Now here she was, embarking on what she was probably supposed to call her twilight years. Well, she'd have to see about that! Smiling, she swirled the whisky round in the mug and drank it down. She had no intention of going quietly into that long dark night and nor was she going to play by the rules expected of her.

As if on cue, Bon-Bon uncurled himself from his wicker basket and after stretching and then shaking, trotted over to her. Putting the empty mug on a side table, Venetia scooped the little dog up in her arms.

'What a perfectly good boy you've been,' she said, 'not a single bark from you the whole day. And it's going to have to stay that way, otherwise you and I will be in big trouble.'

The miniature apricot-coloured poodle tilted his head to one side and looked intently into Venetia's face as though understanding her every word.

Venetia didn't consider herself a habitual rule-breaker, but she'd set her heart on living here and a silly management company rule such as *'No pets allowed'* wasn't going to stop her. Besides, her precious companion would be no trouble to anyone. Nobody would even know he was here. Happily, he wasn't one of those annoying yappy dogs who barked for hours on end and was hardly likely to make a mess.

When it came to a certain type of mess, Venetia had that sorted. As emergency backup, she had trained Bon-Bon to use a litter tray like a cat, but generally she planned to go out when it was dark at night to take him for a walk in the woods. She would do the same early in the morning, the dog hidden in her tote bag until the coast was clear. The thought of all the sneaking about appealed to her, but she knew she would have to be careful and on her guard.

Carrying the dog over to the kitchen area of the large open-plan space, she put him on the floor and retrieved a bag of dried dog food from a packing box. A stainless-steel bowl was in the same box and after pouring in a small amount of food, she set it down next to the bowl of water already on the tiled floor. With his customary delicacy, Bon-Bon sniffed the food and seemingly approving of it, began eating.

It was time Venetia ate something as well. After several attempts to locate the fridge – it was going to take a while to remember where everything was – she found it and although it hadn't been switched on for very long, it was cooling nicely. She helped herself to the last remaining tuna and mayonnaise sandwich which she'd wrapped in cling film. She'd made a huge pile of them earlier for the hungry removal men, along with a stack of cheese and pickle sandwiches, and they'd all but polished them off. They'd also consumed the best part of two packets of biscuits and more sugar in their tea and coffee than she used in a month. Not that she begrudged them so much as a grain of sugar or crumb of bread.

She had only taken a few bites of her sandwich when she heard a knock at the door. It was a discreet knock and other than pricking up his ears and glancing at Venetia to check all was well, Bon-Bon continued with crunching on the dried food in his bowl.

'Good boy,' Venetia murmured. Then going out to the hallway and closing the door to the sitting room behind her, she went to see who was paying her a call.

It was two young women. The shorter one of the two, blonde with a bright and vivacious smile and wearing a lovely 1950s-style dress, cinched in at the waist and full-skirted, held out a bottle of rosé.

'Hi,' she said, 'we thought we'd come and introduce ourselves and let you know that if there's anything you need, you only have to ask. My name's Cassie.'

'And I'm Nina,' the other one said, passing Venetia an envelope, presumably a card. 'We both live on the top floor.'

'Though not together,' the blonde woman said with a laugh. 'We're neighbours. But not the ones from hell.'

'Or so we like to think,' the taller woman said. There was a refreshingly natural beauty to her, her complexion was make-up-free and enviably clear, as were her bluey-grey eyes. Her long reddish-gold-coloured hair put Venetia in mind of a beautiful autumnal day.

'And don't worry, we're not expecting you to invite us in,' the blonde one said, pressing the wine bottle on Venetia. 'We just wanted to make you feel welcome. We've put our contact details in the card and my partner, Ben, is a dab hand with basic DIY jobs if you're ever stuck or need something shifting.'

'That's extremely kind of you both,' Venetia said, accepting the wine and card, 'I'm touched.' If she wasn't hiding a forbidden dog on the premises, she would have stepped aside and asked them to come in, but as it was, she would have to take them at their word, that they didn't expect to be invited in.

They were moving away from the doorway to go back upstairs when she said, 'Forgive me, I haven't introduced myself. I'm Venetia. Venetia Randall-Jones and I look forward to getting to know you both better. When I'm a little straighter, you must come in for a drink some time.'

What she really meant was that when she'd got to know them better and thought she could trust them, then she'd invite them in.

Later, when she had eaten her sandwich and it was dark outside, she fetched her tote bag and put it on the floor. Good as gold,

Bon-Bon hopped inside it – he really was the most well-behaved dog – and she clipped the lead onto the soft leather collar around his neck.

'Time to go exploring,' she said. Her cover story, should she encounter anyone on the stairs, was that she always liked to take a constitutional walk before bedtime.

The large bag hooked over her shoulder, and armed with a torch, she locked her apartment and set off down the wide stairway with its rich mahogany banisters that smelt of lavender polish. It was good to know the colossal monthly service charge the residents had to pay was being put to good use, she thought wryly. The carpet beneath her feet was royal blue and as soft and plush as a feather bed. There were oil paintings in gilt frames on the walls, probably not remotely valuable but they set the tone, which was of luxury and opulence.

It was all a far cry from how she remembered the place when she was here as a child. A child who used to sneak about late at night in the shadows just like she was doing now.

With every step she took, the ghosts of the past called out to her, whispering that she was home.

Home again.

At last.

Chapter Five

It was the first week of July, so the main body of university students had dispersed, and the streets of Cambridge were now thronged with tourists trailing behind tour guides. There were gangs of language students from all over the world, who drifted about in concentrated groups the way that only large numbers of boisterous carefree adolescents do. Buskers also added to the high spirits and cacophony of noise, especially in the tourist hotspots.

But in St Anne's Court, just off Lower All Saints Lane, there was a sense of cool, quiet calm along the narrow cobbled street. With its antique shops and by-appointment-only jewellers and one or two other galleries besides Lavelle's, it offered a pleasing hint of classy Dickensian charm. It wasn't one of the busy thoroughfares for the tour groups and that morning, with no one about, Nina could take her time standing on the empty pavement, checking that the Auguste Bouvard landscape which her assistant Jakob had just placed on an easel in the gallery window looked its best. Satisfied that it did so, she gave him a thumbs-up sign and went back inside.

'It looks perfect,' she said.

'Of course it does,' he agreed, 'and I guarantee it won't be there for long.'

'In that case I should increase the price, if it will be that easy a sale.'

He smiled. 'You're the boss. Coffee?'

'Thank you, that would be great.'

While Jakob disappeared through the swing doors to the small kitchen area at the back of the gallery, Nina sat at her desk and checking her emails on her laptop, saw that there was one from the printers. She had been waiting to hear from them about the new brochure for the autumn show she was planning, and she hoped it wasn't bad news. She was relieved to read that it was just a courtesy email, an update on when they would deliver.

Sending out brochures was a costly and time-consuming business, but clients for the most part were old-school and preferred a physical copy rather than a digital one. Jakob had come up with an excellent idea the other day, that since the physical brochure was so popular, maybe Nina should produce a calendar with each month displaying a painting from her considerable stock. She didn't know why she or her parents had never thought of doing it before. Jakob, it had to be said, was full of good ideas, and she was glad she had taken him on.

Her last assistant had been an art student from Ukraine who had come here to escape the war, but when Oksana received the devastating news that both her father and brother had been killed while defending their country, she returned to Kyiv so she could sign up to fight. The last Nina heard from her she was still alive and was prepared to do whatever it took to help make her country free again. Whenever Nina found herself weighed down with her own grief and worries, she thought of Oksana and her courage and the fear she must live with every day.

In contrast Jakob seemed to sail through life without a care in the world. Perhaps that's why she enjoyed having him in the gallery; he was always so upbeat and positive. He had been with Nina for six months now and with a law degree under his belt along with an MA in advertising, working here as her assistant wasn't exactly a stretch for him.

He was Norwegian and was living in Cambridge, so he claimed, to escape his family back in Oslo and to perfect his English. Neither of which was true because his English was excellent, rarely did he make a slip-up over a word or a phrase, and he was clearly extremely close to his family as he talked about them constantly. He was thirty-two, and very personable and engaging which were great assets when dealing with customers. It didn't hurt for business that he was as good-looking as he was and always immaculately dressed, but not in a show-pony kind of way.

What Nina couldn't understand was why he was happy to work for her as her assistant when he could so easily find a job far better suited to the qualifications he held, and one that paid more. She had to assume that working at Lavelle's was merely a stop-gap until he'd decided what he really wanted to do.

His family back in Oslo ran a shipping company and she imagined that one day they would demand he returned to the fold. For now, though, she would make good use of him. His art knowledge hadn't been all that impressive when he applied for the job, but he proved to be a quick learner. It had crossed her mind more than once that if she wanted to keep him, she could offer him commission on any sales he made. Yet something told her he was not driven by money. Wasn't that often the way when a person grew up surrounded with the kind of wealth his family had generated back at home? The house he lived in, so he'd told her, and which he shared with a couple of student lodgers had been bought for him outright by his parents and would not have been cheap by any stretch of the imagination.

In fact, Nina knew the house well; it was a three-storey townhouse just two doors down from where she and Hugh had lived. Since selling their old home she had deliberately avoided ever driving past the house; it was still too painful. Everyone she knew understood that – everyone except for her mother-in-law. It was no exaggeration to say that Hilary had been outraged when Nina had first mentioned that she was selling the house.

'But you can't!' Hilary had cried. 'It was Hugh's home.'

'It was *my* home too,' Nina had said firmly.

'Then why are you talking about selling it? Surely it would be too painful to be parted from the home you made together? It would be like leaving Hugh, he put so much of himself into the house.'

'As did I,' Nina had asserted, thinking that she was actually the one who had turned the bones of the house into a proper home.

'Then it makes absolutely no sense you selling something that was so special to you and Hugh. It's like you're trying to erase him from your memory.'

There was no reasoning with Hilary who was still desperately hanging on to every scrap of memory about her son and refusing to let him go.

Every first Monday of the month, it was carved in stone that Nina had dinner with her in-laws. Hilary had insisted it should become a tradition for them after Hugh's death.

'Hugh would have liked the idea of us being able to support one another in our grief,' Hilary had said. Nina had gone along with the idea because to do otherwise would have seemed unnecessarily rude. It was, she told herself, Hilary's way of keeping the flame alive.

So after work, and saying goodbye to Jakob as he set off to join friends for a drink and a far more enjoyable evening than the one she was destined to endure, she drove to Madingley with a heavy heart.

But at least she could look forward to seeing Hugh's father. Keith was always pleasant company and Nina's ally whenever Hilary became too overbearing. A people-pleaser, he was the archetypal put-upon, hapless husband who just wanted a quiet life.

Was that the fate of all husbands who wanted to take the path of least resistance; they placated and humoured their wives to avoid any unpleasant altercations? It was hard to picture it, but would she and Hugh have eventually adopted similar roles?

She arrived at The Maples on the dot of six o'clock. When Hugh had taken her to meet his parents for the first time, he had joked that to be late for his mother was the worst crime he could ever commit.

'I could literally be accused of mugging an old lady and she'd let me off with nothing more than a warning. But be late and she'd cut me out of her will!'

'What a splendid sight for sore eyes you are!' declared Keith when he opened the door to Nina and enveloped her in one of his fabulously welcoming hugs.

He was always a good hugger, and she sank deep into his embrace, grateful for his big-hearted compassion. It was so rare these days that she was held like this, and by a man who was affectionate and genuinely empathetic.

She had discovered since Hugh's death that most people who greeted her with a hug did so with little warmth or sincerity. They didn't linger, as if afraid her grief might be infectious. Or worse, a display of emotion on their part might open the floodgates of her grief which they would find acutely embarrassing.

She strongly suspected there was also the fear that a hug from a friend's husband or partner might be misconstrued. *Hands off my husband,* Nina imagined her friends thinking, *you might have lost yours but don't think you can help yourself to mine!*

There was a minefield of unspoken sentiments when it came to grief, and knowing this was one of the reasons she tolerated her mother-in-law the way she did. She understood what Hilary was experiencing and that she was unable to express the real emotional impact of her son's death, other than to come across as unfeeling towards anyone else's grief.

'For heaven's sake,' said Hilary, appearing in the hallway, 'do let the poor girl in before practically suffocating her!'

Same old Hilary, thought Nina, emerging from Keith's embrace. 'Hello, Hilary,' she said. 'You're looking well.' She made no attempt to kiss her mother-in-law. She'd made that mistake the second time Hugh had brought her here. The woman had virtually recoiled at her touch.

'I've been better,' Hilary said flatly. 'Well, don't just stand there. Come through to the kitchen. I'm putting the finishing touches to a salad. Keith is insisting on a barbecue. You know how he likes to mess about with hot coals and a pair of tongs.'

'For you, my darling,' he said, 'I'd walk over hot coals!'

Nina smiled but Hilary tutted and rolled her eyes at her husband.

Slipping her arm through Keith's, Nina fell in step with him. In the kitchen, he presented her with a selection of opened bottles of wine. 'What's your fancy?' he asked.

'A small glass of that Chablis would be perfect, thank you.'

'Darling?' he said, turning to his wife who was wielding a lethally sharp knife to cut into a large watermelon. 'What about you?'

'I'll have my usual. But don't be so heavy-handed with the gin. You know I don't like it too strong. Nina, we've been married for forty-six years, and he still can't make me a drink how I like it.'

'Right you are, my love, message received loud and clear that I must do better.'

Keith's good-humoured response induced another eye-roll from Hilary, but this time Nina detected what felt like a false note to Keith's customary ebullience in smoothing his wife's sharp edges and softening the worst of her barbs. There was no twinkle in his expression and nor was there the exchange of a complicit glance with Nina.

When the drinks were served and Hilary had finished making the watermelon and feta salad with black olives, they went out to the garden. It was a magnificent garden and Nina knew it was Hilary's pride and joy, so she always made a point of asking for a tour around the borders. She did the same now while Keith busied himself with the barbecue, sending clouds of smoke into the warm evening air.

Before Hugh died, father and son would have manned the barbecue together while putting the world to rights with a beer. Listening with only half an ear as Hilary rattled on about what a nightmare it had been to keep the garden from turning into a desert during the hot weather, Nina glanced back at Keith and thought how lonely he looked. And older. He must miss his son so much and yet his grief had undoubtedly been overshadowed by his wife's.

By the time they sat down to eat, Keith had resumed his familiar joviality and was making Nina laugh with his tirade on modern life – how the smug lot in Silicon Valley were determined to make his life a misery with their constant software upgrades that often resulted in his laptop or mobile not working as well as it had before.

'And don't get me started on the hundred and one passwords I'm supposed to remember and all those wretched QR codes,' he went on, warming to his theme. 'As for trying to remember which bin to put out, and for that matter, what we're supposed to put in it, I give up. I long for the days when a man's bin was his own affair; now we're practically facing a term in prison for making an innocent mistake.'

'You do exaggerate,' said Hilary, 'and apart from that, Nina's heard it all before, so climb down from your soapbox.'

'That's all right,' said Nina, 'I always enjoy listening to Keith raging against the machine. It's what we all feel at times, isn't it?'

'But what he doesn't tell you is that it's me who deals with the bins.'

'Aha, in that case, my love, you had better be careful or it will be you who goes to jail and not me,' said Keith with a laugh. 'But I promise to visit you,' he added.

'Oh, do be quiet.'

They drifted into a lengthy silence, and with the golden light of the evening giving way to a deep roseate glow as the sun began to set, Nina asked about Hugh's cousins and the wedding she'd been invited to.

'They were planning to marry next summer but have brought it forward,' Hilary said, 'after Fabian's fiancée, Tigs, discovered she was pregnant.'

'How wonderful for them both,' Nina said, 'they must be thrilled.' She hoped she looked and sounded as though she meant it because mentally she was bracing herself for what she knew would come next.

'It wasn't the order they wanted to do things in, but as it turns out they couldn't be happier.'

'I'm sure,' Nina murmured.

'And dare I ask if you're any nearer reaching a decision about having the child Hugh so badly wanted?' Hilary asked.

Keith sighed and briefly closed his eyes. He looked mortified at the question.

It was just over a week since the letter from the clinic had arrived, and Nina still hadn't replied to it. Every day she thought she knew what she wanted to do only then to change her mind. How could anyone make such a monumental decision and not be consumed with doubt that the decision they made was the right one, morally and personally?

She helped herself to a couple of grapes from the cheese platter in front of her. 'No, I haven't,' she said mildly.

'But time must be running out by now? Didn't you say the clinic would only store things for so long, and it's not as if you're getting any younger?'

Maintaining an impassive tone, Nina replied, 'That's correct, on both counts.

'And?' Hilary pressed.

There was really no need for Nina to say any more, but what the hell, she thought. 'And I've now received a reminder from the clinic that I need to let them know what I intend to do.'

'I don't understand why you're hesitating,' Hilary said. 'Surely the joy of having Hugh's child would give you something to live for. I know it would make all the difference for me, it would give—'

'Darling,' cut in Keith, 'it's none of our business.'

'Of course it's our business,' she snapped back at him, all pretence of polite discourse gone. 'This is our only chance to have a grandchild and she,' she paused to point at Nina, 'is denying us that right!'

'It's not a right,' Keith said. 'A child is a gift, not a right.'

'But I gave our son a lot of money to try for a baby with IVF, so don't you dare tell me I don't have a right to express an opinion!'

Keith looked murderous. 'Just once in your bloody life shut up, won't you!'

Never had Nina heard her mild-mannered father-in-law speak so roughly to his wife and judging by the shocked expression on Hilary's face, it was a first for her too.

But whatever shock Hilary was experiencing it was nothing compared to what Nina was trying to process. Hugh had taken money from his mother so they could have a baby? He'd never mentioned it. He'd said that the money they had used for treatment had come from their joint savings and a particularly good bonus he'd been given at work.

How could he have lied to her?

They'd promised each other that they would do this themselves, that they wouldn't take money from anyone else or put themselves in debt. Her parents had offered to help, but she'd turned them down because of the promise she and Hugh had made together.

Discovering that Hugh had lied to her, she felt sickeningly betrayed.

Chapter Six

Tuesday afternoon and Cassie was busy working. She had a few more tweaks to make to the website she had spent the last three weeks designing and then it would be ready to share with the clients. She was pleased with what she had come up with for the couple who ran a florist's shop. It had been such a pleasure to work with them and she would be sure to use them whenever she needed to send flowers to anyone.

Her work as a website designer was varied and absorbing and, on the whole, creatively satisfying. She had an eclectic mix of clients which included a micro-brewery, a farm shop, a care home, an accountant, an author and an all-female private detective agency. Of all her clients, the detective agency intrigued her the most.

Stretching her arms above her head, then flexing the muscles in her neck and shoulders, she pushed back her chair and stood up. Her office was on the upper floor of their apartment and in the turreted room with panoramic views of the grounds through three arched windows. In the middle of the room was an oak spiral staircase that led to the roof garden and she was sorely tempted to go up there and relax while listening to the current true-crime podcast she was hooked on. In the past few months, she had developed an addiction for podcasts about previously unsolved murder cases. She didn't care to explore too deeply why she found them so appealing, other than she liked the idea of justice being served if the guilty were finally exposed. With great restraint she ignored the spiral staircase and went down to the kitchen to make herself a drink.

When the kettle had boiled, she reached for the box of green tea bags. It was far from her favourite drink, but she kidded herself that it was good for her, so she drank at least two cups every day. As with so much in her life, she always had to add a teaspoon of virtuous self-denial or outright punishment to make good on the many indulgent excesses she enjoyed.

Her latest mission to cleanse and detox her body in the hope of losing weight hadn't lasted long, no more than a pathetic couple of days – her vow of abstinence broken by those glasses of wine she'd had with Nina. The weighing scales daily reminded her that those surplus-to-requirement pounds were not going to disappear without more effort on her part. She consoled herself with the thought that she still had the rest of the summer to lose the weight, so plenty of time yet for a crash diet before her fortieth birthday.

She knew it was shamefully superficial of her to worry about something so insignificant as her weight and a few lines and wrinkles, but a girl had her pride, and she was determined to retain as much of her youth as she could. Nina had clearly managed it, so why couldn't she? It was just a matter of willpower. And maybe a little help. Botox wouldn't help with the weight loss, but it would certainly assist in smoothing out any unwanted lines. Whenever she half joked with Ben that Botox would be an ideal early birthday present, he would frown and say something adorable like loving her just as she was.

And therein lay the problem. *Just as she was.* How about when she was as big as a house, which according to those weighing scales was where she was heading?

Ben was always so supportive of her and often said that if she ever wanted to give up designing websites and do something else, he would back her. Once or twice, she had considered she might like to do something new but could never decide what. Admittedly there were moments when she thought it might be nice to have nothing more complex to think about other than a yoga or Pilates class to attend, or lunch out in Cambridge with a friend, but she knew that would make her even more superficial and horror upon horror, totally irrelevant.

Her website design work had been good to her over the years and generally her clients had been good to her too; many had been with her for a long time as she also managed their websites. Of course, the truth, as Ben was at pains never to say, was that he easily earned enough for the two of them. More than enough. But her work, as modest as it was, represented something important to her: her independence. It was her safety net, just as it had been when she had been on her own with Emily.

Everyone needed a safety net, that was one of the most important lessons she had learnt, and if she was working at something that didn't necessarily bring her one hundred per cent satisfaction but paid the bills, it did at least give her a degree of security in case Ben ever left her. Not that he ever gave her any reason to think he would, but you never knew. Life – Drew-the-Terrible in particular – had taught her never to take anything for granted.

One of the few times Ben had ever really lost his temper with her had been over her fear that he might leave her. They'd been out for dinner with some of his work colleagues, one of whom was a girl called Anneka who was clearly as bright as she was attractive. All the way home in the car afterwards Cassie had dropped hints about Anneka and how Ben must enjoy working with her, going so far as to suggest that she was far more his type than Cassie was. He'd told her she was talking rubbish and that had made Cassie say, 'Well, that's my point exactly, I bet Anneka never talks rubbish!'

From there things had escalated until they were home and Ben had lost it. 'You have no grounds on which to think that I would ever leave you,' he'd exclaimed angrily, 'none whatsoever! Do you have any idea how insulting it is that you could think I'm anything like Drew?'

She'd had no rational argument to offer, other than to apologise and assure him she thought no such thing. The trouble was, deep down there was a small niggling part of her that didn't think she deserved Ben. Or the amazing life they had together.

Carrying her drink, she went back upstairs to her office. Standing at one of the arched windows, she saw a now familiar tall and slender figure heading towards the woods. It was their new neighbour, Venetia Randall-Jones, and she marched along at a surprisingly fast pace.

'There she goes again,' Ben had said yesterday morning when they'd been having breakfast and seen Venetia from the kitchen window. 'Do you think she's obsessed with reaching a daily step target?'

'Maybe so,' Cassie had said. 'I just hope I have the same level of energy when I'm older.'

The Enforcers had referred to the new occupant of the apartment below Ben and Cassie's as an 'old lady' or a woman 'getting on in years' but from what Cassie had seen, that description was very far from being appropriate. The woman she and Nina had met that evening when they'd introduced themselves could have been in her late sixties or maybe early seventies. There had certainly been nothing 'elderly' about her in her denim jeans and silvery-grey linen blouse, a colour that had toned perfectly with her well-cut jaw-length bob of hair. *Alert and elegantly streamlined* had been Cassie's first impression. And considering she had just moved in that very day and must have been tired, the woman looked as fresh as the proverbial daisy.

She thought much the same thing now as she watched Venetia

striding out of the bright sunshine and disappearing into the shadowy gloom of the woods. The funny thing was, Cassie was sure she'd seen her out late last night, the light of a torch glowing faintly in the darkness. It seemed an odd thing for anyone to be doing, never mind a woman on her own who had just moved in.

Hope Hall didn't really seem the obvious choice for a single woman of a certain age, which, Cassie knew, was both sexist and ageist of her, but it wasn't like the woman could walk to any convenient shops; everything was a car drive away. Having said that, Venetia Randall-Jones drove an enviably sporty little number: a beautifully sleek Mercedes SLK.

Cassie had wanted to call on her again, just to be friendly, but she didn't want to come across as an interfering neighbour. That was a job best done by the Enforcers, who doubtless had been at fever pitch making themselves thoroughly well known. As they'd said they would, Cheryl and Joanna had sent out an email inviting everyone to a welcome drinks party for their new neighbour. It was to be held on the lawn this coming Friday evening and everyone had been asked to bring a bottle and a plate of bite-size snacks. Glasses would be provided.

From behind Cassie came the tinkling ringtone of a FaceTime call on her computer. When she saw that it was Emily, her happiness came at her in an instinctive rush of pleasure, but then it was eclipsed by an unforgivable snark of resentment – *Oh, so after more than six days of not hearing from you, you finally have time to call me!*

Pushing the ugly thought away, she warned herself not to utter a single barbed comment about Drew-the-Terrible. As Ben would say, she had to play nicely, so Emily would be encouraged to share more with her.

'Hi, Ems,' she said cheerfully, using the pet name that only she had been allowed to use by Emily, at the same time mentally figuring out the time difference and concluding it was early evening there in Dubai. 'This is a lovely surprise, how are—' But before she could say any more, her daughter's face crumpled and Cassie lurched forward in her seat. 'Ems, what is it? What's wrong?'

It was a few seconds before the poor girl could speak and during those moments, myriad thoughts flew through Cassie's head.

Emily had discovered just what a selfish, hardnosed fraud her father was.

There had been a massive argument, and she had fallen out with Drew's wife, the impossibly perfect Rosalyn.

She was homesick and desperate to come home.

Or . . . worst of all, absolutely the very worst of all, someone had done something unspeakably vile to her precious daughter!

'I thought you should know,' Emily said, her voice barely recognisable, it was so thick with emotion. 'It's Dad, he's . . .' Her voice wobbled and broke off.

Yes! thought Cassie. The veil had at last been lifted and the real man had been revealed.

'Tell me, darling, what's happened, what's he done?'

Emily shook her head and kept on shaking it, her lower lip trembling. 'It's not what he's done,' she said, 'it's . . . there was an accident . . . and . . . he's in intensive care but they don't know if he's going to make—' Her words were swallowed up by an enormous shuddering sob.

Her distress tore at Cassie's heart. 'Take a breath, Ems,' she said, desperately wishing she could put her arms around her daughter and comfort her.

'It was a car accident,' Emily said at length, her voice still shaky. 'He was driving back from Abu Dhabi last night . . . it was raining, and people always joke that they don't know how to drive here in the rain because it hardly ever does. And that's when it happened. It was a lorry. A witness said it lost control and drove straight into Dad's car.'

Filled with heart-pounding relief that Emily hadn't been in the car with Drew, Cassie said, 'Was anyone with him?'

'He was on his own. Rosalyn and Finlay were at home with me. I was with her when the police came to the house with the news. Oh, Mum, it's just too awful. I can't believe he might die.'

Cassie couldn't believe it either. 'It's too soon to know for sure,' she said, wanting to ease the pain her daughter was feeling. 'Your father's tough, he'll make it.'

'You're just saying that to make me feel better. What you're really thinking is that you're glad he's going to die!'

'*Ems!*' Cassie cried out. 'That's a dreadful thing to say.'

'But it's true, isn't it? All my life you've never once said anything good about him so why wouldn't you be pleased?'

As stunned as she was by the accusation, Cassie knew that her daughter was in shock and was merely lashing out as an emotional release. 'Ems,' Cassie said gently, 'you're saying things I know you don't really mean, it's the shock. Now is there anything I can do to help?'

Sniffing loudly, Emily thrust the palms of her hands against her bloodshot eyes and rubbed them hard. She then looked back at Cassie, her expression so bleak it made Cassie want to insist that she take the next flight home. *Come home so I can look after you and make all this pain go away for you.* It was what any mother would want, to have their child close so they could be wrapped in love and protected from anything that could harm them.

'There's nothing you can do,' Emily said flatly.

'If it all gets too much, you only have to say. And if you want to come—'

'Don't say it, Mum! Don't you dare suggest I fly home. I'm staying right here where Rosalyn needs me.'

Hearing those words from her daughter was a direct strike to her jealously possessive heart. She should be proud of Emily caring so much for a woman she barely knew, a woman Cassie had mentally mocked as a fool for having thrown in her lot with a lying, cheating man like Drew, but to her shame she couldn't do it.

'Of course,' she forced herself to say, 'I understand completely. All I was going to say was, if things become too difficult, I'm here for you. Ben too.'

'Well, I'm here for Rosalyn,' Emily said, with what sounded like defiance, 'because if Dad dies, she's going to need me. She's already in a terrible state.'

'What about her family? Can't her parents be there with her?'

'They don't get on. Anyway, I'm her family, aren't I?'

Another strike to her jealous heart. 'But there must be others there in Dubai who can help,' Cassie said. *It's not your job*, she wanted to add. 'Aren't there friends there to support her? And didn't you say there's live-in help, a Sri Lankan maid?'

'She needs more than just practical help, Mum. She needs emotional support.'

But you're just a child! Cassie wanted to say. *You need emotional support too, and I'm the one who's always done that for you!*

'You should be pleased that Emily is being so caring,' Ben said in bed that night.

With her head resting on his chest and listening to the soothing rhythmic beat of his heart, Cassie said, 'I'm trying to be, but I'm fighting against years of resentment, and I'm only too aware how pathetic I sound and that it casts me in a bad light.'

'Hey, I'm not judging you.'

'You don't need to; I can do that all on my own.'

'You're always so hard on yourself.'

'And you,' she said, lifting her head from his chest and kissing him, 'are far too good for me.'

'Can you put that in writing, please?'

She smiled. 'Only if you'll always say the right things at the right time.'

'I'll do my best, but no promises.'

'Then promise me this, you'll stop me from becoming any worse than I already am.'

He kissed her long and hard. Then, 'Enough with the misplaced self-hate,' he said, moving his hands in slow, sensuous movements, his intent clear. She welcomed it, wanting to lose herself in their lovemaking, to forget that somewhere in a hospital thousands of miles away, the man who had caused her so much pain, but had helped create their beautiful daughter, was now fighting for his life. She should feel something for Drew, but she didn't.

What she did feel was a profound sense of fierce love for Emily and for what she was going through. However it had happened, the girl had connected with her biological father and just as she had made that connection, it looked like she was about to lose him. Would she ever get over that? And would she always blame Cassie for not trying harder to bring her and her father together when she was a child?

Chapter Seven

'Don't look at me like that, Bon-Bon, I'll only be gone a short while and you won't be alone, you'll have Adam Frost on *Gardeners World* to keep you company, and you know how you like his quiet soothing voice. It always puts you to sleep.'

His head tilted to one side, the little dog watched Venetia spray Elizabeth Arden 5th Avenue, a perfume she had used for as long as she could remember, onto her wrists and then her neck, his gaze tracking her as she bent down to slip on a pair of white trainers to go with the burnt-orange trouser suit she was wearing. His gaze remained on her as she looked at herself in the mirror that had yet to be hung properly on the wall in her bedroom. It was one of the many jobs on a long list of things to do. But at least she had a functioning landline, a mobile that had a reliable signal with a decent Wi-Fi connection, and a television that had been set up by one of the obliging removal men when she'd moved in over a week ago. It was Bon-Bon who needed the television more than she did, for moments like this when she had to leave him on his own. It worked surprisingly well as a dog-sitter. Her previous neighbours never once said they'd heard him barking.

Generally, it was the more anxious, more stressed-out dogs that barked, but Bon-Bon had always had such a contented nature. Poodles were known to be exceptionally intelligent, and

Bon-Bon had been a delight to train from when he'd first come to live with her as a puppy. He loved nothing better than to be involved in whatever she was doing.

'What do you think, Bon-Bon?' she asked, turning around from the mirror. 'Will I do? Will I impress the good folk of Hope Hall? But the question is, what shall I tell them about myself? Shall I have some fun and tell a few outlandish porky-pies, or shall I stick to the truth?'

With a twitch of his ears, followed by a release of air from his button nose, he sprang up from where he'd been sitting on the rug and trotted off down the hallway to the sitting room, his fluffy pom-pom tail bobbing behind him.

Applying some lipstick, Venetia picked up her handbag and slipping the chain strap over her shoulder, she gave her reflection a final glance in the mirror. It still surprised her when she really looked at her seventy-nine-year-old self. In her heart she was still a young girl with her whole life stretching out before her. A girl who was determined to put the past behind her and do something worthwhile with her life. It was debatable as to whether she had achieved either of those things as the past could never be shut away in a box and forgotten, and who knew what constituted worthwhile?

After a last kiss and a cuddle with Bon-Bon, she placed him on his favourite cushion on the floor in front of the television and took the stairs down to the ground floor, preparing herself for an hour or so of innocuous polite chit-chat. And maybe making a few friends into the bargain, if she so chose.

The question was, how much was she prepared to reveal of herself this evening?

They were gathered on the lawn just below the stone balustraded terrace and clustered around two wooden garden tables that were laden with glasses, bottles, and plates of food.

She stood for a moment on the terrace surveying the scene below her, instantly superimposing it with countless other scenes from a lifetime ago, of children running around, games of chase and hide-and-seek being played, voices shrieking. This had happened to her so many times since she'd moved in and had explored the Hall, while trying to piece together the new layout with what she recalled from before. The bones of the place were the same, it was the flesh that was different. In much the same way she herself was different with the passing of the years. It amazed her how disorientating the changed interior layout was, making it almost impossible to recall where the library had been or where she and all the others had eaten their meals.

The flashbacks she experienced to her childhood, which for the most part had been blissfully happy, were sometimes no more than a sensation of someone or something from those long-ago days. Those were the memories that often came with a heavy sense of loss.

'There you are!' called out a shrill voice from the assembled gathering. Homing in on the source of the salutation, Venetia saw two women coming towards her. They were the ones who had knocked several times on her door since she'd moved in and who had organised this meet-the-neighbours drinks party.

'It was very kind of you to go to so much trouble,' Venetia said when she was level with them on the grass.

'It's no trouble at all,' they chorused in unison.

Venetia knew that one of them was called Cheryl and the other Joanna, but she couldn't remember which was which. In contrast she could bring to mind every name of every person she'd known when she'd lived here before. The two women in front of her had twice invited her to join them for coffee and a chat – coffee and an interrogation session more like it – and she'd politely declined. The first time they'd asked, she'd said she was expecting an important phone call and the other time she'd claimed tiredness, what with all the unpacking. She'd made no attempt to invite them in, and she doubted she ever would. Something about their eagerness to befriend her cautioned her to keep them at arm's distance.

After a glass of white wine was pressed into her hand, she was ceremoniously introduced to the rest of her neighbours, all of whom were full of bonhomie and good cheer. Some of them she'd already encountered on the stairs or over by the garage block or strolling around the grounds and along the river. It was all very convivial, lots of pleasant small talk and with everyone declaring the Hall an idyll, an oasis or a heavenly sanctuary.

To Venetia's relief she had no trouble remembering the name of the pretty blonde now coming over to chat with her. It was Cassie, the friendly young woman who had been the first to knock on her door with her attractive friend, Nina.

'Are you settling in all right?' Cassie asked her.

'It's as if I've always been here,' she said with a wry smile.

'That's very good to hear.' This was from a man standing next to Cassie. He had sandy-coloured hair and very blue eyes and a charming air about him.

'This is my partner, Ben,' Cassie said, 'and if there's anything you want to know about Hope Hall, he's your man. He's fascinated with its history. Isn't that right, Ben?'

He had a lovely engaging smile, thought Venetia, much like Cassie.

'In that case, tell me what you know about the place,' Venetia said to Ben. She had the feeling he was itching to oblige. She was also curious to discover just how much he did know.

'Well,' he began, 'originally it was built in the seventeenth century for Sir William Beauchamp, some bigwig lawyer at the court of James the First, and when he died it passed to his son and then his son who promptly lost it in a game of cards to Thomas Audley, who spent a fortune on making his mark on the place after a fire. That was when the turrets were added as a piece of whimsy. The grounds were also re-landscaped at great expense. When he tired of the place, and the cost of its upkeep, he sold it to Lord John Morton and his wife Lady Felicity.' He paused. 'Are you sure I'm not boring you to death?' he said.

'Not at all,' she said. 'Go on, please.'

'Eventually it was owned by Lady Constance Morton-Granger who turned it into a children's home at the outbreak of the Second World War, and it remained so for some years. After it closed, it went through a series of different uses: a boys' boarding school, a remand centre, a teacher training college, and a Buddhist centre until it finally fell into disrepair.'

'And thanks to an enterprising developer, here we all are,' chipped in Cassie, bringing the story to its conclusion.

'Well then, here's to us all enjoying yet another Hope Hall Renaissance,' said Venetia, raising her glass. 'Now tell me all about yourselves. Oh, and is Nina not joining us this evening?'

'She'll be along later,' answered Cassie, 'she had a client who insisted on seeing her this evening. She runs Lavelle's art gallery in St Anne's Court in Cambridge. Do you know it?'

Venetia shook her head. 'I'm afraid I don't. But I shall be sure to call in the next time I go into town. What about you, do you work in Cambridge?'

'No, I work from home, I'm a run-of-the-mill website designer.' She pointed up at the westerly turret behind them. 'That's my office.'

'How lovely,' said Venetia, remembering how she used to play up there, standing on a chair and peering out of the windows.

'Cassie's downplaying what she does,' Ben said. 'There's nothing run-of-the-mill about her work, she's extremely creative. Her clients love her.'

Cassie groaned. 'Stop it, Ben, you're making my toes curl.' She then went on, and with obvious pride, to sing Ben's praises and the work he did. They were, Venetia thought with an amused smile, very sweet together. She liked them and knew that she would enjoy getting to know them better.

'By the way,' Ben said, 'we're very impressed with your fitness regime.'

'Fitness regime?' she repeated.

'Not that we've been spying on you,' said Cassie, 'but we couldn't help but notice how regularly you like to go for walks.'

'Oh that,' said Venetia airily, 'I'm a stickler for routine. Very boring, I know. But when you're as ancient as I am, it's important to keep moving.'

'If you ever fancy some company, you only have to ask.'

'Thank you, Cassie, I'll bear that in mind.'

'Permission to cut in here?'

Turning to her left, Venetia encountered an exceptionally tanned man in navy chinos and a lemon-coloured Ralph Lauren polo shirt. Silver-haired and with a face as craggy as a rockface, she put him in his early seventies. He held out a large hand to her.

'Ronnie Sharp at your service, Venetia Randall-Jones,' he said with a flourish and instead of shaking hands with her, he smoothly lifted her hand to his lips and kissed it.

'I presume you're sharp by name and sharp by nature,' Venetia said mischievously.

He laughed. 'Now that's not on, that's my line!'

'I'm sorry,' she said, 'it was just too tempting.'

'Watch out for this one,' said Cassie with a smile, 'he's a regular Casanova!'

Ronnie chuckled. 'I don't know where people get this idea about me.'

'How's tricks then, Ronnie?' asked Ben. 'We haven't seen you around in quite a while.'

'It's been a hectic time with the hotel, peak season and all that.'

'Ronnie divides his time between here and Majorca where he's part-owner of a boutique hotel,' Cassie explained for Venetia's benefit. 'We once stayed there and had a fabulous time.'

'So if you're ever tired of the peace and quiet here,' Ronnie said to Venetia, 'let me know and I'll make sure there's a room at El Castilo available for you.'

Ben laughed. 'Don't say we haven't warned you.'

'Warning noted,' she said good-humouredly.

'Ignore them, Venetia, I'm always a perfect gentleman. Now, how are we all fixed for drinks? Who needs a top-up? I know I do! I'll hunt down a couple of bottles, shall I? Back in a jiffy!'

'He seems fun,' Venetia said when he'd gone to fetch more wine.

'He is,' agreed Cassie, 'and his hotel really is beautiful.'

'And all the roguish charm,' enquired Venetia, 'is that what I suspect it is, an act?'

'How very astute of you,' replied Ben. 'We think he rather enjoys playing the part. It probably works well in the hospitality business.'

'In turn,' said Cassie, 'we enjoy our role of playing up to his so-called reputation of charming ladies' man.'

'He certainly has an abundance of charm,' said Venetia.

'Here we go then, chaps,' said the man himself, 'red or white? Venetia, what's your tipple?'

'The white will do nicely,' she said, holding out her glass and hoping he hadn't heard her observation about him. 'Thank you.'

Their glasses topped up and the bottles returned to the tables, Ronnie made a toast. 'To our honoured guest and lovely new neighbour,' he said, raising his glass to Venetia. 'I hope you'll be very happy here.'

'I'm sure I will be,' she said, raising her own glass. 'Here's to everyone who has made me feel so welcome.'

And here's to all those I've loved and lost and who were such a big part of my life here, she silently added.

Chapter Eight

With the sale completed on the Auguste Bouvard landscape which Jakob had correctly predicted would be sold within the week, the clients who'd bought it had insisted on taking Nina for a thank-you drink in the garden of the Graduate Hotel where they were staying. She had wanted to make her excuses and drive home so she could show her face briefly at the welcome drinks party for their new neighbour but Andrew and Christine Kelling, old friends of her parents, were valued customers and so it would have been rude to say no. Jakob had promised to switch on the gallery security system and lock up in her absence. It wasn't like he hadn't done it before anyway.

Now, having said goodbye to the Kellings, and setting off towards Mill Lane, she was glad she had agreed to spend a couple of hours with them. It had been lovely sitting in the hotel garden overlooking the river on such a perfect summer's evening. The sight and sound of people walking along the towpath on the other side of the water, their voices raised with a cheerful vibrancy, had added to the upbeat feel of the occasion.

Since Hugh's death she had found it all too easy to turn down invitations that required her to be sociable. Invariably business situations were manageable because she could ensure the conversation avoided anything of a personal nature. Generally, very few friends pushed her to accept their invitations. Some understood her reluctance, but others she suspected had no desire to get too close to her grief.

Even after more than two years, many old friends still didn't know how to treat her, so it was simply better to distance themselves from her. She didn't blame them. Because let's face it, half the time she didn't know how to treat herself. There were days when she woke up feeling that she had come through the worst, that she was ready to be happy again. Maybe even meet somebody and fall in love. But all too soon that glimmer of hope was snatched away and replaced with guilt that she could even consider the possibility of being with anybody other than Hugh.

She had read something about the importance of shaking off the 'cloak of grief' which mourners wear following the death of a loved one. It was advised to shake it off before it became too much of a comfort blanket and in turn became too difficult to give up. Lately she had begun to wonder if she had left it too late to do that.

A crowd of noisy youngsters blocked her way as they queued at the punt station, and with a stream of cars now appearing from around the corner of Mill Lane, she waited until it was safe to cross. A sudden burst of raucous voices down on the river made her turn to the left where she saw two punts on course for a collision. Everyone else turned to stare too, most raising their mobile phones hoping to catch something TikTok-worthy. But as the near disaster was averted, it was the occupants of another punt that attracted Nina's attention.

At first, she doubted what she was seeing, it was so implausible. But she kept her gaze on the man doing the punting. He was wearing a baseball cap and sunglasses. She then looked at the woman who was seated on the cushioned bench smiling back at him. There was absolutely no mistaking the pleasure on both their faces and Nina found herself unable to tear her gaze away.

With surprising skill, the man manoeuvred the punt into a space and a young lad went to help them out, and all the while

Nina tried to reason that there was an innocent explanation for what she was watching. That there was nothing out of the ordinary in the affectionate glances being exchanged between the couple. Or that the hand that went to the small of the woman's back, and the light kiss that landed on her cheek, was not loaded with familiarity and intimacy.

When the crowd in front of her abruptly dispersed and there was no one to hide behind, Nina hastened away. She didn't want her father-in-law to spot her. She didn't want him to know what she had seen. It was none of her business. If this was his way of coping with his grief, then so be it.

Shock carried her feet at speed along Mill Lane and King's Parade, and then up towards Trinity Street and on to Lower All Saints Lane and the private car park she used. Unlocking her car, and slipping behind the wheel, she told herself she was overreacting.

What had she actually witnessed? Just two people enjoying an evening punt on the river. What was so wrong about that? There were any number of reasons why Keith was alone with a woman Nina didn't recognise. She could be an old friend. Maybe Hilary had been included in the outing but had declined.

None of this satisfied Nina. She knew with her whole being what she'd just witnessed and so what if Keith was involved with another woman? Who in their right mind would blame him when his wife behaved so coldly towards him?

As she drove out of the car park, Nina's thoughts returned to that dreadful scene with her in-laws earlier in the week when Hilary had admitted that she had given money to Hugh for IVF treatment, and that effectively she saw it as her right for Nina to produce the grandchild which she regarded as having paid for and bought.

She hadn't yet decided what appalled her more, Hilary's sense of ownership, or that Hugh had never told her about the money.

It wasn't even as though they'd been hard up. They'd had the money. They would never have embarked on the treatment if they hadn't been sure they could afford to do it. So why had Hugh accepted the money from his mother?

Had it been naive of Nina to believe that they didn't keep secrets from one another? If Hugh had deliberately kept that from her, what else had he hidden from her?

Each time Nina asked herself this question, something in her heart hardened and it wasn't a good feeling.

She was driving between the stone pillars of Hope Hall, when a text appeared on the screen in her car. It was from Cassie.

Party's over. Fancy a bite to eat and a catch up?

The onboard car system asked if she'd like to reply, and she pressed *Yes* on the screen and replied verbally with *Be with you in a few minutes.*

She hadn't seen Cassie since the evening they'd called on their new neighbour and apart from a number of texts in response to the invitations emailed to them about this evening's drinks party for Venetia Randall-Jones, they hadn't spoken. Some weeks were like that.

When Cassie opened the door to her and ushered Nina inside, her first words were: 'I'm going to be a terrible friend and selfishly offload because if I don't, I might explode!'

'That must have been some party,' Nina said, assuming that's what Cassie was referring to and that maybe she'd had a run-in with the Enforcers.

'No, no, it's nothing to do with that, it's personal. Ben's on the running machine and will eat later, so it's just the two of us. Salad with gravlax and some toasted sourdough bread, is that okay?'

'More than okay, but didn't you eat anything at the drinks party?'

'Didn't get a look in, not that I fancied much of it.'

'Is there anything I can do to help?'

'Do nothing but perch on a stool there, help yourself to some wine and I'll do the rest.'

Nina was conscious that whatever it was that Cassie wanted to offload, she would only do so when they were both sitting down. She knew her friend well enough to know that when she was ready to talk it would all come hurtling out in one colossal rush. That was a big difference between the two of them; Cassie needed to get whatever was bothering her off her chest, whereas Nina bottled things up. She always had. She also rarely confronted a situation head-on. It was always after somebody had annoyed her that she could think of any number of smart comebacks, her mind usually buzzing with everything she should have said but hadn't.

It had been the same on Monday evening when her mother-in-law had been so vile. Nina should have told Hilary exactly where she could shove her arrogant assumption that it was her right to be a grandmother because she'd handed over a chunk of money, but she had behaved in her customary very controlled manner by swallowing down her anger and focusing on not escalating the situation. Wasn't that also what she'd just done when she'd hurried away before Keith had a chance to spot her? It had been her way of avoiding an awkward scene and making them both, but especially Keith, uncomfortable.

Sometimes she thought it was cowardice that made her behave this way, but she had always wanted to put other people's feelings before her own. She had believed it was a virtue to do so, but now she thought it could not sound more sanctimonious.

However, none of that was important right now. Her priority was to stop thinking about herself and her shock at seeing her father-in-law with another woman, and instead help her friend. After all, it was always easier to deal with someone else's problem than one's own.

'Was there a good turnout for the drinks party?' she asked, while pouring herself a glass of wine and sitting on a stool at the island unit which was identical to the one in her own kitchen.

'Pretty good. The biggest surprise was Ronnie showing up. He was laying it on a bit thick with Venetia. The man's an incorrigible flirt.'

'How did Venetia react?'

'With amusement. I think she rather enjoyed it.'

'Good for her.'

'That's what Ben said. He reckons they'd make a good match. God love him, he's such a romantic.'

'I thought Ronnie's taste ran to much younger women?'

'Maybe it's time for him to find a more appropriate girlfriend, not some bit of arm candy. Right, here we are, supper, such as it is.'

Nina looked at her plate and smiled. 'This is absolutely divine,' she said appreciatively. 'Aren't you drinking any wine?' she asked, noticing Cassie's glass tumbler contained what looked like water.

'I had two glasses earlier,' Cassie said, 'which was more than I should have had with everything that's going on inside my head, but you know what it's like, we put on a show when we need to.'

'Indeed,' said Nina. 'So is this the moment when you tell me what's wrong?'

'It's my ex-husband,' Cassie said without equivocation. 'Emily called me earlier in the week to say he'd been involved in a car accident and . . . and he might not survive. She called again this afternoon, and the news isn't any better. It's worse in fact. There's talk of switching off the life support machine he's on.'

Choosing her words with the greatest of care, Nina said, 'And you're surprised how upset you are, is that it?'

'Yes and no. Not for Drew, but I'm desperately upset for Emily. I might not have been happy about it, but she'd just started to get to know her father, and now she's going to lose him. I can't begin to think what the effect on her will be. Selfishly, I want her home. I want her here so I can keep her from being hurt.'

'That's understandable.'

'But why do I feel such indifference for Drew? Shouldn't I at least feel some sadness for him that his life is hanging by a thread?'

'From what you've told me about your ex, I don't think you should beat yourself up with guilt. Nobody would expect you to make such a dramatic turnaround with your emotions.'

'I feel as if makes me look like a horrible person that I can't summon at least one tear for him. Just saying that aloud makes me sound sickeningly self-centred, that I'm thinking more about myself than him.'

'Maybe your feelings will change.'

'You mean if he dies, and I'm confronted with the stark reality of it?'

Nina nodded.

'That's the odd thing, I can't imagine him dead. It's like he's been the eternal bogeyman in my life since forever. He's cast this long shadow over everything. I know that's pathetic of me, because I doubt he gave me a single thought, but I've allowed him to live rent free in my head all this time.'

'Even though you love Ben and you're so happy with him?'

Now it was Cassie's turn to nod. 'I've always joked that no one can hold a grudge like I can, I've turned it into an art form.'

'What if now is the time to let that grudge go? Why live the rest of your life with that shadow hanging over you?'

'Because I'm scared what might be left. What if that's all that I am, just a pitiful woman driven by bitterness and the inability to forgive?'

'Come off it, Cassie, that's not you. There's nothing remotely pitiful about you. If you want an example of bitterness, try this for size.'

And suddenly, without meaning to, Nina told Cassie about her latest encounter with her mother-in-law, followed up by what she'd witnessed this evening.

'My God!' exclaimed Cassie when Nina had finished. 'As though you haven't been through enough, but then Hilary acts as though she owns your body and can insist what you do with it. That's the maddest thing I ever heard.'

'To be fair, I think it's because she's mad with grief.'

'That's very forgiving of you.'

'But that's not to say I don't feel angry with her, I do. I'm also angry at the way she treats Keith, he's done nothing but support her and put his own grief aside to help her. The man's a saint.'

'A saint who may or may not be finding comfort in the arms of another woman,' remarked Cassie. 'Not that I'm judging him.'

'Me neither,' said Nina.

'Will you let him know that you saw them together?'

'No. I don't think I should, not when he didn't see me. At the end of the day, it's none of my business, is it? I don't want to get involved. Whatever is going on is between them.'

'On the other hand,' said Cassie, 'and since you've always said how well you and Keith get on, he might be glad of someone in whom he could confide.'

As fond as she was of Keith, taking the role of co-conspirator to such an extent didn't appeal to Nina. It certainly didn't seem like an ideal way to improve her relationship with Hilary. But was that ever going to happen? Wouldn't it be better all round if she cut the tie completely?

Chapter Nine

The following afternoon and while Jakob was delivering a painting to a client over in Newmarket, Nina was deciding which picture to put in its place on the wall.

She had her back to the door when she heard it open and turning around, she was surprised to see Keith walk in.

'I was just passing and thought I'd call in,' he said. He looked and sounded as awkward as she suddenly felt.

'That's nice,' she said. 'Time for a coffee?'

'Only if it's not an inconvenience to you.'

'Don't be silly,' she said. Leaving him to browse she scooted off to the kitchen and set the machine working. In less than a couple of minutes, she returned with two mugs of coffee and found Keith standing in front of a still life by Charles Perron, his expression thoughtful as though he were deep in thought.

'Your coffee,' she said quietly.

Barely taking his gaze away from the painting, he took the mug she offered him.

'Nina,' he said, still not looking her directly in the eye, 'I know that you saw me last night down by the river, and I know what you're probably thinking. But it's not like that.'

'I didn't think you'd seen me,' she said, deciding to dispense with any attempt to pretend she didn't know what he was talking about.

'Just fleetingly, enough though to see the look on your face as you hurried away.'

'Would you have preferred that I stayed and said hello?'

Now he did turn to look at her. 'Can I be honest with you?'

'Are you sure you want to be?'

He smiled. 'Yes.'

'Then let's sit down, shall we?' She pointed to the comfortable chairs grouped around a coffee table and while he sat, she flipped the door sign from *Open* to *Closed*.

'I met Diane through an online bereavement group,' he said when she was seated next to him. 'She lost her daughter roughly the same time we lost Hugh, so she understands. We started by messaging each other, but then we decided to meet up. We share things that Hilary refuses to let me share with her. It helps. It helps a lot. We can even cry together, something I don't feel able to do with Hilary.'

'Is Diane married?' Nina asked. As though that made any difference.

'No. She's been on her own for some years. We're just friends. There's nothing else going on.'

Remembering what she'd witnessed last night, the tender way Keith's hand had touched the woman's back, the smiles they'd exchanged, and the kiss on her cheek, Nina wondered if he was kidding himself, rather than actually lying to her.

'I can talk about Hugh with Diane without worrying,' he went on, 'that I'm going to say the wrong thing and cause a massive scene. You know yourself that Hilary's not entirely rational these days. The way she spoke to you last Monday, it was just awful. I admire your self-control; I really don't know how you didn't let rip at her.'

'I think that you had that pretty much covered.'

He sighed. 'I'm not proud of my outburst. I shouldn't have done that in front of you. I could see how uncomfortable it made you feel.'

'I was uncomfortable already.'

'You know,' he said after a short pause, 'if you ever want to stop our Monday evening get-togethers, you can. Although I'd miss seeing you.'

She put down her mug and placed a hand over his. 'I'd miss you too, Keith.'

'But you're entitled to live your life the way you choose. You mustn't allow Hilary to bully you into doing anything you don't want to.'

'Are you talking specifically about me having another go at IVF?'

'Yes, but not just that. You're young and beautiful and you deserve to meet somebody special who will cherish you. Just as Hugh did.'

She was silent for a few seconds. 'I wish it was as easy as that.'

'But it could be. You owe it to yourself to let go of Hugh.'

'But I don't want to. I don't ever want to forget him. How could you even suggest I do?'

'Oh, darling girl, I'm not. But what I've come to realise is that the depth of real love you feel for another person cannot ever be destroyed by death alone.'

'Is that what you've learnt from sharing your grief with Diane?'

'Yes. As I said before, I can talk about Hugh with her without fear of the consequences. I can talk about the good times, relive the days when Hugh was a child, and all the things he did that made me so proud of him.'

'I'm glad you're able to do that,' she said. She meant it, too.

'Now the question I want to ask you is this,' he said. 'Do you have anyone with whom you can share your real feelings?'

'I did try an online bereavement group, but it didn't help, in fact it made me feel worse listening to everybody else's grief. Which is not very generous of me, I know.'

'I understand exactly what you mean, I felt that too initially. But then Diane and I made a connection and we decided to slip away from the group, or rather form our own self-help group, just the two of us.'

'Does she live in Cambridge?'

'No. Ely.'

'Do you go and meet her there?'

'Usually that's where we meet up, but yesterday she came here. I knew it was a risk, that our friendship could be misconstrued, but I suppose a part of me didn't care. What did it matter?'

'Yet here you are, feeling the need to explain yourself,' Nina said.

'But only because I wanted you to know the truth of what you saw.'

'I think the truth is, it's more than just friendship which you have with this woman, isn't it?'

He blinked and then smiled hesitantly. 'Maybe.'

'And what does that mean in the long term?'

'I have no idea. It seems too cruel to leave Hilary when she's still so consumed by her grief for Hugh. I'm worried how it would affect her. And I'm all too aware that if she knew how I was currently conducting myself, it would have just as grave an effect on her.'

'But you can't put your life on hold forever,' Nina said.

'I agree, especially at my age. I'll be seventy-two next year so I'm more than aware that I need to make the most of what's left to me. But, Nina, the same goes for you. You owe it to yourself to move on. There, I've uttered the dreaded cliché we hate so much, and I can only apologise. The trouble is, sometimes there's nothing more accurate than a cliché, which is why we use them. Now then,' he said with finality, patting her hand and rising to his feet, 'I've taken up enough of your time, and since there's somebody looking at the closed sign on the door, I should leave you to your customers.'

Hugging him goodbye, Nina thought how he walked out of the gallery a different man, his shoulders back, his head up. There was none of the embarrassed awkwardness of when he'd walked in. Confession really is good for the soul, she couldn't help but think.

Chapter Ten

*T*he twenty-three-year-old mother of two young children had been missing for exactly eleven months and three weeks before her body was found in the woods, following an anonymous tip-off to the police. According to the postmortem, Olivia Benlow had only been dead for five days. So where had she been all that time?

Cassie was driving home after spending a girls-only day with her mother and sister. She was listening to a new true crime podcast, and thinking as she often did that she would make an excellent investigator as she had a regular nose for a mystery. Which was why she was going to investigate their new neighbour's late-night and early-morning wanderings. It would be almost dark when Cassie arrived home, and she planned to go up to the roof terrace and wait for Venetia to appear. Then she would run downstairs and, hiding in the shadows, she would follow their new neighbour and discover what she was really up to.

A week had passed since the evening of the welcome party for Venetia, and it was only a few days later that it struck Cassie as odd that the woman had revealed nothing of herself to them. Almost every question had been neatly side-stepped. Ben was of the opinion that the woman was simply naturally private and liked to keep herself to herself. 'Not everyone likes to share personal details,' he'd said.

In contrast Cassie was a world-class sharer; she was probably guilty of over-sharing. But that was how she was, and she was unlikely to change. Yet change, she feared, was something she would have to force herself to do when it came to her feelings towards her ex-husband. She had to change for her daughter's sake, because how else would she be able to offer genuine comfort to Emily if Drew died?

For now though, and from what Emily had told her yesterday, Drew was still in a coma, his life ebbing away. It was a weird sensation, willing him to live if it meant it would protect Emily. Cassie tried to believe that wanting to save her daughter any heartache made her a better person than she really was. That was another of her failings, always trying to ease her conscience. It would be a lot simpler if she could just be a better person.

The truth, and only she really knew the extent of this truth, was that beneath the outward happy-go-lucky exterior she presented to the world, there was a black-hearted, grudge-holding vindictive person who had repeatedly wished her ex-husband dead. She'd wished too that his last dying wish was to beg her forgiveness, only for her to refuse to give it. That's how irredeemably vile she was!

But now that he really did seem to be on the verge of dying, would she give him her forgiveness? She knew what the answer should be, but she didn't think she could make the necessary leap.

While with her mother and sister, Jodie, they had been reminiscing about their children when they'd been babies. Mum had always claimed that both Cassie and Jodie had been model babies up until the age of two and then each in turn had turned into mini-monsters, their tantrums having become part of family lore. Jodie had two daughters, ten-year-old Isla and eight-year-old Sienna, and an abundance of amusing stories about them. For Cassie, all this talk had brought back a host of memories, not all of them good, but foremost was the memory of the fierce protective love she'd had for Emily and how so often it had felt like it was the two of them against the world. She had vowed always to keep her daughter safe, to protect her against the evils of the world. The knowledge that she might not be able to keep that promise did not sit well with Cassie.

During their reminiscing, Jodie had joked that it wasn't too late for Cassie to have another child. 'Last chance saloon and all that,' her sister had said, 'have one while you still can.'

'Thanks a bunch for reminding me that I'm living on borrowed time,' Cassie had fired back. 'You're only four years younger than me, so you'd better make the most of things too!'

Watching her speed as she entered the village of Grantchester, Cassie thought of the choice Nina had to make, whether or not to try one more time with IVF to have the child she and her husband had wanted. Cassie couldn't help but think that if Nina really wanted a child, she would have tried again by now.

When Nina had told her about her mother-in-law's assertion that Nina owed it to Hugh's memory to produce a grandchild, she had gone on to say that she had wanted to make the life-changing decision when she wasn't so consumed with grief, when she felt the time was right and she was better able to cope with having a child on her own.

'Trust me,' Cassie had told her, 'no time is right. But somehow, we women all muddle through and I reckon if anyone could take motherhood in their stride, you could. You're always so organised and calm.'

Nina had disputed this, saying Cassie only saw her on her good days. There might well be some truth in what her friend had said, because most people were like that, they kept the worst aspects of their character hidden. Cassie might wear her emotions on her sleeve – they swung chaotically like a weathervane in a high wind for all to see – but that dark shameful side of her, the side that for years had fantasised about Drew dying was not something she had ever wanted anyone else to see.

When she let herself in at the apartment, all was quiet and there was no sign of Ben. Dropping her bag on the sofa and putting her mobile to charge, she then heard Ben's voice coming from upstairs. He was probably in his office. It was next door to hers and was larger but didn't have the benefit of the whimsical turret. She liked it on the few occasions he worked from home, as they could call through to one another, quoting silly stuff they'd just seen online. She went to let him know she was back.

She was halfway up the stairs when she heard him say, 'Look, I have to go now, Cassie's home.'

There was something in his hushed tone – something furtive – that made her pause. Ben was never furtive. He didn't do furtive. He was as open as they come.

Remaining where she was, she listened to what he said next.

'Yes, of course. I'll speak to you again when I can. But remember, she mustn't find out. No, I'll invent something. Something convincing.'

Knowing that she'd just overhead something she wasn't meant to hear, Cassie crept back down the stairs to the kitchen.

Don't even think it, she warned herself as her mind began replaying a host of painful memories from the past. *It's nothing suspicious. You made that mistake once before. You imagined the worst – an affair – and you put yourself through unnecessary hell. Ben is nothing like Drew. Repeat after me, Ben is nothing like Drew! He's probably just planning a lovely surprise for your birthday.*

Filling the kettle at the tap, she shuddered at the appalling memory from the early stages of their relationship, when she'd found it so difficult to lower her guard and be vulnerable with Ben, to allow herself to believe that he genuinely cared about her. Back then she had sooner believed the worst of him than the best.

'Hi sweetheart,' Ben said, appearing just as she'd plugged in the kettle and effectively plugging the dangerous flow of her thoughts. 'Good time with your mum and Jodie?' he asked.

'Yes,' she answered, trying to sound as normal as possible, 'they sent their love. Who was that you were speaking to upstairs?'

'Just someone from work,' he replied with an easy shrug.

It was exactly the kind of thing Drew had said. 'At this time of night?' she queried, despite the voice in her head yelling at her to stop it. *He's planning a surprise, so leave well alone!*

'You know what it's like,' he said, 'some people never switch off.'

And some people just can't help themselves, she thought miserably. Would she never fully trust Ben's love for her? What the hell was wrong with her?

'You know what,' she said, needing a moment to settle her emotions, 'I think I'll go for a walk.'

He turned to look out of the window. 'But it's almost dark.'

'I won't be long. I just need to stretch my legs; I've been sitting down for most of the day, and I could do with some fresh air.'

'I'll come with you.'

She raised her hands as if to physically stop him. 'No, it's okay, you stay here. I'll be back before you've even missed me.'

She felt badly leaving him standing there in the kitchen looking so baffled, but she really did need a moment to reset herself. It was ridiculous how easily she had been unnerved by overhearing a perfectly innocent snatch of conversation. Of course Ben wasn't cheating on her! She knew that in her heart. All he was doing, because he loved her, was planning a surprise for her birthday.

Without realising the direction in which she had wandered,

she found herself entering the gloom of the woods, and with her eyes adjusting to the darkness, she slowed her pace before coming to a stop. Ahead of her, she saw the horizontal trunk of a fallen tree. Thinking it would be a good place to sit and think, she went over and sat down on it.

She'd only been there for a few minutes when she heard noises coming from behind her, the crackle and rustle of twigs and dried leaves.

Suddenly thinking of the podcast she'd been listening to in the car – *The Disappearance of Olivia Benlow* – and how the woman's body had been found in a shallow grave in the woods, her stomach clenched, and her mouth went dry. Holding her breath, she then heard a low murmuring voice followed by a scampering sound. Then out of the darkness came the faint glow of a beam of light and the figure of a woman and a small dog.

Chapter Eleven

It was hard to know who was more startled, Venetia or her young neighbour sitting on the fallen tree, the spot where Venetia always sat while Bon-Bon, on his extendable lead, poked around in the leaves.

'You have a dog,' said Cassie as Bon-Bon stood stock still in the soft beam of light, emitting a low growl, his ears pricked. She didn't say it in an accusatory voice, more a simple statement of fact.

'Yes,' said Venetia, equally matter-of-factly. 'His name is Bon-Bon.' Then as if the necessary introductions had been completed satisfactorily, the dog went to inspect Cassie. Standing close enough to be petted, he tilted his head back expectantly.

'If he's being a nuisance, or you're not a fan of dogs, just ignore him,' Venetia said.

'How can I ignore him when he's so adorable?' Cassie responded. 'Come and sit with me and tell me all about him. Presumably he's the reason for your late night and early morning walks, isn't he?'

'Guilty as charged,' Venetia said when she was seated next to Cassie. 'Are you going to report me to the management company?'

'Of course not. I'm not a snitch.'

'You'd be perfectly within your rights to do so; after all, it does say quite clearly in the management rules, *no pets allowed.*'

'But who could possibly object to this little cutie?' After he'd been pawing at her, Cassie now had Bon-Bon on her lap, and he was plainly loving the attention. 'But as totally gorgeous as he is,' Cassie went on, 'why have you moved here, where, to put it bluntly, he isn't welcome?'

'I have my reasons.'

'I've noticed you have a habit of never really answering a question,' the younger woman said when a few seconds had passed. 'You did it at the drinks party.'

Thinking that it was quite an astute observation, Venetia said, 'I answered your questions about my dog.'

'True, and I do appreciate I scarcely know you, but it seems to me that you do tend to evade anything of a personal nature.'

Venetia smiled to herself. 'Maybe it's because I'm inherently dull and have nothing of worth to share. I'm much more interested in knowing why you're here alone in the dark.'

'There,' said Cassie, 'that's a classic example of misdirection.'

Venetia turned her head to look at her companion. 'Really? And there was me thinking I was just being a good neighbour.'

A small smile appeared on Cassie's face. 'You are, but you have to admit, you are giving the impression that you have something to hide, quite apart from this delightful little chap.'

Venetia laughed lightly. 'We all do, don't we? I'm no different to anybody else.'

'What will you do if it becomes known by other people here that you have a dog?'

'I'll fight tooth and nail for him to be allowed to stay.'

'And if you lose the fight?'

'Then they'll have to carry me out kicking and screaming. I shan't go quietly, I can assure you.'

'Well, you can count on me to help man the barricades to stop them doing that. I love a rule-breaker.'

Venetia smiled back at her. 'How about in return for that kind gesture, you tell me what's troubling you?'

Cassie frowned. 'What makes you think something's troubling me?'

'Why else are you here on your own in the dark? Or are you communing with nature? Or maybe moon-bathing?' She turned her gaze upwards. 'Not that there's any chance of any moonlight making its way through the thick canopy of leaves above us.'

A long moment passed while Cassie played with Bon-Bon's fluffy ears. Venetia waited. She was good at that.

'It's nothing really,' Cassie said at length. 'Just me being my usual idiotic self.'

'You don't strike me as being idiotic.'

'I promise you, I am. I have this infuriating habit of leaping to conclusions and usually getting it absurdly wrong.'

'And why might that be?'

'Because I'm an—'

'Please don't say it's because you're an idiot. I won't countenance that.'

'Okay then, it's pretty simple really; I have trust issues. And the person I should be able to trust one hundred per cent, I don't seem able to.'

Venetia let a moment pass before saying, 'Would that person be Ben?'

Cassie sighed deeply. 'Yes. And don't jump to any conclusions yourself about him, you mustn't do that. Ben's never given me any cause not to trust him.'

'What's the problem, then?'

'Long story short, it's my inability to believe Ben won't treat me the way my ex-husband did. He was a serial cheater and dumped me when our daughter, Emily, was born.'

'Ah,' said Venetia, 'that would understandably have a destructive effect on you. So how long have you and Ben been together?'

'Ten years. Time enough for me to have shrugged off the doubts, you're probably thinking, aren't you?'

Venetia shook her head. 'Not at all. Something like that would never really leave a person. Trust is such an integral part of a relationship, perhaps the most fundamental part. So what's happened to cause you to have a momentary wobble, if I can put it that way?'

Cassie ran a hand the length of Bon-Bon's body, then repeated the movement before saying, 'I overhead Ben talking to someone on the phone earlier and it was a conversation I plainly wasn't meant to hear, and though I'm sure it was perfectly innocent, no more than him organising a surprise for my birthday, it caught me off guard. It was a reminder of all those times I'd caught my ex cheating on me.'

'And the memory caused a bit of you to leap to the conclusion that Ben was doing the same?'

Cassie nodded. 'It all sounds so pathetic, doesn't it?'

'Far from it. Does Ben know how you feel?'

'Yes. Although perhaps not the full extent. I know it annoys him intensely that I can't let go of the past and trust him completely, so I try to hide my true feelings. I once accused him of having an affair. We'd only been together for a couple of years, and I'd somehow convinced myself that he was being unfaithful and sneaking off to see an ex-girlfriend of his. It drove me crazy imagining him with her. He was doing nothing wrong, of course, the ex had merely contacted him to ask if he had the phone number of a mutual friend as she'd lost her mobile. The mess I made of things could so easily have ended our relationship.'

'But it didn't,' said Venetia, with what she hoped sounded like gentle but no-nonsense firmness, at the same time thinking that Cassie was clearly a lot more insecure than at first she appeared, or how she liked to portray herself. But then wasn't that often the way? We each have our Achilles heel, and for Cassie it was obviously how she'd been made to feel all those years ago. Some things stayed with you forever, you simply had to learn to live with whatever had left its mark on you.

'If I could give you one piece of advice,' Venetia said, 'it would be this; don't ever let the past get in the way of your future.'

Seemingly lost in thought while absently stroking Bon-Bon's head, Cassie eventually turned to face Venetia. 'You've been very kind, listening to me babbling on. I've probably shared way too much with you. Another crime I'm guilty of. You won't tell anyone what I've told you, will you?'

'Absolutely not. The last thing you need is people gossiping about you and I sense that there could be a few here who might derive pleasure in a bit of neighbourly gossip.'

Cassie smiled. 'The Enforcers definitely would.'

'Who?'

'The cabal of Cheryl and Joanne who enforce the Hope Hall rules. You need to watch them. If they find out about Bon-Bon' – Cassie covered the dog's ears with her hands – 'they'll come for you with pitchforks and flaming torches.'

Venetia smiled. 'Thank you for the advice, I'll be sure to heed it. Now, why don't you go back home to Ben while I take Bon-Bon for a wander so he can stretch his legs and do his euphemistic business.'

'If you don't mind,' Cassie said, 'I'd like to walk with you and then we can go back together. Is that okay?'

'More than okay, I shall enjoy your company.'

They'd only gone a short distance, following what had become a regular route for Venetia, when Cassie asked her the question Venetia had known she would.

'What really brought you here to Hope Hall?' asked the younger woman.

Why not tell her? Venetia pondered. It was always going to come out in the end. It was just that old habits die hard. Her natural inclination was always to say as little as possible while encouraging the other to do all the talking. As she just had with Cassie. She'd learnt that as a child, to keep things to herself, to lock them away in her heart so they couldn't be taken or destroyed.

'This was where I grew up a very long time ago,' Venetia said. 'I lived here when it was a children's home.'

Chapter Twelve

Naturally, just as any child couldn't possibly know or remember anything about their very early years, the story Venetia had been told was that in the spring of 1945, a month before the end of the war, she had been found wrapped in a towel inside a cardboard box on the front steps of Hope Hall Children's Home. It was, so she was later told, her ferociously loud cries in the dead of night that announced her arrival.

The police were notified, and a notice put in the *Cambridge Gazette* for the mother of the abandoned newborn to come forward, but nobody did. Being an abandoned wartime baby wasn't an uncommon occurrence, in fact there had been a surge in illegitimate births resulting in unwanted babies, so what was one more to add to the tally?

Some of the children at the home were there because their families couldn't afford to keep them. Sometimes the parents returned months or even years later to reclaim them. Every so often they would all be scrubbed clean and dressed in what passed for their Sunday best with ribbons in their hair for the girls and, for the boys who were old enough to wear them, tightly knotted ties. Encouraged to behave well, they would be introduced to couples who, if they saw what they liked, and having been thoroughly vetted by Lady Constance who ran the home, would be considered prospective parents for the chosen ones. These couples usually wanted a baby, the more attractive the better, not some red-faced goblin, as one of the older children once described Venetia when she'd been a baby.

From red-faced goblin she grew into a quiet, reserved toddler who flatly refused to smile on demand at strangers in the hope they might like her and take her home with them. She wasn't much better when she turned five. She was more than happy to stay where she was. She liked it at Hope Hall. It was home for her, so why would she want to be anywhere else, living with strangers? The older children shared frightening tales of children being put in cages and sent to live thousands of miles away in Australia, where they were put to work on farms where there were snakes and deadly spiders as big as dinner plates. The stories gave her nightmares, and it wasn't until Lady Constance winkled out of her what was worrying her that she was assured no child from Hope Hall would ever be sent to Australia.

Lady Constance Morton-Granger, to give the woman her full name, was well-known for being a wealthy philanthropist who, when she inherited Hope Hall in a dilapidated state, decided to put it to good use and turn it into a home for unwanted children. It was to be a place of hope where they could feel loved and wanted and where they could be educated. She made a point of always telling the children that each and every one of them was special in their own unique way. It was Lady Constance who had given Venetia her implausibly posh name the night she was discovered on the doorstep. The surname of Randall was given to her because Lady Constance had had a brother with that name to whom she'd been very close, but he had sadly died in the war.

A great believer in education, Lady Constance was determined that when it was time for the children to leave the home, they should leave fully equipped with the necessary skills to get on in life. She was what was known as a progressive and believed that girls and boys should learn not just the three Rs, but how to cook and sew, as well as know their way around a set of woodworking tools. She also instilled in them an appreciation of art and music as well as the Classics, literature and poetry. She taught some of the classes herself and in all ways, she was a genuine *tour de force*. The members of staff she employed were extremely loyal and stayed with her for years.

The other hugely important woman in Venetia's life was Edie Buckle. She came to work at the home as a nurse when Venetia was six years old. She was a kindly, rosy-cheeked woman who made a fuss of all the children when they were ill, but she took a particular shine to Venetia, and not just when she was unwell. Many a time when lessons were over, Venetia would slip upstairs to the sickroom just to be with Edie.

Years later, Venetia discovered what drove Edie to be the big-hearted woman she was. She had lost her husband at Dunkirk and then her two children during the Blitz in London, but rather than give in to her grief, she assuaged it by devoting herself to the care of other children. Venetia loved her dearly and there wasn't anything she wouldn't do for Edie. Or Lady Constance for that matter. She was devoted to them both.

In time though, somebody else came into her life, somebody for whom she would also do anything. Which she did. But that was far off into the future. Until then, Hope Hall lived up to its name and really was a place of hope for her.

Not that Venetia told Cassie all of this while they were walking back to the Hall by the light of her torch and with Bon-Bon now safely concealed in her tote bag. The general picture was all that was required, just a few broad strokes to satisfy her young friend's curiosity.

Chapter Thirteen

If the media, with its many hysterical headlines was to be believed, the heatwave that was sweeping across Europe, including the UK, might well herald the end of the world. But to look at Cambridge, as tourists and young folk lazed by the river and on the parched grass of Parker Green, as well as the cafés and pubs with their limited outdoor space, annihilation seemed like the last thing on anyone's mind.

It certainly wasn't on Nina's mind, but then maybe she was guilty of fiddling while Rome burned. Procrastination had, after all, become something of an art form for her. There again, if the end was nigh, then what did any of her worries count for? Maybe she would be better off living for the moment and not caring about tomorrow. That seemed to be Jakob's philosophy, to take each day as it came. But then he had the luxury of knowing that tomorrow was probably taken care of for him, in financial terms that was. Although it was possible she was assuming too much and doing him a disservice. He might be one of those lucky people who never let anything faze him.

They were sitting either side of her desk with a large pile of gallery catalogues for the upcoming exhibition which was to be held at the end of August, and would showcase the work of a Norfolk artist who specialised in seascapes. Most of what Nina sold was fine art, but she liked to support contemporary artists too. While she slid catalogues into envelopes and pressed down the self-sealing flap, Jakob stuck on address labels which he'd just printed.

'We work well as a team,' he said, taking an envelope from her.

'Yes,' she said, surprised by the comment, which had that Norwegian lilt to it that could have made it either a statement of fact, or a question. Was he worried that she was going to say she no longer needed him? She couldn't think why he might think that as he'd more than proved himself since starting work for her. He was always reliable and prepared to go the extra mile.

'We do,' she confirmed, wanting to reassure him. 'We're making light work of these catalogues together.'

A few more envelopes added to the growing pile, he said, 'I was wondering if you would like to go for a drink after work this evening?'

Her hands stilled and she looked up at him. 'A drink?'

'Yes,' he said, returning her gaze with his intensely blue eyes, which one client had described as blue as a Norwegian fjord. 'You know the kind of thing, we sit in a bar somewhere, order a glass of something cool and refreshing and chat.'

'Oh,' she said. If she'd been surprised a few seconds ago, she was shocked now. 'A drink with *me?*' she added, as though needing the clarification that she hadn't misunderstood.

'A drink with *you*, yes,' he replied, his gaze still on hers.

'Wouldn't you rather be out with your friends?' she asked. *God, she was making a meal of this! Why couldn't she just say yes? What was the big deal? He was a work colleague suggesting they have a drink together, what could be more normal?*

'Shall I take it that's a no, then?'

'No!'

An eyebrow raised, he said, 'Now that definitely sounds like a no.'

'I didn't mean it that way, I meant yes, I'll have a drink with you. That's if you haven't changed your mind at my absurd reaction.'

He grinned. 'The offer still stands. Now come on, back to these catalogues. Then I'll take them to the post office before the boss tells us off for slacking.'

Relieved that the awkwardness of the moment had passed, she said lightly, 'I hear she's a terrible tyrant.'

'The worst,' he said with a sigh. 'I don't know how anyone could work for her, she's a real slave driver.'

'Aha, then you'd better watch out!'

'Yes, boss!'

By the time the working day was over, and Nina was setting the alarm system and locking up, she doubted the wisdom of agreeing to go for a drink with Jakob. He was the first man – a man on his own without a wife or partner – from whom she'd accepted an invitation of this sort, and her acceptance was loaded with guilt and an unshakable sense that she was betraying Hugh.

She knew it was an overreaction because no way was Jakob coming on to her. For heaven's sake, why would he, given the age gap? He probably felt sorry for her and thought that she didn't have any kind of a social life. Which wasn't far off the truth.

'I thought we'd go to the Anchor on Silver Street,' Jakob said, 'or would you prefer the Granta? Or somewhere else?'

He sounded so eager to please. 'The Anchor will be fine,' she said.

Away from the cool shade and relative peace of St Anne's Court, they made their way towards King's Parade and as they jostled their way through the crowds, Nina could feel the dramatic change in temperature, both from the sun still beating down from the cloudless sky and the baking heat rising from the pavement.

By the time they reached the Anchor, Nina was wishing she was wearing a light cotton dress instead of her cream trouser suit and teal silk blouse. And just as she'd suspected it would be, the pub terrace was packed. There'd be no chance of a table. But she was wrong. Jakob spotted the only free table and with a hand to her elbow, he steered her to what was a prime position overlooking the river. On the table was a handwritten 'reserved' sign.

'You booked?' she said.

'I did. In the hope you'd say yes.'

'And if I'd preferred the Granta?'

'I would have been in trouble.' He smiled. 'Perhaps I'm in trouble with you for presuming too much?' Not giving her a chance to respond, he said, 'What do you want to drink? I'll go inside and order at the bar.'

'A glass of whatever rosé they have would be good. A small one though.'

'Anything to go with it? No, leave it to me, I'll see what's available.'

She watched him go, noting with amusement that she wasn't the only one observing him. A group of Spanish-speaking girls were openly staring as he passed their table. She couldn't blame them. He was definitely worth a second look of anyone's time. Well-groomed and well-dressed, he was over six feet tall, broad shouldered, slim-waisted, and with an easy-going manner about him. His dark hair was short at the back but long at the front where his fringe dangled almost into his eyes, giving him a preppy look. He was a good catch in anyone's book, as her mother would say.

It was what Mum had said about Hugh when her parents met him for the first time. 'He's a catch and a half,' she had said.

'As is Nina,' Dad had chipped in, ever her biggest fan.

She missed her parents; it seemed an age since she'd last seen them. FaceTime chats, along with regular photos and videos, were all very well, but it wasn't the same as being together. Together was always better. That's what Cassie had said in the first few weeks of her daughter flying off to be with her father in Dubai.

Thinking of Cassie, Nina was reminded that she had been a poor friend to her neighbour and hadn't been in touch with her recently. The last she'd heard from Cassie was that her ex-husband was still in a coma, his life hanging by a thread, and that she was desperately worried about Emily. 'It's a lot for her to cope with,' Cassie had said, 'I just wish she'd never gone to Dubai in the first place.'

No time like the present, Nina thought, taking out her mobile from her bag to message Cassie. But when she looked at the screen of her mobile, she saw she'd missed a call from her father-in-law, which he'd then followed up with a message. Opening it, she saw he'd sent her link to the online grief group he'd found so helpful – the group that had led him to meeting the woman he was now involved with. Did he think it might be a way for her to meet someone? A widowed man with whom she could share her grief? The thought so appalled her, she immediately deleted the email. Then she felt petty. Keith was only trying to help her. He had been helped and he wanted the same for her.

Looking up and seeing Jakob coming towards her across the crowded terrace, she put her mobile away.

'Rosé as requested,' he said, sitting down and passing the glass of wine to her. 'I also ordered some hot honey chicken wings and olives. Is that okay?'

'More than okay,' she said, the thought of food suddenly making her feel hungry.

'Excellent. And now,' he said, sitting back in his chair and raising his glass of beer to her, 'we can relax.'

Yes, she told herself. *Relax!* And amazingly, ten minutes later she realised she was relaxed, and she was actually enjoying herself. Jakob, it turned out, had a hidden talent for mimicry and could put on a variety of accents ranging from Scottish to Geordie, Liverpudlian to Brummie as well as something straight out of *EastEnders*.

'How in the world have you learnt all these accents?' she asked.

He shrugged. 'I hear a voice and it just clicks with me.'

'That's quite a gift. What other talents do you have which I don't know about?'

'I can boast of nothing else, I'm afraid. What about you, what secret talents do you have?'

'I'm double-jointed,' she said, 'look.' She pushed her thumb on her left hand so that it lay almost flat against her wrist.

'That's not human,' he said with a shudder.

She laughed. 'You're not the first person to say that.'

'What else can you do?'

'I can procrastinate for England.'

He drew his brows together. 'What does that mean?'

'It means I'm always putting things off.'

'You don't appear to. To me you always seem so decisive.'

'That,' she said, taking a sip of her wine, 'is because you only see me in a work environment where I'm used to making decisions about the gallery. Those are easy. I find personal decisions far trickier. I never used to.'

'But you moved house, that must have been a difficult decision to make when it was so personal.'

'That's true, but it felt right, so I didn't try to talk myself out of it. I knew it was a step into the future, rather than staying in the past.' She said nothing about the name of Hope Hall instilling in her a sense of optimism for her new future.

'And has it worked?'

'Yes and no,' she said, and before she was expected to elaborate on this, a young girl appeared with their food. She hated talking about herself, so was glad of the distraction.

When the girl had gone, Nina said, 'You know, you've never really explained why you're here in Cambridge when you could be anywhere in the world doing a far more—'

'Don't say it!' he interrupted and with a shake of his head.

'Don't say what?'

'That I could be doing something far more important, or more ambitious. That I shouldn't be settling for what others might think is a cooshy set-up. That's what my parents think, anyway.'

'*Cooshy?*' she repeated.

'Soft. Easy. An easy option.'

She smiled. 'I think you might mean cushy. But *cooshy* does have a certain ring to it. That,' she went on, helping herself to a sticky chicken wing, 'must be the only time I've ever heard you mispronounce something.'

'You see, that is why I have to be here, to perfect my English!'

'Nonsense,' she said with a laugh. 'Your English is excellent already. But I'm still curious. Why are you working in a small provincial gallery. Why not London? Or is there a girlfriend here? It's none of my business, I know, and as your employer I really shouldn't be asking you that.'

'I'm fine with it. But no. There's no girlfriend. There was when I was in London, but that didn't work out. I came here for a fresh start and it's somewhere I feel at home. As strange as it sounds, Cambridge reminds me of Oslo. Obviously without the sea,' he added with a smile. 'And the snow.'

'You wait for when we do have a really bitterly cold, bone-numbing winter, you'll know all about it then.'

'I look forward to it, it will make me feel even more at home.'

'You plan to stay then?'

'If you'll have me, yes. Or do you want me to leave?'

'Absolutely not. You're an invaluable part of Lavelle's now.'

'That's good to know,' he said with a nod.

'It's just that with your qualifications and ability you could do—'

He interrupted her again. 'So much better for myself,' he finished for her while wagging the remains of a chicken wing at her. He hadn't bothered with cutlery, and she wished she'd done the same, instead of messing about with a knife and fork. 'But would I be happy?'

'Only you can know the answer to that.'

'I am happy. Very happy. I like being a part of Lavelle's and I enjoy learning from you. You're a good teacher.'

'And you're a quick learner, and as you said this afternoon, we work well together.'

'So you wouldn't feel it was rude of me to propose an idea I've been thinking about for the gallery?'

Dispensing with the knife and fork, she picked up a chicken wing with her fingers. 'Go on,' she said, intrigued.

'I was wondering if you might consider exhibiting a few paintings by Norwegian artists.'

'Contemporary artists?'

'Not exclusively. In Scandinavian art there is a very particular way the light shines out from a picture; to me it always seems brighter and fresher. In European art, the light is almost subdued in comparison.'

Her interest piqued, she said, 'I know what you mean. I was in a gallery in Helsinki some years ago and I was struck in exactly the way you've just described by the use of light in the paintings I saw.'

'Does that mean you might consider my proposal? My business proposal,' he added quickly.

'I think it's certainly something we should look into,' she said, 'For now, why don't you do some research for me and come up with a list of artists whose work might fit in with the Lavelle's brand?'

'The brand which is classical rather than what-the-hell-is-that?' he said. 'You see, the Boss has taught me well.'

'Indeed she has,' said Nina, wiping her hands on a paper napkin, then sipping her wine and thinking that she was glad she'd agreed to have a drink with Jakob. She felt stupid for feeling guilty about accepting his invitation. What an idiot she'd been! She really needed to get a grip on her emotions. Obviously, his only reason for suggesting they do this was so he could put forward his idea for her consideration in a convivial setting. But fair play to him, she strongly approved of anyone with initiative and who was prepared to seize an opportunity.

Perhaps it was because she was now fully relaxed, and on familiar firm ground talking about work, she found herself letting down her guard and telling Jakob about the family wedding she'd been invited to in a few weeks. 'When I say family, I mean my husband's family,' she explained, 'it's one of Hugh's many cousins getting married.'

'That's nice,' Jakob remarked, 'that they continue to include you in their family occasions.'

'It is, but at the same time I can't help but think they only invite me out of pity.'

'I can't believe that's true.'

'Maybe not, but it's what I feel when I'm amongst them.'

'Then you need to find a way to stop that feeling happening. Why don't you take a plus-one, somebody who is there not so much to hold your hand, which you certainly don't need, but to be on Team Nina?'

'The look of horror on my mother-in-law's face would be priceless,' she said with a laugh.

'Would she really be so shocked to see you with somebody else now?'

'She'd be outraged; in her eyes nobody could ever replace her son.'

'What about in your eyes?'

The question was so unexpected and direct, and hit a nerve so powerfully, Nina wasn't sure how to answer.

'I'm sorry,' he apologised when seconds passed and she hadn't spoken, 'perhaps that was too blunt of me.'

'It's a reasonable enough question,' she said, 'and part of me thinks that I have to look to the future and what I want for my life, but it's . . . '

'Hard to let go of what you once had?' he offered.

'Yes. I know full well that Hugh has gone and that I owe it to him to be happy again.'

'You owe it to yourself too, don't forget.'

She frowned. 'For one so young, you're very wise.'

'I'm not so young,' he refuted, 'I'm thirty-two.'

'Wow, as old as that!'

'Now you're making fun of me. But back to the subject of this wedding, is there a male friend who could go with you?'

She shook her head. 'Everyone I know is partnered up.'

'I'm not. I could be your plus-one?'

Nina had a sudden mental picture of Hilary's jaw dropping to the floor at the sight of Jakob walking in with her and how the rest of the family might react.

Before she'd even processed the thought, and as if reading her mind, Jakob said, 'Wouldn't it be just a little bit satisfying to shock your mother-in-law into seeing you as a person in your own right?'

No, thought Nina, she'd probably think I'd gone mad and accuse me of embarrassing her and everyone else by showing up with someone so much younger than I am.

'But who would look after the gallery if you came with me?' she said without answering Jakob's question.

Which meant she was considering the idea, she thought later when after a tussle over the bill – a tussle which she won, overruling his claim that it was his idea to come here – Jakob insisted on walking her back to her car.

'There's no need,' she said as they set off down Mill Lane.

'Just as there was no need for you to pay the bill,' he countered.

It was dark now but there were still plenty of people about in the illuminated streets, and plenty of good-humoured carousing going on too as people spilled out of pubs and restaurants. Kings College Chapel was looking particularly magnificent, with a silvery-bright moon high above it.

In contrast, when they turned into Lower All Saints Lane it was completely deserted and once again, despite complaints to the council, the streetlights weren't working.

'Here, take my arm,' Jakob said as they entered the darkness.

It was a wholly natural thing for anyone to say, and after a slight hesitation, she did as he said and at the feel of his arm against hers, she once more pictured Hilary's face if she showed up to the wedding with Jakob. Would it be so bad of her to do it?

Wouldn't it, as Jakob had said, show Hugh's family that she wasn't just Hugh's grieving widow? She was Nina Lavelle, a woman in her own right.

Chapter Fourteen

'Cassie,' asked Ben, 'is everything all right?'

'Why wouldn't it be?' she answered, barely able to speak she was so short of breath. She had just mercilessly thrashed Ben three sets to love, and the blood was pounding in her ears, and her heart was thumping violently in her chest from the physical exertion of pushing herself so hard. Every point she'd been so determined to win had been a point scored to shore up her confidence to do what she knew she had to do next.

Eight long days had passed since she'd overheard *that* phone call between Ben and whoever he'd been talking to. Having successfully convinced herself that he was doing nothing more underhand than planning something for her birthday, there had then followed other overheard snatches of phone conversation, as well as times when he'd quickly shut his laptop when she walked in on him. She should have come straight out and asked him what he was up to, but instead she had bounced from telling herself that she was completely wrong, of course Ben wouldn't cheat on her, to letting her thoughts spiral wildly out of control.

They hadn't had sex since that night either. Normally they were equally balanced when it came to which one of them instigated sex, but while part of her wanted to seek comfort and reassurance in the act and the hope that it meant something, she couldn't bring herself to let it happen. Always respectful of when it was a no-go time, Ben hadn't pushed it when she'd claimed she was either too tired or just not in the mood. She'd used the heatwave as an excuse too, claiming the stifling hot weather had sapped her energy.

This Saturday morning though, Cassie had woken with new resolve. She couldn't let the not-knowing go on any longer. It wasn't fair to Ben. Or herself. And so, with the air cooler and fresher than it had been, Cassie had chosen the one place to talk to Ben where she always felt she had the upper hand – the tennis court.

'Because I can't help feeling I've done something wrong,' he said in the absence of a reply from her to his question. 'If I have,' he went on hurriedly, as if needing to get something off his chest, 'will you just say? I've felt for a while now that you're upset with me. I know Drew's accident has been a shock and you're probably still coming to terms with it, but I'm worried that maybe it's made you realise that you still have strong feelings for him. Is that what's going on here?'

She stared at him, aghast. Whatever outcome she had expected from this conversation she'd wanted to have with Ben, this hadn't featured. 'You're joking,' she murmured.

'Do I look like it?' he shot back. 'If I'm right, tell me. I need to know, Cassie.'

'But it's you,' she said, 'you're the one who's been acting strangely. All those secret phone calls I wasn't supposed to hear and . . . and I wanted to believe it was something to do with my birthday, but then . . .' She lost her nerve, unable to say the words.

His expression was now one of bewilderment. Then he slapped a hand to his forehead and groaned. 'You're not going to tell me that you thought I was having an affair, are you? For God's sake, not that again!'

'Yes and no,' she said hesitantly, 'but the more the phone calls I partially overheard, the more I feared the worst. You know what

I'm like, that I . . . ' Once more her words failed her and she could see that he was fighting to hold back his angry disappointment in her, that once again she had failed to trust him. Then with slow and very deliberate movements, he took the tube of tennis balls she was holding and tossed it on the bench beside them. He then stretched out his arms to her, placed his hands firmly on her shoulders and looked at her hard. 'I'm not having an affair, Cassie; I've been arranging a couple of surprises for you for your birthday.'

'But—'

'Enough with the buts, Cassie! I swear on everything I hold dear, and that includes you, that I'm not having an affair. I know Drew hurt you badly, but as I've told you before, I'm not like him and I never will be. I don't know what more I can say or do to make you believe that.'

He sounded so profoundly hurt, and as she took in the painfully earnest expression on his face, and remembering Venetia telling her that she mustn't let the past get in the way of the future, it was suddenly frighteningly clear to Cassie that she had to find the strength to trust Ben, or she would end up destroying his love for her, and hers for him. Filled with regret and compassion, she said, 'I'm sorry, Ben. I'm sorry I doubted you.'

Removing his hands from her shoulders, he shook his head. 'Not as sorry as I am.'

In the awful silence that followed, she said, 'But I don't understand how you could have thought that I still had feelings for Drew? That's just crazy.'

He shrugged. 'I guess it was the timing; it was the only thing that made sense of the change in you.'

'Why didn't you say something?'

He cocked an eyebrow. 'Says the woman who thought I was having an affair and didn't say anything until now.'

'Fair point,' she said.

'And for the record, I haven't lied to you at any stage. I've kept a secret, that's all. But if you want me to spoil the surprises I've planned for you, to convince you that I'm telling you the truth, then I will.'

'No,' she said, 'please don't.'

He briefly closed his eyes and when he opened them, he stepped closer to her and held her tightly. Wrapped in his embrace, she felt instantly soothed by the warmth and smell of him, a familiar combination of sweat mixed with his Tom Ford aftershave.

'Cassie,' he said, 'promise me you'll never doubt me again. And,' he added, tilting her head back so he could look down into her eyes, 'that you'll never slaughter me on the tennis court like that again. Have you any idea how humiliating it is to lose so comprehensively? You wouldn't let me win a single point.'

'I was fuelled up with a week's worth of conflicting emotions,' she said with a small smile, sensing that he had said all he was going to say on the matter.

'No kidding,' he murmured, bending to kiss her. 'But you know, if you have any spare energy still to burn, I can think of a way to put it to good use.'

'Are you sure you have any fuel left in the tank?'

'I reckon I can find some.' He then whispered in her ear, and she laughed at the outrageousness of his suggestion. But something about the way he'd said it and was looking at her made her realise he wasn't joking, and she was instantly aroused.

'I'm game if you are,' she said.

That was how they ended up in the woods with Cassie pressed against a tree and Ben climaxing inside her at the same time as a voice ringing out. 'Well, really!'

Chapter Fifteen

Saturday afternoon, and back from a shopping trip in Cambridge, Venetia was climbing the stairs to her apartment when she was set upon by the Enforcers. It was almost as if they had been lying in wait to ambush her and she braced herself ready to take them on if this was about Bon-Bon. But she needn't have worried because in breathless tones of scandalised horror, they informed her that that very afternoon Cassie and Ben had been seen having sex in the woods.

'In daylight!' Cheryl stressed in case there was any doubt of the depravity of the situation. 'Actual broad daylight and for anyone to see. I saw them with my own eyes!'

'Well, I never,' Venetia said cheerfully. 'But I can't say I blame them as it is a beautiful day and in my experience *al fresco* rumpy-pumpy was always the best fun! And still would be,' she added with a mischievous wink, 'if I were given the chance. You should try it. Toodles for now, ladies.'

At the satisfyingly sharp intake of breath, she swept past the two women, all the while hoping Bon-Bon wouldn't give the game away from inside her tote bag. As always, the zip was undone, and he could have poked his head up at any moment.

Inside her apartment, she lowered her bag to the carpeted floor and Bon-Bon immediately hopped out and gave himself a quick stretch and a shake. After receiving a kiss on the top of his head from her, he trotted off to his water bowl in the kitchen while Venetia dealt with the carrier bags of shopping, taking them through to her bedroom. She'd treated herself to a couple of nice things in a super dress shop in town.

Joining Bon-Bon in the kitchen, she thought of Cassie, hoping that whatever had been witnessed in the woods was a step in the right direction. The dear girl really needed to think more of her future and less of her past. One of the many things Venetia had learnt as a child was that no one should ever let the past define their present or their future. It had been a favourite mantra of Lady Constance.

'Girls and boys,' Lady Constance would say, 'just because you haven't experienced what is considered a conventional family life, you mustn't ever let anyone tell you you're not special and unique, you most certainly are! Each one of you has something only you can offer the world. Never forget that.'

Venetia felt that Cassie could do with a Lady Constance in her life and she rather fancied taking on the role herself, so that she could persuade her young friend that hanging on to an event from her past and nurturing it as a grudge would do her no good.

They had enjoyed another two chats in the woods this past week while walking Bon-Bon and it had revealed much to Venetia about Cassie's insecurities beneath the delightfully bubbly exterior and flashes of humour. Venetia could see that she put on a good show of bravado, but scratch the surface and the fear that history could repeat itself with Ben was all too apparent.

Later that evening, when Venetia had poured herself a tumbler of whisky and was on the sofa with Bon-Bon, there was a knock at the door. She put a finger to her lips to make sure the dog didn't bark, and after putting him in her bedroom, she went to answer the door, peering through the spy hole before opening it.

She was delighted to see that it was Cassie.

'Are you receiving guests?'

'Only those who have been caught in an indecent act in the woods,' Venetia said, stepping aside to let her in.

Cassie rolled her eyes. 'Oh God, word's gone round, then?'

'I'm afraid so. What a wonderfully naughty pair you are! Can I offer you a drink to help with the sparing of your blushes? Not that you have anything to be embarrassed about in my opinion.'

'A drink would be great,' said Cassie, 'I'm not disturbing you, am I?'

'Absolutely not. I'm having whisky but if you want wine, there's a bottle of white in the fridge. Help yourself while I let Bon-Bon out of my bedroom. Glasses are in the cupboard to the left of the window.'

Once they were settled on the sofa, one at each end and with Bon-Bon on Cassie's lap, Venetia said, 'Am I to understand, based on your woodland shenanigans, that you've cleared things up with Ben?'

Cassie smiled coyly. 'You could say that.'

'And?'

'Apparently he really had been planning something for my fortieth birthday.'

'Oh, you silly girl, all that worry for nothing!'

'No need to rub it in, I feel stupid enough as it is.'

'And just to be sure, you believe Ben?' Venetia asked. 'You *trust* him?' She put a heavy emphasis on the word trust.

'I'll be honest,' Cassie said after taking a sip of her wine, 'there was a moment when I struggled to believe him.'

'Was that because you still wanted to hang on to the comforting sense of righteous hurt?'

Cassie's eyes widened. 'Wow, you make me sound like a total grudge-bearing psycho!'

'That's not my intention, but we can all fall into the trap of victimhood, it's a defence mechanism, it gives us an extra layer of protection. It also gives us the moral high ground, which invariably is as stable as shifting sands.'

With a faint smile, Cassie said, 'I'm beginning to regret knocking on your door. I only came to say thank you for listening to me.'

'I'm sure any of your friends and family would have done the same. Although I do appreciate that sometimes it's harder to talk to family or close friends because they're not objective enough. Too often they tell us what they think we want to hear.'

'I guarantee they would have said I was crazy to imagine Ben having an affair, that I was being paranoid.' Her hand stroking Bon-Bon as the dog looked up at her with his soppily adoring eyes, Cassie went on to say, 'I know I have trust issues, but if I could be so easily triggered, who's to say it won't keep on happening?'

'I think you're looking at this the wrong way. From all that you've told me about your ex-husband, he was the real trigger. You had him neatly consigned to the past, and then he resurfaced.'

'Yes,' agreed Cassie, 'he barged his way back into my life by convincing Emily that he was a changed man and wanted to be a part of her life.'

'You didn't believe that he was?'

'No. Even if I did, it doesn't change the past, does it?'

'But it changes the future. Especially for your daughter.'

'I get that, I really do, but I'm worried that he'll hurt Emily, just as he hurt me. In fact, it's happening right now because he's already hurting her by bloody well dying!'

'I hate to play devil's advocate, but I doubt he deliberately involved himself in a potentially fatal accident just to get one over you.'

'Yeah, that's the logical approach, but inside I'm screaming that he should have been more careful, and I'm all too aware that makes me sound like a heartless bitch.' She took a gulp of her wine. 'For years I fantasised about him dying and then dancing on his grave, but now I desperately want him to live for Emily's sake.'

'That, if I may say, is not the wish of a heartless bitch.'

'It's a selfish wish.'

Venetia smiled. 'Most wishes are.'

At the thoughtful expression on Cassie's face, Venetia said, 'I think that's quite enough serious talk, let's get down to your scandalous behaviour in the woods.'

'Let's not!' said Cassie with a laugh.

'Spoilsport. But I hope you put on a decent show for the Sisters Grim.'

Cassie laughed at Venetia's moniker for Cheryl and Joanna. 'Cheryl was on her own, thank goodness, although it doesn't sound like she wasted any time in rushing to share what she'd seen.'

'Did she say anything directly to you at the time?'

'There was an initial expression of disgust but then she disappeared, leaving us collapsed on the ground in near hysterics. I might add that we've never done anything like that before, we're not a pair of kinky exhibitionists who regularly get up to this kind of thing, it was a totally spur-of-the-moment thing, and at Ben's suggestion.'

'The million-dollar question is, was it a good suggestion?'

'Let's just say, it was a bonding moment.'

'Wonderful!' declared Venetia.

'But as wonderful as it was,' Cassie said, 'Cheryl and Joanna are no doubt going to share our escapade with anyone who will listen. They're such a pair of mean girls!'

'Then you're going to have to hold your head up high and brazen it out. Rest assured though, spreading tittle-tattle doesn't show Cheryl and Joanna in a good light. And I guarantee their husbands will be as jealous as hell! Who knows, you might have set a trend and there'll be no end of woodland romps going on.

Which will be a nuisance for me,' she added with a smile, 'when I need to take Bon-Bon for his walks.'

Cassie stroked the dog's head, paying extra attention to his ears, which he always loved. 'Do you really think you can keep up the secret of having him here with you?' she asked.

'Time will tell. But I'm a risk-taker at heart and pretty good at keeping secrets.'

'Well, as I told you before, your secret is safe with me, and with Ben too. I told him earlier about Bon-Bon and he was very amused. We'll both back you if anyone starts making trouble for you and we'll approach the management company to have the rule changed if needs be. I'm sure others will feel the same way. Ronnie Sharp will definitely be an ally.'

'I certainly don't want to be the cause of any friction or division. Besides, as much as I appreciate your support, I'm used to fighting my own battles.'

'Such as?'

'Oh, numerous battles,' she said with a careless shrug. 'Everyone has them; it's life.'

'But given the start you had in life, in a children's home, that must have meant you had more than your fair share of battles to overcome in the early days.'

'A few, but we were taught to regard them as challenges.'

'Are you still in contact with anyone from those days?'

Venetia shook her head. 'No.'

'So no reunions?'

'Goodness me no.'

'Have you never wanted to arrange one?'

'People change and some might not want to be reminded of those old days.'

'You seem to look back on that time with fondness, it's why you're here, surely? Why shouldn't they feel the same way?'

'Because not everyone is the same.'

'Did you have a best friend here, someone with whom you could confide and share all your secrets and do silly things together?'

Venetia smiled. 'I did.'

'What was her name?'

'Actually, my best friend was a boy, and his name was Lucien.'

Chapter Sixteen

December 1957

Whenever a new girl or boy arrived at Hope Hall, Lady Constance would assign one of the older children to take them under their wing and show them the ropes. The child she selected for the task was always carefully chosen. It wasn't just that Lady Constance hoped they would be a sympathetic match to the newcomer, but would also benefit from the process themselves by gaining a sense of responsibility and maturity. Sometimes it was a way to bring that child out of their shell and encourage them to be more sociable.

This was why, on a freezing cold afternoon in December with snow falling from a leaden sky, and while she was on duty in the library, Venetia, who had a reputation for being something of an introvert, was asked to report to Lady Constance's study. There she found Lady Constance sitting in a wingback armchair by the fire with a dark-haired boy seated opposite her. Above the fireplace there was a framed embroidered sampler with the words *Hope Hall is a place of hope*. Lady Constance had sewn it herself and the words summed up her philosophy at Hope Hall. The slogan appeared throughout the Hall whether it was painted in art classes, sewn in needlework classes, carved in woodwork classes, or engraved in metalwork classes.

'Ah, there you are, Venetia. How are you today?'

'I'm very well, thank you, Miss Constance,' she replied politely.

If there was one thing Lady Constance demanded of the children in her care, it was courtesy and respect, but what she didn't want was a lot of bobbing, bowing, and tugging of forelocks, just because she had a fancy toff title. In spite of that, Venetia always thought of her as Lady Constance. She was a tall, statuesque woman with a regal way about her – that was breeding for you – and wore her pretty reddish-gold hair in a messy chignon with bobby pins poking out. Yet for all that regalness, she was often the first to offer comfort to a crying child, taking them to her ample bosom and soothing them until their tears had stopped. She had never had children herself, in fact she'd never been married, but she was such a kind, motherly sort.

'I'd like to introduce you to Lucien Barnes,' she said to Venetia. 'He's joining us here at Hope Hall and I thought the two of you would get on famously well together. You're both twelve years old and from what Lucien tells me he's a big reader just like you, so you're kindred spirits. Perhaps you'd like to give Lucien a tour around the library and then take him for tea in the dining hall?'

Venetia nodded. 'Yes, Miss Constance.'

Lady Constance turned to look at the boy sitting opposite her, who didn't seem to have moved since Venetia had entered the room. 'It's sausages and mash today, followed by treacle pudding with custard and then later there's hot chocolate before bedtime,' she said. 'How does that sound to you, Lucien?'

The boy seemed incapable of forcing a smile to his lips, never mind open his mouth to speak. His gaze didn't seem to reach further than the end of his nose. His answer, such as it was, was a sullen shrug of his shoulders, which appeared to satisfy Lady Constance, but not Venetia. *This boy was going to be hard work unless he sharpened up.*

'You'll probably find it feels a bit overwhelming to begin with,' Lady Constance explained to the boy, 'but you'll soon get the hang of the place. Especially with Venetia to help you. The important thing to remember is simply to be yourself. Everyone is different and here at Hope Hall we strongly believe in fostering uniqueness.' She abruptly clapped her hands together which was a signal that the meeting was over. 'Now, off you go, you two, and have fun.'

Fun looked like the last thing Lucien Barnes was capable of as he stood up and left the room with Venetia. She led the way down the corridor towards the library, neither of them speaking. From the far-off kitchen, the engine room of the Hall as Lady Constance referred to it, came the smell of tea being cooked. They all joked that it didn't matter what was served, there was always the smell of boiled cabbage. From the rec room she could hear a crescendo of shouting and a piano being played, and from somewhere else a door slammed hard. She noticed the boy beside her jumped at this last sudden noise. *Better get used to that,* she thought, *noise is part of Hope Hall.*

The only quiet place was the library, which was why she enjoyed spending so much time there. Some of the other children said she was stuck-up because she didn't want to join in with their games that usually consisted of a lot of yelling and shrieking. Most of the time they knew to leave her alone, that if provoked she could more than fight her corner. But this boy didn't look like he could defend himself; he looked like a gust of wind might carry him off.

He had a serious face with a pointy chin and large dark eyes with smudgy shadows beneath that made his pale skin look paler still. There seemed so little of him, as though he hadn't eaten properly in a very long time. Maybe he hadn't. Some children arrived here in a terrible state, thin as anything and in filthy threadbare rags. Venetia hated to see the little children arrive like that and she always counted herself lucky that she'd never experienced anything but the loving warmth of Hope Hall. Yes, she'd been an unwanted baby and abandoned on the doorstep, but she had no memory of it, so what she didn't know couldn't hurt her. In contrast, some of the children here had awful memories of their lives before, of terrifying neglect and abuse. Perhaps this boy did too. With that in mind, she made herself think kindlier towards him, to give him the benefit of the doubt.

'Lady Constance was right when she told you it might feel a bit overwhelming here to begin with,' she said, 'most feel that way at the start. But everyone settles in eventually.'

There was no response from him, which annoyed her. Didn't he realise she was trying to be nice to him? It made her not want to share the library with him, which she regarded as her very own special place. Why should she share it with this pathetic boy?

The library wasn't her only favourite place to be, she loved being upstairs with Edie Buckle in her cosy office just off from the sick room. She also loved being outside in the grounds where she liked to sit on her own with a book, often in the woods where she wouldn't be disturbed. Some of the other children had convinced themselves that they were haunted and wouldn't go near them. Venetia didn't believe in ghosts, not for a second, but she actively encouraged the myth so that she would have the woods to herself.

Finding your own private space at Hope Hall was important, as was having the freedom to do as you liked at times. Lady Constance insisted that during their free time they were allowed to have as much freedom as possible, whether it was playing tennis, swimming in the river (under strict supervision), climbing trees, playing football, rounders, or cricket, or just sitting quietly under a tree.

There was nobody else in the library and closing the door after them, Venetia stood back to let this strange elfin-like boy explore the bookshelves himself. But he didn't. He just stood rooted to the spot as if waiting for something to happen.

'We're only allowed to have one book at a time, and we can keep it for just two weeks,' she explained, moving away from him, and going over to the large bay window through which she could see the snow was coming down even harder now and settling thickly on the grass. 'Sometimes you have to put your name down on a waiting list for a book that's really popular,' she continued. 'What kind of books do you like to read?'

She was prattling on, something she never did but this peculiar boy with his unnaturally quiet stillness was having an odd effect on her; he was making her nervous, something she rarely felt. Usually, it was the other way around, with some of the younger children feeling nervous when in her company, not because she was nasty to them, but because she didn't chatter on nineteen to the dozen like most others. Perhaps this boy was the same. Was that why Lady Constance had said they were kindred spirits?

The boy was staring at her now, the first time he'd looked at her properly, and she was taken aback at his unblinking gaze, almost as though he was staring right through her. But as uncomfortable as it made her feel, she wasn't going to give him the satisfaction of turning away. *No chance, mister,* she said to herself.

Seconds passed. Long drawn-out seconds with neither of them moving, not until he narrowed his eyes which gave him a slightly menacing appearance, as if he might lurch forward and strike her.

Let him try, she thought. For starters she was taller than him and doubtless stronger, given how slight he was. But just then the boy with his weirdly narrowed eyes moved towards her, and she took an involuntary step away from him.

'I like the Narnia books,' he said.

'Oh,' she said, surprised at the sound of his voice which was low and gruff, 'me too.'

'Can you show me where they are?'

She slipped around him and went over to the shelves where the books of C. S. Lewis were kept.

'They're here,' she said.

Standing next to her, his nose just inches away from the shelf, he ran a hand slowly along the row of books, touching each one on its spine before pulling out *The Lion, The Witch and the Wardrobe*.

'Is that your favourite of the series?' she asked.

'Yes,' he replied, and without looking at her.

'Mine too.'

'Can I have it?'

'You can borrow it, yes. I'll need to make you a library card and then stamp the book for you. I'm allowed to do that.' She made no effort to hide her pride in this admission.

'You work in here?' he asked, his eyes now meeting hers.

'I help Mrs Mackenzie, our librarian, to organise the books and the card indexes. She also lets me use the stamp.'

'Could I help in here, if I wanted to?'

'Lady Constance decides what we all do. I used to help in the laundry and then the kitchen, and I've also helped in the greenhouse, which was fun, but I prefer it in here. I like the peace and quiet and putting everything in order.'

He scowled. 'It sounds like she makes children work as slaves instead of paying somebody to do the job.'

'No, that's not fair,' Venetia said, keen to defend the woman who was so good to them all. 'Lady Constance likes everyone to carry out a job here, it's to give us a sense of responsibility. She likes us to learn skills that will be useful when we leave. In exchange we're given pocket money to spend in the tuckshop.'

'It still sounds like cheap labour,' he muttered.

'You can think what you like,' she snapped, 'but Lady Constance is one of the nicest and most generous people you will ever know, and you should consider yourself lucky to be here, and if you're too stupid to realise that, I pity you.' And with that, she snatched the book out of his hands and returned it to the shelf. 'It's time to go for tea now.'

'But I want the book.'

'Tough!' she said. 'You need to learn some manners before you can borrow anything from this library.'

His scowl increased. 'It's not *your* library.'

'It is while I'm on duty!'

'I thought the war was fought to stop dictators like you from bullying the rest of us.'

'The war was fought to defend democracy and our freedom to respect the rules that make life fairer for everyone!' She'd learnt that from Mr Butler who was a friend of Lady Constance. He'd been a pilot with the RAF and had lost a leg when his plane had been shot down by the Luftwaffe in the Battle of Britain. He came in twice a week to teach them history. He wasn't a proper teacher, but the boys loved hearing his stories about the war and of the planes he'd shot down and the girls stared at him all dreamy-eyed because they thought he was so handsome. Even if he did only have one leg.

'There's nothing about life that is fair,' the ungrateful boy said. 'If life was fair, we wouldn't be here.'

'There are worse places you could be,' she said, her tone now softened.

For a few moments he remained silent. 'If I said sorry, would you let me borrow the book?'

'I might, if it was a genuine apology.'

'I'm sorry,' he said.

As sullen as he sounded, she decided to accept his apology. Taking the book he wanted, she carried it over to Mrs Mackenzie's desk, pulled out a drawer and found a library card for him. 'How do you spell Lucien?' she asked.

'L U C I E N,' he spelt out for her, joining her at the desk.

In her best handwriting, she wrote his name in the space

provided and beside that in another column *The Lion, The Witch and the Wardrobe*. She then wrote his name on a small buff-coloured ticket. 'This is yours,' she said, handing it to him, 'keep it somewhere safe.' With a flourish – she always enjoyed doing this part – she stamped the book and gave it to him.

'Thank you,' he said, clutching the book to his chest as though it were the most precious thing in the world. 'And I meant it when I said I was sorry.'

'Good,' she said and being faithful to Lady Constance's instruction, she added, 'time for tea now. You'll learn that it's better not to be late.'

'Yet more rules?'

'No,' she said firmly, 'it's good manners to be on time.'

'Are you always so—'

'So what?' she prompted when he broke off.

'So grown up?'

'Better that than being a stupid idiot who can't read properly unless his nose is pressed against the bookshelf!'

'I'm not stupid!' he said. 'It's because . . . because I can't see properly.'

That stopped Venetia in her tracks. 'What do you mean you can't see properly?'

'Now who's being stupid by being unable to understand plain English?'

'But if you can't see, how are you going to read that book?'

'I can manage,' he said tersely. 'If I hold it up close.'

'Why don't you wear spectacles, then?'

'I had some but . . . but they got broken.'

'When was that?'

'Ages ago.'

'So you need new ones? Have you told Lady Constance?'

'No. And anyway, it doesn't matter because I won't be here for long. When she's better, my mum will come for me.'

This wasn't the first time Venetia had heard something like this. Children often arrived with some story or other that a member of their family would show up one day and take them home with them. The older a child was, the less likely it was to happen.

Feeling sorry for the boy, she checked the clock on the wall and decided there was just time before tea to take him upstairs to meet Edie Buckle. She would know what to do about him needing spectacles. Venetia couldn't bear the thought of him struggling to read the way he'd just described.

'Come with me,' she said.

'Where are we going?'

'You need to be kitted out in the Hope Hall uniform and to do that, you must meet Mrs Buckle. She's our matron but is also in charge of arranging what you have to wear. We all wear the same shirt, sweater and dungarees, boy or girl.'

'I just told you I won't be here for long, so I don't need a uniform.'

'But while you are you here,' she said patiently, 'even if it's only a week, you might as well fit in. That's important.'

His frowned deepened and he narrowed his eyes, perhaps to see her better. 'I thought Lady Constance said uniqueness was to be encouraged. Wearing a uniform makes everyone look the same, doesn't it?'

Clever-dick, she thought. 'It's what is inside a person that matters,' Venetia said, 'and right now you're proving to me that what's inside you isn't worth a fig! And besides, didn't you wear a uniform at the school you used to go to?'

'Yes, but not one as stupid as the one you're wearing.' He gave her dungarees a long and disapproving look. 'You look like some kind of farm worker.'

'Oh, and I suppose you're too posh to wear something like this? What would you rather wear, Little Lord Fauntleroy, velvet breeches and a frilly white shirt?'

He stared angrily at her, gritting his teeth, but at the thought of him prancing about in velvet breeches she suddenly snorted and then she laughed. To her surprise, he smiled back at her, and he laughed too. It was a funny gravelly kind of laugh, as if he wasn't used to laughing and hadn't yet worked out how to do it properly. Or maybe he was recovering from a sore throat. It was none of her business anyway.

He was staring at her now, his eyes narrowed in a distinctly weird way. She supposed he was trying to focus on her, which had the effect of making her feel self-conscious about her appearance, which normally she never much cared about.

'Come and meet Edie Buckle,' she said, wanting him to stop looking at her. 'You'll like Edie, there's nobody nicer than her in the whole wide world.'

'You think everyone is nice.'

'And you think everyone is horrid, don't you? Including me probably.'

'No,' he said, as she opened the library door to let them out. 'I think you're okay. You say what you think. I like that. I don't like people who say things they don't mean.'

That, she thought, *sounded almost like a compliment.*

They found Edie on the top floor in her cosy little office sitting by her small electric bar heater with a mug of tea in her hand. If Lady Constance was tall and statuesque, Edie Buckle was like a lovely soft round dumpling. She was always so comforting and never had a harsh word for anyone.

'Is this our new lad you've brought to see me, Venetia?' Edie said.

'Yes, Mrs Buckle. I've shown him the library and then I thought we just had time before tea to come up and see you so you could sort out a uniform for him.'

'A very good idea. Now then, Lucien,' she said, turning to

look at him, 'I'm delighted to meet you and my first piece of advice I'm going to give you is that I can't recommend a better friend for you than Venetia. I can see from the way you're clutching that book, you're fond of reading like she is.'

Venetia had manoeuvred herself so she was standing behind Lucien and pointing to her eyes, she shook her head. On her feet now, Edie gave her a puzzled look and gesticulating again with her hands, Venetia pointed at Lucien, then circled a thumb and forefinger around each of her eyes. Just as the woman appeared to understand what she was trying to tell her, Lucien whipped round, but quick as a flash Venetia had already lowered her hands and was fiddling with the cuff of her woollen sweater underneath her dungarees, looking for all the world a picture of innocence.

'Right then, young man,' Edie said, while smoothing down her snowy-white apron, 'let's go and see if we can find you a smart uniform for you to wear. Then I'll need to book you in for a few tests tomorrow.'

'What kind of tests?' he asked warily.

'Oh, nothing to worry about, just the usual things. Come along now.'

It was two weeks later, following a visit to an optician in Cambridge that Lucien returned to Hope Hall wearing a pair of heavily black-rimmed NHS spectacles. He said he hated them, that they weren't as nice as his old ones, but by then Venetia was more than used to his ways. 'Don't be so ungrateful, Little Lord Fauntleroy!'

By now they were firm friends and Lady Constance had welcomed Venetia's suggestion that Lucien help in the library with her. He was, in truth, her first proper friend of her own age. A friend who eventually confided in her why he had ended up at Hope Hall.

'My mother is never going to get better and come for me,' he said. 'She's dead and so is my father.'

'Wasn't there anyone who could take you in and give you a home? Your grandparents?'

'All dead,' he'd said bluntly. 'Or as good as.' He never mentioned his family again. Not for all the time she knew him.

Chapter Seventeen

'So, tell me why the bride is called Tigs, it's a name I have never heard before. It's very unusual.'

'Unusual is the word,' said Nina. 'Her real name is Antigone, which I'm told she hated as a child and from the age of eight she was determined that she should be known as Tigs.'

It was Saturday morning, the day of Fabian and Tigs's wedding and Nina was sitting in the passenger seat of Jakob's car as he searched the car park for a space.

All the way here to the Dangley Court Hotel in Hertford she had been fighting the urge to tell him to turn around and drive them straight back to Cambridge. How on earth had she talked herself into believing this would be a good thing, that flaunting Jakob like some young trophy boyfriend would help her mother-in-law realise she had a perfect right to move on? No doubt Hilary, and everyone else for that matter, would think she was making an embarrassing fool of herself. And perhaps they'd be right.

It had been her need to release herself from Hilary's possessive hold on her that had made her email Fabian and Tigs to ask if it would be all right for her to bring a plus-one. She hadn't specified who it would be, and in return, doubtless snowed under with all the last-minute arrangements for a hastily thrown-together wedding, they hadn't asked for any more information.

Almost immediately she had regretted sending the email, and she blamed Cassie for her part in convincing her that it would be great fun to go to the wedding with Jakob. Her encouragement had been offered during a perfectly idyllic evening at Hope Hall. Along with Ben, they'd been enjoying a picnic supper on the riverbank, complete with setting sun and a couple of swans in the water relishing the odd titbit thrown to them. During the picnic, and while Ben had wandered off to take a call on his mobile, Cassie had admitted that she'd recently had the ridiculous notion that Ben had been cheating on her, and all because she'd overheard him planning a surprise party for her fortieth birthday.

'I let my insecurities get the better of me,' she'd further admitted, 'it just came out of nowhere. One simple misunderstanding and it led me to believe the worst of Ben. Even now,' and she'd turned her head to look at Ben who'd had his back to them while talking to whoever it was who had called him, 'there's a part of me that thinks, *but what if?* What if he's as convincing a liar as Drew was?'

Nina had been in on the secret – Ben having invited her to the surprise party he was arranging – so if Cassie had approached her, it would have been difficult to assure her friend that Ben was completely innocent without giving the game away. But that evening on the riverbank, she did her best to assure Cassie that Ben really wasn't the cheating sort. 'He's crazy about you, completely devoted, you must know that in your heart,' she'd said.

'We never know for sure, do we?' Cassie had said sadly. 'There's always something we keep from those we love. Look how Hugh kept from you that his mother had given him money to use for IVF.'

Reminded how angry it had made her feel when Hilary had literally demanded her right for a grandchild because she believed she'd paid for that right, Nina had shared with Cassie what she was tempted to do, to have Jakob as her plus-one for Fabian and Tigs's wedding. 'It would be the most effective way to show Hilary she can't hold me hostage to the past.'

'Does that mean you've reached a decision about the letter from the clinic?' Cassie had asked.

'No. I still haven't made my mind up. Maybe once this wedding is out of the way, I'll be able to think more clearly,' she'd said.

'For what it's worth, you should absolutely go with your handsome Norwegian. Remember, I met him in the gallery not long after he'd started working for you and I can personally vouch for his appeal.'

'He's not *my* Norwegian!' Nina had remonstrated. 'But what if people think I've hired him for the day from an escort agency? Think of the humiliation!' She was in danger of talking herself out of the idea once again.

'Nobody will think that, Nina. You're a fabulously beautiful woman who could have any gorgeous man on her arm as a plus-one.'

'But the age gap, Cassie. There's no getting away from that, Hugh's family will think I'm some kind of ghastly cougar.'

'Rubbish! The women will all be mad with jealousy and the men, well, they'll be jealous too. Just go and have some fun. That's my final word on the subject. But I'll want all the juicy details on your return, especially your mother-in-law's reaction!'

That was now very near to being experienced, thought Nina as Jakob nosed the car in between a Range Rover and a BMW. He had insisted that he drive as he wanted to give his new car a decent workout. 'Boys and their toys,' he'd said with a smile when he'd arrived at Hope Hall to pick her up earlier that morning in a shiny black Porsche 911.

'I clearly pay you too much,' she'd joked as he'd pressed his foot on the accelerator, and they'd roared off down the driveway.

'Don't be too impressed,' he'd said, glancing at her over the top of his sunglasses, 'it's second hand.'

It was hard not to be impressed by Jakob, she thought now as after pushing open the passenger door to step out, and before she had both feet planted firmly on the ground, he had magically appeared at her side to help her, his hand outstretched. Then while she smoothed down the skirt of her pink Chanel suit – it was her one and only Chanel suit and it never failed to make her feel strong and confident when wearing it, which was why she had chosen it for today – Jakob retrieved his own suit jacket and pulled it on.

'Will I do?' he asked, adjusting the cuffs of his white shirt so they protruded the sartorially correct half an inch to show off his cufflinks, and then tightening his silk tie so that the knot was perfectly positioned. Still wearing his sunglasses and an outrageous quantity of head-turning sex appeal, he was the perfect companion for such an occasion, if only the circumstances were different. And if only he didn't look so young!

'You'll do very well,' she said, picking up the gift bag from the footwell of the Porsche.

'I hope it would not be considered a workplace offence to say how lovely you look,' he said.

Goodness he was disarming! 'Since we're not at work,' she said with a smile, 'the usual rules don't apply, so thank you.'

'Excellent.' He locked the car and raised his arm for her to take.

When she hesitated, he said, 'Just while you negotiate the gravel in those heels; I know from my sisters how treacherous it can be. You don't want to risk twisting an ankle and have me carry you in, do you?'

Recognising that he was teasing her, she did as he said and once they were inside, she left him in the reception area while she went to look for the ladies. She found there was quite a party going on when she stepped into the opulent cloakroom. It was crowded with attractive young girls wearing an assortment of skimpy barely-there dresses. Laughing and joking, they were taking selfies and applying make-up, at the same time passing around a bottle of champagne. Not recognising any of them and feeling about a hundred and ten, Nina decided they had to be friends of the bride.

Back out in the foyer, Jakob was waiting for her by the reception desk. A member of staff then directed them through to the ballroom where the ceremony was being held and which was due to start in ten minutes.

In the entrance to the ballroom, they were greeted with a clamour of voices from the assembled guests, some of them seated but most of them on their feet and mingling. Two ushers flanked the entrance, one of whom asked if they were for the bride or the groom, and the other pointed over to a large table where a mountainous pile of gifts had been deposited. It was just as Nina had placed her present on the table that she heard her name being called.

'Nina, there you are!'

Turning around she saw her father-in-law bearing down on her, a smile of delight on his face.

'Hello, Keith,' she said after he'd swamped her with one of his big hugs, 'good journey?'

'Not bad. Usual hold-ups with roadworks and diversions. You probably encountered the same.' Before she had a chance to answer, his gaze slid enquiringly towards Jakob standing next to her.

'You remember Jakob from the gallery, don't you?' Nina said. 'You met him on one occasion when you called in to treat me for lunch.'

For a split second Keith clearly didn't know what to say. Then: 'Yes, of course, silly me,' he said, extending his hand. 'I didn't recognise you out of context. So . . . erm . . . you're Nina's plus-one, are you?'

'Yes,' Jakob said, 'she kindly invited me to join her. I feel very honoured.'

'Well . . . that's . . . that's very nice, I hope you enjoy yourself. These . . . erm . . . family get-togethers can be a bit overwhelming. It's like marrying into the mafia. That's what Hugh's best man said in his speech on your wedding day, didn't he, Nina?' Keith gave an uncomfortably hearty laugh, but then perhaps realising how inappropriate his comment was, looked as if he wished the ground would open beneath him and swallow him whole.

'You make it sound like I'm in some sort of danger,' Jakob said lightly.

'No, not at all, of course not, it's just that they're a close-knit bunch,' Keith blundered on.

'How's Fabian coping?' asked Nina, feeling she should come to Keith's rescue, at the same time glancing to the front row of gold-painted chairs where she could see the groom on his feet talking to another man, presumably his best man. 'Any nerves?'

Keith shook his head. 'No, you know what they're all like on Hilary's side of the family, nerves of steel, terrifyingly fearless.'

Nina remembered how Hugh had always joked that he came from fearless stock, warriors to the last. When he'd been diagnosed with a brain tumour the family had said, 'It'll be fine, the tumour won't last two minutes in a tussle with Hugh!' It had been fighting talk designed to reassure themselves, to arm themselves against the inconceivable that one of their own could be taken well before his time. Especially someone as invincible as Hugh, whom the younger cousins looked up to. At his funeral there had been much talk in the eulogies of Hugh's sporting ability, his prowess on the rugby and cricket pitch, his daringness on the ski slopes and his all-round likability. Someone had even joked that the man was just so damned perfect they should have hated him and not loved and admired him the way they had. Not one person had mentioned that it was a small entity, a tumour the size of a walnut, that had beaten Hugh.

'We'd better go and sit down or she-who-must-be-obeyed will be on the warpath,' Keith said, breaking into Nina's painful memories of Hugh's funeral. 'I'm afraid we only saved you the one seat.' His gaze flicked towards Jakob. 'If we'd known that you were bringing someone, we'd have—'

Suddenly irritated by Keith's customary act of hen-pecked husband, she cut him off. 'That's all right,' she said, 'Jakob and I will sit at the back, there's plenty of room there.' It seemed particularly unworthy of Keith to keep making his wife the butt of his jokes when he was seeing someone behind her back. Feeling sorry for Hilary was a first for Nina, not something she ever thought she'd experience.

'You won't be able to hide from her once the ceremony is over, you know.'

Keith's remark was only just audible to Nina above a noisy burst of laughter from the group of girls who had earlier been in the cloakroom and were now entering the ballroom en masse, but she caught the underlying tone of what he was accusing her of.

'I'm not hiding, Keith,' she said sharply. 'What's more, I'm certainly not the one here with anything to hide. I would simply prefer to sit at the back and let the immediate members of the family be closer to the action.'

He stared at her with a stricken expression on his face. 'I . . . I didn't mean anything, Nina, I was joking. I merely meant that . . .' His voice tailed off.

'It's fine, Keith,' she said. 'Enjoy the service and we'll see you afterwards.'

'That wasn't at all awkward,' Jakob said when they were seated. 'Do you want to tell me what just happened?'

'I behaved badly,' she muttered, 'that's what happened.'

'Is it me, my being here with you?'

Gripping the wedding order of service in her hands, Nina tried to compose herself; she was shaking with shame that she had been so rude to Keith. It had been appallingly judgemental of her, and she knew she would have to apologise just as soon as the opportunity arose. But everything about the encounter had provoked her. She had counted on Keith being entirely relaxed about her bringing a plus-one, that he of all people would think it was the most natural thing in the world that she should have a companion by her side today. Had she assumed too much? Was she, in the eyes of Hugh's family, forever destined to remain the heartbroken, grieving widow who mustn't ever be unfaithful to his memory? His *sainted* memory, she thought with a flare of white-hot anger.

It was not the first time she had felt angry since Hugh's death. There had been many gut-wrenching days of raging anger when she'd wanted to scream and shout and hurl things at the wall, to smash everything within sight. She had been advised to find an outlet for the anger and so she'd joined a running club in Cambridge. When that hadn't been enough, she'd tried boxing, but she'd hated that.

She'd read about the so-called five stages of grief – denial, anger, depression, bargaining and acceptance – and which could roll up in no particular order. She'd never experienced the bargaining stage, but the others she was well acquainted with. Even moments of acceptance.

Acceptance was why she was here today with Jakob, she realised. Hugh was dead. He was never coming back. He was never going to be her companion again. And it was time that she was treated not as a widow, but as a woman.

'Nina,' Jakob said quietly beside her. 'Are you okay?'

Realising she hadn't answered him, she threw him a tight smile. 'I'm fine,' she whispered, just as an excited hush fell on the room signalling that the ceremony was about to begin. That was when Hilary turned around, craning her neck to get a better look at Nina. And Jakob. Keith must have just told her that Nina wasn't here alone.

The ceremony was over. It had been one of those woo-woo affairs as Hugh used to call them, when the formal gravitas of the service had been jettisoned in favour of a more personal but perhaps less meaningful approach.

At one point Fabian had vowed not to squeeze the toothpaste tube in the middle or mislay his keys quite so regularly. In exchange the bride had promised to curb her addiction to online shopping. Their vows had drawn chuckles from the guests, but it had made Nina feel old and out of step. Just as she had in the cloakroom earlier.

With guests now on their feet, it was time to go outside to the marquee where, they'd been informed drinks and canapés would be served while the photographer got to work with the bride and groom.

This was it then, thought Nina. Now the curious glances and questions would really begin. And without realising she was doing it, she slipped her arm through Jakob's and in response, he pressed it firmly and reassuringly against his side.

'It will be fine,' he said out of the corner of his mouth. 'It will be a walk in the park. A breeze. Child's play. A piece of your finest Victoria sponge cake.'

She laughed. 'Any more idioms up your sleeve?' she said.

'Oh, I'm sure I can think of something if the moment presents itself.'

Inside the fuggy warmth of the marquee, they were met with the smell of crushed grass and the richly extravagant scent of cut flowers. Every table was decorated with a beautiful display of white and lilac blooms. There were silver balloons too, which, no doubt, knowing Hugh's family, would not make the end of the night.

They'd just been handed a glass of champagne each when Hugh's aunt Lindsay approached. She was Hilary's oldest sister and was a no-nonsense woman who was a retired headmistress of an all-girl's school. Her default setting was straight out of the Mary Poppins handbook, spit-spot and best foot forward, no slouching, no slacking, even in the face of adversity. Nina had often wondered at the army of girls who must have passed through her hands and who were now out in the world.

'How lovely to see you, Nina!' she exclaimed, landing a kiss on Nina's cheek with such force it nearly tipped her backwards. 'And how well you look. Now then, who's this you've brought along with you? Introduce me!'

'This is Jakob, Jakob, this is Lindsay, one of Hugh's many aunts.'

Lindsay gave a deep-throated chortle. 'Be warned, Jakob, when you throw in Keith's side of the family, there's a lot of us!' She then leant in towards Nina. 'And what does Hilary think about this?'

Nina played dumb. '*This*? What do you mean?'

'You, having a chap.'

'I think we might be about to find out,' Nina murmured, seeing Hilary fast approaching and with Keith trailing in her wake.

Chapter Eighteen

Hugh used to joke that when his mother was on the warpath, she took on the handbagging persona of Margaret Thatcher and could deliver a scathing insult before you knew she'd even taken aim. 'She might be small of stature,' he'd say, 'but she's a giant when it comes to a putdown and as Dad and I have learnt, it's best to ignore what she says, it's just her way.'

With Hugh's voice in her head, Nina braced herself by greeting her mother-in-law with a smile and a ready supply of the accepted social niceties of the day.

'Hello, Hilary,' she said as the woman as good as shoved Lindsay out of the way, 'that's a lovely outfit you're wearing. Did you enjoy the ceremony? Tigs and Fabian looked so charmingly adorable together, didn't they?' *Charmingly adorable*? Since when had she started saying things like that?

Hilary's glinting gaze bore into Nina's as though seeing right through her pretence. As well she might.

'I suppose this—' she swivelled her head towards Jakob, 'this *young man* you've brought with you today is the reason you were so evasive when I suggested we could come together. You could at least have been honest.'

'I wasn't evasive,' Nina said, 'I just hadn't finalised my plans. Anyway, this is Jakob who I don't believe you've met in the gallery before. Ever since joining Lavelle's he's been my invaluable assistant. I really couldn't manage without him these days.' Her choice of words was as loaded as those of Hilary's when she'd referred to Jakob as this *young* man.

Seemingly unfazed by the situation, and all credit to him, Jakob held out his hand to introduce himself. But Hilary rudely ignored him.

'Everything makes sense now,' she said. '*Everything.*' She then inhaled deeply, and with her nostrils flaring, she turned her back on them and walked away. Keith gave an apologetic shrug and went after her.

'That was intriguing,' remarked Lindsay with a raised eyebrow. 'What could my sister have meant by *everything makes sense now*?'

'You'd have to ask her,' Nina muttered, suspecting that Lindsay's question was entirely disingenuous. Nothing in this family was secret, they told one another everything and no doubt Hilary had grumbled to them how Nina was dragging her feet about producing the grandchild she wanted so badly. Very likely Hilary now believed she had just been presented with the reason why Nina was selfishly refusing to play her part, that she was daring to replace Hugh and his baby was the last thing she wanted.

She was about to suggest that she and Jakob should circulate when members of the family were requested to pose for photographs.

'That includes you too,' Lindsay said, grabbing hold of her arm and nearly spilling her glass of champagne.

'I shouldn't think I'm needed,' she said.

'No arguments! Once a member of this family, always a member. Isn't that what we've always told you?'

'But I can't abandon Jakob.'

'Oh, I think your delightful companion can fend for himself for a while. Am I right, Jakob?'

He smiled. 'Go ahead, Nina, I'll see you later.'

Knowing it was futile to resist, Nina downed her champagne in one long swallow and after handing the empty glass to a passing waitress, she set off with Lindsay and all the other guests now leaving the marquee and heading across the lawn.

'Is it serious between you and Jakob?' Lindsay asked as they approached a magnificent yew tree where the photographer was directing guests to line up in two rows, 'because if it is, if there is the chance of it being something lasting, you shouldn't take anything to heart that Hilary says. It's just that she can't accept that anyone could replace her darling boy.'

'I know that, but does she have to be so vile and so possessive of me?' Nina said. 'It's like she wants me to remain as miserable as she is. Can't you speak to her?'

Lindsay gave a short laugh. 'Sorry to disappoint you, but that's way above my pay grade. Hilary doesn't listen to anyone, she's always been like that, even as a child, she always knew best and would dig her heels in for the stupidest of reasons. It was a defence mechanism then and still is.'

'Against what?'

'Against being overlooked. In an ideal world she should have been an only child and not one of three, then she would have been a much happier person. Did you know that she never wanted Hugh to have a brother or a sister?'

'No,' replied Nina, surprised at the apparent swerve in their conversation. 'Why was that?'

'It would have meant she had to share him,' said Lindsay. 'And that's something Hilary was incapable of doing.'

'I was led to believe that she was given medical advice that another pregnancy was too risky.'

'Risky for whom?' said Lindsay archly. 'Of course that was the party line she told everyone, but I never believed that was the whole story.'

'Did Keith want more children?'

'Of course he did. But you know Keith, anything for a quiet life.'

'Yes,' Nina said absently, thinking of the man she thought she knew and the one she'd seen getting out of the punt in Cambridge and the intimate exchange between him and the woman he was with. The memory of their undeniable closeness suddenly made her long to be treated with the same tenderness.

'Like I said,' Lindsay continued, 'don't put too much store on what Hilary says. We all know Hugh's death hit her hard. He was her life. That's why she takes it out on everybody around her, to lessen the pain of losing him.'

'But he was my life too!' Nina said crossly. 'He was my husband, the man I loved! Why does Hilary's grief eclipse everybody else's, including mine?'

Lindsay came to a standstill and while other guests surged past them, their happy chatter at odds with the flood of emotions threatening to burst through Nina's self-control, Lindsay put a hand on her arm. 'I'm sorry, that was clumsy of me. What I meant is that you can have another husband. You can love again. Hilary can never have another son. You can move on and enjoy a whole new life. She can't. She simply can't.'

'She could if she wanted to,' Nina said, stubbornly, not wanting to relinquish the angry hurt she felt.

'That's the whole point,' Lindsay said gently. 'She doesn't want to.'

To her relief, Nina was positioned at the opposite end of the line-up from Hilary and as soon as they were dismissed by the photographer, she hurried back to the marquee. A quartet of musicians had set up and were now providing background music. More waiting staff had materialised and were buzzing around the beautifully decorated tables making sure all was in order. For a wedding arranged at the last minute, thought Nina, there didn't seem to be any corners cut. Goodness knows how Tigs and

Fabian had done it. Maybe there had been a cancellation which they'd been able to take advantage of.

It took Nina a while to locate Jakob amongst the guests. Like bees to a honeypot, the pack of young girls she'd earlier encountered had him surrounded, and when he spotted Nina over their heads there was no mistaking the relief in his face.

'There you are, babes,' he said, reaching out a hand to her, 'I thought you were never coming back!'

As one, the girls turned to see who he was talking to and then reluctantly parted to let Nina through. She heard one of them mutter, 'I wouldn't mind being in her shoes.' Followed by another saying, 'Some have all the luck.'

'Seriously, that was the longest moment of my life,' he said when the girls had wandered off to hunt down some new prey.

'I'm sure it wasn't anything you couldn't handle,' Nina said with a smile. *'Babes.'*

He cringed. 'You didn't mind me saying that, did you? Was that very wrong?'

'It did sound funny coming from you.'

'It felt funny saying it. I promise I won't do it again. But if I do, it will only be in self-defence.'

She laughed. 'In that case, let's go in search of the table plan so we can make sure you're not sitting anywhere too hazardous.'

'I've already done that, we're together on your—'

She groaned. 'Please don't say we're on Hilary and Keith's table.'

He nodded. 'I'm afraid so. That's if my name for the day is Plus One. We could try rearranging the names while nobody is looking.'

'As tempting as that is,' she said, 'the whole purpose of coming here today was to make a point. A point I intend to make. That's if you can bear to be caught in the crossfire.'

'I didn't realise it was a war you were fighting?'

'You saw how Hilary treated me, and you.'

'True. So, do we have a game plan in mind for our mission? What is my role? Friend or something more?'

Realising that she should have thought of this well before now, she said, 'I think we should be enigmatic and let people speculate.' She thought of Lindsay asking if it was serious between her and Jakob, and how she hadn't actually given an answer. She hadn't needed to, because Lindsay had reached her own conclusion. It was what everyone would do.

Lunch was a whole lot better than Nina had feared it would be and for one reason: someone – presumably Hilary herself – had changed the place cards on the table and had opted to sit elsewhere with Keith. She was still within eye range though and occasionally, if Nina turned to her left, she would catch Hilary two tables away looking daggers in her direction.

The meal and speeches over, there was a lull in proceedings while yet more photographs were taken of Tigs and Fabian, then the DJ – hot from Ibiza if he was to be believed – announced that it was time for the bride and groom to perform their first dance. The announcement was met with rowdy cheers and tables were pounded enthusiastically.

'Things are hotting up, I think,' said Jakob to Nina.

'Are weddings like this in Norway?' she asked.

'In some ways, yes. The last one I went to was quite traditional, a church service with the bride and groom led down the aisle by violin players and a lot of the guests wore their bunad, the traditional national costume.'

'Did you wear it?'

'Sure.'

'Do you hire the outfit?'

'No, I have my own. It's what we like to wear for special occasions.'

'Do you have any photos of you wearing it?'

He smiled. 'I'll show you another time,' he said just as another cheer went up and everyone stood to watch Tigs and Fabian take to the dancefloor. With diamond-bright lights bouncing like stars off the glitter ball above them, they swayed in perfect unison to 'Lover' by Taylor Swift.

Nina was thinking how radiantly beautiful Tigs looked, and that she was hardly showing her pregnancy, when Jakob said, 'They look very happy together, don't they?'

'They do,' she said. 'More than that, they look right together.'

'Does it make you sad, being here when it must bring back so many memories for you of your own wedding day?'

Touched by his thoughtfulness, she said, 'A little.'

There was a lengthy pause between them, until Jakob said, 'How would you feel about dancing with me? It seems that everyone is now allowed to join the bride and groom.'

He was right, guests were now flooding onto the dancefloor, but Nina faltered. She hadn't danced with another man since Hugh. Not that he had been much of a dancer. If he could get away with it, he had preferred to stand with his mates at the bar leaving her to dance with her girlfriends.

Was this her cue to say that maybe they should go? But why leave when the party was only just getting going? Why be so boring? She remembered Cassie telling her to have some fun today and thought it was high time she did. To hell with worrying what anyone might think, and for playing his part so well, didn't Jakob deserve a dance at the very least? And if she were honest, she'd had just enough to drink to make her think she might actually enjoy it.

'Yes,' she said decisively, 'let's dance.'

'Excellent,' he said, removing his jacket, then his tie and undoing the top button of his shirt.

'Wow,' she said, 'you look like you mean business.'

'I do! I love to dance!'

'In which case I'd better remove my jacket too.'

Laughing, they made their way to the dancefloor where he slipped his arms around her waist and after an awkward few moments when they neither seemed to know where to put their feet or their hands, they settled into the rhythm of the song which the happy couple had chosen for their special day.

Hours later and having danced not just with Jakob but also with Hugh's cousins, and several men she didn't know, as well as an all-female crowd that had swarmed the dancefloor to 'It's Raining Men', Nina was filled with the pleasurable sensation that she was thoroughly enjoying herself. She had forgotten how much she liked to dance. Dancing, especially with Jakob, was so freeing. Joyously freeing and exhilarating! With Abba's 'Dancing Queen' now thrumming through her and everyone singing along, and Jakob twirling her round and then bringing her in close again, her body felt energised in a way it hadn't felt in a very long time.

When 'Dancing Queen' came to an end there was a swift change of tempo to Ed Sheeran's 'Thinking Out Loud'.

'Do you want to sit this one out?' she asked breathlessly.

'Do you?'

She shook her head. She didn't want this wonderful moment to end. She didn't want to go back to feeling how she did before, trapped in a suffocating bubble of widowhood. Here on the dancefloor, in this conjured make-believe world with its flowers, ballons and flickering lights, she was a different Nina. It was such a cliché, but God she felt so gloriously alive!

They came together and because she now felt at ease with him, she let herself sink into his embrace. Closing her eyes, she pressed her hands lightly against his shoulder blades, her head touching the side of his neck while his hands encircled her waist. She could feel the thud of his heart beating and the subtle movement of his hands in the small of her back. It seemed that each time he moved his hands, her own mirrored the exact same thing.

She must have known instinctively what would happen next because she wasn't at all shocked when it did. Nor did she try to stop Jakob. Or more importantly, stop herself. Instead, as he placed a hand to her neck, she tipped her head back so he could kiss her. And so that she could kiss him.

Chapter Nineteen

What followed next shocked not just Nina to her core, but to everyone who saw the drama unfold. Or what they thought they saw because, and to coin a phrase, *recollections may vary*. But however the story was destined to be pieced together, it would become the stuff of wedding lore, a tale that would be embellished with every retelling of it.

By the time an ambulance had arrived, the incident had already found its way onto social media and had racked up hundreds of likes which had rapidly multiplied into thousands and then hundreds of thousands. Who knew what number it had since reached.

Now, and back at Hope Hall with dawn not far off, and her Chanel suit exchanged for a pair of pyjamas, Nina was in bed with a thumping headache. There was a dressing applied to the back of her head beneath which, so she'd been informed, were four stitches, along with a small shaved area of her scalp. The hair would grow back but Nina wasn't so sure about her pride and self-esteem.

And what about my mother's pride and self-esteem? asked a quiet voice from inside her thumping head. It was Hugh. *Imagine how she must feel. Imagine how ashamed she must be feeling.*

I don't care about her, thought Nina, turning to look at the framed photograph in the lamplight on the bedside table. It was of her and Hugh on their honeymoon in the Maldives, the two of them looking golden and carefree and with not a clue of what lay ahead for them.

I'm sorry, Hugh, murmured Nina, *I'm beyond caring what your mother thinks or feels. I don't owe her anything, certainly not my forgiveness. What's more, I did nothing wrong. I really didn't. I'm allowed to be happy.*

She moved the photograph so she couldn't see Hugh smiling at her and swallowing down the threat of tears, she squeezed her eyes shut. But it was the wrong thing to do because now she was back inside the wedding marquee and hearing a very different voice. It was Hilary's, and it wasn't her usual measured tone undercut with a steeliness that brooked no argument, this was more of a demonic screech with Hilary grappling to wrench Nina out of Jakob's arms.

'How could you?' Hilary shrieked above the music, her hate-filled face just inches from Nina's. 'How could you make such a spectacle of yourself? What would poor Hugh think of your disgusting behaviour, and in front of his entire family?'

Stunned at the virulence coming at her from Hilary, and not wanting to escalate things, especially as guests around them had now stopped dancing and were watching, Nina turned to Jakob to suggest they discreetly get off the dancefloor.

'Don't you dare turn away from me when I'm talking to you!' Hilary screamed.

Nina inhaled sharply. 'You're not talking to me,' she said, 'you're screaming at me like a mad woman and embarrassing yourself into the bargain.'

'It's you who's embarrassing yourself, coming here and deliberately flaunting your boyfriend. A boyfriend who looks young enough to have still been at school when you married my darling Hugh! Do you have any idea how ridiculous you look with him?'

'Not half as ridiculous as you're making yourself look right now,' Nina said, squaring up to her mother-in-law. 'Now leave me alone. What I do is none of your business. My life is my own and I'll do whatever I want to do, and that includes being with somebody new. You have no rights over me. None whatsoever!'

'Then all I can say,' Hilary hissed savagely at Nina, 'is that you were never worthy to be the mother of my grandchild.'

'Good, because why would I want any child of mine to have a grandmother as rude and viciously spiteful as you?'

Whether or not Hilary had run out of ammunition at that point, she fell quiet, and in that moment, Nina noticed that an array of mobile phones had magically appeared all around them and were being held aloft to record the exchange in all its hideous awfulness.

That was when Jakob intervened and with calm authority, he put a hand to Nina's elbow to guide her away. But his gesture seemed to reignite Hilary and with a swiftness that took Nina completely unawares, the woman came at her and pushed Nina so hard in the chest, her feet went from beneath her and she felt herself flying backwards until her head hit the floor with an excruciating thump.

It was all a bit blurry after that. She had a vague sense of everything spinning around her, of Jakob holding her and something icy cold pressed to the back of her head. Her next memory was of being in an ambulance with a paramedic asking if she could tell him her name. To her embarrassment, her answer was to be horribly sick.

Not long after that, things became less blurry and by the time the ambulance arrived at the hospital she was fully *compos mentis* and able to deal with the admissions procedure herself. Jakob then arrived, having driven himself to the hospital and was a great support during the interminably long wait before she was examined and stitched up.

While Jakob had driven them home, Nina had scrolled through the messages on her mobile, having been alerted by various members of Hugh's family to keep away from social media. Which meant there was nothing on earth that could stop her from looking. What she'd found horrified her. Keith had tried ringing her and had left several messages on her voicemail, none of which she'd listened to. They could wait. It could all wait, even Cassie's message asking how things had gone and wanting to know – oh, the irony – if she'd had fun.

The lightest of knocks at the door had Nina opening her eyes. 'Come in,' she said.

'One peppermint tea, as requested,' Jakob said, stepping into the room and placing the mug on the bedside table. She'd forgotten she'd asked for it but thanked him anyway.

'Aren't you going to join me with a drink?' she enquired when he moved towards the door.

'I will if you'd like me to.'

'I do,' she said softly.

He returned a few minutes later, mug in hand and with a strip of paracetamol. 'For your headache,' he said. 'It must be time for you to take some more.'

'Probably. I'm sorry about your shirt.'

He looked at the bloodstains on his sleeve. 'It will be fine when I've washed it. I'm not so sure about your suit though.'

They both looked over to the built-in wardrobes where her skirt and jacket had been put on a coat hanger and hooked over a door handle. She had no recall of having put it there herself, Jakob must have done it while she was in the bathroom. There was a dark red stain on the left shoulder of the jacket – the blood from the back of her head must have found its way there down her neck.

He sat on the chaise longue in front of the large sash window that was hidden by the curtains he'd drawn when he'd helped her into bed, despite her protestations that she wasn't an invalid. He hadn't helped her undress, that would have been unbearably embarrassing, but he'd been most solicitous in his attention, as though he were worried she was going to keel over at any minute.

He had the same look of concern on his face now.

'You've been very kind,' she said.

'It's the least I can do,' he responded, 'after all, this is my fault. I should never have kissed you. I should never have suggested that I be your plus-one. It made a difficult situation for you far worse.'

He looked so solemn, so full of anxious regret.

'If anyone is at fault, it's my crazy mother-in-law,' Nina said, 'she's the one who attacked me. And for the record, I kissed you as much as you kissed me.' Her memory might have failed her when it came to certain parts of the evening, but the memory of how she'd felt while dancing with Jakob and the delicious moment their lips had touched had not been lost.

'Your mother-in-law needs help,' Jakob said gravely. 'Her behaviour was not that of a well woman.'

'I agree,' said Nina, after taking a few seconds to tear herself away from remembering how shockingly she'd desired so much more than just a kiss from Jakob. 'But I don't think I covered myself in glory.'

He looked at her puzzled. 'Glory?' he said.

'I mean I behaved badly in what I said to her. I went too far.'

'You were provoked into saying what you did.'

They sipped their drinks in silence.

Then Jakob said: 'I know it's nothing to do with me, but what was all that business about a grandchild?'

'It's a long story,' Nina said with a sigh. 'And it's late. You really should go home; it will be light soon.'

'I'm not going anywhere. I shall sleep on the sofa in the sitting room.'

'There's no need.'

'There is,' he said firmly. 'You might have delayed concussion. You shouldn't be alone.'

'I think I've had all the concussion I'm going to have.'

'I'm still not leaving you. Unless . . . unless it's too awkward for you with me being here.'

'It's not awkward, I'm very grateful to you.'

He frowned. 'I know now is not the time to discuss it, but I just want you to know that if I've ruined everything, I will understand if you feel it would be better if I no longer worked in the gallery for you anymore.'

'You're right,' she said wearily, exhaustion suddenly catching up with her, 'now is not the time.'

Chapter Twenty

Monday morning and minutes after Ben had left for work, Cassie was at her desk and updating a website for one of her long-term clients. Andrea J. Matthews was an author of half a dozen self-help books and, in Cassie's humble opinion, a specialist in waffly wellness BS. Her new book *Mindfulness Meditation for the Nonbeliever* appeared to be just another take on what most of the author's previous books had been about. But fair play to Andrea J. Matthews, her books sold and according to the latest batch of testimonials Cassie had just uploaded, she had helped thousands of people over the years, if not hundreds of thousands if the claims were to be believed. Cassie had no idea if the testimonials were genuine, but that wasn't her concern.

Just as it wasn't her business to pester Nina about the wedding on Saturday, so Ben had said while they'd been having breakfast.

'I take exception to the word "pester",' Cassie had responded, 'I just want to know that Nina's okay, it's very unlike her not to reply to a message.'

'If Nina had anything she wanted to share, she would have done so by now,' Ben had said in that annoyingly reasonable voice of his, while continuing to read the news headlines on his iPad.

'That is such a typical male thing to say!' Cassie had retorted.

'And that, right back atcha,' he'd said with a smile, 'is such a typically female thing to say!'

'Don't be so smug.'

'But you have to admit, I do it with such aplomb.'

Why were men so incurious about certain things, Cassie thought now while she uploaded the last batch of testimonials to Andrea J. Matthews's website. Wasn't it the most normal thing in the world to want to know how Nina's day had gone when she had been so anxious about attending the wedding with Jakob? Wasn't it also perfectly normal to want to know all the details, such as how did the ghastly mother-in-law react to Nina having a plus-one at her side?

The last of the testimonials now uploaded, Cassie moved on to the quote the client wanted added to the welcome page of the website:

You no longer have yesterday, and nor do you have tomorrow. You only have today, so let me teach you how to make it not just a good day, but an exceptional day.

It might not have been wholly original, but it was a sentiment Cassie could get behind. She spent far too much time worrying about what had gone on in her life previously and if there was an easy way to stop herself from doing it, she would. No doubt Andrea J. Matthews, and countless others, would say it was a straightforward choice – you either let go of the hurt or hung on tight to it.

Venetia had said something similar when Cassie had asked her about her time here at Hope Hall when it was a children's home, something about never allowing the past to become a weapon to use against others, or yourself. The woman genuinely didn't seem to have a negative bone in her body and yet for someone who had been abandoned as a baby it would be understandable if she harboured any number of grudges. Did that kind of resilience and acceptance come with age, or were some people born with an innate ability to accept the hand they'd been dealt?

What intrigued Cassie most was that Venetia had never tried to discover who her mother was, or her father come to that. With all the resources available on the internet these days, surely it would be possible. And what about the children with whom Venetia had grown up, in particular her friend, Lucien, why hadn't she wanted to find out where they all were now?

Or was Cassie merely letting her own curiosity get the better of her, as well as projecting her obsession with not letting go of the past?

The question brought her back to Nina and the wedding on Saturday. Had going with Jakob given Nina a taste of what her life could be like in the future, released from the past and her dead husband and his family? Frankly, the mother-in-law sounded a total control freak and a prime example of someone who was determined not to move on and, while she was about it, chain everyone down with her.

The pot calling the kettle black, Cassie thought with a shake of her head. How easy it was for her to see the mistakes others made but do nothing about her own. Which wasn't quite true because she knew the mistakes she made, she just didn't know how to stop herself from repeating them.

The jingling ringtone of a FaceTime call jolted her out of her thoughts and seeing that it was Emily, she took a moment to prepare herself before speaking to her daughter. She needed to ensure that she sounded positive and sincerely reassuring for Emily. It should come naturally to her, of course it should, but because Drew would be part of the conversation it simply wasn't that easy.

She clicked on Accept and straightaway the bleakness of Emily's face staring back at her told Cassie that she was going to need to dig deep if she was going to say the right thing.

'Mum,' she said, 'I . . . I thought you ought to know, Dad died last night. I know you won't exactly be heartbroken at the news, but—' Her voice cracked and she pressed a fist to her mouth.

'Oh darling, I'm so very sorry.'

'Are you? Are you really?'

Recoiling at the sharpness of the accusation, Cassie said, 'I'm sorry for *you*, Ems, that you're going through this.'

'If you hadn't hated him so much, I would have been able to know him better and for longer, but you denied me that!'

Her instinct was to launch herself into fighting back, to dismiss what was being thrown at her, but Cassie knew that right now her daughter needed someone to blame for the unfairness of losing her father when she'd only just started getting to know him. 'Ems,' she said gently, 'tell me what happened.'

'Why, so you can gloat?'

God forgive her, Cassie would have felt precisely like that once upon a time. 'Of course not,' she said, 'that's a terrible thing to say. How's his wife coping?'

'Like you care!'

'Please, Ems, don't keep thinking the worst of me.'

Emily sniffed and then rubbed the tears from her eyes. 'If you must know, she's not coping at all. She's a wreck and it's a wonder she's held up for as long as she has.'

'You've probably been a great support to her,' Cassie said. 'I'm proud of you. And I'm sure Drew would have been proud of you too.'

It was the wrong thing to say. The girl's face crumpled, and Cassie longed to put her arms around her daughter and make all this wretched heartbreak go away. If only Drew had left well alone! If only he hadn't had some kind of mid-life crisis of conscience and invited his abandoned daughter into his life! He'd wrecked Cassie's life all those years ago and now he'd done it all again with his second wife and little boy, and Emily.

Reining in her emotions, and knowing that she wasn't being entirely rational, Cassie focused on her precious daughter who was far too young to have to deal with all this. But was Emily right, should Cassie have hated Drew less and done more to make him a proper father to his daughter?

But how? How could she have done more when Drew had been the one to make it so clear he hadn't wanted to play any part in his daughter's life until recently? How was it always the woman's fault?

'*Mum!* Are you even listening to me?'

Cassie snapped to attention. 'Sorry, sweetheart, the connection went a bit fuzzy then,' she improvised. 'What were you saying?'

'I have to help Rosalyn repatriate Dad's body back to the UK. The laws here are a bloody nightmare and because she doesn't work and can't support herself, they'll kick her out.'

'Not immediately, surely?'

'No, but she knows she'll have to leave when the authorities say time's up. But she has nowhere to go. She's frantic with worry.'

Knowing that Drew's parents were long since dead and were therefore not a source of help, Cassie said, 'Rosalyn must have friends and other members of family here in the UK who she can turn to?'

'I told you before, she hasn't had any contact with her parents in years.'

'Then this might be the moment to resolve whatever issues there are. In times of crisis that's usually when families put their differences aside and come together to help.'

Minutes later and, as unbelievable as it was, Cassie realised the trap she'd walked into. She realised too, that if she said no, then it would damn her for evermore in her daughter's mind.

Chapter Twenty-One

Keith woke to the thoroughly annoying sound of wood pigeons flapping their wings noisily in the lilac tree just yards from the open window of the spare room. He'd been sleeping in here ever since the awful day of Tigs and Fabian's wedding.

He'd driven home to Madingley that night unable to bring himself to speak to Hilary as she sat grim-faced and silent in the passenger seat beside him. He'd told her that he thought it best that he slept in the spare room. She didn't try to dissuade him. At breakfast the next morning, they had sat like strangers at the table, neither willing to break the silence that lay heavily between them. For his part he didn't trust himself to be civil and as for her, he couldn't begin to fathom what delusional web she was spinning inside her head. He didn't much care. She could stew in whatever sanctimonious self-deception she wanted to wrap herself in.

Two very long and very miserable weeks had passed since then with Keith doing his best to avoid spending any time with his wife. When they were in the same room together there was a large elephant there too, its ominous presence reminding him of the moment when Hilary had lost control. What she did that night was unforgivable and whenever he so much as attempted to raise the subject, when he trusted himself not to lose his temper, she shut him down by accusing him of not caring about Hugh and his memory.

Rather than confront her and unleash God knew what, he escaped to the golf course as often as he could or went for long brooding walks and twice he met up with Diane in Ely. He'd also been to see Nina to apologise for what had happened, not at the gallery, but at her apartment. He had phoned her in advance to check that he was welcome, and she'd said it would probably do them both good to clear the air between them. She'd been right, and he'd taken comfort in being with her while strolling around the beautiful and serene grounds of Hope Hall. He could quite understand why she had moved from the centre of town to live there; it was a soothing balm to the soul, an answer to a mad world.

Outside the window of the spare room, the wood pigeons continued to make their irritating noise in the lilac tree, cooing and flapping their wings – it was like Chinese water torture, waiting for the next coo or the next flap. Suddenly he could bear it no more and he threw aside the duvet and went to the window, banging it shut loudly, scaring the wretched birds out of the tree.

Opening the window again, he stood there looking at the garden, knowing that after today no more would he enjoy the view. They had moved here nearly forty years ago when Hugh had been a small boy. Keith could remember the day as though it were yesterday, when he'd climbed the beech tree at the far end of the garden and fixed a rope swing to one of the lower branches. The rope had rotted years ago but just as Hilary had hoped for a grandchild, he too had wanted one and had pictured a smiling child playing on a newly installed swing. But instead of Keith climbing the tree, Hugh would probably have done the job of fixing a rope to the branch. At the thought of Hugh and what might have been, he felt the familiar ache of wishing his son was still alive.

What in hell's name would Hugh make of what his mother had done and what Keith was about to set in motion? With a heartfelt sigh, he supposed he should be grateful, if it didn't sound too illogical, that his son wasn't here to witness the aftermath his death had caused.

Today was August Bank Holiday Monday and he'd chosen the day to do what he had been putting off for far too long. If he didn't do it now, when would he?

His marriage had been failing for so many years he couldn't recall when he'd last felt anything remotely like love for his wife. He had been on the verge of leaving her when Hugh was diagnosed with a brain tumour. He'd been shattered by the news and would have willingly traded his own life for that of his son's. So, he did the next best thing, and he made a pact with whatever god he futilely hoped might exist. He vowed to stay with Hilary and do his best to support and love her in exchange for Hugh surviving the diagnosis he'd been given. For that, he would do whatever it took.

But then Hugh had died, and he knew he couldn't abandon Hilary to her grief alone, she needed him like never before. He'd help her over the worst of it, he told himself, and then he'd go when she was strong enough to handle the divorce. Part of his decision to delay leaving her was rooted in the disagreeable knowledge that he didn't want the family and their circle of friends to think badly of him for being so cruelly selfish. They might have publicly made excuses for him, blamed his out-of-character behaviour on grief, but privately they would have been disgusted by his actions. If he were honest, he was disgusted with himself for not having the guts to do what he knew he had to do before now. By not being stronger he'd been complicit in allowing Hilary to take out her grief in ways that should have been checked ages ago. He was a coward. And a liar and a cheat.

He hadn't physically cheated on his wife, but the relationship he had with Diane was a heartbeat away from becoming more than just companionship grounded in the emotional support they gave each other.

He'd known very early on in their online friendship while still using the grief support group that he was guilty of obfuscation, but what the hell! He believed he deserved to be happy. Everyone deserved to be happy, even Hilary. Nina too. Life was for the living; Hugh would have been the first to agree with that.

He showered, shaved, dressed, and went downstairs. There was no sign of Hilary and when he looked out of the hall window, he saw that her car had gone from the driveway. He had no idea where she'd gone, but he was relieved to have the kitchen to himself while he made himself breakfast.

When he'd eaten two slices of toast and drunk a mug of strong coffee, he placed his mug, plate and knife in the dishwasher and went back upstairs to retrieve the suitcases he'd packed last night. After he'd stowed them in the boot of the car, he awaited Hilary's return. He had no idea how long she would be. He was tempted to pour himself a glass of Dutch courage, but he wasn't sure he could stop at just the one glass.

At half past twelve he heard Hilary's car on the drive. He breathed in deeply, listened for her key in the lock, the door closing, and then her sharp staccato footsteps on the oak flooring in the hall.

'We need to talk,' he said, uttering the cliché of all clichés when she came into the kitchen where he'd been waiting.

'I have nothing to say to you,' she said, dumping her handbag on the dresser.

'Too bad, I have plenty I want to say to you and for once in your life you're going to listen. You might just as well sit down.'

She stared at him as though not quite believing the way he'd spoken to her. But she ignored his instruction to sit down.

'I've tried my hardest to be sympathetic towards you, Hilary,' he said, 'but no more. I'm all out of sympathy, it's time now for me to do what's right for me, not you.'

Her expression flipped from disbelief to one of deep scorn. 'You've always done what's right for you. You're a weak man, Keith and I despise you for that.'

'I agree with you, I've been shamefully weak, and I'll have to live with that knowledge. But what I won't stand for is how disgracefully you behaved towards Nina.'

'I did nothing wrong,' she asserted, her body ramrod stiff, her gaze steely.

'How can you say that? You assaulted her! You attacked your son's wife . . . our daughter-in-law! She could have pressed charges against you. The fact that she didn't speaks volumes about the kind of decent woman she is.'

'She's no longer my daughter-in-law,' Hilary stated almost robotically. 'She's nothing to me.'

'I'm sure the feeling is mutual from Nina's perspective.' He shook his head. 'I can't imagine how appalled Hugh would be at what you did.'

She flinched at that. 'And what would my darling Hugh have thought, seeing his wife flaunting herself the way she did! Kissing another man, and in front of his family!'

'That's the whole point,' Keith said, and going over to her. 'Hugh wasn't there, he's dead and gone and I thank God that he is.' He paused before going on. He swallowed and forced himself to continue. 'Hilary,' he said, 'it pains me to say this, but you're unwell and you can't go on like this. *We* can't go on like this,' he added. 'I can't stand by and watch you destroy not just yourself, but me as well. I'm leaving you. I should have done it before, but I didn't have the courage then.'

That was when Hilary raised her hand to strike him, just as she had with Nina. He caught hold of her slender wrist, gritting his teeth as he did so, scarcely containing his own need for physical violence. They stood there locked in a moment of seething silence, each staring at the other with what he recognised as intense loathing.

Yes, he'd reached the point where he loathed his wife. No more could he pretend he was easy-going Keith prepared to tolerate the put-downs, batting them off with self-deprecating comments.

That Keith was dead.

As dead as his marriage.

And as dead as their dear son, Hugh.

Chapter Twenty-Two

September had proved to be one of the warmest on record, but there were signs now that the intensity of the long hot summer was coming to an end. The light had assumed a gentle golden hue, casting far-reaching shadows across the landscape. Parched and curled-up leaves on the trees whispered conspiratorially on the warm breeze. It really had seemed as though autumn would never come, that these endless days of summer and soft cornflower-blue skies would be with them forever. But change was coming and that made days like this feel such a gift, a chance to take a breath and simply be in the moment.

That was how Venetia felt, dreamily in the moment and wholly at peace as she stretched out her legs on the comfortable sun lounger. She was with Nina on her splendid roof terrace that was furnished with stylish garden furniture and a couple of olive trees in large planters.

Being in the moment was what she had implored Nina to do, to live her life just as she wanted to live it and to hell with what anyone else thought. Especially that mother-in-law of hers. From all accounts, the woman needed professional help to get over the death of her son. Maybe some anger management wouldn't go amiss!

Nina's father-in-law had apparently tried to help his wife but had bailed out and for the time being, at Nina's invitation, was staying with her until he found a more permanent arrangement. Venetia had met him several times since he'd moved in with Nina and had found him to be a very agreeable man. Nina said he was an easy guest to have around and was even helping at the gallery.

After the summer exhibition at Lavelle's, Jakob had resigned and had gone to Oslo for a holiday and to consider his future. Venetia suspected there was more to it than that, but she wasn't going to pry. Very likely Nina had shared more with her parents who'd come over from the States for a couple of weeks. Venetia had met them just before they flew back to the US and had liked them enormously. It was plain to see that Nina took after her mother in looks, who was tall, slender and elegance personified.

Today Keith was seeing his 'lady friend' as Nina coyly referred to the woman with whom Keith had struck up a relationship through an online grief support group. In his absence, Nina had invited Venetia for an al fresco lunch, during which Venetia had been struck, from this high vantage point, by how little the view of the grounds below them had changed since her childhood days.

She and Lucien often used to climb the rickety fire escape ladder and sneak up here, usually when they had wanted to make a change from going off to the woods to sit and chat. They had lain on their backs counting the stars and whispered their hopes and dreams to each other.

Venetia had thought of Lucien a lot since she'd told Cassie about him; well, in truth she'd thought a lot of him before and since moving here. How could she not? He'd always been there in the background of her life. A forever presence. A lingering shadow. She couldn't quite decide whether coming back to Hope Hall had been an act of closure for her, or more an act of hope, a way to relive the happy times they'd spent together. Before it had all gone wrong.

A dainty sneeze followed quickly by another from Bon-Bon who was curled up on Nina's sun lounger with her, had Venetia turning to look at him.

'That dog is such a little tart,' she said, good-humouredly, 'he's so free and easy with his affections.'

Nina laughed. 'I know perfectly well that I'm a poor substitute for his true love,' she said, 'and that's Cassie.'

Venetia laughed too. 'Like any male of the species, he'll take his pleasure where he can.'

Reaching over Bon-Bon for the bottle of wine on the low table between them, Nina tilted it towards Venetia. 'Top-up?' she asked.

'Why not? But only if I'm not outstaying my welcome. I know how busy you are.'

'You're fine to stay, it's Sunday, my official day of rest. Your being here gives me the excuse to do nothing, otherwise I'd be compelled to deal with the VAT paperwork for my accountant.'

'I'm glad to have saved you from that,' Venetia said when her glass was replenished. 'Any time you need the excuse to be lazy, I'm only downstairs. Not that I want you to think I'm one of those awful neighbours who can't respect boundaries.'

'You've never given me cause to think that you would,' Nina said, 'it's always a pleasure to spend time with you. And this handsome little chap as well,' she added, gently cupping Bon-Bon's head in her hands. 'I'm still amazed that you've managed to get away with concealing him as well as you have.'

'People mostly see what they want to see,' Venetia said. 'Nobody expects me to have a dog here, therefore I don't have one. It's a classic case of hiding in plain sight. And who would suspect a respectable old woman like me of defying the rules?'

'Who indeed?' responded Nina, staring off into the distance. 'It's always interesting how other people perceive us, and how we perceive ourselves. I've thought about that a lot recently.'

'In what respect?'

Nina swung her gaze back to meet Venetia's. 'I feel like I'm in danger of not knowing who I am anymore. One minute I was Hugh's wife, then I was his widow, now I'm the kind of woman who makes a disgusting spectacle of herself at weddings.'

Venetia tutted. 'That, my dear girl, if you're referring to what you told me about your mother-in-law when she went berserk, is blatantly not true! And you'll be doing yourself a great disservice if you give an ounce of credence to anything she said. You kissed an attractive man, who from what I've seen of him sees you as a beautiful woman to whom he's more than a little attracted. No, no,' she said, lifting a hand to stop Nina from interrupting her, 'I saw the way his eyes barely left you the evening of the exhibition at the gallery, and I know what I saw!'

With a light laugh, Nina said, 'You make him sound like a creepy stalker.'

Venetia smiled. 'That wasn't my intention. But my word, he's a fine chap and I would definitely throw my cap into the ring if I were fifty years younger.'

'He seems to like an older woman, so don't rule yourself out.'

Venetia tutted again. 'Good Lord, am I really going to have to waste my breath disabusing you of the absurd notion that an age gap is of any consequence? Two of my husbands were younger than I was and not for one moment did I let it bother me!'

'Two? How many were there?'

'There were three in all,' answered Venetia, amused at the surprised expression on Nina's face. 'And yes, I fully accept that to lose one husband might be considered unfortunate but to lose three smacks of wilful carelessness. They died, if you're wondering what happened to them, and not by my hand I might add!'

'The thought never crossed my mind,' said Nina smoothly. 'But I don't recall you ever mentioning being married before now.'

'Oh, I'm far more interested in other people. After all, I know everything there is to know about me and my dull old life.'

'I doubt your life has ever been dull. And it might seem an odd thing to say,' Nina continued, her hands now fondling Bon-Bon's ears, 'but you always give the impression of having travelled through life alone. You seem so self-contained.' Her gaze slid towards Venetia's left hand. 'You never wear a ring on that finger.'

'Occasionally I do, it depends on my mood and the situation.' Venetia's own gaze glanced towards Nina's left hand. 'I notice you always wear your rings. Would I be right in thinking you can't bring yourself to take them off?'

Nina nodded. 'They're like a comfort blanket.'

'I'm sure they are, but do you really need a comfort blanket? Is there not a danger that the rings are anchoring you to the past? Which I can understand you needed in the beginning, but that was then, and forgive me if I'm wrong, but I believe you're in a very different place now.'

Seconds passed before Nina replied. 'You're right, but sometimes I hate the thought that I am in a different place. It feels wrong.'

'That's only human. Whatever happens, Hugh will always be with you in your heart; but your happiness depends on you being able to imagine a new future for yourself, which may or may not include a new partner. And there, my dear girl, endeth today's lesson. Apologies for going on so much.'

Nina drank from her wineglass, her eyes seemingly fixed on a faraway point in the sky. 'You're not saying anything I haven't thought or been told before,' she said at length, 'I know what I'm supposed to do, just as I know Hugh wouldn't want me to be stuck in this . . . this awful ninth circle of hell.' She took another sip of her wine. Then: 'Sorry, I'm being overly dramatic and that's not me at all.'

'Or perhaps it is,' suggested Venetia. 'Maybe that's a side of Nina Lavelle that's never been allowed to reveal itself before now?'

'Implying I've repressed the real me all my life?' Nina looked doubtful, even a little defensive. 'We're getting very deep all of a sudden.'

'Blame it on the wine,' Venetia said airily. 'That and the exquisite beauty of the day.'

'No,' said Nina with more than a hint of firmness, 'that would be a cop-out because actually there's some truth in what you're suggesting. That day of the wedding when I was dancing with Jakob, I felt the real me again. I felt happy and carefree, like I used to be. I was Nina. It was the purest and most wonderful of emotions. Almost, I would imagine, like taking a drug and being high on it, and then came the crash,' she added with a weighted sigh.

Venetia chose her next words with care. 'If your mother-in-law hadn't behaved the way she had,' she said, 'what do you think might have gone on to happen?'

'That's a very good question, and if I'm honest, the answer scares me.'

'No bad thing to be scared, if by that you mean challenged.'

'Oh yes, it challenges me all right, it makes me doubt I can be trusted to make an objective decision.'

'Objective?' queried Venetia. 'Whoever made an objective decision when it came to the important moments in life? Was it an objective decision on your part to fall in love with Hugh?'

'Of course not, it just happened because it felt completely right.'

'Exactly how it should be.'

'In contrast, and ever since Hugh's death, I've had to overrule my emotions to avoid making a misstep. The result being, everything now seems forced and I'm constantly second-guessing the future.'

'And that way lies madness.'

'I know. And it's exhausting constantly asking myself the "what if" question. It's why I've put off making the biggest and scariest decision of all, what to do with the embryos the clinic has been storing all this time.'

This was a subject that Nina had never spoken in great depth about before; it was after all a very personal matter, but Venetia had the gist of it and didn't envy her friend the decision she had to make. Despite her three marriages, Venetia had never had children – there were a couple of stepchildren floating around somewhere, but they'd never had anything to do with her – so she didn't consider herself qualified to give advice on motherhood. It was a hell of a dilemma, and she didn't envy Nina the choice she had to make.

'Do you think you're any nearer knowing what you're going to do?' she asked.

'After the wedding debacle I was one hundred per cent certain that I was going to tell the clinic I didn't want to use the embryos. But my certainty was for all the wrong reasons. I wanted to hurt Hugh's mother after what she'd done to me, and I knew that by destroying her wish to become a grandmother was the surest way I could do it.' She looked directly at Venetia. 'Are you shocked at me for saying that?'

'No, not at all. It seems perfectly reasonable in the circumstances, but I imagine you rejected that course of action because you're essentially a decent person and don't go around deliberately hurting others.'

'Something along those lines,' Nina murmured, 'but don't get carried away with the idea that I wasn't seriously tempted, I was. Then an even worse thought came to me. That I'd have Hugh's child and never let Hilary see her only grandchild. Now you are shocked, aren't you?'

'Shocked to my toes and wondering how you sleep at night!' Venetia said with an amused lifting of an eyebrow.

A faintly sardonic smile passed across Nina's face. 'As cowardly as it sounds, I wish I didn't have to decide what to do, that the decision could be taken out of my hands.'

'I might be wrong, but it strikes me that you know what you want to do, but you're afraid of committing yourself to doing it.'

Nina frowned at that. 'Am I that obvious?'

Without answering her, Venetia said, 'Is your real dilemma how to assuage your guilt at *not* having Hugh's child?'

Nina lowered her gaze. 'More or less,' she murmured.

'Being a mother doesn't appeal?' asked Venetia.

'Not as much as being a father appealed to Hugh. He used to joke about creating his very own dynasty.'

'Yes, it's funny how so many men love the idea of a big family without ever putting themselves forward to take on the hard work involved.'

Her wineglass now empty, Venetia placed it on the table next to her. 'You know, the sooner you inform the clinic of what you want to do, the sooner you can get on with making a new life for yourself.'

Nina gave a small shrug of her fine-boned shoulders. 'You're right,' she said, 'I know you are. And you make it sound so easy and so straightforward.'

'I don't mean to, and I certainly don't mean to influence you one way or another or downplay the enormity of what you have to decide.'

'I know that.'

'Well, and before I do say anything untoward and you throw me over the parapet for my impertinence, it's probably time I went.' Slipping on her sparkly flip-flops, Venetia stood up.

'You haven't been at all impertinent,' replied Nina, carefully lifting Bon-Bon off her lap and rising to her feet. 'I appreciate your candour. And,' she added, 'your friendship.'

'That's the nicest thing you could say to me,' said Venetia, 'thank you. I value your friendship too. As does this cheeky little chap,' she added, bending down to gather up Bon-Bon and put him into her tote bag. He'd just hopped inside it when Venetia's attention was caught by the sound of a child's shrill voice. It reminded her of being a child here herself, when the voices of children were always to be heard.

She and Nina went over to the stone parapet, and down on the lawn beneath them was a pretty blonde-haired girl in skimpy shorts and a sun top trying to teach a small boy how to fly a kite. It was Cassie's daughter, Emily, with her half-brother, Finlay. The boy's widowed mother was nowhere to be seen.

'I do hope Cassie and Ben are having a good time,' said Venetia.

'Yes,' agreed Nina. 'They both fully deserve the break. I'm not sure I could have done what Cassie has.'

'Just goes to show what a big heart she has,' replied Venetia.

Chapter Twenty-Three

The book she'd been reading, *The Great White Palace* by Tony Porter, now cast aside, Cassie watched Ben swimming in the Mermaid Pool. His front crawl was infinitely better than hers and she observed his steady strokes with admiration. She might be able to beat him at tennis, as she had after breakfast that morning on the hotel's court, but he was a far stronger swimmer than she was.

They'd arrived here at the renowned Art Deco hotel on Burgh Island two days ago, Ben having booked a beautiful suite with fabulous sea views. His arranging this mini break for her birthday had been one of the surprises he'd planned for her, knowing as he did that the hotel had been on her wish list ever since watching Agatha Christie's *Evil Under the Sun* with David Suchet which had been filmed here. He'd even managed to organise excellent weather for their stay and although it was September, it was warm enough to sunbathe as well as swim in the sea. Some guests had said that the water at this time of the year was at its warmest.

The combination of the Devon sea air, the stylish comfort of their suite and the excellent food and drink they'd consumed, together with the complete absence of stress and worry, had done wonders to restore her equilibrium, as well as her sex drive, which had dwindled to nothing in the emotional fallout – and upheaval – of Drew's death.

When her daughter had begged Cassie to help Rosalyn and Finlay, she'd had the nerve to use emotional blackmail.

'Mum,' Emily had said with tears in her eyes, 'Finlay's my half-brother, how can we not help? When I was little you had Gran and Grandad. Rosalyn and Finlay have no one.'

'But they must have somebody who can take them in,' Cassie had tried.

'Not anyone who matters. Come on, Mum, what do you say? Rosalyn's really nice. I know you'll like her.'

Emily didn't have a clue what she was asking of Cassie. But then she was still full of the youthful and naive belief that black could be white and vice versa if you said it often enough. Give it time and Emily would be battle-hardened like the rest of them. But was that the problem? Was Cassie so embittered that she couldn't see the world the same way her daughter did? Couldn't, or *wouldn't?*

'I can't make an important decision like that unilaterally,' she'd told Emily. 'Ben's hardly going to be overjoyed at the prospect of welcoming strangers into our home.'

'Let me speak to him,' Emily had said. 'I'm sure I could talk him round.'

Cassie hadn't doubted that for a minute; Ben had always been a big softie when it came to Emily. Many a time the two of them had ganged up against Cassie when Emily had wanted to do something and Cassie had deemed it too risky, or too expensive or just plain unsuitable.

'No, Ems,' Cassie had said firmly, 'I'll speak to Ben, but please don't go getting your hopes up, or Rosalyn's, it wouldn't be fair to her.'

'I knew I could rely on you, Mum,' Emily had said triumphantly when ending the call. 'Love you!'

Before speaking to Ben, Cassie had checked online what the legal situation was in the UAE for a newly widowed partner, and she discovered that there wasn't the urgency Emily had inferred. She'd as good as said that Rosalyn and her son could be deported any minute from the country. But Cassie knew that to point that out would only serve to make her look petty.

Naturally, being the generous and compassionate man he was, Ben had said yes, but only if Cassie was in agreement, and on the clear understanding by all parties concerned that it was a temporary measure.

'We must keep in mind that Emily is grieving for her father,' he'd said, 'and perhaps this is her way of dealing with it, of doing something positive and not dwelling on what she's lost.'

'But you're her father!' Cassie had remonstrated. 'Emily knew Drew for no more than a blink of an eye.'

'Semantics,' Ben had said mildly.

Why did he have to be so infuriatingly reasonable and kind, she'd wanted to scream, why couldn't he have exploded and shouted that no way did he want a strange woman and her child living in their apartment with them? But if he'd been that type of a man, he wouldn't have been Ben, and she wouldn't love him the way she did.

The trouble was, his generosity and compassion underscored her lack of it and worse still it fuelled her insecurity, made her feel as though she were unworthy of his love and that it wouldn't be long before he realised his mistake in sharing his life with her.

Then step to and be a better person, a stern voice commanded inside her head, *stop whingeing and do something that would make your daughter and Ben proud of you!*

Once Cassie had given Emily the go-ahead, the girl had swung into action, dealing with the British Embassy and the local authorities in Dubai, including the coroner.

'You wouldn't believe the paperwork involved with repatriating Dad's body back to the UK,' she'd complained to Cassie. 'And then there's all the packing to do. Rosalyn says she couldn't have coped without me. Oh Mum, it's so awful for her, and she's so grateful to you and Ben for what you're doing.'

The grieving widow herself had phoned Cassie to express her tearful thanks and to say just how amazing Emily was.

'She's a wonderful girl,' she had said, 'but then I'm sure I don't need to tell you that.'

From thousands of miles away, Rosalyn's breathily thin, watery voice trickled down the line and Cassie had known a moment's guilt that she had harboured so much resentment and animosity towards this unknown woman.

Cassie had known Rosalyn was fifteen years younger than she was, but she hadn't expected her to look quite so young in the flesh. In all her Instagram and TikTok posts, Rosalyn had come across as a generic, heavily contoured version of the millions of young women who had ever pouted and posed in front of a camera, but Cassie's first glimpse of her at the airport revealed a fresh-faced girl who looked almost as young as Emily. What make-up she wore was the bare minimum, just a little smudgy dab or two around her eyes and a touch of lip-gloss on her pillowy lips.

Cassie had driven Ben's SUV to Heathrow to meet Emily and her charges and at some point, while they were collecting the luggage from the carousel, Drew's body had been discreetly removed from the plane by the appointed funeral director. Their job had also been to deal with sorting out the mundanity of Customs Clearance and Airline Handling charges. That was a week ago and it would be some weeks before a funeral could take place as a coroner in the UK had yet to decide if a further inquest or postmortem was required.

Ben had been waiting for them when they arrived at Hope Hall, and with his help they'd hauled the luggage from the boot of the car and carried it up to the apartment. In the days that followed, more luggage arrived and went straight into storage until Rosalyn knew where she was going to live.

It rapidly became clear just how dependent Rosalyn was on

Emily, leaving most of the care of her son to the girl while she spent much of the day in her room in bed. Also clear was that Emily treated Rosalyn more like a friend or a big sister, rather than a stepmother. Observing this closeness as Emily fussed around Rosalyn, willingly fetching and carrying for her, it filled Cassie with an emotion she wasn't proud of: envy. She was profoundly jealous that Rosalyn had usurped her role as Emily's big sister, a role that Cassie had enjoyed ever since Emily had become a teenager and people who didn't know them would assume they were sisters and not mother and daughter. It was a role she'd treasured.

In deference to the situation in which they now found themselves – a grieving widow and confused little boy living with them – Ben hadn't felt it was right to go ahead with the surprise party he had arranged for Cassie's birthday. It seemed disrespectful. But he'd insisted that they still go away for the surprise trip he'd planned. Emily had been quick to agree with him.

'Mum, you not being here for a few days will help Rosalyn relax, as you can be a bit reactionary and give off, you know, a bit of an intense vibe at times,' Emily had said. 'It will give her some, you know, head space.'

Cassie had taken offence at that and had been on the verge of saying, 'Well, pardon me for breathing in my own home!' when Ben had given her a warning look. Swallowing back her outrage at the injustice – *she did not give off an intense vibe and was not reactionary!* – she'd suggested a game of tennis to Ben as the safest way to vent. The poor man had known he was in for a beating but had gamely complied.

I'm a bad, bad woman, she thought now as she watched Ben swim to the pebbly shore of the man-made pool which they had to themselves. While a pair of seagulls wheeled overhead, she kept her eyes on him as he made his way up the short strip of beach to where she was sitting on the raised platform of decking.

'I know what you're thinking,' he said, when he was standing in front of her and shaking the water from his hair before grabbing the towel from the sun lounger next to hers.

'You do?'

'Yes, that I'm the spitting image of Daniel Craig emerging from the sea in his sexy blue swimming trunks. It's the rippling muscles, isn't it?'

'Got it in one, Mr Bond,' she said with a happy laugh.

Wrapping the towel around his boyishly slim waist, he said, 'How about a kiss then, Miss Moneypenny?'

'Oh, *James!*' she said in a girlish voice, mimicking myriad Bond conquests as Ben bent down and kissed her long and hard on the mouth.

In their suite later, they lay languorously satiated in bed, their bodies slick with sweat and their hearts still pounding in their chests. A half-empty bottle of champagne stood in an ice bucket on the bedside table along with two empty glasses.

'I've always been partial to sex in classy hotels,' Cassie murmured, playing her fingers over Ben's chest, 'can we stay here forever, please?'

He turned his head to look at her. 'I'm not sure I'd have the stamina,' he said, smiling. 'You'll have reduced me to a dried husk of a man within weeks. Not that I'm complaining, but we've certainly upped the ante since arriving here.'

'It must be the sea air,' she said contentedly, still luxuriating in the lightheaded afterglow of the climax Ben had so expertly brought her to. 'That and the privacy.'

'Yes,' he said, 'having guests around at home isn't entirely conducive to an afternoon given over to champagne and sexual pleasure, is it?'

When she didn't say anything, he said, 'It won't be for much longer, Rosalyn will soon find a place of her own and then everything will go back to normal.'

'Will it?' she said doubtfully. 'I'm not so sure.'

'Why?'

'I don't think Emily is going to let things go back to normal,' Cassie said. 'She wants Rosalyn and Finlay in her life, maybe ours too; she wants them to be her family. *Our* family.'

'Finlay is her half-brother,' Ben said after a pause, 'so it's understandable. But equally she's on a crusade right now.'

'What an odd thing to say.'

'But it's true; this is the first time in her life she's had a real cause to fight for. Her generation love that.'

'Don't let her catch you talking about her that way, she'll have you up on a charge of gross patronising condescension.'

'Very true,' he said with a laugh. 'But don't forget, putting her energy into helping Rosalyn and Finlay is part of her grieving process.'

'But what then? When Rosalyn is building a new life for herself and no longer needs Emily in the way she does now, what will she do then?'

'She might go back to university. Or find she has a taste for helping others by sorting out their lives. She seems pretty good at it.'

'Dear God, you make her sound like Mary Poppins meets Mother Teresa!'

'Admit it, you're proud of her. If Rosalyn was any other woman and not Drew's widowed wife, you'd be banging the drum for that girl.'

Cassie sighed. 'You're right. Is it wrong that I can't quite bring myself to be the bigger person towards Rosalyn? You can do it, but—'

'But I'm not burdened with a ton of top-quality Louis Vuitton baggage like you are.'

'Don't mock me.'

'I'm not, but stop giving yourself such a hard time. You're doing a great thing helping Rosalyn. How many ex-wives would do what you have?'

'But my heart isn't in it, and you know as well as I do, I'm doing it under sufferance to please Emily.'

'That's as good a reason as any, and for what it's worth, I'm bloody proud of you and I couldn't love you more.'

'If only you were a little less perfect,' she said with a smile, putting a hand to his face and kissing him. But at the same time and for no real reason she could think of, a humorous one-liner she'd once heard popped into her mind, that no good deed went unpunished.

They'd booked to have dinner in the Grand Ballroom that evening and were suitably attired, Ben in a black velvet dinner jacket and bow tie and Cassie in a full-length dress of embroidered ivory-coloured organza, which had been yet another birthday surprise from Ben, along with a little help from her sister.

Their cocktails finished while selecting what they were going to eat and chatting with a fun couple from Sydney who were on a walking tour, they were now being shown to their table in the ballroom where a jazz band was playing.

'I could definitely get used to this,' Cassie said when they were seated, and after Martine, their favourite waitress who had looked after them every evening, had poured their wine.

'Me too,' Ben said when they were alone.

Reaching for Ben's hand across the table, Cassie said, 'Thank you for arranging this, it's been the best birthday.'

His fingers entwined through hers, he said, 'I'm glad. I wanted everything to be perfect for you.'

'You've achieved that with bells on. It's been a blissful few days.'

'Well, it's not over yet, I still have another surprise up my sleeve for you.'

'But you've given me so much already.'

He grinned. 'One more surprise won't hurt though, will it?'

'Is it a birthday cake? Have you asked the chef to make me a cake?'

He tutted and rolled his eyes. 'You had to go and spoil it, didn't you?'

'I'm sorry,' she said at the crestfallen expression on his handsome face.

'Just be sure to act like it's a total surprise,' he said.

As the evening progressed, and between courses, their fellow diners took to the dancefloor.

'Shall we risk a shuffle?' asked Ben when they'd finished their main course of sea bass.

'I think we should,' said Cassie, 'as we're never going to have a more romantic moment than this.'

'Exactly what I was thinking.'

On their feet, Cassie slipped a hand through one of Ben's and a little self-consciously, they joined the other couples who were gracefully gliding around like *Strictly* pros.

'I hope we're not disgracing ourselves too much,' she whispered as they navigated their way around the other couples.

'We're doing just fine,' he murmured, 'and you look sensational in that dress. Did I say that earlier?'

'You did. Several times.'

'Well, I'm saying it again. You're easily the most beautiful woman here.'

'And you, my darling, are the sexiest man here. You look even more like James Bond in your dinner jacket. You should wear it more often.'

'I will, but only if you promise to help me out of it later.'

'It's a deal.'

They were both laughing when the music came to an end, and everyone began drifting back to their tables.

Ben surprised her by saying, 'Let's go outside for a minute. It's our last night here and I want to make the most of it.'

She followed him out to the terrace. Her eyes adjusting to the darkness, she held his hand firmly to ensure she didn't topple over in her impractically high-heeled sandals. He led the way up the sloping path that led around the island. It was the clearest of nights and the velvety black sky was peppered with stars. The moon was a sharp thin crescent and not large enough to provide any tangible light.

'Where are we going?' she asked, puzzled that Ben seemed intent on walking some distance away from the hotel, which was brilliantly lit up against the night sky. 'Hey, this isn't some ruse of yours to tip me off the cliff edge and claim the life insurance, is it?'

He didn't say anything but then coming to a stop, he looked about him as if taking in the starlit view. She did the same while listening to the rhythmic swishing of the sea below and the rumble of the sea tractor making its way across the causeway, perhaps performing its last duty of the day. Next to her, and letting go of her hand, Ben suddenly bent down as if to tie a shoelace. She waited for him to straighten up, but he didn't and then from nowhere he'd produced a small box and was holding it towards her.

'Cassie,' he said, lifting the lid of the box and revealing a beautiful diamond ring, 'will you marry me? I know you've said in the past that marriage wasn't important to you, but I find it matters to me. I want to be your husband. I want it more than anything in the world.' In the silence that followed, he said, 'Say something, please.'

She stared at the ring. She stared at him.

'I can't . . . I—'

'Is it a terrible idea to you?'

She shook her head. 'No! It's a wonderful idea, but—'

'But what?'

She dropped down to her knees to be on the same level as him, but not before lifting the front of her dress to save it from being ruined with grass stains. 'But are you sure? Are you really sure about us? About *me?*'

'Oh God yes, I'm absolutely sure!'

'In that case, yes. Yes, I will marry you!'

Smiling, he removed the ring from the box and with shaking hands slipped it onto her finger.

'I'll never forget this moment,' she said, kissing him. 'I love you so much, Ben.'

Then with a mischievous grin, remembering how he'd fooled her earlier, she said, 'Does this mean there's no surprise birthday cake made by the chef?'

Laughing, he helped her to her feet, held her hand and led her back down the pathway. To her amazement, when they re-entered the dining room, she saw that not only was there a bottle of champagne on their table but a beautiful birthday cake, and as if they'd been in on the surprise, the other diners started clapping and the jazz band struck up with a jaunty rendition of 'Happy Birthday' and everyone sang along.

'I can't believe you did all of this for me,' Cassie said to Ben, tears of happiness filling her eyes, 'and in secret. Thank you so much.'

'I told you before, I wanted your birthday to be special for you. Something you'd always remember.'

Chapter Twenty-Four

It was Sunday morning and marriage was very much on Venetia's mind, as it had been during the night when a kaleidoscope of memories flitted through her dreams. It was the fault of that chat with Nina over lunch yesterday that had raised the spectre of the three men to whom she'd been married, and with varying degrees of happiness.

Looking back on her life, no one was more surprised than Venetia that she'd been married so many times. It certainly wasn't how she'd imagined her life. But then who really did have the life they expected or hoped for? Not Nina, that much was obvious. Cassie too could not have pictured the way her life was turning out. Temporarily sharing her home with her ex-husband's widow and child could not have ever featured in her wildest imaginings.

With the radio on and listening to Classic FM, Venetia was doing her ironing. It was one of those tasks she enjoyed, pressing out all the wrinkles and creases of her clothes and bed linen, resulting in a satisfyingly satin-smooth finish. Every now and then she would look up from the ironing board and watch Cassie's daughter, Emily, playing on the lawn with her half-brother – they seemed to be having a game of chase that involved a lot of running around in circles. She could recall doing the very same thing as a child. Observing Emily and the boy, it struck Venetia that they looked like they didn't have a care in the world, which given the circumstances couldn't be true. Just as yesterday, there was no sign of the boy's mother.

Cassie and Ben were due back tomorrow evening and Venetia very much hoped that they'd had a wonderful few days away. Cassie had sent Venetia a couple of photos of the hotel, and it looked like the perfect getaway destination. Lawrence, her last husband, had often suggested they should book a couple of nights at the famous Art Deco hotel, but they'd never made it. They'd run out of time.

Returning her attention to the job in hand, she delved into the laundry basket and selected a bedsheet to iron next. It was Egyptian cotton and supposedly easy-care which was anathema to Venetia. She didn't care what anyone said, there was no such thing as iron-free or crease-free when it came to cotton. After spraying the sheet with laundry starch and getting to work, her thoughts returned to what she'd been thinking about before: her marriages. Not by anyone's standards could she be considered to have been lucky on that score.

Her first had been a colossal error of judgement on her part. She'd married a divorced man with two young children whom he never saw, claiming their mother had poisoned their minds against him. Harold ran an upmarket antique shop on Fulham Road in London – a purveyor of fine antiques was how he'd described himself when she'd met him. She'd been thoroughly taken in by his apparent *savoir faire*. That and his Jaguar, the fashionable clubs he took her to and the clothes he lavished on her, including a mink coat. He promised her the world and she believed him. But he'd turned out to be a con man and would have sold his own grandmother if he'd thought he could get away with it. Older than her by almost seventeen years, he called her his queen, and while he loved to show her off whenever they went out, woe betide if she so much as spoke to another man.

She had, it's worth saying, developed in her late teens from an ugly duckling into something of a swan, or what was deemed a swan back in the sixties when Jean Shrimpton and then Twiggy were all the rage. To her amazement heads turned when she walked into a room, something she never got used to. Her gamine looks attracted the attention of a couple of modelling agencies, but Harold wouldn't hear of it. He didn't really approve of her continuing with her job as a secretary for an import and export business in Piccadilly.

They'd been married for three years when he was arrested for money laundering and selling stolen goods. Everything he'd ever given her had been stolen. Everything he'd ever said to her had been a lie. Edie Buckle had warned Venetia not to rush into marriage, but she was eighteen and thought she knew best. What eighteen-year-old doesn't believe that?

She'd fallen for Harold and the dream life he'd sold her (miss-sold her it turned out!) believing it would give her the security she so badly craved. They would build a home together – a conventional home with a husband and wife and maybe a child. But more importantly, it would be a future that would stop her looking over her shoulder at the past and what had happened at Hope Hall.

Harold died in prison after getting into a fight, his temper, flashes of which she'd personally seen and physically experienced, finally getting the better of him. In no hurry to marry again, especially if the man turned out to be anything like Harold, Venetia focused her energy on doing well in her job. She was still working for the same business in Piccadilly which had expanded to include precious and semi-precious gemstones, and she was now the owner's personal assistant, a role she took great pride in. She would be forever grateful that she'd learnt to type and do shorthand at night school classes.

In 1970 and when she was twenty-five, she met Alan. He was

the boss's son who, after going to university and then drifting around Europe (that's how Mr Bailey referred to his son's inability to knuckle down) had now decided to join the firm. He was charming, articulate and extremely handsome, and all the women who worked in the offices at S. J. Bailey Ltd. couldn't take their eyes off him with his sapphire-blue eyes, soft curls of collar-length blond hair and tight trousers, turtleneck sweater and velvet jacket. He was a sight to behold, a breath of fresh air compared to his father and the other two middle-aged men who wore boring suits and ties.

Younger than her by two years, Alan proposed to her a year later. She said no three times before finally accepting. It was after she'd lost the one person in the world who meant everything to her – Edie Buckle – that she agreed to marry Alan. Edie's death meant the only connection she had with her childhood and the only real home she'd known was gone. Alan had a genuinely caring nature and was so tenderly supportive while she was coping with the loss of dearest Edie, that she cast aside her fear of marrying the wrong man again and agreed to be his wife.

They married on a cold winter's day at Marylebone Town Hall in 1972 and went on honeymoon to Paris. It was Venetia's first time abroad and she loved everything she saw. Alan was the perfect guide, taking her round the Louvre and sharing with her his favourite paintings. They stayed in a modest *pensione* in Montmartre, and she was shocked at some of the sights she saw in nearby Pigalle, but Alan took it all in his stride.

They didn't consummate their marriage during the honeymoon, Alan claiming he wanted to wait until they were back in London and settled in as newlyweds in the lovely mews property his parents, Wendy and Stephen, had bought for them as a wedding gift. Venetia had been puzzled at his reticence to make love to her in what was known as the city of love. She felt slighted, worried that perhaps Alan didn't find her sexually attractive. They'd been at home for some weeks, and still their marriage hadn't been consummated, when Alan admitted that he had trouble in that department but promised to see a doctor.

But months later and with her suspicions growing, and having nothing more intimate from him than a few kisses, hugs and hand holding, she asked him to be completely honest with her. He broke down when he confessed to the truth and now it was her turn to comfort him. The strange thing was, she wasn't shocked. More than likely she had already known deep down that he wasn't attracted to women. He said he was desperately sorry, that he never meant to hurt her. She believed him. She also believed him when he said he loved her, but as a friend, or a sister.

She knew that he had used her; a wife gave him respectability and effectively a hiding place, but maybe she had used him too. Marrying him had given her security and a more than comfortable lifestyle.

After she'd laid down the rules of how they would proceed, they remained married and lived together in loving and companionable acceptance – he had his discreet 'friendships' as they referred to his male companions, and she had the occasional equally discreet affair. In all respects it was a marriage of convenience, but it was cemented with a true bond of trust between them. If there was one thing Venetia knew, it was that a secret bound people together like nothing else.

Following his father's death, they became even more of a partnership when the two of them took over the running of S. J. Bailey Ltd., changing the name to Bailey & Co International. The firm went from strength to strength throughout the 1970s.

Alan died of AIDS shortly after their thirteenth wedding anniversary and his illness remained a secret between them and the private nursing staff Venetia employed to look after him. His mother, who'd died eighteen months before, never knew of her son's illness, which Venetia thought was a blessing: the poor woman would have been heartbroken.

Alan's death meant that Venetia was now in charge of the business and working all hours she kept it going until she received an offer she would have been foolish to refuse. She signed the contract, ensuring that all existing employees were kept on, and she walked off into the sunset a wealthy woman, now in her fifties.

Lawrence – Husband No. 3, as he always jokingly referred to himself – came into her life on a cruise around South America. She'd never been on a cruise before and had been anxious when she'd boarded the ship in Ushuaia in Argentina whether it was really going to be her cup of tea, but had decided to do it because so many of her friends had told her she'd love it.

She met Lawrence during dinner on her first night onboard. While chatting with him and the other diners around the table, she learnt that he did this kind of holiday two or three times a year, as did many of the other passengers.

She enjoyed his easy-going company and down-to-earth personality and agreed to have dinner alone with him the following evening, and the evening after that. He told her that he was a retired builder, having started out in life as a jobbing brickie in the East End of London but had gone on to set up his own building company. He'd been happily married to just the one woman until seven years ago and while they hadn't any children of their own, they'd fostered over twenty. He described how their home had been open to any child who'd needed a safe space. His words had touched an unexpected nerve with Venetia, and she'd found herself becoming quite emotional and told him about Hope Hall.

When they were back in England in their respective homes, she in London, and he in Essex, they met up on a regular basis and six months after meeting, not only had they been on another cruise together and shared a suite, Lawrence asked her to move in with him. She hesitated. She liked her house in Richmond. She liked her independence. She'd been single for so long, and had become quite selfish in her ways, doing precisely what she wanted and when. But being with Lawrence was such fun and she found she genuinely enjoyed sharing her life with him. She was now in her late sixties and he a couple of years younger, so why not share the rest of her life with him?

But instead of just living together, they took the plunge and tied the knot. Why hang about at their age, they decided.

Looking back on it, those precious few years spent with Lawrence were some of the most enjoyable she'd experienced. It had been a refreshingly care-free time. Perfect in fact. But then Lawrence died of a heart attack. There'd been no warning signs, nothing to indicate his heart was about to give out. The suddenness of his death was the worst part; if she'd had time to prepare, she would have coped better, or so she believed.

It was after Lawrence's funeral that she had acquired Bon-Bon. The puppy had instantly given her some much-needed comfort and had helped to fill the huge gap in her life; he had given her a purpose and sense of routine.

Lawrence had left her his large, rambling Grade II cottage which he had beautifully renovated. It was far too big for her on her own and then one day, while at the hairdresser and flicking through an out-of-date magazine, and glancing idly at the property pages, she had spotted Hope Hall. Amazingly the place had been converted into apartments and there was one yet to be sold.

Following her instinct, she'd made enquiries about the last remaining apartment for sale only to be told that it had just been sold. Disappointed, but not thwarted, and having now convinced herself that she should definitely move, she kept an eye on the property market. She considered all types of property, both in

London and in Essex, Suffolk and Cambridgeshire, but nothing appealed to her as much as that apartment had, and what it represented to her.

Eventually her patience was rewarded when she saw that an apartment at Hope Hall had come back onto the market. She didn't hesitate to put in an offer. It was only once she had exchanged contracts that she realised pets were not allowed. No matter, she told herself, this was destiny and red tape be damned! What could make more sense than to complete the circle and go back to where her life had started and live amongst the ghosts of the past?

There had been a time when she would have been too frightened to return, fearful that everything might unravel and the shocking secret she'd carried all her life might be revealed. She had sworn that she would never tell a living soul what had happened, and it was a promise she'd kept. Only two other people knew what had happened that night. One of them, Edie Buckle, was long since dead and who knew whether Lucien was still alive?

Chapter Twenty-Five

March 1960

Terry Sands arrived at Hope Hall in the spring of 1960 after Bert, their cheery old groundsman and handyman, retired. Bert had been with them ever since Venetia could remember and he had been very much a part of the place; he was like a grandfather to them really. Every Christmas he would dress up as Father Christmas and give them presents from a large hessian sack. The books, toys and sweets were all paid for by Lady Constance and selected with Edie Buckle's help. The older children, once they'd realised that it was Bert in a padded suit and a white beard, had been sworn to secrecy never to let on to the younger children that it wasn't the real Father Christmas.

Bert's replacement was a much younger man and could not have been more different. He was tall and powerfully built with hands like shovels and a slightly flattened and crooked nose. He had a tattoo on both of his forearms – a dagger on the left and a skull on his right. Rarely was he seen without a cigarette dangling from the side of his mouth, whether he was lolling on a bench in the sun or climbing a ladder to fix something.

In no way, in Venetia's opinion, could he be described as good-looking, yet somehow he attracted the attention of some of the girls. He would whistle at them when they passed by or give them a wink which would have them stupidly giggling.

He didn't impress Venetia in the least. Lucien didn't like him.

'He looks like he's a gangster from the East End of London,' Lucien said one day.

'Or trying to pretend he is,' Venetia had said.

It turned out that Lucien hadn't been that far wrong. Terry had been taken on by Lady Constance in one of her many generous acts of altruism and it soon became known that he had been to borstal for assault and robbery and had recently been released. Working as a handyman at Hope Hall, so Edie Buckle told Venetia, was his chance to prove that he had learnt his lesson and turned his back on a life of crime.

He might well have deceived Lady Constance into believing he could become a transformed character and that he was grateful for the chance to make a new life for himself, but he didn't fool Venetia. Not when she'd heard him boasting that he'd once met the Kray twins and that just as soon as he could, he'd leave and go back to London and get a job more fitting to his talents. Being a handyman, he said, wasn't for him, he was destined for bigger and better things. His grandiose tales of what his life would be like once he'd completed his time here, making it sound like Lady Constance's generosity in taking him on was akin to serving a prison sentence, added to his attraction in the eyes of the girls silly enough to be taken in by him. He was the Bad Boy they had all been warned about, the type to avoid. Clearly for some that was his appeal.

Venetia knew what kind of a person Terry really was, she'd seen him shoot a rabbit in the garden of his cottage in the grounds – Bert's old house – and that he hadn't killed it instantly like Bert used to, not wanting the animal to suffer unnecessarily. Terry had put the wretched animal in a cage and then smoked a cigarette with a twisted smile of pleasure on his face, while he watched the rabbit writhing in pain. Only somebody with the blackest of hearts could have done that.

Terry's time at Hope Hall coincided with Lady Constance

marrying Mr Butler, their history teacher, and the two of them going away on an extended honeymoon around Europe. Their marriage had surprised no one, the wonder was why it had taken them so long to get around to doing it. Mind you, no one wanted to think what they might do on their honeymoon. Lucien had reckoned they were far too old for sex – a subject they had learnt about by sneaking a look at one of Edie Buckle's medical books.

'They'll spend all their time looking at churches, art galleries and museums,' he'd claimed.

Venetia wasn't so sure. She'd seen Mr Butler kissing Lady Constance when they didn't think anyone was around. And it hadn't been a polite peck on the cheek.

'You make them sound ancient,' she'd said to Lucien, forever protective of Lady Constance, their benefactor. Despite his being at Hope Hall for three years now, Lucien still harboured an element of resentment at where he was, as if Lady Constance was personally responsible for his presence there.

'They *are* ancient,' he'd asserted. 'Work it out for yourself. Mr Butler was in the Battle of Britain, so that must make him in his forties.'

'But that's still not what you'd call ancient.'

'If you say so,' Lucien had said, nudging at his spectacles on his nose. It was one of his many gestures which she knew and loved. In fact, she knew his face as well as her own, maybe even better because she seldom spent any time looking in the mirror at herself if she could help it. Sometimes she even found herself copying his gestures, like the way he frowned or shrugged or tilted his head when he was concentrating on something. Mimicking him made her feel closer to Lucien, a part of him.

'Have you ever thought that we're two sides of a coin,' she said now as they lay in the darkness on a soft cushiony bed of leaves in the woods while listening to the owls hooting out to one another. Lucien's right hand was wrapped around her left and as he squeezed her hand gently, she turned her head to look at him and found herself staring into his eyes just inches from her own.

'I'd never thought of it quite like that,' he said. 'But I know what you mean. It means we can never be separated.' He squeezed her hand again, then kissed her. They kissed for the longest time and Venetia could feel the familiar flare of his desire for her. It matched her own for him, but they knew the rules – thanks to that medical book – they would never go further than just kissing and touching. Going all the way, they both agreed, and as much as they loved each other, was to be avoided at all costs. They had discussed it many times and neither wanted to take the risk of her getting pregnant. The thought of her having to confess such a shocking thing to Edie Buckle or Lady Constance was just too awful to contemplate. Besides, she and Lucien had plans.

Next year they would both be sixteen and with Lady Constance's encouragement and support, they were going to be allowed to stay on at Hope Hall and be privately tutored so that they might be the first ever children from here to go to university.

'It will be a marvellous feather in our cap,' Lady Constance had said, 'and would show all those doubters that my unique approach to nurturing abandoned children is the right course, that a poor start in life is absolutely no obstacle.'

Lucien wanted to study medicine and be a doctor and Venetia had her sights set on studying history. Mr Butler said she had a real grasp of the subject and that she could appreciate the importance of understanding the past to understand the future. Never did Venetia imagine just how prophetic those words of Mr Butler's would be.

They had been so lost in the exquisite pleasure of kissing they had been deaf to the sound of approaching footsteps. Either that or he had been deliberately furtive in his approach, because the first they knew of Terry's presence was when he was standing in the clearing just a couple of yards from where they lay.

'Now, ain't this just lovely,' he said in an ugly, mocking voice, 'a pair of kids at it like rabbits in the woods. And you know what happens to rabbits, don't you, they get shot, skinned and thrown into a pot and cooked for supper.'

That was when Venetia and Lucien, having scrambled to their feet and straightened their clothes, realised that Terry had been holding a shotgun at his side and was now raising it straight at them.

'You shouldn't point guns at people, only an idiot does that,' Lucien said in his most authoritative tone, the one he used when he was helping in the library and insisting the younger children behave and keep quiet. Venetia didn't think it would have the same effect on Terry.

She was right. Terry laughed nastily at Lucien. 'Listen to you with your fancy I'm-better-than-you-voice! You think you're so 'igh and mighty, but you ain't. You're nothing. You're not even the dirt on my boots. Now get down on your knees and say sorry for speaking to me the way you did.'

'Why should I?' said Lucien defiantly.

Terry raised the gun so it was aimed directly at his head. 'Well, Lucy-Boy, I'll give you one good reason.'

'And what then after you've killed me? What comes next? Because as far as I can see, you'll just get yourself into a load of trouble and you'll be sent to prison. Or better still, you'll be hanged. So go ahead, shoot me and do society a favour by being rid of you.'

Venetia wanted so much to be proud of Lucien for his bravery, but she feared it was misplaced. Terry didn't look or sound like someone who gave a damn about consequences. He looked and sounded like he was mad enough to do anything.

'You're a cocky little sod, aren't you?' Terry responded with a snort. 'But how about I blow your girlfriend's head off instead?' He swung the gun so it was pointing at Venetia now. 'Still wanna call my bluff? And I'll tell you for nothing, Lucy-Boy, pulling the trigger on this shotgun will be the easiest thing in the world for me. I ain't afraid to kill you both and then I'll bury your bodies so no one will ever find them.'

'You're crazy!' Venetia shouted, her frightened voice ringing out loud and shrill in the night air. Then grabbing Lucien's hand, she yelled at him to run. And they did run. They ran as fast as they could, weaving their way around trees, jumping over tree stumps but all the while they could hear Terry bearing down on them.

'You can't get away from me,' he said in a terrifyingly menacing voice. He seemed to know the woods as well as they did and then, just as they had almost reached the outer perimeter of trees, Venetia tripped and cried out as an agonising bolt of pain shot through her ankle.

Lucien stopped running and bent down to help her up. 'Come on, we haven't got far to go,' he said with an urgent wheezy gasp. She recognised the rasp in his voice as the onset of an asthma attack. It was something he'd started suffering from in the last year.

'It's no good,' she said, 'I can't—' She broke off as from behind them Terry pounced out of the darkness.

'Gotcha!' he said, grabbing hold of Venetia's ponytail and yanking it so viciously he lifted her off the ground. Lucien hurled himself at the man, but Terry was stronger than the two of them put together and he shoved the butt of the gun at Lucien's chest, sending him flying, and then dropped her like she was a puppet whose strings had just been cut. Falling onto the ankle she had just twisted, and recalling the rabbit in the cage and how Terry had enjoyed watching it slowly die, she stifled a cry, not wanting to give him the satisfaction of knowing he'd hurt her.

As though proving he really was as dangerously cruel as Venetia believed him to be, Terry threw back his head and started to laugh, saying he was going to enjoy making their lives a living hell for the rest of the time he worked at Hope Hall.

'You'll be looking over your shoulders the whole time just waiting for me to do something to one of you,' he crowed, 'or maybe both of you, depending how I feel.'

Venetia thought that for as long as she lived, she would never forget that sickening laugh, and his vile threat.

Chapter Twenty-Six

'You must believe me when I say I'm sorry for what I did,' Hilary said. 'I behaved atrociously, and I know that Hugh would have been thoroughly ashamed of me. I'm ashamed of myself. If there's any way in which I can make it up to you, please tell me.' She paused, swallowed, then carried on. 'As misplaced as the hope might be, I want to believe that when you accepted my invitation to come here this evening it was because there was a chance we could put that awful night behind us.'

Throughout the speech, for that was what it felt like to Nina, a very formal and well-rehearsed speech, Hilary wrung her hands and twisted the rings round on the third finger of her left hand, never once actually meeting Nina's eyes. In place of her customary cool demeanour there was a brittle awkwardness to her manner. She held herself ramrod-straight in her kitchen chair and while her ash-blonde hair bore its usual appearance of being freshly washed and stylishly swept back from her forehead, it revealed a face which, despite the make-up applied more heavily than usual, was drawn and pinched. She had tried to mask the dark shadows beneath her eyes with too much concealer and it had only served to make things worse by caking and enhancing the lines and pouches of lose skin. She had lost weight since the fateful wedding day six weeks ago and dramatically so, thought Nina, if the looseness of her rings with which she was constantly fiddling was anything to go by. Nina was sure they never used to fit so loosely.

Hilary was clearly suffering and if it had been anyone else, Nina would have felt sorry for the poor woman and comforted her. What held her back from doing that, from reaching across the table and giving a reassuring squeeze to one of Hilary's hands, was the fear that the gesture might trigger a total collapse in her mother-in-law's physical and mental state. It seemed to Nina that she was dangerously close to the edge of some sort of breakdown.

In the days immediately after the wedding debacle Nina would have been more than happy to witness her mother-in-law's downfall, to see her grovel and beg forgiveness, but seeing her now struggling so hard to retain just the flimsiest veneer of self-control brought Nina no satisfaction. She could see that Hilary was broken. She had lost her son and probably her husband, and all semblance of dignity. She had nothing left.

Nina had agreed to come here this Monday evening, not for supper as she had in the past, but for the purpose of the two of them saying what needed to be said. Whatever that might be.

Until last night Nina had resolutely ignored any of Hilary's attempts to contact her; it was an act of petty revenge on her part which she wasn't proud of. But we all protect ourselves in any way we can, she thought now as she sipped from the glass of fizzy water Hilary had poured for her.

'I think we've both said and done things which we're ashamed of,' she said, placing the glass on the table. 'And I shouldn't have ignored your messages or phone calls. That was contrary and unhelpful of me. I'm sorry.'

Hilary pursed her lips and finally looked at Nina. 'You were perfectly entitled to be as contrary as you wanted. But I must confess to being curious as to why you did answer my call last night.'

'I was tired of it all. It takes too much mental energy to be angry, or hold a grudge,' she added, thinking of Cassie. Cassie had always made light of admitting that nobody could hold a grudge like she could, that she had spent nearly two decades harbouring a fierce hatred for the man who had abandoned her when she'd needed him most. 'And look where it's got me,' she'd said the day before Ben had whisked her away for her birthday surprise down in Devon, 'I'm now looking after his bloody widow and child! That's what I get for holding a grudge! If I hated Drew before, imagine how I feel now. Honestly, even in death he can screw up my life!'

Poor Cassie, she had sounded so irrational and so consumed with bitterness and it had made Nina realise that she didn't want to hate Hugh's mother. It was such a waste of emotional energy.

Not that she was setting herself up to be better than Cassie, she wasn't. Cassie was full of warmth and fun and was so very big-hearted and engaging, and Nina envied her friend's emotional openness.

In comparison, Nina was far too controlled. Ironically, much like her mother-in-law. Maybe that's why they had never truly warmed to each other, they saw themselves in the other and didn't much care for it. And wasn't it true that sons are often attracted to women who resemble their mothers? Nina shuddered at the possibility.

'Are you cold?' asked Hilary.

'No, no,' said Nina, 'I'm fine. It was just one of those involuntary spasms,' she lied.

'We always said it was someone walking over your grave when that happened,' Hilary said absently, 'I don't suppose your generation believes in such nonsense.'

'My mother used to say it when I was a child,' Nina replied, 'along with, *you should never put new shoes on a table* as for some reason that would bring instant bad luck.'

'I said some unforgivable things to you that night of the wedding,' said Hilary, picking up her glass of gin and tonic, the ice cubes rattling noisily. Shocked, Nina realised Hilary's hand was shaking and that was why the ice cubes were rattling.

Perhaps realising it too, Hilary quickly put the glass down. 'There hasn't been a day since when I haven't wished I could unsay what I said,' she continued. 'As for hitting you the way I did—' She broke off as though the memory was still too painful for her to recall. 'I have no defence. Keith said it would have served me right if you'd made a formal complaint to the police and I'd been arrested for assault.'

'I didn't think it would have helped either of us if I'd done that,' said Nina.

'How is your head?'

'It's healed well enough.'

'Which is unquestionably more than our relationship ever will,' Hilary murmured with a slight tightening of her lips as if to stop the unthinkable from happening: a display of emotion.

Nina couldn't think of a suitable response to this, so she deflected. 'What about you and Keith? Are you trying to put things right with him?'

If Hilary was surprised by the question, she didn't show it. 'I don't think there's much chance of doing that,' she answered.

'But have you tried?'

Her chin raised, Hilary said, and with a flicker of defiance, 'If he doesn't love me, then that's an end to it, isn't it? He's made his choice, and whether I like it or not, I must accept it.'

Nina could see how it was costing Hilary dearly to put such a brave front on. Her body was so taut with constrained emotion she was like a house of cards, one nudge and it would come tumbling down.

'But you kept on trying with me, didn't you?' Nina said. 'And here I am.'

'That was different.'

Nina opened her mouth to query the statement, but then snapped her mouth shut as an awful thought occurred to her. Was Hilary forcing herself to apologise because she was still clinging desperately to the hope that she might yet become a grandmother if she convinced Nina that she was genuinely sorry for what she'd done? But surely that was too Machiavellian even for Hilary?

'Why is it different, Hilary?' she asked, her voice firm.

'It just is. I did it for Hugh's sake.'

Because you want his grandchild? was on the tip of Nina's tongue, but checking herself, she said, 'Surely for Hugh's sake you need to sort things out with Keith. He's hurting just as much as you are.'

Hilary shook her head. 'I doubt it.'

Nina had to admit that currently Keith didn't give the impression of a man in any real degree of hurt. Seeing as much of him as she did, both at home and at the gallery where he was helping her, he seemed to be enjoying life just a little too much. She put it down to him experiencing the initial heady glow of imagining a new life for himself, free of the burden of carrying his wife's overbearing grief as well as his own.

Nina knew the feeling all too well, because for a few crazy moments at the wedding when she'd been dancing with Jakob, she had felt the same thing, a wildly liberating sensation of being truly alive and without a care in the world. When they'd kissed, her every sense had been awakened sending an intense pulse of desire racing through her, and she'd wanted to go on kissing Jakob, to lose herself in the moment forever, for it never to end. But it had ended, and just as whatever it was Keith imagined he felt towards Diane, that would probably end too. The woman was not the answer to his problems, she was merely a pleasant distraction.

When Jakob had handed in his formal resignation to Nina, explaining that if she was happy, he would remain at the gallery to help her through the exhibition and then leave, she had experienced a wave of guilty relief. It had been combined with gratitude that he appreciated that the situation simply wasn't tenable now; a line had been crossed that inevitably made them both uncomfortable around the other. There was a very good reason why office relationships were frowned upon.

On a purely business level, which was all she allowed herself to contemplate, she missed Jakob's efficiency in the gallery and his enthusiasm to learn about the world of fine art. Finding a replacement as good as he'd been would be hard. As a temporary measure, having Keith lending a hand worked well enough, but a more permanent arrangement had to be put in place. She hadn't rushed to find anyone else because she suspected Keith needed to keep busy, to stop himself from thinking what he was going to do next.

'I know Keith is staying with you,' Hilary said, breaking into Nina's thoughts, 'he told me you'd invited him to use your guest room. Before he left me,' she went on, 'he explained all about the woman he'd met. He seemed to think it would help me to understand things better, my knowing how they met.' Her voice took on a hard sarcastic edge. 'A classic case of my-wife-doesn't-understand-me. Could he be any more of a cliché?'

'I doubt it will last between them,' said Nina. 'It's grief Keith is running away from, not you.'

Hilary frowned. 'Has he told you that?'

'No. He doesn't need to. It's obvious what's going on, he's found someone with whom he can talk about Hugh. You wouldn't ever let him do that, would you?'

The Hilary of before wouldn't have let Nina get away with such an impudent question, but then if it had been the old Hilary sitting opposite her, Nina wouldn't have dared launch such a direct hit.

'I couldn't,' murmured Hilary, 'it was too painful. Whenever he broached the subject, I had the feeling all he wanted to do was put Hugh's death behind him and move on. He made it sound so mundane that we had lost our son, as though I just had to pull myself together and we'd get over losing Hugh.'

'I don't believe for one minute that's what Keith thought. He wanted to share his grief with you, not trivialise it.'

'You're saying I drove him away, straight into the arms of another woman who would let him share his grief? Is that it?'

'Not entirely. But grief can be so divisive, and it hits people in different ways; it can drive a wedge through the most stable of relationships. You might not believe it, but I think you and I are quite similar in how we've tried to deal with Hugh's death, we both shut down a part of ourselves in the hope it would protect us from the worst of the pain. I buried myself in working at the gallery and you buried—'

'Myself in what exactly?' Hilary cut in abruptly, as if ready to be offended.

'You buried yourself in every memory you had of your son and . . . ' Nina hesitated, but forced herself to go on because if she couldn't say it now, she never would. 'You buried yourself in dreaming of having a grandchild, maybe a little boy who would be just like his father and then you'd have something worth living for and some of the heartbreak might be eased.'

In the crashing silence that followed, and from the terrible look of anguish on Hilary's face, Nina feared she had gone too far. But to retract or apologise would negate the truth and for too long Hilary had been allowed to avoid the truth. She had to accept that no amount of denial or angry grief would ever bring Hugh back. Nor would a grandchild.

'Is it really so wrong of me to want something of my son?' asked Hilary. 'Isn't the desire for a grandchild the most natural thing in the world, a necessary part of the circle of life?'

'Not wrong at all, of course it isn't.'

'Then why won't you give me a grandchild?' Hilary cried out pitifully with a tearful choke in her voice.

'You know it's not as simple as that,' Nina said gently. 'Hugh and I put ourselves through the soul-destroying misery of IVF four times, and now you want me to do it again but on my own.'

'You wouldn't be on your own,' Hilary said, 'I'd be there for you. You'd have your parents too, and your friends.'

'I'm sorry, Hilary, but it's too late.'

'You're not too old, if that's what you mean. Plenty of women older than you have had babies this way.'

'It's not my age,' said Nina, 'although admittedly it's a small part of the decision I've at last reached.' She took a breath and willed herself on. 'I wanted you to be the first to know this, because I appreciate how much it matters to you, but I've decided that I'm not going to use any of the embryos which the clinic has been storing. The dream of having a child was always Hugh's more than mine. Because I loved him so much, I was happy to have a family with him, but without him, it wouldn't be the same.'

Hilary stared back at her, her eyes dark with sadness. 'You're not doing this to spite me, are you, to pay me back for what happened at the wedding?'

'Of course I'm not. You should know me better than that.'

'Is there nothing I can say to persuade you to change your mind?'

'It's taken a long time for me to reach the decision I have and it's not one I've made lightly.'

'Is it because you want to be with that man from the gallery?'

'Jakob, you mean?'

'Yes. Are you in love with him? Is it his child you want rather than Hugh's?'

Nina shook her head vehemently. 'There's nothing between us. He isn't around anymore. He's gone.'

'You looked very *close* at the wedding when you were dancing together,' said Hilary. There was an archness to the way she'd phrased the remark.

'I'd had too much to drink,' Nina said lightly, 'and lost myself in the moment.'

Hilary looked at her with shrewd penetrating eyes. 'That doesn't sound like you at all,' she said.

'You and I both behaved out of character that day.'

'Quite.'

They sat in silence for a few awkward seconds until Hilary said, 'Are you sure you wouldn't like a proper drink, or maybe have a bite to eat? I'd be happy to cook something.'

'I'm fine with water and I had lunch with a client today so I'm not that hungry now.' She glanced at her watch. 'And really I should go.'

Hilary looked disappointed. 'Must you?'

'You know how it is,' Nina said, finishing her drink and getting to her feet, 'there's always a ton of emails to deal with.'

'Of course, I know how busy you are. Hugh was always so proud of you, how you took on the gallery and threw yourself into it with such dedication.'

They were in the hall now and Nina was rummaging in her bag for her keys when Hilary said, 'What will happen to the embryos you and Hugh stored at the clinic?'

Thrown by the question, Nina said, 'That's another decision I have to make.'

'If I understand things correctly,' Hilary said, 'you have two choices, donate the embryos to another couple or have them destroyed.'

'Or they can be used for research,' said Nina.

Hilary looked appalled. 'You mean part of Hugh could be tinkered with, like . . . like some hideous Frankenstein experiment?'

Nina wasn't surprised at Hilary's reaction; she had expected it. 'I think that's a little extreme, don't you? And what would you have, your grandchild being brought up by an anonymous couple?'

'It's not what Hugh would have wanted.'

'None of this is what Hugh wanted,' Nina said grimly, 'but I'm left with the mess to sort out and I have to do it my way because I'm the one who has to live with it.'

And with that, she said a curt goodbye and drove home.

Chapter Twenty-Seven

On returning to Hope Hall, it didn't take long for Cassie's soaring spirits to be brought back down to earth with a monumental crash.

During the journey home from Dorset where they'd stayed the night at a charming hotel to break the long drive from Burgh Island, Cassie had promised herself that nothing would spoil her mood when they arrived home. No matter the mess or general awkwardness of having a woman whom Cassie was predisposed to dislike on principle living with them, she would retain the loved-up happiness she was running high on. But within minutes – *no, make that seconds!* – of letting themselves in, her mood took an immediate nosedive.

They'd found Emily stretched out on one of the sofas, mobile in hand, thumb scrolling. She'd looked up tiredly when Cassie greeted her with all the excited brightness of somebody bursting with news to share, namely the reason for the ring on her finger. But at the lacklustre welcome, Cassie had felt peevishly cheated of her happy *ta-daa* moment and had determined not to say anything unless the ring was actually noticed.

There was no sign of Rosalyn or Finlay, but the polished streamlined perfection of the open-plan sitting and dining area had been decimated. Painting and colouring things were spread over the large glass-topped table, lumps of brightly coloured Play-

Doh appeared to have been flung far and wide as though fired with the aid of a scatter gun. The rugs and wooden flooring had been turned into a minefield of toy cars, pieces of jigsaw puzzles and bits of Lego. Over in the kitchen area, the worktops were covered with pots and pans, opened packets of pasta, biscuits and unwrapped cheese. The sink was crammed full of dirty dishes.

The sight of the chaotic mess incensed Cassie but Ben smoothly took charge and suggested she go and unpack while he and Emily tidied up.

'Don't make any noise, Mum,' Emily said, making a half-hearted attempt to haul herself off the sofa, 'Finlay and Rosalyn are both in bed asleep.'

'But it's only eight o'clock,' said Cassie, 'why is Rosalyn in bed? Is she unwell?'

'Way to go, Mum!' Emily said with a roll of her eyes. 'Of course she's unwell, the man she loved has died and she's worried sick about the future. I'd have thought it was obvious, even to you, that she would be exhausted and would need to take care of her mental health by sleeping as much as she can. Doing anything is just too much of a strain for her right now.'

'Right,' said Cassie, thinking how lucky Rosalyn was to have the luxury of being able to sleep all her worries away. When Cassie had been on her own all those years ago with Emily to care for and a job to hold down to pay the bills, she hadn't taken to her bed like some pathetically incapable Victorian heroine.

'What's that supposed to mean?' demanded Emily.

'What?' said Cassie.

'Right' Emily mimicked. 'It was judgey and loaded with sarcasm and micro aggression.'

'Rubbish!' responded Cassie, furious at the accusation. 'And if I was implying anything, it would be that maybe mollycoddling might not be the answer. In the long run it won't help Rosalyn get herself back on her feet.'

Emily rounded on her. 'Not everyone is as tough or as heartless as you.'

Over by the table where Ben was tidying up the painting things, he cleared his throat. 'Your mother is not heartless, Emily. If she was, do you think she would have invited Rosalyn and her son to stay here with us?'

'Dad said she was,' Emily muttered. 'He said that was why he was never allowed to see me when I was little. He told me that.' She pointed a finger at Cassie. 'You stopped me from knowing him properly and now that he's dead I never will!'

At the downright unfairness of her daughter's words, Cassie wanted to let rip with a torrent of angry denial, but she knew that to unleash even an atom of it would make things worse. 'That's absolutely not what happened,' she said calmly, 'and I'm sorry that Drew lied to you.'

'He didn't lie!' roared Emily. 'You're the liar!'

Enough was enough, and deploying a salvo of sarcasm, Cassie said, 'I thought we weren't allowed to make any noise for fear of disturbing our guests?'

Emily glared at her and from behind them, Ben said, 'I don't think you're being fair to your mother, Emily, and I'd sooner you didn't raise your voice to her like that.'

Turning her glare on him now, Emily said, 'Why, what will you do, send me to my room for being naughty?'

Never had Emily spoken to Ben like that and Cassie wasn't going to stand for it. 'Ems, I can see that you're tired and upset, and that's hardly surprising if you've been running around looking after Finlay on your own while we were away, but apologise to Ben this instant.'

'*No!* And don't you dare accuse me of being tired and emotional, that's beyond insulting!'

But then as if to prove Cassie right, her face crumpled, and she burst into tears.

Seeing her daughter so distressed tore at Cassie's heart and her anger instantly evaporated. She went to her, but when Emily tried to push her away, Cassie held her close, just as she had countless times in the past when her precious baby girl had needed her. Emily was still so young and in so much pain and it appalled Cassie that she hadn't realised that sooner. 'It's okay, Ems,' she quietly soothed, feeling Emily's rigidly stiff body gradually relax against hers as she rubbed her back in small circular movements, 'it's all right, you let it all out, cry as much as you want.'

'We should have seen that coming,' Ben said much later when they were in bed, their bedroom door shut, the lights switched off, and their voices lowered.

'I feel like such a bad mother the way I went on the attack when she was rude to you,' said Cassie. 'How could I have not understood the state she was in with so much to cope with?'

'No point in beating yourself up over that, the important thing is we're here for her now.'

Yes, thought Cassie, recalling how Emily had allowed her to put her to bed and sit with her while stroking her hair until she fell asleep. That had always been Cassie's go-to way to calm Emily when she'd been anxious or overtired and unable to sleep as a little girl.

'She's taken on so much with trying to support Rosalyn and look after Finlay,' said Ben, breaking into Cassie's thoughts. 'And on top of that she's also trying to deal with her own complicated emotions about Drew.'

Cassie sighed. 'That's very true. And I didn't react the right way, did I, when she said Rosalyn was in bed? All I could think of was how pathetic Rosalyn was being and how she was using my daughter as her personal slave, and I know it's wrong, but I can't stop being angry with Drew for putting Emily through this nightmare.'

'That's not surprising,' said Ben. 'Like Emily, you need someone to blame for the situation we're now in. That's what Emily was doing when she had a go at us, she just needed to release the build-up of emotions she's carrying around inside her.'

For some minutes they lay on their backs in silence. Was she, Cassie wondered, as heartless as Emily had earlier accused her of being?

Maybe she was, because that would explain why she was so irritated by Rosalyn's inability to be the mother her little boy needed instead of handing over his care to Emily. Why wasn't Rosalyn doing something about planning her future and getting Finlay into school somewhere, instead of lolling around in bed and literally pulling up the covers over her head and hoping somebody else would solve all her problems?

I must be heartless, Cassie concluded, *to regard Rosalyn so critically*. Why couldn't she be a better person and feel genuine compassion for Rosalyn, especially, and as ironic as it was, since they had something in common – they had both been abandoned by the same man and left to pick up the pieces.

'Fancy a quickie?'

At the unexpectedness of Ben's question, Cassie laughed.

'You know, just to take your mind off things?' he said.

'In need of rekindling our Burgh Island exploits?' she asked, snuggling up to him.

Turning to face her, he placed a hand gently to her cheek. 'I wasn't being serious, I just wanted to say something to distract you. I could hear the gears grinding away inside your head.'

'I'm sorry.'

'Don't be. It's completely understandable in the circumstances, but I bet you anything you like, everything will feel better in the morning.'

'I wouldn't count on it.'

'Why do you say that?'

'Tonight, when Emily was so upset and I helped put her to

bed, that was the closest we've been ever since she connected with Drew. I'm worried that it'll be a one-off moment, and we'll never really get back to how we were.'

'How about you stop worrying about something that hasn't happened, and probably never will happen?'

'But—'

He hushed her with a kiss.

'I love you so much, Ben,' she said, her lips moving against his.

'I know you do.'

She gave him a playful nudge. 'Oh, Mr So-Sure-Of-Himself knows it, does he?'

'Yeah, that's why you agreed to marry me. Because you *lurve* me so much.'

Smiling, she said, 'I still can't believe you did that, got down on one knee.'

'Hey, I can't believe it either.'

'I'll never forget that night, or our time away. It was magical. It's just such a shame what we came home to. I'm sorry that you're caught up in it all when it's not even your problem.'

'It's not really yours either, but that's how partnerships work, we shoulder the problems together. Your trouble is that you expect to solve everything yourself, because you had to when Drew left you, but you're not on your own. You have me.'

Her heart quickened at the loving sincerity in his voice. 'I wish I'd met you before Drew ever came onto my radar.'

'But then you wouldn't have Emily, and you wouldn't be without her for anything, would you? She's been your world since the day she was born.'

Which was so very true and was the reason her daughter's apparent defection to Drew had been so painful to Cassie. What was worse, his death had effectively now turned Drew into a martyr in Emily's eyes.

Okay, that was an exaggeration but there was a degree of truth to it, because Emily wanted to believe in the myth that Drew would have been a perfect father if only he had been given the chance to be in her life. If only he hadn't been so cruelly excluded by Nasty Wicked Cassie.

Sensing that Ben had fallen asleep, that his breathing was slower now and his arm lay heavily across her chest, she very carefully, not wanting to disturb him, rolled onto her side, and waited for sleep to come to her.

Inevitably, given the tsunami of disagreeable thoughts threatening to overwhelm her, sleep eluded her, so she thought back to two nights ago when Ben had surprised her with his wonderfully romantic proposal.

She felt for the ring on her finger. She loved the feel of it; it already felt a part of her, as though it had always been there, and always would be. She had so badly wanted to show off the ring to Emily and tell her that she and Ben were finally going to marry. Not so long ago and Emily would have been delighted to hear it, and the two of them would have hugged and squealed and probably danced around the apartment like a couple of hysterical idiots.

But now Cassie didn't know how Emily would take the news. Would she think it was inappropriate to talk about marriage when Rosalyn was grieving for her dead husband?

'Read the room, Mum,' she imagined Emily saying in her most censorious voice, 'do you think that banging on about wedding dresses and wedding venues is in any way suitable right now?'

Not that Cassie planned to bang on about anything that related to her marrying Ben, but what was she supposed to do, put her life on hold until Rosalyn and Finlay had moved out?

Well, she wouldn't! If Rosalyn felt uncomfortable here, then there was a simple solution: she could find her own place to live.

Nothing, absolutely nothing, was going to spoil Cassie's happiness at marrying Ben.

It was funny that marriage had never really felt like a big deal to either of them before, but now it felt hugely important to Cassie. She wanted the security of it, because with everything else going on, she needed the certainty she believed – and hoped – marriage would bring.

Chapter Twenty-Eight

Hilary was bored to tears and wishing she was at home. In fact, she wished she was anywhere but here. She'd only agreed to come because she'd been afraid what the group would say about her behind her back if she didn't join them.

Lunch with 'the Girls' – Susanne, Lynne, Julie and Gabriella – was a tradition that had begun over four decades ago. Back then, they'd been young twenty-somethings who'd met at NCT classes when they were all expecting their first baby. After a month of classes, the five of them had broken away from the original group to form their own as an antidote to the fearmongering fostered by their teacher, a middle-aged earth-mother type. Every session she'd instructed them on what they could and couldn't eat and drink or what they should and shouldn't do while pregnant, as well as highlighting the myriad dangers of giving birth. The way the woman had gone on, they'd be lucky to survive!

Finding the sessions unhelpful, the five of them had declined to attend any more and instead had met up for lunch to share books and magazines on pregnancy, labour and motherhood, and usually with a glass of wine to go with their meal. It was their only glass of the week, they would claim, but all knowing they were lying. Their get-togethers had been fun, and they'd supported each other every step of the way. When their babies had arrived, they'd continued to meet up, now sharing their anecdotal horror stories of labour, breastfeeding and lack of sleep. As support networks went, it was the best and had seen them through all the many years and major life events.

But where was that support now when Hilary needed it most? They'd been supportive enough in the early weeks of Hugh's death, but as time had passed, they'd drawn back from her, seldom asking how she was. Keith had once commented when she'd remarked on their lack of interest and sympathy that perhaps they'd grown tired of hearing the same answer from her. It had been such a cruelly insensitive thing to say, and it should have warned her that there was worse to come from him. Just how callously he would ultimately behave, she would never have imagined.

The Girls had been shocked when she'd shared with them that Keith had left her, but Gabriella had had the temerity to say, and quite offhandedly, that it was common for a marriage to break down following the death of a child, because in some cases it had only been the child keeping them together in the first place. Hilary had been incensed and hadn't spoken to Gabriella again until she'd apologised, no doubt at the request of the rest of the Girls.

And what a joke that was, she thought, glancing around the table at the lined and wrinkled faces, that they still called themselves girls when they were well into their sixties, two of them nearer seventy than sixty! It was ridiculous. Just as it was ridiculous that she was putting herself through this charade of all-friends-together over lunch at their regular haunt, the Green Man in Grantchester. These women weren't her friends anymore. If they were, they'd be more understanding. They'd show genuine compassion.

But why would they understand what she was going through when their own lives were so blessedly untouched by the profoundest of loss: the loss of a child? The problems they'd experienced didn't come close. Susanne's son had had a gambling problem for a while and Julie's daughter had had a drugs problem five years ago, but all was hunky-dory now and Julie and her husband were thrilled that a grandchild – their first – was now on the way. No, none of those trifling little so-called problems came anywhere close to what Hilary had suffered.

The news that Julie was at last going to be a grandmother meant that Hilary was the odd one out, the only one of the group who would never know that pleasure. Whenever they met, photos of cherubically adorable grandchildren were relentlessly shared on their mobiles and ooh-ed and aah-ed over. Although in Hilary's opinion, Lynne's granddaughter was never going to win any best-baby prizes; she looked like an angry, piggy-eyed, red-faced troll.

It was now the middle of October and two weeks since Nina had shattered Hilary's hope of ever being a grandmother. She had watched Nina drive away that evening, somehow still holding on to the faint hope that her daughter-in-law would reverse up the driveway, rush to the front door and say she'd changed her mind, that she would try one more time to have Hugh's child.

But Nina had gone and after Hilary had closed the front door, she had sunk onto the bottom step of the stairs and wept, her head resting against the wall, her heart breaking for Hugh and all that might have been. For him. And her. She had stayed there until it was dark and then she had gone up the stairs to Hugh's old bedroom and where she kept all her guilty but very precious secrets. Holding one of them to her chest as a comforter, she had lain on the bed and wept some more until she had finally fallen into an exhausted sleep.

Remembering now, and with a painful jolt to her heart, how alone, empty and bereft she'd felt that night, Hilary slipped her hand into her handbag, found her wallet and picked out what she was sure would cover the cost of her share of the lunch, most of which she hadn't been able to eat. She couldn't remember when she'd last experienced hunger, or enjoyed anything she ate.

'I'm sorry,' she said, slapping the money down onto the table and getting clumsily to her feet, 'I'm not feeling well, I need to go.'

And she did. She fled, before anyone could try to stop her or ask if they could help in any way. She was in such a desperate hurry to escape, she almost tripped over a small apricot-coloured poodle with a couple sitting at a nearby table.

She drove out of the car park as fast as she dared, vowing never to put herself through another of these unbearable lunches.

She wasn't one of the Girls anymore.

And that was something else she'd lost.

Chapter Twenty-Nine

Lunch with Ronnie Sharp at the Green Man in Grantchester, followed by a stroll along the river in the beautifully mild October weather had made for a very pleasant outing. Bon-Bon had had a high old time nosing around in the long grass, although he hadn't been so happy inside the pub when that rude woman had tripped over him, and she hadn't even apologised. It was as if she'd barely noticed him.

Ronnie was back from Majorca to sort out what he referred to as a few business odds and sods. He had knocked on Venetia's door earlier in the week and asked if she was free for a drink that evening. Later, and leaving Bon-Bon watching *The Great British Bake Off*, she had taken the stairs up to the top floor and made her way along the carpeted corridor to Ronnie's apartment, her steps triggering ceiling lights to come on overhead. It was hard to believe, but this was the very same route she had followed as a child when going to see Edie Buckle in her cosy office-cum-sitting room next door to the sick room. In those days there hadn't been a plush royal-blue carpet, just a worn stretch of curling linoleum the colour of vomited pea soup, as all the children had described it.

From what she had seen of Ronnie's apartment that evening it was very much a bachelor pad and lacked any real heart, or even a sense of home. There were a few items of statement furniture in the sitting room and some rather unfathomable abstract pictures on the walls which served to add to the sterility and transient feel of the place; it could have been a soulless hotel room. While Ronnie had poured her a glass of wine, he'd confessed to having employed an interior designer to kit out the apartment when he'd bought it. 'I was lazy, and just let the woman get on with it while I was in Majorca,' he'd explained.

As the evening had progressed, she'd felt that he was quite a different Ronnie to the one she'd met the evening of the welcome drinks party when she'd moved in. It was as if when not in front of a crowd, he didn't need to live up to the role of Ronnie-the-Rogue which was how he'd come across before. But in Venetia's experience everyone played a role depending on the situation, no one was immune from playing up to an audience.

It might have been the excellent quality of the Alberiño they were drinking, but by the second glass she had entrusted Ronnie with her secret about Bon-Bon. He'd been tickled pink that she had a stowaway dog in her apartment and had assured her that his lips were sealed.

'I'm more than happy to keep your secret,' he'd said with a laugh. 'Anything to get one over those two bossy women who think they run the show here.'

He'd shared with her that he'd had a personal run-in with the Enforcers last year when he'd let a friend keep a campervan in the parking area by the garage block. Apparently, even though Ronnie had said it was a temporary arrangement, Joanna and Cheryl had described the vehicle as an eyesore, claiming it made the place look like a cheap campsite.

'Which naturally,' Ronnie had told Venetia, 'made me want to install a wreck of a campervan of my own just to really annoy those stuck-up whinge-bags. And you know what,' he'd gone on, 'there's nothing in those management rules about not being allowed to keep caravans or campervans here. Not a word. *Nada!*'

The more they'd chatted, the more Venetia had enjoyed

Ronnie's company, but she'd sensed that it wasn't just business loose ends that he was here to tie up. She'd been proved right over lunch today when he'd mentioned he had an appointment at Addenbrooke's Hospital. She didn't feel she knew him well enough to ask what it was for, other than to say she hoped it wasn't anything serious. He'd avoided answering her by steering the subject onto something else.

Now, back from Grantchester, and after inviting Ronnie in for a cup of coffee, Venetia let them into her apartment. Setting her tote bag down on the floor in the hall, Bon-Bon hopped out, shook himself from his nose to his tail, then trotted through to the kitchen and his water bowl. They followed behind the little dog.

Taking in his surroundings with an appreciative nod, Ronnie said, 'Your apartment feels much more of a home than mine.'

'Thank you, but there's nothing like a ragtag collection of squashy old cushions and faded rugs to make a place feel lived in. Make yourself comfortable, while I put the kettle on. I apologise for not having one of those fancy coffee machines, the best I can do is a cafetière.'

'Hey, no standing on ceremony with me,' he replied, 'instant will do perfectly.'

'In that case I shall take you at your word.'

Having ignored her invitation to sit down, Ronnie prowled around the room, then went over to the window to look out at the grounds in the autumn sunshine. 'You have a better view than I do from my apartment,' he said when a few moments had passed. 'I missed the boat when the apartments with the best views came up for sale.'

'You have a view of the woods though,' she said, 'that's not so bad, and it's not like you live here permanently.'

He shrugged, then pushed his hands into the pockets of his trousers. 'True. But life changes.'

'That sounds rather like you're considering making changes?'

'Sometimes,' he said quietly, almost more to himself than her, 'change is thrust upon us, whether we want it or not.'

The coffee made, Venetia took the two mugs over to the sofa, pondering on what Ronnie had said, or more accurately the reflective way in which he'd said it. It made her wonder if he was worried about something. His hospital appointment perhaps?

When they were both seated, and feeling that she would like to help if she could, she said, 'You could tell me to mind my own business, but if there's anything I—'

'*Whoa!*' he said, holding up a hand to interrupt her. 'Whenever a woman says that, I know jolly well she has no intention of minding her own business. So go on,' he added with a chuckle, 'do your worst.'

Amused at what she'd been accused of and knowing it was true, as it simply wasn't in her nature to let something go, she said, 'Do you currently find yourself in a position of having unwanted change thrust upon you?'

'I might do,' he said evasively, levelling his gaze with hers over the rim of his coffee mug.

'Change is fine when we're in control of it,' she said. 'When we're not, that's a different matter.'

'That's very true,' he agreed, 'especially when life doesn't play fair.'

'Now that sounds like a man who has something very specific on his mind.'

'Ah, perceptive as well as beautiful.'

Recognising a classic conversational swerve, she tutted and wagged a finger at him. 'You can stop that silly nonsense right now. I've been around the block far too often to be fooled by any flimflam flattery.'

He smiled. 'But you are a very attractive woman.'

'I'm also an old woman and you are certainly old enough to know better than to try your tricks on me.'

'But you can't blame a chap for chancing it when he's trying to wriggle out of being cross-examined.'

'There now,' she said, 'finally some honesty from you.'

'Coffee was what you invited me in for, you didn't say anything about gouging great chunks out of my self-esteem.'

'Nothing but a friendly nibble or two to keep you on your toes,' she said lightly, 'nothing untoward.'

'But you won't stop until you have it all out of me, will you?'

'I'll stop if you want me to.'

He sighed. 'Clever. Now if I don't confess to you, it'll look like I'm trying to hide something.'

'We all hide something.'

'You're a regular Miss Marple, aren't you?' he said good-humouredly. 'You won't be satisfied until you've winkled every detail out of me.'

She smiled. 'A gross exaggeration. I just feel you're worried about something and a problem shared is—'

'A problem halved. Yeah, yeah, I know how all the clichés go. If you really want to know, I have problems coming out of my ears.'

'I'm sorry to hear that,' she said.

'Not as sorry as I am. You see, and this must go no further, but for a while now my hotel has been losing money like water running through a sieve and I've only recently discovered the reason for that; my business partner and so-called financial expert has been siphoning money off to clear his gambling debts. He'd done a bang-up job of covering his tracks, and now he's vanished into thin air. I blame myself; I shouldn't have trusted him to the extent that I did. Then to top it all,' Ronnie continued, putting his coffee mug down on the table in front of them, 'the quack I saw in Palma last week reckons the cancer I was treated for some years ago might have resurfaced.' He puffed out his cheeks and sank back into the cushions of the sofa, as though the confession had exhausted him.

'Putting the hotel to one side,' Venetia said, 'your priority must be your health. Presumably your appointment at Addenbrooke's is to see a specialist, an oncologist, when is the appointment?'

'The day after tomorrow.'

'I'd be happy to accompany you. Or I could drop you off at the door if you'd prefer and then return when you're finished.'

His expression, which until then had been one of stoic resilience, softened. 'That's kind of you, but there's really no need.'

'Good,' she said, brooking no argument. 'That's settled then, I'll take you. As for your financial difficulties, have you involved the police? After all, it is fraud what your business partner has been up to.'

He rubbed a hand over his face. 'I haven't gone to the police yet; I don't want any bad publicity for the hotel. Not when things are so precarious.'

'Who's taking care of the hotel while you're here?' Venetia asked.

'The manager.'

'Can you trust that person?'

'Trust,' he repeated with a roll of his eyes, 'is a luxury I can no longer rely on.'

'Do you have a plan?'

'*Hah!*' He exploded with a raucous laugh which had the effect of making Bon-Bon raise his head where he'd been curled up in his basket throughout the conversation. 'You're one tenacious lady, aren't you?'

'You should see me when I'm out of first gear,' Venetia said with a smile.

'I look forward to it,' he said, matching her smile with one of his, 'but in answer to your question, the only plan I have is to pay off those who are owed money, sell the hotel while making a loss, then slink away with my pride and reputation shot to pieces.'

'Slinking away be dammned!' Venetia snapped. 'You've done nothing wrong, so let's not have any cloying self-pity.'

'Not even a little?' he said.

'Absolutely not.'

'I had a feeling you might say that.'

Chapter Thirty

'Sorry I was so long,' said Cassie, shutting the door behind her and putting her umbrella in the umbrella stand, having already shaken it outside. 'But the queue at the post office was a mile long. Only one counter open, of course, because obviously it was lunchtime and the most popular time for anyone in town to want to use its services. And then,' she continued, while shrugging off her wet coat, 'it's as if after all the good weather we've had before now people have forgotten how to walk in a straight line when it's raining. You wouldn't believe the number of times I was pushed into the gutter.'

'You should have waited until the rain eased.'

'What, and not have anything to complain about, where's the fun in that? You know I can't function unless I have something to moan about.'

Nina laughed. 'That's why I hired you.'

'And I love you for it, my darling! It's great fun being your part-time office junior, it's a lot more interesting than being on my own doing my website work.'

'I don't think Jakob ever saw himself as the office junior,' remarked Nina.

'No,' said Cassie with a sly grin, 'I'm sure he didn't.'

Nina tutted. 'Any more comments like that and I'll have to fire you.'

'And I'll report you to HR for unfair dismissal.'

'Good luck with that!'

Their exchange reminded Nina of a similar exchange with Jakob; it had been the day he'd suggested they go for a drink together after work. How long ago that hot July summer's evening at the Anchor now seemed. And how misguided. For if she hadn't said yes to him, she would never have agreed to his subsequent suggestion that he be her plus-one for the wedding and everything that followed. One simple error of judgement on her part and look what it had set in motion – Hilary had experienced a total meltdown, Keith had left her, and Jakob had handed in his notice.

The last she'd heard from Jakob was that he was in Oslo and he was sorry to let her down by leaving the way he did, but he was sure she would agree with him that it was for the best, all things considered. He'd added a postscript to his email along the lines that his parents were keen for him to join the family firm, just as they'd always expected him to. *'Perhaps it is time for me to be the dutiful son'*, he'd written.

Nina had emailed back saying that she wished him well in whatever he decided to do. She said nothing about missing him in the gallery, or that some of the regular customers often asked after him, as well as some of her fellow shop owners in St Anne's Court who had been used to seeing him around. She supposed that if Jakob really was going to be the *dutiful son* he would sell his house in Cambridge, there would be no reason to keep it on if he was to be permanently living back in Oslo. She was embarrassed to admit it, but she had checked Rightmove once or twice to see if the property had gone on the market.

'What would you like me to do next?' asked Cassie, breaking into her thoughts. 'What about those invoices in your in-tray, shall I deal with those upstairs?'

'That would be great. Thank you. I have a backlog of emails to deal with, but first I have a shipment to Canada to sort out. Then I need to decide on a date for the next exhibition in the run-up to Christmas.'

Cassie groaned. 'Oh please, don't start talking about Christmas, it's surely much too soon, we haven't even had Halloween yet.'

'Hardly too early. I've already organised the gallery Christmas card at the printers, I did that in August.'

With Cassie now in the upstairs office, Nina settled herself at her desk to do the necessary paperwork for the charming Helen Allingham watercolour that would soon be on its way to Toronto. The couple who had bought it had been on holiday touring around the UK and had instantly fallen in love with the painting. It was another favourite of hers and Nina would be sorry to see it go, but business was business. Letting things go was much easier in her work life than it was in her personal life, but she was making progress with the latter.

Following her visit to see Hilary three weeks ago, when she had informed her mother-in-law that she would not be using the embryos stored at the clinic, she had finally decided what should happen to them. A family conference on FaceTime with her parents and brother and sister-in-law had helped chase away what remained of her indecision. They completely appreciated the moral dilemma in which she found herself and could see it from the many perspectives involved, and gave her the space and time to air all her doubts and what-if scenarios. Her parents had never once applied any pressure for her to provide them with any more grandchildren, but then as her brother had once joked, his own children were quite enough for any grandparent to deal with.

She could have chosen the ultimate altruistic option and donated the embryos to be used by other couples desperate to have a child, but selfishly Nina didn't want to spend the rest of her life wondering if there was a child of hers, and Hugh's, out there in the world. A child who might one day want to know Nina. She couldn't bear to live with that uncertainty, the not knowing. And what if that child accused Nina of not wanting them, of her having given the child away like an unwanted parcel?

Donating the embryos for fertility research appealed even less to Nina. Hilary had shown her disgust at the idea by likening the process to a Frankenstein experiment and Nina was not without sympathy because if she were entirely honest, she too felt slightly squeamish at the thought.

Which left her with only one solution, the only one that would bring an end to the dilemma once and for all. She wished she and Hugh had discussed this part of the process in more detail when they'd embarked on the process of IVF, but the question of death had been very far from their thinking at that stage. Then it had been all about life, not death. What to do with unwanted embryos had been briefly touched on at the clinic, but it had seemed so hypothetical, one of those way off in the distance things they wouldn't have to deal with.

Last week she had given formal instructions to the clinic to dispose of the embryos. She had hoped to feel a sense of relief, but it had yet to come. If it ever would. But it was done, and it was time to let go of the enormous weight of the decision that had hung so heavily over her. There was no going back now, it was time for her to concentrate on her future.

This was something that she had implored Cassie to do ever since she and Ben had returned from their time away with the wonderful news that they were going to marry.

'You must stop focusing on what's going on now with Rosalyn and Finlay,' Nina had said. 'Look to the future when your life gets back to normal, and you and Ben marry. Rosalyn and Finlay won't be with you forever.'

'But it feels like we'll never be rid of them,' Cassie had said miserably. 'I wish I had an office to go to,' she'd then said. 'At least then I'd be able to escape Rosalyn and the cloud of doom she carries around with her. Which is cruel of me, I know, but I can't help it. And then there's Emily, she's still intent on blaming me for her not knowing her father better when he was alive. As though I could have done anything more!'

Nina had suddenly seen a way to help Cassie, and herself too. 'Why not come and use the gallery as an office?' she had suggested, 'there's a room upstairs which you could use and maybe you could help me out now and then.'

'But I thought Keith was helping you?' Cassie had said.

'No, that's all stopped now that he's moved in with Diane in Ely. He has better things to do with his time these days.'

'He didn't hang about, did he?' commented Cassie.

That was putting it mildly in Nina's view, but as much as she'd wanted to caution Keith not to be too hasty, she really didn't think it was her place.

The next morning Cassie joined Nina at the gallery with a smile on her face and a spring in her step. No sooner had she organised her workspace with her laptop upstairs, than she was down in the gallery with Nina, answering the phone, making drinks, running errands, and chatting with customers.

'You are managing to do your website stuff, aren't you?' Nina enquired some days later, feeling bad that maybe Cassie was prioritising the novelty of helping in the gallery over her own work.

'Oh, don't worry about that, I'm going through a quietish spell. It's fine. Being here with you has been the perfect distraction. Just what I needed.'

Now, and after Nina had dealt with the backlog of emails, she steadily worked through everything else on her To Do list.

She soon had everything done, all except for speaking to the artist whose work she wanted to exhibit in the run-up to

Christmas. The exhibition was going to be entitled Echoes of the Fens, and she was sure it would prove popular. She was about to ring the artist when her mobile rang; it was Keith.

'How's my favourite daughter-in-law?' he asked.

'I'm very well, thank you. And how is my favourite father-in-law?'

The greeting was a new way of addressing each other and had started when he'd moved out of her guest room and in with Diane. The exchange had a falseness to it, as though they were both playing a part.

'I'm extremely well,' Keith replied, 'but I was wondering how you got on last week with the clinic and how you're feeling about it now.'

Nina had told him what she'd planned to do and was surprised he'd thought to ring her about it. 'I'm fine,' she said, which sounded carelessly dismissive of her, but what else could she say?

'That's good,' he said, 'and for what it's worth, you've made the right decision and—'

'Please, Keith,' she said, stopping him short as a tightness suddenly filled her throat, 'don't say any more, I want to put it behind me now. Besides, I'm at work and therefore . . . ' Her voice trailed off as the tightness increased.

'Of course,' Keith said, 'I'm sorry. I shouldn't have blundered in like that. You were on my mind, that's all.'

'That's okay,' she managed to say, just as the door opened and a couple came in, their umbrellas dripping on the wooden flooring. 'I'll speak to you another time.'

She ended the call, shocked that she had reacted in the way she had, that from nowhere her emotions had bubbled up and threatened to spill over.

Her head lowered and pretending to focus on the screen of her laptop so she could compose herself, she listened to the couple grumbling that everything on the walls was stupidly overpriced. Feeling more herself, Nina asked if they were looking for anything in particular. She knew full well they weren't interested in buying anything she had for sale. They'd probably only come in to shelter from the rain.

'Not at these prices,' the woman answered rudely.

Nina smiled politely and said no more. They left, leaving the door wide open. Nina got up to go and close it and saw that the rain was coming down even harder now. Looking out of the window, she saw that the cobbled street, slick with rain, was deserted and she doubted there would be any more customers that afternoon.

She was back behind her desk when Cassie reappeared.

'Invoices all done,' she said brightly, 'and I've even done some website work, so I'm feeling very virtuous.'

'Good for you,' Nina said. 'I was just wondering whether it's worth staying open any longer, punters are few and far between with this awful weather. You're more than welcome to go home if you want.'

Cassie grimaced. 'I'd sooner stay here than face what's at home.'

She plonked herself behind the other desk and swung to the right and then to the left in the swivel chair, much like a child would.

'You're going to have to sort things out with Rosalyn,' Nina said. 'She can't expect to stay with you indefinitely. It's not fair on you.'

'You try telling Emily that without starting World War Three.'

'Maybe Ben should be the one to do it.'

'He's already said he's happy to be the bad guy.'

'Let him do it then.'

Cassie frowned. 'Are you trying to get rid of me?'

'No, of course not,' Nina said with a laugh. 'I've enjoyed having you here but your generosity towards Rosalyn can't be indefinite, surely she has to accept that. Emily too. After all, you have a wedding to plan.'

'You're right, I know you are. I also know that I'm the one who must talk to her, not Ben. I wouldn't do that to him. Indirectly, I've caused the problem, so I'm the one who must put it right.'

As much as she was encouraging her friend to do it, Nina didn't envy Cassie the task ahead of her. 'Have you decided on a date yet?' she asked.

'What, when to talk to Rosalyn?'

Nina smiled. 'No,' she said. 'Your wedding.'

Cassie shook her head. 'Ben and I want life to feel more normal before we set a date.'

'What about the venue, have you given that any thought? These places get ridiculously booked up, years in advance some of them.'

'Not really,' Cassie began, just as Nina was distracted by the ping of an email arriving on her laptop. Force of habit made her look to see if it was important. She did a double-take when she saw who it was from.

It was Jakob.

Chapter Thirty-One

The rain had eased, it was no longer coming down in monsoon fashion, but there was still plenty of it, and it pattered a loud tattoo against Cassie's umbrella as she held it above her head. Her laptop bag slung over her shoulder and banging against her hip, she hurried along the cobbled street to where she'd left her car. Some days she and Nina drove in together, but this morning Nina had asked Cassie to open the gallery for her as she had a dental appointment.

Behind the wheel of her car, it was slow going getting out of Cambridge with the traffic moving at a snail's pace in the dwindling light. Stuck behind a bus, her windscreen wipers swishing back and forth, Cassie drummed her fingers impatiently on the steering wheel but instead of passing the time by listening to the current true crime podcast she was hooked on – *Tyler Walker, The Missing Boy of Idaho* – she mulled over the sudden change in Nina's manner in the office just now.

One minute they'd been chatting quite normally and then Nina had turned her head to read an email that had just landed on her laptop and the next thing she'd practically hustled Cassie out into the rain, insisting she go home early. Admittedly a short while before that Nina had said they might as well shut early because they weren't likely to see any more customers when the weather was so awful, but the haste with which Nina wanted Cassie gone, and how flustered she'd seemed, had been plain weird.

With her sleuthing antennae up, Cassie sensed a mystery; not that it required a detective to suss that the abrupt change in Nina had been caused by reading that email, which had to be the reason her pale complexion had unexpectedly bloomed with a delicate shade of pink. Nina had then turned away from the screen, shuffled some papers on her desk, randomly opened and closed the drawers in the filing cabinet to her right as though looking for something and then announced that Cassie should go home and leave Nina to lock up. 'Go now to beat the worst of the traffic,' she'd said.

Cassie had been left in no doubt that Nina wanted to be alone so she could respond to the person who had just emailed her.

Now who could that person be?

Who could cause that beautiful porcelain complexion to blush so charmingly?

It had to be Jakob!

Cassie had no evidence to support her theory, but the only time she'd previously seen that look on her friend's face had been when Jakob had been around. Was the Handsome Norwegian coming back to Cambridge, was that what had upset Nina's usual flawlessly self-possessed equilibrium? And if so, what did that mean?

The pleasurable intrigue kept her mind occupied all the way home and after parking her car, the rain having now stopped, she waved up at Ronnie who was standing at one of the windows in his apartment. The room behind him was brightly lit so he was clearly visible. He waved back at her.

Her sleuthing antennae had also detected that Ronnie and Venetia had been spending time together since his return from Majorca and it pleased Cassie enormously. Maybe her own happiness after Ben's romantic proposal was making her want everyone else to be as happily loved-up as she was. She had believed she couldn't love Ben any more than she did already, but the surprise long weekend away he'd planned for her birthday, and then his asking her to marry him had caused her to love him even more profoundly. He was truly the best of men.

When Emily had spotted the sparkly new ring on Cassie's left hand – she'd seen it when Cassie was making her breakfast the morning after her worryingly tearful breakdown – she had seemed genuinely pleased, if a little subdued. She had then apologised to Ben and Cassie for what she'd said the night before. 'But don't expect me to dress up in some hideous bridesmaid dress on your big day,' she had then gone on to say, sounding more her normal self. She had, however, made Cassie promise that she wouldn't discuss their wedding plans in front of Rosalyn.

'I'm not as insensitive as you think I am,' Cassie had said defensively, 'and anyway, we've decided not to rush things.' Which was only true in as much as they wanted Rosalyn gone as soon as possible so they could start planning their big day.

Key in hand, and as she now did every time she returned home to the apartment, Cassie steeled herself for what she would find the other side of the door. She so badly longed for the harmonious times of before – before Drew died and when she didn't have to tiptoe around Rosalyn or smile indulgently when Finlay made a mess or ignore Emily giving her the stink-eye if she so much as grimaced while once again scrubbing at a stain on the cream sofa or mopped the floor after yet another drink had been spilt. She'd never known a child to knock over so many drinks!

She'd also never known a child to produce so many unnerving drawings and paintings. The pictures all seemed to have a theme, a very dark theme. Cassie had asked Finlay one day what he'd painted. 'It's Daddy when he crashed his car,' he'd said. 'Look, there's his head and that's his blood.'

A child psychologist would have a field day with that!

Hanging up her coat in the hallway and putting her umbrella to dry, Cassie was surprised at the lack of noise. It was as silent as the proverbial grave. An unfortunate analogy, given their houseguests. But it certainly made a nice change not to have her every nerve jangled by a TV blaring, an iPad playing music, and Finlay and Emily talking loudly over the cacophony of noise. It was funny that they could make all that noise, but if Cassie raised her voice by so much as a decibel her daughter told her not to disturb Rosalyn.

But when she took the short flight of stairs down into the main living area she was taken aback at the sight of Rosalyn in the kitchen with a knife in her hand. She was chopping onions at the island unit, and it was hard to say whether the tears in her eyes were caused by grief or the onions.

'Rosalyn,' Cassie said by way of greeting. She never knew what to say to the woman, or how to go about saying it. Several times Emily had accused her of being excessively upbeat and therefore coming across as obtuse or patronising, like she was talking to a child, a dim-witted child at that. Another time Emily had said Cassie had sounded too sombre and was in danger of dragging Rosalyn down even further. Basically, she couldn't win, whatever she did was wrong.

'You're back early,' said Rosalyn, pressing her forearm to her face, the knife glinting in the overhead pendant lights.

'Yes,' said Cassie, as she watched Rosalyn put the knife down and go over to the sink to wash her hands.

'It's the onion,' Rosalyn said, 'it's making my eyes sting.'

'Yes,' Cassie repeated. Could she sound any more taciturn? In any other situation she was never stuck for words, but Emily had made her excruciatingly self-conscious of her every utterance.

It still rankled that she was expected to feel comfortable around Drew's widowed wife, that she should even view Rosalyn as a potential friend. As if that could ever happen!

With what felt like a flash of conversational brilliance, given the lacklustre of it so far, Cassie said, 'Where are Emily and Finlay?' She looked around in an exaggerated way, as though the little rascals might suddenly pop up from behind a sofa or a curtain. But as she took in the room, and their obvious absence, she realised that the place was actually tidy. There was no maelstrom of clutter strewn as if flung from a vortex, and come to think of it, Rosalyn herself looked a lot less like she'd just reluctantly dragged herself out of bed.

It would be fair to say, Rosalyn appeared to have undergone a dramatic transformation. She was wearing faded blue jeans with the knees artfully ripped and a loose-fitted dove-grey cashmere sweater. The sleeves were pushed up to her elbows, revealing the slenderest of wrists. Her hair was washed and swept up into a messy ponytail, and her movements possessed an energy not seen before. She had, Cassie noted, recaptured something of the attractive young woman from her many Instagram posts before Drew's accident. Until now, Rosalyn had shuffled about in a towelling robe like an elderly invalid in need of a bath or shower.

Dabbing her eyes with a square of kitchen roll, Rosalyn glanced back at Cassie. 'Ems has taken Finlay to see your neighbour's dog,' she said. 'He's always wanted one but in Dubai it wasn't . . .' Her voice trailed off as though it was too painful for her to continue.

But instead of feeling sympathy for Rosalyn, Cassie experienced a sharp jab of betrayal. Rosalyn's use of the shortened version of Emily's name crossed a massive line. Emily had never allowed anyone but Cassie to call her Ems; now Rosalyn was making free and easy with that privilege!

What also annoyed Cassie was that Emily and Finlay were

now privy to Venetia's secret. It was Ben who had let the cat out of the bag, or more precisely, the dog out of the bag last night when he'd been reading a bedtime story to Finlay. That had been a new thing from the boy, his wanting Ben to read to him. Did he see Ben as a potential replacement for his father?

'You don't have to do it,' she had told Ben privately last night, 'you're under no obligation.'

'I know that, and I really don't mind,' Ben had said. 'I've always enjoyed reading to your sister's children as well as my nephews and nieces. It's no big deal.'

But it was a big deal to Cassie because it roused within her the old familiar emotion: ugly jealous possessiveness. Ben was *her* Ben! And he wasn't to be divvied up any old how because he was too good-natured to say no. Worse still, and because he seemed so patient and at ease with Finlay it was a reminder that maybe Ben might have liked to be a father. A father to his very own child.

'Rosalyn,' she said, forcing the thought from her mind, 'Finlay mustn't ever tell anyone that Venetia has a dog here, you and Emily have explained that to him, haven't you? If certain people here found out, they'd complain, and Venetia would have to get rid of Bon-Bon.'

'Sure,' Rosalyn answered with a careless shrug, making her cashmere sweater slide down a skinny shoulder. 'Can I make you a drink?' she asked.

The question, as polite and doubtless as well-intentioned as it was, thoroughly narked Cassie, as though it were she who was the guest here and not Rosalyn.

'That's okay,' Cassie replied curtly, her fists clenched behind her back, 'I'll go and change and then I'll make myself a drink to take upstairs to my office. I don't want to interrupt your culinary industry here,' she added. 'What are you cooking? Something for Finlay?'

'I'm doing peppered steak and mushroom tagliatelle for everyone.' Rosalyn smiled. 'Ems mentioned that it was a favourite of Ben's.'

A million thoughts buzzed around inside Cassie's head as she went to change, and none of them were good. Not a single one.

Chapter Thirty-Two

Sunday morning and the church bells were ringing out across the city of Cambridge, the glorious sound carried on the chilly autumnal air as Nina waited at the punt stop on Mill Lane.

The exquisite pearly opalescence of the sky and the joyful peal of bells were quite at odds with how she felt. She was jittery with nerves, wondering if agreeing to meet Jakob was such a good idea.

When he'd emailed on Friday afternoon asking if he could ring her, the request coming so completely out of the blue had thrown her. It had stirred up the confusion of emotions she'd believed she had dealt with. But one simple email and that belief had been swept away. All she could think of was how to get rid of Cassie from the gallery as quickly as possible so that she could be alone to think. Which was ludicrous. There had been nothing to think about. It had taken her no more than a few seconds to email Jakob and say she was free now if he wanted to ring her. Which was also absurd, because what was the hurry?

The phone had rung a few minutes later, but Jakob hadn't been able to say much as he'd just boarded a plane to fly back to the UK. What he did manage to say was that he had something important he needed to discuss with her, and could they meet?

Now here she was waiting for him in the agreed spot so they could go for a walk along the river. The walk had been her suggestion. It had seemed a safe option.

And there she went again. Why did she feel she needed a safe option? What did she think was going to happen?

Leaning against the wooden rail of the bridge and watching a pair of swans gliding elegantly by and a couple in a punt braving the chill on the water, she recalled that day in the summer when she had seen Keith and the unknown woman in a punt. She thought of their smiling faces and how happy Keith had looked, and the caring way he'd helped the woman out of the boat. Nina had never witnessed a gesture of that nature pass between him and Hilary.

Poor Hilary, Nina thought sadly. How alone and abandoned she must be feeling. Because of what had happened at the wedding, Nina couldn't help but feel partly responsible for that. She wished she could put things right and get her in-laws back together. But how? And what might be right for Hilary might not be right for Keith now. He seemed to have made up his mind that his marriage was over. He was, he'd told Nina, happier with Diane than he'd been in a long time with Hilary. He had no idea if it was permanent being with Diane, but what he did know was that he couldn't tolerate being with Hilary. All this he'd shared with Nina when she'd called him last night to apologise for ending the conversation so abruptly when he'd phoned her at the gallery on Friday.

'Nothing to apologise for,' he'd said, 'it's quite reasonable that you'd find it difficult to talk about closing that particular chapter of your life.'

'Do you think Hugh would have wanted me to make the decision I have about the embryos?' she'd asked Keith.

He had hesitated before answering. 'I couldn't say, but he would have been very proud of the way you've coped so well. That much I do know. And he wouldn't have wanted you to remain on your own for the rest of your life,' Keith had then added. 'Heard anything from that nice Norwegian chap?'

Not liking his thought process, Nina had lied. 'No. And what you're implying is out of the question.'

'I don't see why,' he'd said. 'The two of you looked as though you were having a great time together at the wedding. You probably won't thank me for saying this, but a few members of the family who were there that day have since asked me if the two of you were serious about each other.'

Nina had groaned. 'What did you tell them?'

'I told them I didn't know, but that we shouldn't be surprised if you did start seeing someone seriously as it was only right and proper that you should. And now, because I can hear that you're cross with me, I shall say goodbye.'

Nina hated the thought that she was the focus of speculation within Hugh's family, and it made her wonder, as she had before, whether it wouldn't be better to cut all ties with them. How else could she ever be free of feeling their judgement, or be free of the guilt that she was keen to move on with her life?

But would liberating herself from Hugh's family be cutting her nose off to spite her face? Shouldn't she just accept that all families enjoyed gossiping about one another and that judgement went hand in hand with that?

Hilary had certainly given the family plenty to talk about with her *Wedding-Gate* meltdown. For all Nina knew, the captured moment was still doing the rounds on social media. It was an appalling thought and made her wince.

It also made her wonder why on earth she was waiting here for Jakob. Why put herself through any more emotional turmoil? For that was what it would be, she was sure.

Undeniably she was attracted to him, and he seemed to be attracted to her. Or he had been. It would be so different if he was the same age as her, but convention – and even her own perception of what constituted the ideal relationship balance – dictated that she could be in danger of making a spectacle of herself. She had always believed that her feminist ideals, when it came to equality, were of sufficient strength to cut through this sort of archaic prejudice, but when push came to shove, it was plainly evident that she couldn't walk the talk when it came down to it. Ethics and principles were all well and good on paper, but in this case the reality was quite another matter. She was not cut out to be the older woman.

Chiding herself for wasting her energy in going over what she now considered old ground, she decided that Jakob probably only wanted to see her to discuss the idea he'd had when he worked at Lavelle's, that of her stocking a selection of paintings by Norwegian artists. Well, she was more than happy to explore that business proposal with him.

This thought had just firmly taken hold in her head when she saw Jakob striding purposefully towards her. He was dressed in an unzipped black quilted jacket and a red beanie hat, black jeans and chunky soled laced-up boots. He looked even younger than she remembered. He also looked strangely apprehensive.

'You came,' he said. 'I wasn't sure that you would.'

'Why would you think that?' she asked.

'For all the obvious reasons,' he said, his gaze meeting hers.

Reluctant to pursue this, she suggested they cross to the other side of the river, and they set off at a steady pace along the towpath.

'It's good to see you again,' he said. 'You look radiant. Autumn suits you. It must be the chestnut colour of your hair.'

'Goodness, what a very unBritish thing to say,' she responded with a nervous laugh.

'A few weeks back in Oslo and I'm once more very Norwegian,' he said. 'But it's true, you do look great.'

'You look well too,' she said.

'I suppose you're wondering why I'm in Cambridge.'

But before she could answer, he pointed to a bench just ahead of them. 'Let's sit for a while, then I can focus on what I need to say.'

'Is this about the gallery?' she asked.

He cleared his throat. 'Yes and no,' he replied ambiguously. 'The thing is, I imagined that being in Oslo and being surrounded by my old life I wouldn't think about the life I'd left behind here, but I was wrong. I thought about it even more.'

'You missed Cambridge?' she said.

'Yes,' he said. He turned to look at her. 'But I especially missed you, Nina. I missed seeing you every day. I missed how it used to be between us in the gallery.'

She swallowed anxiously. The thought that he'd come here to discuss Norwegian art with her now seemed preposterous. 'Go on,' she murmured.

'Meeting you has changed everything for me and in ways I never imagined,' he said. 'So I'm here because I want to know if there's a chance we could make it work between us. And not as work colleagues, not as friends, but as lovers. Do you think there is?'

The use of the word 'lovers' made the colour rise to Nina's face and she felt as gauche as a teenager.

'I know you're concerned about the age difference,' Jakob went on, 'but who really cares about that? I don't. And you shouldn't either. That day at the wedding, you didn't care, did you? What happened then was real. Unless—' he broke off as a couple with a prancing red setter straining at the leash passed them.

'Unless what?' Nina said when they were alone again and he stared at her, the intensity of his cornflower-blue eyes creating a fluttering sensation in her stomach. She wanted to look away, but she couldn't.

'Unless you were only using me to get at your mother-in-law. I know that was the plan in the beginning, to prove something to her, but I always believed that what happened between us was genuine. When we were dancing and we kissed that was real, wasn't it?'

'Yes,' she said quietly, 'it was very real.'

'What do you think would have happened if your mother-in-law hadn't behaved the way she had? Would we, when we were alone later, have let our feelings take their natural course?'

Remembering how Venetia had asked her the very same thing and how she had encouraged Nina not to overthink her emotions, or fear them, she forced herself to be as honest with Jakob as he had been with her.

'I think there's a very strong possibility that we would have done a lot more than kiss,' she said, 'but I would have probably regretted it afterwards.'

'Yes,' he said solemnly, 'I believe you would have, and that is why I resigned and went back to Oslo. I didn't want you to feel as though you had done anything wrong, or were at risk of doing anything wrong.'

'That was very understanding of you.'

'It was selfish too; an act of self-preservation.'

Nina sighed. 'That's how every day feels to me, an act of self-preservation as I guard against my emotions getting any more battered than they already are. I know I'm over the worst of my grief, but it occasionally still has the power to stop me in my tracks.'

'How does it . . . ' Jakob hesitated as if searching through his extensive English vocabulary for the right word, '. . . how does it manifest itself?'

'Mostly as guilt. I know Hugh is dead and I'm alive and that means I must get on with my life. I know all that, but grief isn't linear, it goes round and round in never-ending circles with me caught at the centre of it.'

'I apologise for stating the obvious, but you need to break out of that cycle.'

'I know I do,' she said. 'As you say, it is obvious and I think, or rather I hope, I've now taken a positive step to break the cycle.' She was thinking about the clinic and how she'd brought matters to a close there. But she didn't want to talk about that now.

A group of students in their running gear with *St Catharine's College* emblazoned across their sweatshirts pounded by and when they had disappeared into the distance around a bend in the river, she said, 'I'm sorry you felt you had to leave. I shouldn't have accepted your resignation. It was a mistake, and I was a coward not to try and talk you out of going.'

'You were under enough pressure already without me adding to your problems. But I wish now that I had stayed and talked to you properly.'

'So do I. I've missed you,' she said, forcing herself to be honest again, but then tempering the admission by adding, 'The clients have too.'

'I could come back if you think the clients would like it,' he suggested with smile. 'Or have you found a replacement?'

'Not a permanent replacement, but the job is yours if you'd like it. What about the family business in Oslo, don't you have commitments there? Won't your parents be disappointed if you return here for a job for which they know you're overqualified?'

'They know why I'm here. I told them all about you and they agreed that I should return to Cambridge to try and convince you that we could make things work. They said if I didn't come, I'd always regret it.'

'But do they know that I'm so much older than you?'

He frowned. 'You're not that much older. And anyway, my mother is older than my father, so for them it is no big deal.'

Like father like son, she thought. And how easy he made it all sound. So tempting too. What was stopping her from saying what did it matter what anyone might think? Why not be tempted? What was the worst that could happen? Surely the worst had already happened to her, she had lost Hugh. Or was she frightened to be with someone new because she feared she might lose them as well?

Her brain was whirling again with a rush of *what ifs*. She couldn't live like this though. Living in fear of what each day could bring, she might as well be dead. She had to be brave and make herself vulnerable all over again. It was the only way.

'Come on,' she said, abruptly rising to her feet, determined to banish the *what if* demons from inside her head. 'Let's walk, it's too cold to sit still for any length of time.'

When Jakob stood up, he reached for one of her hands. It made her remember the day of the wedding when they'd just got out of his car, and he'd given her his arm to lean on so she could safely negotiate the gravel in her heels. She had hesitated at the time, even though it had been a perfectly natural gesture on his part, just as this was now. But this time she didn't hesitate; she happily placed her hand in his.

They'd only walked a short distance when, and as if both driven by the same spontaneous desire, they came to a stop, turned and gazed at each other.

'Is this when we risk kissing again?' he asked.

His voice was low, and drawn in by the powerfully magnetic pull of his blue eyes, Nina saw in them the raw strength of his feelings for her. 'I think it is,' she said. 'What's more, I don't think we'll come to any harm this time.'

'Speak for yourself,' he said, 'my heart is ready to explode!'

His arms moved to hold her close, and their mouths met. Despite the cold, his mouth was invitingly warm and soft, and she pressed her lips against his, sinking deeply into his embrace, finally giving in to the potent ache of her feelings for him.

The kiss only came to an end because from behind them came the sound of heavy breathing and thundering feet. Hastily standing to one side to let the runner by, a juggernaut of a man who didn't look like he was built for running, Jakob grinned at Nina. 'We survived a second kiss and nothing bad happened to us,' he said.

With a lightness of heart, as if a huge weight had been lifted from her, Nina laughed and they began walking again, her hand in his. His hand felt good. Strong, reassuring and . . . right.

They'd been walking for a few minutes when Jakob squeezed her hand gently and Nina instinctively sensed that he was about to say something important. She was right.

'I know a new relationship won't be easy for you, Nina, but I want you to know that this is not easy for me either. I've never had a girlfriend whose partner died, so I know I have to be careful and not say or do the wrong thing that will scare you away.'

Nina had never looked at it from his perspective before. She had only ever thought of the risk to herself in being in a relationship with somebody who wasn't Hugh. She pondered what he'd said as they continued to follow the path that was a patchwork of fallen leaves. After they'd slowed their step to allow a trio of girls to jog by, she turned to look at Jakob.

'Thank you for being so honest with me,' she said, 'I really hadn't thought how difficult it might be for you.'

'It was one of the reasons why I went back to Oslo,' he said, 'I lost my nerve. I suddenly became worried that I could never give you what your husband did. Or be like him.'

She was shocked to hear him say this and thought carefully before replying. 'You don't have to be like Hugh,' she said firmly, 'just be yourself. It's what we both must do. The worst thing we could do is lose sight of who we are as individuals. If we can't be our natural selves, then a relationship will never work.'

When she fell quiet, he stopped walking and put his hand to her cheek. 'Then we must try very hard not to fall into that trap. I'm not used to failing, Nina. And I don't believe you are either.'

He was right, she hated to fail, she always had. It was one of the many things that had upset her about Hugh's death. She'd felt she'd failed him, that if she had only loved him more, he might have lived. In her more rational moments, she knew that that was nonsense, yet in her darkest moments she'd believed it.

But now was not the time for dwelling on her darkest moments. Not when Jakob was staring at her the way he was, making her legs feel like they were about to dissolve into the ground. She moved her head and kissed the palm of his hand that still rested against her cheek. 'Let's walk across the meadows to Grantchester,' she then said, 'and have a pub lunch there. I'm suddenly hungry.'

She was, she realised, suddenly hungry for life, and a life lived to the fullest.

Chapter Thirty-Three

It was Sunday evening and emerging from King's College Chapel with the rest of the congregation, Venetia buttoned her coat and glanced around to see where Ronnie was. They'd managed to get separated in the mêlée of worshippers filing out, many of whom looked like tourists and probably there for the sense of theatre, which was not in short supply in such splendid surroundings. She for one had enjoyed the display of such a time-honoured ritual immensely. The choir had sung beautifully, their voices combining with the swell of the organ notes soaring as though to heaven itself through the magnificent, vaulted roof.

She had never been a regular churchgoer, but she was certainly partial to what might be termed as the high notes of the religious calendar – Christmas and Easter, along with weddings, baptisms, and funerals – the latter occurring increasingly more frequent for her these days.

When Ronnie had asked her if she'd like to attend Choral Evensong with him, she'd been surprised, and he'd known it.

'What, you thought I was too much of a philistine to want to do something like that?' he'd said.

'Do not put words into my mouth, Ronnie Sharp,' she'd told him sternly. 'I'm merely surprised that you would want me to join you.'

He'd laughed. 'Good recovery, I'll grant you that. So how

about it, do you fancy an hour of mystical malarky with me? We could go for dinner afterwards if you're up for it.'

'When you put it like that, how could I possibly refuse?'

Still waiting for Ronnie, a brisk wind sweeping across the great court that led down to the River Cam, Venetia scolded herself again for the assumption she had made about him. She, of all people, should know better than to pigeon-hole anyone too hastily. The more time she spent in Ronnie's company, the more she liked him. She saw herself in the role of friend, a friend to whom he could talk quite openly because she was outside of his normal circle of friends, acquaintances or business associates.

When she'd driven him to Addenbrooke's for his appointment to see the consultant he had been as fidgety as a child in the passenger seat next to her, and from the tiredness etched on his face, he'd looked like he'd passed a sleepless night. She had suggested she accompany him inside, but he'd pursed his lips and shaken his head. 'No need,' he'd said gruffly, 'I'd sooner face my fate alone.'

At his pessimism she'd given his arm a reassuring squeeze, hoping to transmit support and encouragement through the sleeve of his coat. She'd then watched him walk away, shoulders hunched, his hands pushed deep into his pockets. Wishing he had allowed her to go with him, if only to hang around a waiting room while he saw the consultant, she had reluctantly driven away. To fill the time, she'd driven the short distance to Wandlebury Country Park where she'd taken Bon-Bon for a walk.

When she returned to the hospital, after receiving a text from Ronnie that the 'quack' had now finished with him, she could see at once the change in his bearing; the twinkle had come back into his eye, and he was smiling broadly and clutching a small paper bag.

'Cancer be damned, it's nothing but a stupid stomach ulcer, and it'll take more than that to finish off this old fella!' he'd joked with cheerful bravado. 'Let's go and celebrate,' he'd then said.

'Will your stomach cope?' she'd asked with a frown.

'Sure it will, mind over matter now that I know what's wrong. Plus, I'm fully loaded with medication which the consultant has prescribed for me.' He'd waved the paper bag in front of her.

That had been earlier this week and as if imbued with a new sense of gung-ho energy, Ronnie had been busy sorting out his affairs in Majorca. He hadn't elaborated on what he was discussing with the lawyers whenever Venetia spoke to him, and she hadn't pursued it.

'There you are,' she said when Ronnie finally appeared through the doorway of the college chapel.

'Sorry about that,' he said, 'I got chatting with a couple of Americans. How about dinner? Shall we risk it at The Ivy, seeing as it's a short hop away?'

'What's the attraction of Choral Evensong for you?' Venetia asked when they had ordered their meal, and a waitress had brought them their drinks – a Diet Coke for Ronnie and a Bloody Mary for her.

His eyes crinkled as he smiled. 'Are we back to you thinking that I don't seem the sort?'

'If I'm honest, yes.'

'Well, to satisfy your curiosity, it's always had an appeal for me, ever since I sang in the school choir as a boy treble. Yeah, I know, it's hard to imagine me as an angelic choirboy, isn't it?'

She smiled. 'Where was that?'

'Home was in Middlesex, but I went to a very minor public school in Derbyshire. It was pretty bleak, your typical institution where you either swam or sank, and for me, not being particularly sporty or academic, the one thing I did seem good at was singing in the choir. But then my voice broke, and it was never the same again and I became more interested in earning money. And girls. Of course.'

'Both of which you excelled at I don't doubt,' she said with a raised eyebrow.

'I couldn't possibly comment,' he replied with a laugh.

'Did you never go back to singing again?'

'Only in the shower or in the car on my own. But enough about me, tell me some more about your time at Hope Hall when it was a children's home.'

She had only recently shared with him that she had grown up at the Hall but hadn't gone into too much detail with him, merely satisfying his initial show of interest and then changing the subject.

'I'm not sure there's much more to tell you,' she said, just as a waitress brought them their food – they each had chosen the turbot with shrimps and a dish of fries to share.

When the girl had gone, Ronnie said, 'Was it a happy time for you? I ask the question out of genuine curiosity, given that we were both institutionalised at a young age, so in some ways I would imagine we had similar experiences.'

'It was a happy time,' she answered, 'but then you have to understand, it was the only life I knew, I knew no other way of being. It was harder for children who came to Hope Hall when they'd previously experienced what you might call a proper home environment.'

'We never miss what we never know, so goes the old adage,' Ronnie commented thoughtfully.

'Exactly. I was definitely one of the lucky ones.'

'But weren't you interested about your origins, your mother who abandoned you and whoever your father was?'

'I'm often asked that,' she said, 'and my answer is always the same, that I just accepted my life for what it was.'

'Because you were happy?'

'Yes. If the woman who gave birth to me hadn't wanted me, then I didn't want or need her. That was how I felt. Which you probably think was harsh of me, even judgemental, but I was a child, and children always see things very simplistically.'

'Did your attitude change as an adult?'

'Not really. I was busy getting on with my life, trying to look forwards rather than back.'

'What about friends?' Ronnie asked, adding salt to his fish, then helping himself to some fries, and making Venetia wonder if he shouldn't be taking more care, given he had an ulcer. 'Was it easy to make friends in that environment?'

'I was something of a loner and naturally self-contained,' she said, 'I still am really. Back then I never looked at the world through a lens of *me*, as I would venture to say so many young folk do today. For most of us at Hope Hall, it was always a case of *we*, and what *we* could do to make life better for those around us. That was Lady Constance's philosophy, she taught us to look outwards, beyond the self. In many ways, she was ahead of her time, a visionary.'

'It sounds like she was a huge influence in your life.'

'She was.'

'I can't say that I experienced anyone at my old school who influenced me so inspirationally. But I did have one really good friend. We're still in touch, all these years on. What about you? Did you make a close friend, even though you were something of a loner?'

'There was one,' she replied. 'He became a very special friend from when I was twelve.' Venetia then explained about Lucien coming to the Hall and Lady Constance appointing her to take care of him and how close they became. 'We were practically inseparable,' she said, 'kindred spirits you could say.'

'Was he your first love?'

Venetia found herself blushing, which was ridiculous after all this time. 'Yes,' she said.

'Did it go the distance?'

'That would depend on how you measure distance, or what it implies.'

'First kiss, then?'

She nodded.

'First time—'

'I'm certainly not going to answer that,' she interrupted him severely.

He smiled. 'I'll take that as a yes, then.'

'Take it any way you like, you cheeky devil.'

Wiping his mouth with his napkin, he said, 'So what happened next, did your childhood romance fizzle out all of its own accord?'

'Not exactly.'

'Did the lad break your heart? Or,' he said as if hit with sudden insight and inspiration, 'perhaps you cruelly broke his? Yes, I can see it now, the beautiful young Venetia spurning the boy's ardent affection for her!'

She tutted. 'What a lot of nonsense you do speak, Ronnie.'

'I can't help it, I'm a hopeless romantic at heart.'

'Well, it was nothing as silly as you've just suggested. No hearts were broken,' she lied. 'We grew up and drifted apart.'

Chapter Thirty-Four

May 1960

Ever since that night in the woods when Terry Sands had threatened to make their lives hell, Venetia and Lucien had tried their hardest to keep out of his way.

But it soon became clear that it was Lucien who was the real target of Terry's taunts and jibes, often in petty ways, like deliberately knocking into him when he 'just happened' to be passing. Other times he lay in wait when Lucien and the other boys were out on a cross country run. Lucien hated cross country, he could see no point in it and was hampered by his asthma, and was usually to be found at the back of the group of runners. Terry would be lying in wait for him and with no one else around, he would pounce and knock Lucien to the ground. He would then stand over him and laugh his sickeningly sadistic laugh while kicking him. After it had happened three times, Lucien complained to their games teacher, but Mr Grafton didn't believe him. He accused Lucien of making up something to get out of doing cross country.

Venetia wanted to tell Edie Buckle what was going on because she was sure Edie would believe them, but Lucien wouldn't have it. He didn't want anyone knowing what was happening. Venetia only knew about the cross-country incidents because she'd forced Lucien to tell her how he had so many bruises on his legs.

'If we make a big deal of it,' Lucien said, 'we might end up having to explain how all this started in the first place, and Terry will say we were doing more than just kissing in the woods when he found us. I don't want to risk that. And if we do tell Edie and she makes a fuss and Terry loses his job, who knows what he might do. He's a dangerous thug. I don't care what he does to me, but if he hurts you, well . . .' he paused, 'just never mind what I'd do then.'

Venetia could see the sense in what he was saying, and was touched how protective he was of her, but she didn't like the thought of letting Terry get away with bullying Lucien.

For a couple of weeks, it seemed as though Terry had grown bored of baiting Lucien and left him alone, but then out of the blue, Lucien was summoned to Lady Constance's office. Lady Constance was still away on her extended honeymoon around Europe with Mr Butler and so in her absence it was Miss Selby who was in charge. With Terry in the office with her, she explained to Lucien that he was there to come clean for what he'd done and then apologise.

Venetia was hovering outside, her ear pressed to the door, and she clearly heard Terry accuse Lucien of sneaking into his cottage and stealing a tin of money. What was more, Terry had said, he'd actually seen Lucien do it.

So why didn't you try to stop him? Venetia wanted to scream through the door.

Lady Constance would never have believed such a blatant lie, especially not of Lucien, but Miss Selby urged him to own up to his crime and return the money.

Quick as a flash and suspecting that Terry would insist that a search be carried out, Venetia dashed up the stairs to the dormitory that Lucien shared with ten other boys. She knew that his bed was by the window and that he kept what few possessions he had in a cupboard to the side of the bed. She rifled through it and in amongst his games kit and books, she found an old Holborn tobacco tin which rattled when she shook it. Prising off the lid, she was amazed to see a thick wad of one pound notes and an assortment of shillings, thrupenny bits and ha'pennies. It seemed an awful lot for a groundsman to have in his possession.

Not for a minute did she think Lucien was guilty of stealing the money and hiding the tin in so obvious a place. More likely, and determined to cause trouble, Terry must have slipped up here when nobody was looking, just like Venetia had, and put the tin in the cupboard. Placing it inside the bib of her dungarees, she took to her heels and sped back down the stairs, pushing her way through a group of children on their way up, and then outside. She ran like the wind, the coins rattling inside the tin against her chest. Her intention was to return the tin to Terry's cottage, but when she got there, she found the door was locked. She yanked on the handle, rammed her shoulder against it just in case it was jammed shut rather than locked, but the door remained firmly closed.

She went round to the back of the cottage, but the door there was also locked. The two small windows either side of the door were shut too. She thought about smashing a window and placing the tin on the ledge inside, as though it had always been there, but how to explain the broken glass?

There were three options open to her: leave the tin in the garden as though the culprit had returned it, hide it somewhere in the grounds, or hurl it in the river where it would sink without trace.

The first option was the most tempting and certainly the easiest, but what if Lucien was still accused of the crime and the reappearance of the tin only served to prove his guilt, that he had returned it once he knew the game was up? Then there was the chance that she would be accused of being his accomplice and she had returned to the scene of the crime to cover their tracks?

Better, she decided, to hide the tin and its contents. But where? The woods! It had to be there.

When she'd completed her task, she ran back to the Hall, just in time to hear the lunch bell being rung. After scrubbing her hands, paying attention to her nails which were filthy after burying the tin without the aid of a spade or trowel, she nonchalantly joined the queue. Everybody, so it seemed, was talking about Lucien and how he'd been caught stealing.

'I didn't think he was the sort,' said one of the girls who had been stupid enough to have her head turned by the odious Terry.

'That's because he's not,' said Venetia staunchly, 'Lucien would never do anything like that. He's completely innocent.'

Her defence of her friend was met with sniggers and eye-rolling.

'We all know you'd do anything to defend your precious sweetheart,' said the girl.

Yes, thought Venetia, that much was true. Taking her tray of food over to a table where nobody else was sitting, she waited for Lucien to appear in the dining hall. But he didn't come.

When lunch was over, she went to look for him in the library. That was often where he went when he wanted to be alone. Sure enough, he was there, sitting at the table farthest from the door, but not with his head in a book as he usually was but staring with what looked like furious concentration out of the bay window. He had to have been so deep in thought he didn't hear her rubber-soled shoes squeaking on the wooden floor.

He started when she said, 'Why didn't you come for lunch?'

'I wasn't hungry,' he said with a husky wheeze when she sat down in front of him. Clasped in his right hand was the asthma inhaler he had to use to keep his attacks under control.

'I overheard part of what was said between you and Miss Selby,' she admitted.

He looked at her. 'Only part?'

She explained what she'd done, that she'd found the tin of money in his bedside cupboard and had buried it.

'I'm not sure that will be of much help,' Lucien said morosely. 'Terry made Miss Selby take me upstairs to search my things for the money which I'm supposed to have stolen. When she couldn't find the money, he claimed that of course I wouldn't be so stupid as to leave it where it could be found so easily.'

'Does Miss Selby really believe you did it?'

He nodded with an expression of grim pessimism. 'She's given me twenty-four hours to do, what she calls, the right thing and return the money to Terry and apologise to him.'

'But that's so wrong when you're completely innocent! And why would Miss Selby believe an ex-convict over you? Anyone can see that Terry Sands is trouble and the last person on earth to be trusted!'

'I can only think Miss Selby is scared of him. But I'll tell you this for nothing, I'm never apologising to that bastard!'

But the next morning Miss Selby, accompanied by Mr Grafton, as though she needed back up, told Lucien that Terry was now saying that if he didn't receive an apology in person, he would go to the police. It was laughable, an ex-convict threatening to go to the police!

The conversation had taken place in Lady Constance's office and once again Venetia had been the other side of the panelled door, her ear pressed against it.

'The last thing we need is for the police to be involved while Lady Constance is away,' Miss Selby said. 'It wouldn't do at all.'

'You just need to admit what you did and say sorry,' Mr Grafton said. 'I know from what you've said in the past that you don't like Terry and that you've deliberately made up things about him, but you have to be more of a man now and admit to what you did. Do that and you won't have a black mark against your name.'

'But I didn't do anything!' Lucien had shouted angrily.

'That's enough,' intoned Miss Selby. 'Mr Grafton has offered to accompany you to Terry's cottage after tea today. And that's an end to it.'

'I don't have any choice, do I?' Lucien said to Venetia a short while later. 'If I don't do as they say, this will go on and on and what if the police believe Terry's story and not mine? I could end up in a borstal!'

Desperately upset for Lucien, Venetia went up to the sick room to confide in Edie Buckle in the hope that she might be able to help. 'It's not fair,' she said, 'how could anyone believe a word that horrible man, Terry, ever says, he's vile!'

Jiggling a whimpering baby on her shoulder, a recent arrival to Hope Hall, Edie sighed and let out a series of alternate tuts and oh dears, none of which really helped.

'He just wants to humiliate Lucien,' Venetia went on.

'But why? What has Lucien done to invite such dislike from Terry?'

'I can't say,' said Venetia, 'it might make matters worse for Lucien and me.'

'Come on now, tell me what's been going on,' Edie said, her hand tenderly patting the tiny baby's back. 'Otherwise, how can I help you?'

Wanting so much for Edie to do just that, to make everything right again, Venetia forced herself to give her all the details, how she and Lucien regularly went up on the roof even though it was strictly out of bounds, and of their time spent alone in the woods late at night. Then she explained how Terry had caught them kissing and that it had looked far worse than it really was.

'Worse?' Edie had enquired. 'In what way?'

Venetia knew she had to be brave. 'We've never done . . . you know . . . *it*. We swore to each other we would never take that kind of a risk, no matter how much we wanted to.'

'I'm very pleased to hear that,' Edie said with a rare look of sternness on her face.

'So you see how bad it is for Lucien and me. When it comes out that we've broken these rules, which Lady Constance is so strict about, nobody will believe us when we say that Terry is lying about what he saw us doing, and about the tin of money. Lady Constance might decide we can't stay on to finish our education. She might think we're not worth it because we didn't respect the rules.' She was babbling now, but she couldn't stop herself. 'You do believe that Lucien didn't steal the money, don't you? He would never do anything like that.'

Putting a finger to her lips to hush Venetia, Edie gently laid the now sleeping baby into a crib. 'I do believe you,' she said quietly. 'Lucien is a decent young man; I've always thought that. A little headstrong at times, and stubborn like you, but he's not a thief. I'm disappointed though that you've both been up to . . . to no good,' she added. 'I thought you knew better than that.'

'I'm sorry,' Venetia said, and meaning it. She hated knowing that Edie was disappointed in her. 'But will you go and speak to Miss Selby?' she asked. 'She'll listen to you. Please say you will!'

'I'll try.'

'Thank you,' Venetia said. 'You have to make Miss Selby and Mr Grafton realise that it's Terry who's lying. Because if Lucien does apologise for something he didn't do, Terry will only do something similar in the future. Or maybe something worse. He enjoys inflicting pain.' She then went on to tell Edie about the rabbit Terry had shot, but not killed outright, and which he'd put in a cage and watched it slowly die with cruel enjoyment. 'He's a sadist and he's clearly got it in for Lucien and me. It's like he's put us in a cage and is watching us squirm. And he'll keep on doing it until he's stopped!'

Her voice had risen to a shrill peal, and she was near to tears.

'There, there,' soothed Edie, putting her comforting arms around Venetia. 'We'll soon have all this sorted out. You're not to worry.'

But Venetia did worry.

Even more so when Lucien didn't appear in the dining hall when the bell rang for tea. She waited for a short while and after hanging around at the end of the queue with the clatter of plates and cutlery going on in the background, and too anxious to eat anything herself, she went to look for him.

It was now five-thirty and at six he was supposed to be going with Mr Grafton to Terry's cottage. Passing by Miss Selby's office and peering in through the open door, she could see that it was empty. But then beyond the desk and filing cabinets, and through the window, she caught a flash of movement: it was Mr Grafton striding across the lawn with a reluctant Lucien following behind.

Not missing a beat, Venetia hurried along the passageway, down the steps, past the toilets and their strong smell of Jeyes fluid and carbolic soap, then the laundry room and then out through a fire exit door. From there she sped across the cobbled courtyard and stable block and continued towards Terry's cottage. Ahead of her, she spotted Mr Grafton and Lucien.

Keeping her distance, Venetia followed discreetly behind. She might not be able to stop the humiliation Lucien was being forced to go through with, but she could at least be there for him when the ordeal was over.

Carefully positioned behind a large oak tree, she peered out and watched Mr Grafton bang the knocker on Terry's door. Lucien stood to one side, his shoulders hunched, his arms folded across his chest.

The door opened and Terry appeared wearing only a singlet vest on his top half and a pair of workman's trousers with a pair of braces dangling from the waistband.

Words which Venetia couldn't hear were exchanged and then to her concern, Mr Grafton shoved Lucien through the doorway, then turned and walked back up the path. He gave a brief glance over his shoulder as the door shut and then set off in the direction of the Hall.

Venetia held her position, fearing for her friend who was now entirely alone with an evil monster. Why hadn't Mr Grafton stayed with Lucien? When ten minutes had passed, surely that was long enough for Lucien to make his apology, she crept out from behind the tree and moved slowly towards the cottage.

Not wanting to risk being seen going up the path, she hugged the perimeter of the laurel hedge, staying low to the ground so her head wouldn't be seen above it. When she reached the back, she squeezed through the smallest of gaps in the hedge next to a brick-built shed. The door of the shed was open, and she could see that it was the outdoor privy. The stench coming from it turned her stomach.

Moving up the ramshackle garden, she went and stood to one side of a window, and then very warily she peered into the kitchen, no more than a tiny scullery really. The stone sink and wooden draining board were covered in unwashed pots and pans and empty beer bottles. Shifting her gaze around the small gloomy interior she gave a small start at the sight of a dead rabbit strung up on a hook on the wall to the side of the range.

Cupping her hands around her eyes she strained to see beyond the kitchen, through the open door that led to the front of the cottage. At once she saw the outline of a large man. It was Terry and he was on his feet with his head tilted down as though looking at something.

At first Venetia didn't understand what she was seeing, she couldn't make sense of it. Why was Lucien kneeling in front of Terry like that? Was he being made to beg for forgiveness as a further act of humiliation?

But then it dawned on her what was happening and as the violent need to be sick consumed her, she clamped a hand over her mouth and not caring about the consequences, knowing only that she had to stop what her poor friend was being forced to do, she banged on the window. That was when Terry whipped round, his ugly face as black as thunder. But worse than that was the expression on Lucien's face. It was a combination of horrified alarm and shame.

Everything happened very quickly after that. Lucien sprang to his feet and shoved Terry so hard that, even though there was no comparison between their body weight, Terry lost his balance and fell backwards. Perhaps it was the sheer bulk of his body that caused him to fall with such force, but he went down like a sack of coal.

'*Run!*' Venetia screamed through the window to her friend and then trying to open the back door but without success.

By the time she'd raced around to the front of the cottage, Lucien had flung open the door and was already running, not towards the safety of the Hall, but in the direction of the woods. She yelled at him to slow down as she charged after him, but he didn't. She upped her pace, twice looking over her shoulder to see if Terry was coming after them, but there was no sign of him.

When she finally caught up with Lucien, he'd come to a stop in the densest part of the wood and was bent double trying to catch his breath, a painfully ragged wheeze coming from his chest.

She put a hand out to him, to try and rub his back, to calm him so his breathing could return to normal. But he shuddered at her touch.

'Just go!' he rasped at her. 'Leave me alone!'

'No,' she said firmly. 'I'm staying.'

'But I don't want you anywhere near me. Everything is going to be so much worse now. Don't you understand that?'

'We have to tell someone what . . . what Terry made you do. He'll lose his job and will be forced to leave.'

Tears began streaming down Lucien's cheeks. 'Nobody must ever know!' he cried. 'You must promise not to tell anyone. I couldn't bear the shame. I only did it because he said he'd force you to do it to him if I didn't.'

Dismayed and sickened at Lucien's words, and wanting more than anything to undo the damage Terry had caused him, she said, 'Everything's going to be all right now, Lucien. You'll see. That vile man isn't going to hurt you ever again.'

How naive she was to think that it could be as simple as that.

Chapter Thirty-Five

'Can you believe the outright nerve of the woman? She's only cooking his favourite meals and forcing him to be like a bloody father to Finlay! And if she thinks for one minute I'm going to stand by and let her steal Ben from right under my nose, just like she's stolen Emily, she'd better think again!'

There was a resounding silence in Cassie's ear and she was on the verge of asking if her mother was still there, when, and with infuriating predictability, her mother said, 'Darling, are you sure you're not letting your . . . '

'Go on, Mum,' Cassie said when her mother's voice tailed off, 'say it, don't hold back as though I'm going to fall apart at any implied criticism.'

'It's not a criticism, merely an observation. A concern.'

'Go ahead then, just say it. What's your concern, that I'm allowing my insecurities to get the better of me, that I'm so scared of losing Ben that I see danger in every woman who comes onto his radar? That's what you're thinking, isn't it?'

'Of course I don't think that, don't be silly.'

'What then?' demanded Cassie, childish defensiveness crackling like static through her at being called silly. *What was silly worrying about the threat of another woman making a move on your partner?*

The man in front of her in the self-service checkout queue

turned around to look at her. She gave him a ferocious death-stare and indicated none too politely that one of the self-service tills was now free. He made a beeline for it, leaving her to realise that she had turned into one of those hateful people who conducted overly loud discussions on their mobiles while forcing anyone within range to hear what was being said.

Tuning back into what her mother was saying, Cassie heard: 'It's nothing but pre-wedding jitters you're experiencing, every bride feels anxious before their big day.'

Cassie had to admire her mother's nerve at resorting to that tried and tested old cookie, but she wasn't falling for it. They both knew that Cassie had huge trust issues and doubts could so easily railroad her from the path of rational thought. She knew all that, she knew it with every fibre of her being, but she just couldn't stop herself from imagining the worst. And right now, the worst was a she-wolf in designer sheep's clothing currently living in the hen coop. That was probably a muddle of a metaphor, but Cassie knew what she meant.

'We haven't even set a firm date for the wedding,' she said, 'so why would I be experiencing pre-wedding nerves?' This was another area of annoyance and concern for Cassie. She was all for setting a date and making plans, but recently when Cassie had raised the subject, Emily had responded with an expression of distilled condemnation.

'Really?' she'd said. 'You want to talk about that when we've only just had Dad's funeral?'

'She's like an evil genius,' Cassie had whispered to Ben in bed that night. 'She turns everything I say into a weapon against me. And it's more than ten days since the funeral, so not *just* after. She seems to think that because Drew is dead life has to stop for everyone, especially us!'

As soon as Drew's body had been released following the lengthy process of effectively rubber-stamping that he was actually dead, his funeral could then go ahead. Emily had been adamant that Cassie wasn't to attend the service at the crematorium.

'It would be hypocritical of you to be there,' she'd asserted, 'and you'd only be doing it to look good, like you were trying to do the right thing. And that would stink.'

While it was true that Cassie was relieved that she didn't have to go through with the charade, she was miffed that she was being told what she could and could not do by her daughter. She had tried making a case for being at the crematorium to support Emily, but had been rewarded with an epic roll of the girl's eyes.

Ben had been his usual accepting self, of course he had, and had proposed they hold fire for a little longer. 'We've waited this long to marry, what are a few more weeks?' he'd said.

Just how many more weeks, though? Cassie had privately questioned. At the rate they were going, Rosalyn and her son were never going to leave and move into a place of their own. Every day that went by, and now that Rosalyn was no longer hiding under the duvet, the apartment felt more and more claustrophobic. Was it so very bad of her that Cassie wanted her lovely home back? Surely that wasn't unreasonable?

'Date or no date,' her mother said, hauling Cassie back up from the darkest depths of her thoughts, 'it's a big step for you, isn't it, so it's only natural that you might be worrying, you know, subconsciously?'

'Yes, you're probably right, Mum,' Cassie said tiredly. Sometimes it was easier to give in and agree with her mother.

Plonking her basket of shopping on a self-service till that was now free, and trying not to resent the fact that she was doing a job she wasn't paid to do, she began scanning the items with one hand while holding her mobile to her ear and listening to her mother saying it was ages since she and Dad had seen her.

'It's not that long, Mum,' Cassie said.

'It feels like it. Anyway, why don't you and Ben, and Emily, come for lunch on Sunday? Maybe your sister and Simon and the children could come too if they're free. It might be just what you need, a nice family get-together. Especially Emily at this tricky time for her.'

'That's a lovely idea, Mum,' Cassie said, 'but I wouldn't be surprised if Emily says something like it wouldn't be fair to leave Rosalyn and Finlay on their own.' Cassie could just imagine Emily saying, *Oh, that's right, rub it in for Rosalyn that she doesn't have any family!*

'Well, I suppose we could always—'

Cassie nearly dropped the bottle of wine she had just scanned. 'No, Mum!' she hissed. 'We are not including them into what you've just referred to as a *family* lunch. *They* are not family.'

'But Emily thinks of little Finlay that way, doesn't she? And technically he is.'

Since when had Drew and Rosalyn's son become *Little Finlay* in her mother's head? Cassie wanted to ask, but wisely didn't.

Her shopping now bagged and paid for, Cassie ended the call and set off for her car with her mother's last words reverberating inside her head.

'Try talking to Rosalyn, it's probably what you both need, a proper clearing-of-the-air conversation. It can't be easy for her, accepting charity from Drew's first wife. Imagine yourself in her shoes.'

Yeah right, thanks for that, Mum, thought Cassie, *like I want to spend a second of my time in that woman's shoes!*

She'd made it as far as the sliding doors to go out into the rain and chilly darkness, but as though she needed to prove to herself that she really wasn't such a terrible person, she stopped to buy a poppy from the man and woman sitting behind a table festooned with poppies and Royal British Legion leaflets.

Resting her shopping on the floor at her feet so she could dig out her debit card, she realised that the man behind the table was the one who had been on the receiving end of her death stare.

'I'll have a poppy, please,' she said, and then as if trying to make a good impression, added, 'second thoughts, make it two of the bigger ones.' *Now she just sounded flashy!* Waving her card over the payment machine, she glanced at the man, guessing he was about the same age as her parents. Which compounded her shame, that and the medals pinned to his jacket.

'I'm sorry about earlier,' she said. 'I'm not normally like that, so rude to people.'

He acknowledged her apology with a slight dip of his head. 'We all have bad days,' he said. 'I hope yours gets better.'

'Thank you,' she said, feeling suitably chastened.

Outside it was chucking it down and as she dashed to where she'd parked her car, she wondered what the man's perspective on a bad day was compared to hers. He'd probably fought in a war somewhere. He was too old for Iraq or Afghanistan, she decided, so maybe he'd been in the Falklands? That's where an uncle of Ben's had served when he'd been in the navy. He never spoke about what he had seen or done but Cassie knew Ben's family was very proud of him.

She drove out of the supermarket car park and joining the traffic in the glow of car lights she headed for home, her mood as dark as the November night sky. She had to do better. She had to change the narrative of her thoughts.

But how? How could she rid herself of the fear that she could lose what meant most in the world to her: Emily *and* Ben. If she wasn't careful, she was in serious danger of pushing them both away. Not that Ben had shown the slightest inkling of dissatisfaction with her or their relationship. Quite the contrary. He was as loving as he'd always been.

She sighed heavily, and not in the right frame of mind to listen to the latest true crime podcast she'd started late last night when she couldn't sleep, she wondered how Ben was getting on. He was in Lucerne attending a symposium on genetics and today he was giving a keynote speech about leukaemia, specifically regarding children. He was easily the cleverest person she knew and her awe of his intelligence together with her pride for the work he did were two of the many reasons she loved him.

Ben hadn't been the first man to come into her life after Drew, but the ones before him had been of little consequence in comparison. Cassie had always loved telling the story of how they'd met at Linton Zoo. Cassie was there with Emily and it was Emily who had noticed Ben first in the aviary area. He was with two small children, both younger than Emily, and he was holding a very in-depth conversation about DNA with a parrot inside a large cage. Or more precisely, he was faking the conversation as the parrot's responses were limited to the occasional squawk, which the attractively smiley man interpreted as agreement with what he was saying. He did it in such a convincing way that the children with him, and also Emily, were spellbound. He had his audience in the palm of his hand and in a charmingly unconscious way. He appeared to be enjoying himself as much as they were.

Cassie had assumed he was the father of the small boy and girl, but when he suggested it was time to go and see something else, they chorused, 'No, Uncle Ben, talk to the parrot again!' It was then that Cassie looked at him with slightly more interest. Fresh-faced. Slim. Sandy-gold hair. Faded jeans. Hoodie. Trainers. Attractive. Yes, definitely attractive.

He caught her eye and smiled. 'Yes, you did hear right,' he said, 'I'm Uncle Ben and I've heard all the jokes about rice that you could possibly imagine.'

She'd smiled back at him and asked if he was always as chatty with parrots and was he any relation to Dr Doolittle?

They'd later bumped into each other when buying ice creams and again when queuing for the toilets.

'If I gave you my mobile number, would there be any chance of hearing from you?' he'd asked.

'There might be,' she'd said.

She'd called him the next day and the rest, as the cliché goes, is history. From very early on in their relationship, and after she'd explained about the absence of Emily's father in her life, he understood that the only way she would trust him was to prove himself to her. And he did. Everything about him was so genuine and caring, not just with her but with Emily. He was completely reliable, which may not sound an obviously attractive character trait, but to her, it was. And not once did he ever lie or patronise Cassie for her insecurities or use them to gain an advantage over her.

So why, why, *WHY* was she so ready to believe the worst of him, that he could be taken in by Rosalyn with her ah-poor-little-me routine? Or was that what appealed to Ben, the desire to be a gallant knight coming to the rescue of a damsel in distress?

The wind was gusting, and the rain was coming down even harder when she drove through the illuminated stone pillars of the entrance to Hope Hall. It had rained so much since the start of November the level of the River Cam had risen dramatically, and flood warnings kept being given.

Ahead of her lights glowed at windows in the stately building that she was lucky to call home. She always found the sight of the Hall at night especially spectacular and she still marvelled that she lived here.

She was living her best life, and in so many ways, she reminded herself firmly, so it was time to knuckle down and make sure she didn't lose it through doubting Ben's love for her. With her mother's words still playing on a loop inside her head, she decided she would talk to Rosalyn. Or, as a more apt way of putting it, she would *open negotiations* with Rosalyn.

She made sure to park exactly within their apartment's allotted space – the Enforcers had made a fuss at the latest residents' meeting about parking infringements and incorrect use of bins. They'd also complained about the fireworks Ben had set off for Finlay on bonfire night earlier in the week. God, they were petty!

She was just carrying the bags of shopping across the illuminated courtyard towards the arched oak doors, when one of the doors was flung open, followed by a tumult of raised voices. Surprised to see Emily and Rosalyn, Cassie was then even more surprised to see they appeared to be in the midst of an almighty row.

'How could you have been so careless?' screamed Rosalyn. 'You were supposed to be looking after him!'

'I've told you a million times already, I took my eye off him for no more than a couple of seconds!' Emily shouted back.

'And that's all it takes, you stupid bitch!'

'What the hell's going on?' demanded Cassie, instinctively rushing to protect and defend her daughter from the onslaught of vitriol coming at her from Rosalyn.

A third figure then appeared through the open doorway; it was Venetia. 'He won't have gone far,' she said calmly, 'we'll find him and Bon-Bon in no time at all.'

At that, Rosalyn started frantically screaming her son's name at the top of her voice. 'Finlay! Finlay where are you? Finlay! *Finlay!*'

Darting about the courtyard in the wind and rain, Rosalyn looked and sounded completely crazed, but having guessed what had happened, Cassie didn't blame her. When Emily had been a toddler and had wandered off in a busy shop, Cassie had experienced several heart-stopping minutes when she had been petrified with sheer terror that her precious child had been snatched. There was no bigger fear for a parent.

'If Finlay's missing,' she said, 'we need to look for him in the most efficient way we can. We need to find the brightest torches we all have as well as have our mobiles to hand, that way we can spread out and call one another when we've found him. How long has he been missing?'

Emily opened her mouth to speak, but then clamped a hand over it and started to cry.

It was Venetia who spoke. 'We're not entirely sure. One minute he was playing with Bon-Bon in my apartment when Emily brought him down to me, and the next we realised they'd both gone.'

'At a rough guess, how long?' asked Cassie.

'Twenty minutes, maybe more,' replied Venetia.

'Have you searched the building for them?'

Venetia nodded. 'It was the first thing we did. Finlay probably got it into his head to take Bon-Bon for a walk.'

'What if he falls in the river, Mum?' Emily suddenly wailed. 'If he drowns it will be my fault.'

There was no time for Cassie to hug or reassure her daughter, the priority was to find Finlay and Bon-Bon.

Chapter Thirty-Six

Within no time Cassie had organised a search party, having rounded up some of the neighbours, including the Enforcers, as well as Nina who was just back from work. Unsurprisingly, the Enforcers were scandalised when they learnt about Bon-Bon.

'What?' cried Cheryl, 'you've had a dog living with you all this time?'

'But it's against the rules!' exclaimed Joanna.

Stemming the flow of petty outrage, Cassie said, 'You can sort that out later, for now finding Finlay and Bon-Bon is all that's important.'

With everyone equipped with torches and mobiles, Cassie marshalled the party into an effective task force, directing them to search in couples the vast area of grounds. She sent the Enforcers and their husbands to search the bin store area and garage block, also inside any unlocked garages.

Rosalyn was still vociferously blaming Emily and Venetia for Finlay's disappearance, so Cassie decided it would be better for neither of them to accompany the distraught mother, and so she asked Nina, always the most composed of people, to pair up with Rosalyn and search the stretch of riverbank where the lower branches of the willow trees were now deeply submerged by the raised level of the water. There was a chance that Finlay could have taken shelter from the rain within the canopy of the branches, although it was beyond her why the boy had decided to go out into the dark when the weather was so horrendous.

The Gilburns from No.8 hurried away to search the area around the tennis court and the Bennetts from No.7 set off for another stretch of the riverbank, and the Atkins from No.3 offered to search the huge expanse of lawn, leaving Cassie, Emily and Venetia to search the woods. As Venetia said, she knew the woodland area better than most, so it made sense that she led the way.

'It could be that Bon-Bon ran off to the place where we always walk and then Finlay chased after him,' Venetia explained. 'It would be so easy to get lost in amongst the trees, it would be like a maze to such a young child.'

As plausible as this suggestion was, it upset Emily more than she already felt. 'He'll be so scared if he's lost,' she said in a small tight voice, sounding like a scared child herself.

The cold rain stinging against her face, Cassie caught hold of her daughter's hand and squeezed it reassuringly. 'We'll find him,' she said, 'I promise.'

'But what if—'

'No!' Cassie said sternly, stopping Emily from saying the unthinkable, 'we're not going to consider any what-ifs, because they're not going to happen.'

With Venetia striding on ahead while calling out to Bon-Bon, and Cassie and Emily sticking as close to her as they could and shouting Finlay's name, the light from their torches flashed off the trees. It gave Cassie *Blair Witch Project* chills, a film she hadn't thought of in years.

High above their heads, the tree branches creaked and swayed in the fierce wind and gripping her daughter's hand more firmly to chase off the fear that was growing in her, Cassie shouted louder still to Finlay. Emily did the same, combining her voice with Cassie's, but the wind was so wild even in the relative shelter of the woods, their voices were snatched away, and Cassie doubted they'd be heard. She doubted too that they would hear a small boy cry out to them or hear Bon-Bon barking in response to their shouts.

It was good that Venetia knew the woods as well as she did because after what felt like a lifetime of searching and shouting until they were hoarse, Cassie had the unsettling sensation of being thoroughly disorientated. She didn't have a clue where they were in relation to the Hall or the river.

Just as she was going to check with Venetia that she still knew where they were and that they weren't going round in useless circles, the trees thinned, and their torches picked out a large area of overgrown grass lined on one side by towering rhododendron bushes that loomed out of the darkness like enormous unworldly monsters and demons.

'We've reached the river,' Venetia called back over her shoulder, her voice barely audible in the wind and the rain that lashed down on them, now they were away from the shelter of the trees. In the beams of light from their torches, Cassie saw that Venetia was right, for there ahead of them was indeed the river. She had no idea how they'd reached it but as they drew near the swell of the water, it looked black and oily and eerily menacing in the darkness. It had none of its usual benign charm when the sun was shining on it.

'What was that?' asked Emily urgently.

'What was what?' answered Cassie.

'I think I heard something . . . a voice. A cry.'

All three of them came to a stop.

'There!' cried Emily, pointing ahead of them. 'It's Finlay!' She broke into a run through the long sodden grass and Cassie chased after her, the pair of them dodging around Venetia, the light from their torches bouncing high and low as they went.

The nearer they got to the river, the more clearly Cassie could hear and see that Emily had been right. They had found Finlay! He was crouched on the ground and crying hard. Crying was good though. It meant that nothing seriously bad had happened.

But another glance at the river told Cassie something seriously bad *had* happened.

Leaving Emily to deal with Finlay, she dropped her torch, pulled off her sopping wet parka, removed her shoes and waded into the blackness of the water.

Surprised how deep it was and gasping at the icy coldness of it, she had to swim the last few yards to where poor Bon-Bon's lifeless body was caught in a tangled mass of driftwood and river debris. Scooping him up in her arms, and clutching him against her chest, she swam on her back to the riverbank using just her legs. From behind her, she could hear Finlay crying even harder and then there was another cry, a deeper and throatier cry and it tugged at Cassie's heart.

Before she had reached the bank, Venetia had waded into the water and was taking Bon-Bon from Cassie. Cradling her beloved dog tenderly in her arms, the woman let out an unbearably piteous moan of anguish.

Chapter Thirty-Seven

In the short space of time Nina had known Venetia, she had grown immensely fond of the older woman and valued their friendship. Nina had particularly appreciated Venetia's opinions and gentle offerings of advice, and above all, her positivity.

But to see her now so forlorn and dazed, as though quite literally overnight the stuffing had been knocked out of her, was unbearable to witness. The pain Venetia was experiencing was a palpable reminder for Nina of what she had gone through in the days after Hugh had died.

Selfishly, she didn't want to feel that all over again because in the last few weeks, having convinced herself that she really was allowed to step out of the role of widow and take the first tentative steps of being in a relationship with Jakob, she had felt genuinely happy. Yet here she was, with Cassie's help, and before it was even fully light, digging a grave and feeling with each shovel of earth she dug up and tossed to one side that she was losing herself back down into that familiar dark hole of heartbroken despair. Grief never left you, that was the truth of it. Time didn't heal, you merely learnt to live with the pain of loss. Death, she thought grimly, was simply a way of life.

'Do you think it's deep enough now?' asked Cassie.

'No, not yet,' said Nina, then lowering her voice so that Venetia wouldn't hear, 'we don't want to risk an animal digging Bon-Bon up, do we?'

Cassie shuddered. 'Good point. But it's hard going with all these tree roots.'

'I know, but we promised we'd make a proper job of it, and we will.'

'It's a shame Ben isn't back yet from his trip,' Cassie said, 'we could have done with his extra muscle. If that doesn't offend our feminist sensitivities.'

Nina stamped her booted foot down extra hard on the shoulder of her spade. 'I'm all for girl power,' she grimaced as the spade hit what sounded like a stone, 'but common sense trumps every time in my book. If Jakob had been around, I might have roped him in to help.'

When Venetia had said she was going to bury Bon-Bon here in the woods at Hope Hall, Nina had volunteered to dig the hole for her. She had stayed with Venetia for most of last night, only returning to her own apartment when she was convinced that Venetia was all right.

'You only have to call me, and I'll come, it doesn't matter what the time is,' she'd said when preparing to leave.

'That's kind of you, but I'll be fine,' Venetia had said mechanically.

When Nina left the poor woman alone with the body of her precious dog wrapped in his favourite old blanket and placed in his basket, Nina's heart had been heavy with sadness. The sight of Venetia earlier lovingly drying Bon-Bon's wet apricot fur with a towel was an image she didn't think she would ever forget. Back in her apartment and before getting ready for bed, she had texted Cassie to ask how things were going with her.

A bit shaky, Cassie had replied. *V awkward between Emily and Rosalyn, but Finlay sleeping now.*

Nina had then told Cassie that she had offered to bury Bon-Bon in the morning and Cassie had immediately said she'd help. Nina had gone on to explain that they had to do it in secret, that Venetia didn't want anyone else to know, especially not the Enforcers who would probably cite some rule that under no circumstances should the grounds of Hope Hall be used as an unauthorised burial place.

She had just got into bed when her mobile rang and expecting it to be Cassie with something she'd forgotten to say before, she was surprised, and pleased, to see that it was Jakob. He was back in Oslo for a big family occasion, his grandfather's ninetieth birthday, as well as sourcing paintings by Norwegian artists which might fit with the Lavelle brand. He had invited Nina to go with him to meet his family, but she hadn't been ready for that step. He'd said he understood and that there was no hurry.

They had agreed to take things at Nina's pace, which was slow. Very slow. And that meant they hadn't gone public with their relationship.

'I need to adjust to this new me before we invite others into our relationship,' she'd explained to Jakob. 'In my experience, no relationship is just about two people, there are families involved, friends too. All of whom will have an opinion to offer, good and bad. I don't want to have to cope with that just yet.'

'Having met your husband's family, I understand completely,' he'd said astutely.

It felt odd hearing Jakob refer to Hugh in that way, but how else could he refer to Hugh? *Your dead husband* would sound too blunt and clinical. And *your ex* wasn't accurate, because a dead husband wasn't an ex, he was forever destined to be *The Husband*. *First Husband* if there was a second one.

Nina had told Jakob last night on the phone about the search party for the missing boy and the tragic discovery of Venetia's little dog in the river. Jakob had been a good listener and Nina had felt better for chatting with him. He'd cheered her up by telling her a few stories about his grandparents whom he was clearly very fond of, and about some of the interesting paintings he'd found which he hoped she'd like. He also said how much he missed her and was looking forward to seeing her when he returned. She'd admitted that she missed him too. The words had slipped from her effortlessly and were entirely true. She did miss him. She really did. She missed the fun he'd brought into her life. Part of her wished that she had closed the gallery and gone with him to Oslo, but if she had, then Cassie would have had to do this gruesome task alone.

The two of them were still digging, the hole almost large enough now to contain the old champagne crate which Venetia had previously used for storing hats and was now to be Bon-Bon's coffin. Nina was thankful that last night's storm had blown itself out, so at least they weren't doing this awful task in the wind and rain.

'When is Jakob coming back?' asked Cassie, once again breaking into Nina's thoughts.

'Next week.'

'And?'

'And what?'

'Is distance making the heart grow fonder?'

Cassie was the only person in whom Nina had partially confided about Jakob. Cassie had been absurdly pleased at the news that Nina was allowing him into her life and Nina couldn't help but be caught up in her infectious delight, thinking how easy it was to talk to a new friend, a friend who hadn't ever known Hugh, than an old one who might view things differently.

'Let's talk about that another time,' Nina said quietly, glancing over her shoulder to where Venetia was perched on the fallen tree, which according to Cassie was where she had always sat when she took Bon-Bon for his late-night walk. It was why Venetia had chosen this spot to bury the dog. The champagne crate with its precious cargo was on her lap, her hands holding it firmly as though she might never let go of it. Her face bore an expression of pained bewilderment. It was the face of grief and was an expression that Nina knew all too well.

'Sorry,' said Cassie, 'not the time and place. I'm just talking for the sake of it. I need something to think about other than the catastrophe that Rosalyn's presence here has caused. I wish I'd been firmer and said she couldn't stay, then Bon-Bon would still be alive.'

'You mustn't blame yourself,' Nina said, 'it wasn't your fault. It really wasn't.'

'Why don't you two take a break for a few minutes?' Venetia called over to Nina and Cassie. 'Or at least let me have a go at digging.'

Nina shook her head. 'We're okay to keep going, aren't we, Cassie?' she said.

'Absolutely,' Cassie replied. 'Another ten minutes and we'll have it done.'

In fact, they had it done in less time and Nina knew that they were now facing the most difficult part of what they had come here to do. Going over to Venetia, she said, 'Are you ready, or do you want to wait a bit longer?'

Venetia held the box out for Nina to take from her so she could stand up. Once she was on her feet, she took the box back and went over to the hole. 'It's so much bigger than I imagined,' she said faintly.

'We thought the deeper the better,' murmured Nina. She and Cassie were now standing either side of Venetia. 'Would you like to do this part on your own?' she asked.

Venetia nodded, her lips tightly compressed as though she couldn't speak. Tears were pooling in her eyes and giving her the space she needed, Nina and Cassie went and sat on the fallen tree.

Her own eyes filling with tears, Nina could hardly bear to watch Venetia stoop and then get down on her knees to lower the wooden box, oh, so carefully, into the hole. Next to Nina, Cassie sniffed then searched her coat pockets for a tissue. Nina had come prepared, and she dug out a small packet of Kleenex from her own coat pocket and passed a tissue to Cassie.

Both dabbing their eyes and trying to blow their noses as discreetly as possible, Nina was drawn back to the day Hugh's body had been cremated. Hilary had wanted her son to be buried, for everything to be done 'properly' as she saw it, but Nina had insisted that Hugh's wishes were respected. He had made it clear from the day he was diagnosed with a brain tumour, and should he not survive it, exactly how he wanted his remains to be dealt with. The service at the crematorium had been efficient and quick, perfunctory even. Hilary had hated it and had told anyone who would listen that it was simply dreadful, and Hugh had deserved better.

A week later and they assembled again, a much smaller group this time, to carry out the final part of Hugh's wishes, which was to hire a boat from Fen Ditton, and then scatter his ashes on the River Cam. The whole thing had been rather beautiful, tranquil, and moving. The company Nina had used had organised everything, a two-hour trip with a picnic hamper and what they referred to as a water ceremony set; it included a biodegradable water urn for the ashes and flower petals for each member of the party to throw onto the surface of the water. The trip had been timed for when the sun slowly dropped from the sky and, as it set on the distant horizon, that was the exact moment Nina had cast the urn into the water. She had been told it would float for a few minutes and her eyes never once left it until she'd watched it slowly disappear beneath the surface of the water.

For once Hilary could find no fault and went as far as saying that Hugh would have approved. She was also grateful to Nina for allowing her to have some of Hugh's ashes for her to keep. Nina could have done the same, but she hadn't wanted to do that; it felt too morbid. Keith had shared with Nina that Hilary kept the vial of ashes on her bedside table, next to a photograph of Hugh when he'd been a boy, so that it was the last thing she looked at before turning out the light and the first thing she saw when she woke in the morning.

'We should take over now,' whispered Cassie.

'You're right,' Nina said, seeing that Venetia had picked up one of the spades and was beginning to shovel the earth they'd dug out back into the hole.

They went over to her. 'We'll do that,' Nina said gently, 'you go and sit down and open the hamper you put together.'

Venetia handed over the spade to her and left them to it. Together, Nina and Cassie made short work of filling in the hole, tamping the rich earth down with their booted feet, then adding a layer of leaves and twigs. Afterwards, they joined Venetia where she'd opened a bottle of champagne, and they drank a toast to Bon-Bon.

'To the darlingest of companions,' Venetia said before dissolving into tears, with Nina and Cassie doing the same.

Chapter Thirty-Eight

There were so many flowers in the apartment, Venetia had run out of places to put them. As kind as everyone had been to express how sorry they were about Bon-Bon, she really would have preferred to be left alone. She had felt the same when her husband, Lawrence, died four years ago.

The steady stream of neighbours calling at her door had begun late that morning. Some of them she had exchanged no more than a few words with since she'd moved in, but they had wanted her to know that they were thinking of her. One or two admitted that they wouldn't object to a rule change and that people should be allowed to have a well-behaved pet if that's what they wanted. Their thoughtfulness had been well-meant but just the sheer act of being polite to them had made the day even more emotionally draining than it already was.

After returning from the woods where they'd buried Bon-Bon at first light that morning, Cassie had offered to stay with Venetia, to keep her company, but she had declined the offer because she desperately wanted to be alone. As she had last night when Nina had been so reluctant to leave her. But she saw now that she'd made a mistake, for if Cassie had stayed with her, her friend would have dealt with the neighbours and the weight of their sympathy.

It was the horrible manner in which Bon-Bon died that really upset Venetia; it was just too awful. She couldn't understand why he'd gone into the river; he'd never once been tempted so much as to dip a paw into the water whenever they'd walked along the bank, and in the very same spot where he'd drowned. In fact, he'd hated to be wet. Whenever she had washed him in the bath, he'd looked at her with such sad, reproachful eyes, even though she made sure the water was warm. His body would shake with disapproval at such ignominy. He would only cheer up when she was drying him with a towel and a hairdryer on a lowish setting. For some reason, he'd loved the hairdryer, perhaps because it restored him to his beautifully fluffy state.

The memories were suddenly too much for her, especially combined with the thought of how she'd dried him last night before wrapping his lifeless body in his favourite blanket and putting him in his basket. She had to fight to retain her composure, but it was no use and collapsing into the nearest armchair and covering her face with her hands, she rocked back and forth, the tears flowing. She rocked and cried, rocked and cried until her tears finally gave way to a different emotion: anger.

Anger was something she rarely succumbed to, but whenever she thought of Finlay sneaking out of her apartment with Bon-Bon and literally taking the dog to his death, she wanted to seize that boy by his shoulders and shake the truth out of him, to make him tell her exactly what had happened. Was it simply an accident, or . . . or had the boy forced Bon-Bon into the water? Had he imagined it would be fun to see if the dog could swim? Could a child of his young age be so sickeningly cruel?

Forcing herself to get a grip on her emotions, Venetia dried her eyes and took a deep inhalation of breath. Tormenting herself with these thoughts wouldn't help in the slightest, Bon-Bon would still be dead, and her heart would still be broken. She had to accept that she might never know the truth.

Cassie had promised that she would try to get to the bottom

of what happened. 'It might take a bit of time,' she'd told Venetia in the woods this morning, 'but I'll do my best to speak to Finlay when he and his mother have calmed down.'

Venetia found it hard to imagine Rosalyn ever calming down. After Finlay and Bon-Bon had been found, everyone had gathered in the communal hallway. For Rosalyn it should have been a moment to thank her lucky stars that her son was safe, but holding him so tightly he complained that she was hurting him, she had screamed at Emily that if Finlay had drowned as well as the dog, it would have been her fault. The colour had drained from Emily's face, and she had fled up the stairs, her sobs loud enough for them all to hear.

'That was unnecessary,' Cassie had said to Rosalyn. 'I don't care how upset you are, you have no right to speak to my daughter that way.'

Perhaps embarrassed and not wanting to witness a scene that might turn nasty, people had drifted away, one or two giving Venetia sympathetic looks as she carried the bedraggled body of Bon-Bon upstairs to her apartment, Nina following closely behind.

The loud ringing of her phone had Venetia glancing around her for it. She eventually located it over by the kettle where she'd made herself a cup of tea but had forgotten to drink it.

She answered the phone with a gruff 'Hello.'

'Venetia, it's me, Ronnie. I've just heard the terrible news. I'm so very sorry.'

Venetia was stunned. 'How?' she said. 'How have you heard?'

'Cassie sent me a message. She thought you might need, well, you know, a friend to talk to.'

For a moment she couldn't speak, so touched was she by Cassie's thoughtfulness, Ronnie's too.

'You still there, Venetia?'

She forced the words out. 'Cassie shouldn't have bothered you when you have so much going on there with your hotel.'

'Quit all that nonsense!' he said hotly. 'I know how much that little dog meant to you and that means more to me than dealing with a bunch of useless lawyers and accountants here. Is there anything I can do?'

'That's very sweet of you, but there's nothing anyone can do. I just need to pull myself together. And don't you dare say otherwise or I'll start blubbing again, and I've done quite enough of that already.'

'Is this the bit when I say, that's the spirit old girl, stiff upper lip and best foot forward and other assorted phrases designed to buck one up?'

She had to smile at that. 'Maybe not. But I do appreciate you taking the time to call me.'

'Look, here's a suggestion you might like to mull over. Why don't you hop on a plane and come here for a break? Getting away for a few days might help. Give you something else to think about. A change of scene and all that. I can't guarantee the weather will be that good, but I'll wager it's better than Cambridge right now. What do you say?'

'I think that's a lovely thought on your part, but I'd rather stay here. I don't think I'd be very good company right now.'

'Okay, I shan't press you, but if you change your mind, you only have to give me a call. Promise?'

'Yes,' she said.

'Did you have your fingers crossed behind your back as you said that?'

'Are you accusing me of lying?'

'Damned straight I am!'

Again, she smiled. 'Thank you,' she said.

'What for?'

'For doing the impossible, making me feel slightly better.'

'In that case, I'll give you another tinkle tomorrow.'

No sooner had she said goodbye to Ronnie than there was a ring at the doorbell. Dreading yet another neighbour bearing flowers and condolences, she was tempted to ignore whoever it was, but good manners forbad her from being so rude.

When she opened the door, it was the last person on earth she wanted to see standing in front of her.

'Can I come in?' asked Rosalyn.

'No,' Venetia said, holding the door firmly in place. 'I'm not at home to visitors.'

The young woman frowned. 'What do you mean? You are at home. You're standing right in front of me.'

'I mean,' said Venetia very slowly as though she were dealing with a very stupid child, 'I don't want to see anyone right now.'

'Oh. Well. I get that. But I just wanted to say, you know, I'm sorry about your dog.'

'I don't want your apology. And if you want to apologise to anyone, say sorry to Emily. You were wrong to blame her for what your son did. He's your responsibility, not Emily's.'

Rosalyn looked aghast. 'I had every right to blame her,' she fired back loudly. 'She should have been keeping a better eye on Finlay and apart from anything else, I was out of my mind with fear and panic! Do you have any idea what it's like to lose your husband and then discover your child is missing and all the time be terrified that his body might be found in the river? Do you have the slightest understanding of what that might feel like?'

'I'd appreciate you not raising your voice at me,' Venetia said sternly. 'Or giving me a lecture on how I might feel. Thanks to your son, my dog is dead.'

'It's hardly the same thing,' Rosalyn responded. 'You can easily buy another dog! My son is irreplaceable.'

'Then maybe you should take better care of him. What's more, you should teach your son that it's not right to steal someone's beloved pet.'

'He didn't steal your dog.'

'What would you call it, then?'

'He thought it would be nice to take the dog for a walk instead of it being cooped up in your apartment, where he shouldn't have been in the first place!'

Steadying herself and her left hand gripping the door firmly, Venetia said, 'For a person who came here to apologise, you don't sound the slightest bit sorry.'

'You didn't want my apology, so what else can I do?'

'I want to know the truth. I want to know what your son did with my dog. Bon-Bon would not have gone into the river, he hated water, so tell me why he ended up drowning in the river.'

Rosalyn's eyes blazed and she looked like she might actually strike Venetia. 'If you're suggesting what I think you are, then you're deranged! It was a dreadful accident. Finlay isn't even five years old, he wouldn't harm a fly, never mind a dog. What you're implying is disgusting!'

'I still want to know what happened. Something, or someone, made Bon-Bon go into the water and your son is the only person who knows the truth. If he's told you anything, you should tell me. You owe me that much because if it wasn't for your son, my dog would still be alive.'

Her face flushed, Rosalyn said, 'This is harassment. You need to stop saying these awful things.'

'And you need to leave.'

Chapter Thirty-Nine

Hearing the door to the apartment slam shut, Cassie swung round from the full-length window where she'd been watching Emily jogging. She'd been out there for ages, pounding along in the squelchy rain-sodden grass, pushing herself at a punishing pace, doubtless trying to exorcise last night from her mind.

Cassie had offered to keep her company, but Emily had said that she needed to be on her own. Not that Cassie had really wanted to go for a run with her daughter, she'd wanted to take advantage of Finlay not having his mother around for a few minutes so she could discreetly interrogate him. She'd promised Venetia that she'd try and talk to the boy in the hope of throwing light on what had happened last night and so the minute Rosalyn had gone to see Venetia, and at Cassie's suggestion, she'd done just that.

But what she'd managed to get out of the boy had shocked her and she didn't know what to do with the knowledge she now had.

'Your friend and neighbour is a crazy psycho!' blasted Rosalyn, stomping into the room.

'You can't surely be talking about Venetia,' Cassie said.

'I certainly am. She's as good as accused Finlay of killing her dog! Can you think of anything more sick or twisted?'

In view of what she now knew, Cassie said nothing. But then Rosalyn suddenly looked around her.

'Where's Finlay?' she demanded. 'You said you wouldn't let him out of your sight while I went downstairs. You promised!'

'Calm down, he's—'

'Don't you dare tell me to calm down in that irritatingly patronising way! My son is all I have left in the world!'

'I'll say it again,' Cassie said patiently, alarmed at the 0-to-60 speed of Rosalyn's temper, 'calm down and listen to me. Finlay is in his bedroom watching *Bluey* on his iPad.'

Perhaps not trusting Cassie, Rosalyn glared at her and hurtled across the room and to the bedroom at the farthest end of the hallway.

Murmured voices followed and Cassie was left wondering how to break it to Rosalyn what Finlay had just shared with her. And should she tell Venetia what she'd learnt? She shuddered at the thought. Wouldn't it be better that Venetia never knew what really happened so she could hang on to the belief that it was no more than a tragic accident?

Because the truth was repugnant. So shockingly repugnant Cassie now regretted involving herself. Playing at being detective had been a mistake. She'd done it with the right motive, but it had backfired on her badly for she was now embroiled in something that could have appalling repercussions.

To begin with, when she'd gone into Finlay's room and sat on the bed with him, subtly dropping leading questions into the conversation, he'd barely looked at her while replying, his eyes focused on the screen of his iPad. She'd wondered if he was making it up, but when she'd probed further, it became all too hideously clear what he was saying.

'The dog was naughty,' he'd said. 'He barked. He barked lots. Then he was naughty, and he bit me.'

That was when Finlay had shown her what appeared to be bite marks on his leg; a small circle of tiny pink indentations. Had his mother seen the marks? If so, why hadn't she said anything?

'And then I smacked him,' Finlay had continued, matter-of-factly. 'Because it was naughty to bite me.'

'Then what did you do?' Cassie had asked with a sense of dread.

'I picked him up and told him to be good. But he wouldn't be good. He barked in my ear and tried to bite me again. So I threw him into the water to make him be good. That's what you do when children are naughty.'

'What, throw children into the river?' repeated Cassie, horrified at what he'd said. Surely the boy had to be making things up now.

He'd looked up from the iPad screen at her question and shaken his head. 'No. A swimming pool. That's what happened to me when I was naughty. It was to make me be good.'

'Really? When was that?'

'At home. Before Daddy died.'

'And who threw you into the pool?'

He lowered his gaze, returning it to *Bluey* on his iPad. 'It's a secret,' he mumbled.

'Why is it a secret?' she asked, cautiously.

'Mummy said it was. She said Daddy would be cross if I told anyone. And if I told anyone then something really bad would happen to her.'

'Are you saying Daddy would be cross with Mummy?'

When he didn't answer her, Cassie said, 'Finlay, would Daddy have been cross with Mummy?'

He gave an imperceptible nod, and Cassie could see he was growing bored with the conversation. But she had one more question.

'So you threw Bon-Bon into the river to make him behave, just like what happened to you? Is that what you did last night?'

He rubbed his nose then slipped an exploratory finger inside a nostril. Pulling it out and wiping it on the front of his T-shirt, he said, 'Yes. But he still barked . . . and then he stopped barking, so that meant he was being good. And I called his name, but he didn't come out of the water, and I couldn't see him. I looked. And then I was scared because I was all on my own and I didn't know how to get home. And then I wet myself and I cried. Don't tell Mummy I did that.'

Cassie swallowed. 'What don't you want me to tell Mummy?'

'That I wet myself. I'm a big boy now and big boys don't wet themselves.'

'I'm sure Mummy wouldn't be cross with you for having a little accident. All children do.'

He shook his head. 'Mummy said Daddy wouldn't like it if I had an accident. He'd be cross.'

With a disturbing image of family life in Dubai now fast developing in her mind, Cassie knew that she had to talk to Rosalyn, to tell her what Finlay had shared with her. But ever since last night the boy's mother was so volatile. Would it be better to wait until things had settled down?

What was absolutely clear was that Finlay needed to speak to a professional, some kind of therapist who would teach him that you didn't go around drowning dogs to make them behave! If he could do that at so young an age, what would he do when he was a grown man?

Or was she overreacting? Was she too quick to give credence to what the boy had said because she still hated Drew and wanted to believe he was capable of being an abusive father and husband?

The answer could wait until Ben was home that evening, she decided. With his wholly rational and objective way of looking at things, Ben would know exactly what they should do.

Chapter Forty

Once more it was raining and as Nina stood at the gallery window looking out at the deserted cobbled street, she was grateful that the weather had held that morning while she and Cassie had been in the woods with Venetia burying Bon-Bon. To have carried out their sad task in the pouring rain would have been so much worse.

Cassie had originally planned to come in to the gallery today but had opted to stay at home to be with Emily. Nina had understood perfectly, and besides there really wasn't much to do. Other than worry if things would ever pick up again. Even during the pandemic when everything was shut during the various periods of lockdown, it hadn't felt as bad as this. People had still wanted nice things, perhaps more so when life had suddenly felt so fragile and ephemeral, and in consequence Lavelle's online sales had been remarkably buoyant.

But now, and following weeks of dreadful weather and endless news reports of the economy stalling, business was far from brisk. Nina wasn't the only one to feel the lack of customers; her neighbours in St Anne's Court – Jeremy who owned Quantock's Antiquarian Bookshop on one side and Philip who owned Blythe's Antiques directly opposite – had both complained bitterly that if things didn't improve, they might just as well pull the shutters down and go home. For good. To ease their boredom, they had taken to popping in to chat with Nina. She knew them of old as they'd both been great friends with her parents. They had known Nina since she was a child and still occasionally treated her in much the same way, especially so since Hugh's death, seeing it as their duty, in the guise of avuncular uncles, to ensure she was all right.

Today was Philip's seventy-first birthday and he and Jeremy were coming in later to drink to the passing of yet another year. She really wasn't in the mood for company, not after the events of last night and this morning, but it would have been churlish to disappoint the two old friends.

However, within no time of their arrival on the dot of three o'clock, and armed with a bottle of Veuve Clicquot and some of Jeremy's delicious homemade cheese straws, her mood was pleasantly improved as they traded insults with one another in their customary fashion. They continued in this way for some minutes while topping up their glasses until Jeremy turned his attention on Nina.

'So what's happened to the delectably handsome young Jakob?' he enquired. 'We enjoyed having him around again, he brightened the place up a treat.'

Nina winced at the word 'young'. 'He's in Oslo for a while,' she said, non-committally. Then more teasingly, 'And are you saying I don't brighten the place up enough for you?'

'Darling, you're the brightest star in St Anne's Court, and always will be,' replied Philip, 'but please say that Jakob is definitely coming back to us.'

'He is, indeed,' she said, 'he's working at Lavelle's on a permanent basis now.'

'That's excellent news!' said Philip, helping himself to another cheese straw.

'Now, now, don't you go getting any ideas about him,' Jeremy said warningly. 'You're far too old for the likes of Jakob.'

'You silly old fool,' Philip remonstrated, 'I'm not in the slightest bit interested in him, why would I be when he only has eyes for our darling Nina?'

Nina spluttered on a mouthful of champagne which she'd just been about to swallow, narrowly avoiding spitting it across her desk.

Philip laughed. 'Touched a nerve, have I, sweetie?' he said with a playful drawl.

'Don't be ridiculous,' she replied.

'Come off it, Nina, we all know that the boy is besotted with you, and who could blame him?'

'He's not a *boy*,' she said firmly. A little too firmly. 'He's a grown man.'

'To a pair of old duffers like us, he's but a fledgeling, as are you, petal,' remarked Jeremy. 'Now tell us all. Are you as madly in love with him as he is with you?'

Conscious that she was blushing furiously – this was the very kind of 'going public' she still wasn't ready for – Nina shook her head. 'Honestly,' she said with a tut, 'what have you two been drinking before coming here, a magnum of crazy-juice?'

Philip clapped his hands. 'The lady doth protest too much!'

'Spill the beans, dear one,' encouraged Jeremy. 'Don't make us beg, not when we're so fond of you.'

'I wouldn't dream of making you beg,' she said, 'but seriously all I can share with you is that—' She broke off.

'Go on,' Jeremy urged, leaning forward in his chair.

But Nina didn't. Because there in the pouring rain out on the street looking in through the window was a pitifully bedraggled Hilary. Next to her was a man in a high-vis jacket and he appeared to have a hand placed firmly on Hilary's arm.

'Is that Hugh's mother?' asked Jeremy, following her gaze and frowning.

'Somebody should tell her about timing,' muttered Philip, 'because hers is decidedly off!'

Sensing that something awful must have happened, Nina went to the door.

Hilary sat in stony silence while Nina drove her home to Madingley. To anything Nina said, the woman kept her mouth rigidly shut and her gaze ahead of her. On her lap, she clutched her handbag as though terrified it might be snatched from her grasp. It reminded Nina of Venetia that morning in the woods when she had held on so tightly to the wooden box which had contained her beloved dog.

On the drive at The Maples, she brought the car to a stop in front of the garage, switched off the engine and released her seatbelt. She looked at Hilary, expecting her to do the same, but the woman continued to sit there staring blankly at the garage doors.

'The doors need repainting,' she murmured vaguely. 'Keith said he'd do it. He'd been saying that ever since . . . ever since Hugh died.'

'Come on,' Nina said encouragingly, 'let's get you inside and changed out of your wet clothes. I'll make you a hot drink and light the fire in the sitting room. You'll feel better then.'

Hilary shook her head. 'I'll never feel better,' she said bleakly. 'Never.'

Deciding she had to be more resolute, Nina stepped out of the car and went round to the passenger side. She opened the door and after leaning across and releasing Hilary's seatbelt, she took the woman's left arm and eased her to her feet. Locking the car, Nina then very carefully, as though her mother-in-law was now a fragile old lady who couldn't walk without support, helped her to the front door. Once there, she pointed to Hilary's handbag and asked for the front door key.

'I can do it myself,' Hilary muttered, looking over her shoulder to the houses on the other side of the road, worried perhaps that her neighbours might see her in this uncharacteristically dishevelled state.

Once inside, and after kicking off her wet shoes and removing her sodden cashmere coat which had done little to protect her from the heavy downpour of rain, Hilary seemed to regain some of her former self and insisted she could go upstairs on her own to change.

Nina watched her climb the stairs, one slow step at a time, her hand on the banister. When she'd reached the landing and crossed it to go to her bedroom, Nina went into the sitting room and started work on getting a log fire going. The house didn't feel cold, the central heating must have come on, but if nothing else the effect of a real fire would be a comfort.

Putting the fire guard in place, she then went back out to the hall and into the kitchen to put the kettle on. There she was met with a sight she never dreamt she would ever see at The Maples. It looked like nothing had been put away or cleaned in a very long time. There was a foul smell coming from somewhere and after tracking it down to the bin, she lifted out the offending and overflowing bag and holding it at arm's distance, she took it outside to the bin store. The black bin was full, and Nina had a hard job squeezing the bag into it. Had Hilary been forgetting to put the bins out, as well as not bothering to clean the kitchen?

Nina felt awful now that she hadn't made more of an effort to check in with Hilary. It was weeks since she had spoken to her. The last time had been to tell her mother-in-law that the embryos at the clinic were going to be destroyed. There had been no contact between them since.

So what had been going on in the intervening weeks to push Hilary over the edge and lead her to do the unthinkable today, to shoplift in John Lewis? All things considered; she'd been lucky to be let off so lightly.

The security guard who had witnessed Hilary stealing a Babygro from the baby department had been very understanding. 'We've seen it before,' the man had told Nina in a quiet voice, 'women getting on in years and who . . . well . . . you know . . . lose touch with reality.' He'd tapped the side of his head as if that explained and justified everything. It's the shame, that's what always gets them, and distresses them, when they suddenly realise what they've done and what people will think. My old gran did it once, got herself in a right old state after my granddad died. She nicked a load of chocolate bars, couldn't help herself. Anyway, your mother-in-law mentioned you, so I accompanied her here, just to make sure she was okay. I did the right thing, didn't I?'

'Of course,' Nina had said. 'Absolutely. And thank you for being so good about it.'

Back in the kitchen she washed her hands and contemplated where to start with tidying up but decided it could wait until she'd made a pot of tea. Which was a challenge as she couldn't find any clean mugs and the teapot was nowhere to be seen.

Eventually she found it buried under a pile of used hand towels and after washing a couple of mugs, she opened the fridge for some milk. There was one carton of milk, but the shelves of the fridge held nothing more than a tub of spreadable Lurpak, a couple of wrinkly apples, a piece of cheese that looked dried out and an opened bag of withered carrots.

There was work to be done here, thought Nina. Hilary reaching out to Nina, of all people, had to represent a significant and desperate cry for help.

What was more, Keith needed to know what was going on. He might have imagined he'd cut himself free from his wife, but he would have to step up and pitch in.

Chapter Forty-One

Hilary was exhausted. She was sick with tiredness at the whole futility of her life. More than anything she wanted to get into bed, pull the duvet up over her head and sleep away the shame of what she'd done. Or rather the shame of being caught for what she'd done. Until today, she'd always got away with it. She must have been careless on this occasion, made her move too clumsily.

She knew it was a compulsion she had, a desperate way to ease the pain of her loneliness. When the impulse made itself felt, there was nothing she could do to stop it. Compelled to act, she would drive into town and head straight to John Lewis or wherever else that sold baby clothes.

Today she'd made a beeline for the selection of prams and pushchairs in John Lewis, asking an assistant to let her try some out to see how they handled. She'd made a little joke about sounding like she wanted to buy a new car and take it for a test drive. She'd explained that she was researching prams because she'd promised to buy one as a present for her son and daughter-in-law. The assistant had smiled brightly and remarked how lovely it was when grandparents-to-be did this, especially as prams were so expensive these days.

'When is the baby due?' the assistant had asked.

'Quite soon,' Hilary had replied proudly, enjoying playing the role. 'It's a boy. He'll be the spitting image of his father; I just know it.'

This was the best part, being able to talk about Hugh and describe how much he was looking forward to being a father and how excited she was to be a grandmother. In those precious moments it felt so very real, as though Hugh was still alive with the rest of his life ahead of him. In those moments, the pain of her grief was gone, and she was happy. Just like she used to be. Before her world had ended.

When she'd thanked the assistant for her help, she had wandered off to complete the real reason she was here. She could hardly walk out of the shop with a pram, not when it would set off any number of alarms, but an item of clothing would be easy and safe.

She'd had a difficult time deciding what to take, there were so many lovely things and the temptation to help herself to more than one item was overwhelming – *because why not, why not have double the pleasure?* – but she had resisted. The item she'd slipped into her bag had been a blue-and-white-striped Petit Bateau body suit. Practically identical to the ones Hugh had worn as a baby, it had brought back so many wonderful memories of him as an infant, fresh out of the bath and smelling as sweet as a summer peach.

The surge of emotions she'd then experienced as she prepared to leave the shop fizzed through her and gave her the sensation of walking on air. It was a delicious feeling and added to the prospect of imagining how, when she was home, she would hold the bodysuit to her face, rub the soft fabric against her cheek while breathing in the newness of it and imagine being a mother all over again and cradling Hugh.

She'd been so lost in the fantasy that initially she hadn't realised the man was addressing her. He'd appeared out of nowhere and her first thought was that he reminded her of a Jack-in-the-box toy Hugh had loved as a toddler. Oh, how he'd laughed when the lid had sprung open, and the clown had jumped out on its bendy spring. He did that every time, laughed like a gurgling drain whenever she tapped on the lid and made the clown appear.

But with her stomach lurching in alarm, she'd realised that the man who had sprung out on her wasn't going to make her laugh. Instead, she'd known in an instant what his job was, it was to catch shoplifters, like those awful hooligans she'd read about in the *Daily Mail* who stormed into shops and stripped the shelves bare. She wasn't like that. She wasn't some common thief. She hadn't stolen anything, not really. She'd only borrowed what she'd taken. She'd always planned one day to give everything back. Or maybe donate the clothes to a charity. That would make everything right, wouldn't it?

When the security guard had asked to see inside her bag she'd tried telling him that she'd simply got into a muddle and forgotten to pay for the Babygro. She'd told him that she would go straight back upstairs to the baby department and put things right. He'd surely believe a respectable woman like her? But at the serious expression on his face, she didn't think she was going to get away with that and the shock of what might happen next, that the police would be called, filled her with horror and her legs began to tremble and then shake so much she thought she was going to fall to the ground. The man had reached out to her and held her arm firmly, which only increased her fear that he was going to march her off to a back room where she would be duly arrested.

Picturing the mortifying scene, she'd thought of her darling Hugh and what he would think of her. That she had come to this. She'd begun to cry and once she'd started, she couldn't stop. People were staring at her now and that made her cry all the more and she just wanted to curl up on the floor and die. That was when the security guard had taken her away to meet her fate.

But the police weren't sent for. A woman with a kind face sat her in a chair and handed her a box of tissues, and when Hilary had calmed down enough to speak, she'd apologised for what she referred to as her confusion. She'd blamed it on the death of her son, saying that she hadn't been coping well and she was sorry for the trouble she'd caused. She'd promised it was the first time she'd ever done anything like this, and it would never happen again; she couldn't be more ashamed.

The woman must have taken pity on her. 'I can see how upset you are,' she'd said, 'and I don't know how you came into town today, but if you drove in, I wouldn't advise you drive yourself home right now. Is there someone I can telephone to come here for you? Your husband perhaps?'

Hilary had shaken her head at that. 'There's no one,' she'd murmured.

Hearing herself say this had brought on a fresh wave of tears and self-pity. How had she reached such a pathetic state that she was so entirely abandoned with no one to turn to? Her husband had left her; her friends no longer wanted to spend time with her, she couldn't blame them, not when she didn't really want to spend time with them, and even her family had distanced themselves after the way she'd behaved at Fabian's wedding. Her sisters had lost patience with her, particularly Lindsay who had been the most hurtful, describing her as unhinged and in need of professional help.

But then, as if to prove she wasn't so pathetic, she'd blurted out that she had a daughter-in-law who ran an art gallery in town. She had immediately wanted to snatch the words back, horrified by the admission. How could she bear for Nina to know what she'd done? But at the same time, the thought of Nina and her steady calmness and her clear-eyed way of looking at things acted as a soothing balm. Nina never overreacted to any situation, she always seemed to be above any unnecessary display of emotion. In the past, Hilary had viewed her as being too cool and detached to be worthy of her precious son's love. But in that moment she would have given anything for Nina – capable Nina – to take control of this nightmarish situation in her discreetly understated way and make it all go away.

The woman sitting the other side of the desk had eagerly seized on this piece of information about a daughter-in-law within walking distance of the store and whether it was to be rid of the problem, or maybe believing that a family member could ensure nothing like this happened again, but within minutes Hilary was being escorted by the security guard to St Anne's Court. They'd almost reached their destination when Hilary lost her nerve. She didn't want Nina to see her like this. To know what she'd done. To know the worst of her.

She'd come to a standstill in the rain and contemplated turning on her heel and running away. Perhaps sensing this, the security guard had smiled at her. 'Come on, love, let's not hang about and get any wetter than we already are.'

At some stage she'd lost her umbrella; maybe it had dropped out of her bag when she was looking at the prams. Which felt a lifetime ago. If only she could turn back the clock.

She thought the same thing now as she sat on the edge of her bed, that if only she hadn't gone out today. If only she hadn't succumbed to that powerful impulse to feel connected to Hugh and the grandchild she would never have.

She looked around her bedroom, seeing it through fresh eyes – through Nina's eyes. The room was a mess; clothes were strewn about the place, mostly unwashed clothes that she couldn't be bothered to deal with. What was the point? She didn't see anyone these days. There was no reason to dress up. No reason to do anything really.

From downstairs she heard Nina moving about in the kitchen;

doubtless she would be shocked at the state of it. Not so long ago, Hilary would have been appalled at anyone seeing her house in anything other than pristine order, but after today what did any of that matter?

With a colossal effort she stood up and went downstairs.

'Ah, there you are,' said Nina. 'But you haven't changed out of your wet clothes.'

'No need,' Hilary said tiredly. 'They're almost dry now.'

'Fair enough. I've made some tea and the fire's going nicely in the sitting room, let's go in there, shall we?'

'And then you can cross-examine me, is that what comes next?' Her voice was flat, drained of emotion. She was all out of emotion now.

'I wouldn't put it quite like that,' said Nina, 'but I think you should tell me what's been going on here since I last saw you.'

Hilary waited until they were seated, she on one sofa and Nina on the opposite one the other side of the coffee table. It felt like there was a yawning chasm between the two of them, as though they inhabited completely different worlds and in a way they did. Nina had moved on, she had dealt with her grief, just as Keith had; they were both forging ahead with their new lives, whereas she was left behind sinking ever deeper into the quicksand of her grief.

'I know what you're thinking,' Hilary said after Nina had passed her a mug of tea, 'that I've let things go.'

'Well, it had crossed my mind that for a woman normally as houseproud as you, things aren't quite as orderly as usual.'

'It's okay, you can be as blunt as you like. The house is a tip.'

'Isn't your cleaner coming in anymore?'

'No. We fell out. I snapped at her one day and she didn't come back. It was entirely my fault. I was quite rude to her.'

'We could find a replacement, if you'd like.'

'*We?*' Hilary repeated.

Nina smiled. 'I'd like to help if I can. I feel guilty that I haven't been in touch since September.'

'You have your life to live.'

'So do you.'

'I'm not sure it's worth living any longer,' Hilary said dully. She looked up from the mug of tea in her hands. 'I suppose you're shocked by my saying that.'

'No. Because I know exactly how that feels. I experienced the same thing in the months after Hugh died.'

'But you don't *now*. That's the difference between us. And Keith. You've both found a way to accept that Hugh's gone, but I haven't, and I doubt I ever will.'

'Has Keith been in touch recently?' asked Nina following a lengthy pause.

Hilary shifted her gaze from Nina to the fire and the flames licking around the logs. 'He's left a few messages on the answerphone,' she said, 'but I haven't listened to any of them. He wrote to me as well, but I didn't read the letter, I threw it on the fire.'

'You should talk to Keith,' Nina said. 'There are obviously important matters which the two of you need to discuss.'

'I'm not ready to do that. And I'm aware that I'm sticking my head in the sand.'

'Maybe in his own way he's doing something similar and not tackling what needs to be tackled.'

'That's his business.'

After another silence between then, Nina said, 'Do you feel up to talking about what you did today?'

This brought forth a shuddery sigh from Hilary and after fortifying herself with several sips of tea, she embarked on her confession. Perversely she wanted to see if she could shock Nina out of her cool self-possession.

But it seemed that Nina was unshockable, she barely blinked as she listened.

'So where have you been storing all the baby clothes?' she asked when Hilary fell silent and the only sound in the room was the pop and crackle of the fire.

'They're in Hugh's old bedroom,' she answered. 'In the ottoman at the foot of the bed.'

'And having them brings you comfort?' Nina enquired.

'Yes. Which probably confirms in your mind that I'm deranged.'

'No, it confirms that you're desperately unhappy and something needs to be done to help you. Why don't you come and stay with me for a few days? A change of scene might be good for you.'

'No,' said Hilary, disconcerted at the suggestion. Was Nina worried that she might go out on another shoplifting spree? Or did she think Hilary was a risk to herself if left to her own devices for too long?

Chapter Forty-Two

Everyone else was in bed, but Cassie was up and waiting anxiously – *no, make that frantically!* – for Ben to come home. She'd passed the day in what her sister would call indulging in a spot of recreational freaking-out. Frankly, she'd gone well beyond that level of worry; she was now at the catastrophising stage.

But when Ben arrived home just after eleven o'clock, and despite being desperate to unburden herself the second he walked through the door, Cassie forced herself to wait. She could see how tired he was after his trip and knew that he needed a period of decompression before discussing anything of a serious nature. Adopting as calm a demeanour as she could, she plied him with questions about the bio-tech conference he'd attended while she poured him a tumbler of Coke Zero and made a jam sandwich. It always amused her that a jam sandwich was his go-to snack whenever he'd been away, or when he wanted something quick and easy to eat. It was a childhood favourite of his.

They sat at the island unit, and he'd taken no more than a few gulps of his drink when he said, 'What's up, then, what aren't you saying?'

She affected a laugh. 'Nothing's up,' she lied.

'Cassie,' he said, staring intently at her in the glow of the pendant lights, 'tell me.'

'Eat your sandwich.'

He shook his head. 'Not until you've told me whatever it is you're not saying. I know you; I can see in your face that something's very wrong. It's not about us getting married, is it? Have you changed your mind?'

'No, of course not!'

'Are you annoyed that I thought we should wait before planning anything until Rosalyn has moved out?'

'It's not that. It really isn't.'

'Then what is it?'

There was no point in lying to him, so she told him everything, from her organising the search party last night to find Finlay who'd mysteriously gone off with Bon-Bon, and then to this morning when she and Nina had helped bury the little dog.

'Why on earth didn't you message me about all this?'

'I didn't want to bother you when I knew you were busy.'

'Not so busy I wouldn't have wanted to know. Poor Venetia, she must be in a dreadful state.'

'She is. But there's worse to tell you, and I need your advice.'

He leant forwards now. 'Go on.'

Keeping her voice low, she shared with him, word for word, or as near to it as she could, the conversation she'd had with Finlay that afternoon.

All the time he listened, and with small, barely perceptible movements, he shifted the glass and plate in front of him, a classic gesture on his part that he was thinking hard. 'And you believe Finlay?' he asked when she'd finished.

'I do. Why else would such a young child make up something as twisted and sick as that, and be as matter of fact about it? That was what I found so disturbing, that he didn't seem to have any idea that what he'd admitted to was so terrible. He wasn't at all upset that Bon-Bon was dead because of him; instead he was more concerned about me not telling Rosalyn that he'd wet himself.'

'Surely it was obvious that he had?'

'He was drenched from all the rain, so probably no, it wasn't obvious.'

Ben sipped his drink and took a bite of his jam sandwich, chewing on it thoughtfully. 'Have you said anything to Rosalyn about this?'

'God no! That's what I need your advice for. *Do* I tell her? But what are the chances she refuses to believe me, accuses me of making things up about Drew because I hated him or—?' Cassie threw her hands in the air. 'Or thinks I'm jealous of her for having made him happy when I couldn't.'

Ben frowned. 'She doesn't strike me as the sort to think anything like that.'

'You didn't see her last night. Undeniably she was out of her mind with fear and panic when Finlay was missing, but the way she turned on Emily, she was so vicious about it. Even when Finlay was found, she was still incredibly nasty to Emily. And she turned on me this afternoon because she thought I wasn't taking good enough care of her son. It's like she's suddenly a different person. She's scarily volatile.'

'It could just be shock,' Ben said. Then: 'Do you think she has any inkling about the way Drew disciplined and punished Finlay?'

'I haven't a clue. For all we know, maybe he treated her similarly.'

'Treated who similarly?'

The question came from Emily who, wearing a cropped T-shirt and a pair of cotton pyjama shorts, had appeared in the kitchen without either of them noticing.

'Oh, it's nothing,' Cassie said with a shrug. 'I thought you were having an early night, love?'

'I couldn't sleep.' She came and sat on the stool next to Cassie. 'Is that what I think it is,' she said, pointing at Ben's jam sandwich.

He smiled. 'Sure is. Want a bite?'

Emily pulled a face. 'Nah, you're fine. What were you both discussing so quietly, like you didn't want anyone to hear?'

'Your mum was telling me about Finlay going missing and Bon-Bon drowning in the river,' Ben said. 'It must have been a horrendous experience for you. How are you feeling?'

'I'm okay, thanks.'

'Really?' he said.

His voice being soft with concern filled Cassie's heart with love for him. He'd always been so good at cajoling Emily into opening up in a way that Cassie sometimes failed to do.

'It was horrible,' Emily admitted. 'I can't stop thinking about it.'

Cassie reached over and covered her daughter's hand with one of her own. But she didn't speak.

'I was so scared that Finlay might have fallen in the river,' Emily continued, 'and it would have been my fault. As it is, Venetia probably thinks I'm to blame for Bon-Bon drowning. If I hadn't taken Finlay to go and see her little dog, none of this would have happened.'

'I doubt very much that Venetia holds you responsible in any way,' Ben said.

'You're wrong, I *am* responsible for what happened and there's nothing anyone can say to change that.'

This was too much for Cassie. 'Ems, you only feel that now because it's all still so very raw for you.'

'I know you're trying to make me feel better, Mum, but the truth is I did take my eye off Finlay. I was chatting to Venetia about what I planned to do next, about getting a job, and I was . . . well . . . never mind that. The bottom line is that I messed up and now Bon-Bon's dead.'

Cassie didn't push it, but changing tack, and knowing that she was entering hyper-dangerous territory, she said, 'Ems, has Finlay ever said or done anything that has given you cause to be concerned about him?'

Both Emily and Ben looked at her, and for quite different reasons. Ben clearly was wary of what Cassie might be going on to say and Emily just looked puzzled. 'In what way?' she asked.

'Oh, you know, little things like . . . like . . . ' Cassie bottled it and fell silent.

'Like what, Mum?' pressed Emily.

'Maybe this is a conversation that can wait until the morning,' suggested Ben.

Emily looked at him sharply. 'This has something to do with what you were talking about when I came in, doesn't it? Why don't you just come right out and say whatever it is you're tiptoeing around?'

Ben caught Cassie's eye as if to say: *Over to you. Your call.*

'The thing is, Ems,' said Cassie, deciding to jump in and to hell with the consequences. 'Finlay told me something this afternoon that has shocked me and I don't know what to do about it. Not that I have to do anything, but I feel I should. It would be the right thing to do. For his own good, really.'

'For God's sake, Mum, what is this? Is this one of your mountain-out-of-a-molehill moments? Don't you think we've had enough drama?'

'It's rather more than that, Ems.'

'Then just frickin' well tell me!'

Cassie did just that while Ben silently observed Emily, as though studying her face to see how she would react.

Her response was to ask the same question Ben had posed when Cassie had said her piece. 'Do you believe Finlay?'

'I find I can't *not* believe him,' Cassie answered, 'purely because he was so matter of fact about it and seemed to think that behaviour like that was perfectly normal.' She gave a little shiver. 'There was something disturbingly cold-blooded about his admission.'

'Wait, can we just circle back to the fact that we're talking about a four-and-a-half-year-old boy, and children that age aren't capable of being cold-blooded. It's not in their nature.'

'You weren't there when he was saying all this,' said Cassie.

'But children are always making things up or telling lies,' Emily said. 'Maybe he's just seen something on his iPad or the TV that made him invent this story.'

'Or he could be telling the truth and as adults we would be doing him a great injustice by not believing him.'

This was from Ben, and Cassie could have hugged him for backing her. It was such a relief she was no longer dealing with this singlehandedly. She'd had all afternoon and evening to go over everything that had happened in the last twenty-four hours, and the one thing she kept coming back to was that she felt uncomfortable around Finlay, knowing what he'd told her.

It chilled her to the marrow every time she pictured the boy thinking it was perfectly reasonable to throw Venetia's beloved dog into the river to make him behave. It chilled her too that whenever she looked at him now, she wouldn't be able to rid herself of the thought that he was a dangerous sadist in the making. She didn't dare voice this for fear of being accused of overreacting. She could just imagine Emily saying that she'd been listening to too many true crime podcasts and saw the worst in everyone, even a small boy.

'I remember when I was at junior school,' Ben said, getting to his feet and going over to the dishwasher to put his plate and glass in the racks, 'there was a girl who was something of an oddball, she rarely said anything and was as jumpy as hell. She just didn't fit in and one day, when she was yet again picked on by a group of girls, she went berserk, broke one girl's nose and kicked another so hard on the ankle, the girl was on crutches for a week.'

'And the point of that tale?' asked Emily.

'It turned out all was not well at home,' Ben explained, closing the dishwasher and turning to face them, 'the father ruled with a rod of iron and the mother regularly had accidents, like falling downstairs or walking into doors. She ended up killing her husband and being sent to prison for it. I never knew what happened to the girl. I've often wondered.'

'Right, so let me get this straight,' said Emily. 'You think that Drew, my dad, was some kind of abusive monster and has turned Finlay into a mini version of himself? Is that what you're both saying?' She flipped her defiantly challenging gaze between the two of them.

'It's something we have to consider,' Cassie said. 'Surely you can see that?'

'Then what? When we've considered it from all angles, what do we do?'

That, thought Cassie with a heavy heart, was the million-dollar question.

Chapter Forty-Three

Her eyes thoroughly accustomed to the darkness, Venetia listened to the few remaining leaves rustling on the tree branches above and around her. There was no more than a faint stir of wind on the frigid night air, but it was enough to create a muted swish and rustle. The familiarity of the sound was a soothing comfort to her.

Directly in front of Venetia and where she had often sat in the clearing while Bon-Bon enjoyed himself sniffing and snooping, was where he now lay in the ground. The place was easy to spot as Cassie and Nina had done their best to ensure the hole was not only deep but well earthed up and covered with a thick blanket of leaves and twigs.

Twenty-four hours had passed since her darling dog had been taken from her and the pain of his death was still excruciatingly raw to her. She knew from the many moments of loss and heartache in her life, the worst of the pain would eventually lessen, but there would always be a scar left. And the memories. Good and bad.

She rarely cried but she had wept copiously for Bon-Bon. She was conscious that she wasn't just mourning the loss of her precious dog; she was grieving for so much more, the loss of the years that were gone and everything that never had been, and never would be.

Once again, the tears flowed freely down her cheeks and as the sound of the rustling leaves intensified around her, it seemed that it was the murmur of ghostly voices from the past calling to her.

Chapter Forty-Four

May 1960

Lucien didn't show up for supper that evening. His absence didn't surprise Venetia, in fact she would have been more surprised if he had appeared and sat down to eat as though he didn't have a care in the world.

Following the events of the afternoon when poor Lucien had been forced to carry out that unspeakable act on Terry Sands, her stomach was a bubbling cauldron of fearful unease. The sight of food filled her with nausea, and unable to eat a thing, she left the dining hall and went in search of Lucien. Drawing a blank in all their usual haunts, an alarming thought occurred to Venetia. What if Terry Sands was right now punishing Lucien for shoving him the way he had? What if he'd dragged him back to his cottage and—

No! She refused to think of that.

There was another possibility, though.

What if angry humiliation drove Lucien to take his revenge on Terry and bring an end to the bullying once and for all?

Driven by a wave of sickening dread at what Lucien might do, and with the light fading and not caring that she should be in the dorm getting ready for bed, she hastened towards Terry's cottage.

When she reached it, she found that there weren't any lights on, and the front door was ajar. Her heart hammering against her ribcage, she summoned all her courage and pushed the door further open and crept inside. She'd only taken a few steps when she heard a noise. Or she thought she did. Her heart pounding even harder, she stood very still and heard another noise – a wheezy cough – which she immediately recognised.

'Lucien, what are you doing here?' she whispered urgently when she went through to the front room. But before he replied, and in the semi-darkness, she took in the scene of Lucien with a large kitchen knife in his hand, staring down at Terry's enormous body lying on the floor. The man's head was resting on the edge of the fireplace, and a puddle of what looked like blood surrounded it. It had soaked into the shabby hearth rug as well.

'I came to kill him,' Lucien rasped, his voice barely audible as he struggled to breath. 'But he was already dead. I think that when I pushed him earlier, he must have cracked his head on the hearth when he fell. Which means . . . I murdered him anyway.'

Her head spinning, Venetia tried to marshal her thoughts. She reasoned that a dead Terry was better than a live Terry, because a dead Terry could never hurt Lucien ever again or make foul accusations about him. But equally, a dead Terry might lead to Lucien being accused of killing him.

'Are you sure he's dead?' she asked.

'He's not breathing,' Lucien wheezed, 'and I can't find a pulse. So yeah, he's dead all right.'

Venetia trembled at the reality of the two of them standing either side of a dead body and as much as she hated Terry, it was shocking to think that his life had ended because of their actions. Lucien might think he was solely responsible for this, but she was as culpable as her friend. She might not have been the one to push Terry, but had she been in the room she would have done more than push the evil monster.

'Did you hear me?' Lucien rasped, his chest heaving with the effort of speaking. 'I said he's dead.'

'I heard you,' she replied, her own chest tightening in sympathy with Lucien's. 'Where's your inhaler?'

'I've used it.'

'Then use it again.'

'I can't, it's almost empty. You need to get out of here. Now.'

'I'm not going without you.'

'Don't argue with me; I need to do something and I don't want you around when I do it.'

'No way, Lucien, I'm not going anywhere without you.'

'For God's sake, just do as I say!'

'*No!*' she shouted back at him. 'Whatever it is you think you're going to do, I'm doing it with you. We're in this together.'

'We're not! This is my problem. Not yours.' He paused, and her heart went out to him as he desperately tried to fill his lungs with air. 'But if you want to be helpful,' he continued, pressing a finger to the bridge of his spectacles and pushing them up his nose, 'tell me exactly where the tin of money is which you hid.'

'Why?'

'I have to disappear, and I need money to do that.'

'You're running away?'

'Of course I am. I can't stay here.'

'In that case, I'm coming too.'

'*No!* I'm not going to ruin your future by you coming with me, you have to stay.'

'But I don't want to. Not without you.'

'Don't say that, Venetia. One person is easier to stay hidden than two. I need you to stay here and cover for me.'

She decided to humour him, if only in the hope that it would help ease his asthma attack. Agitating him would only make things worse. 'Tell me what you're going to do and then I'll tell you where the tin of money is.'

His face flushed, he considered her offer for a moment. 'I'm going to set fire to the cottage,' he said, 'that way it should look like Terry was drunk and set the place alight by accident.'

'How are you going to do it?' she demanded. 'You'll have to make it look realistic.'

'I know that!' he said with exasperation.

'So how will you do it?'

'If you'd shut up and give me a chance to think, I'd tell you!'

Ignoring him because she didn't trust his ability to come up with anything convincing while he was fighting against a severe asthma attack, she said, 'This is how I'd do it. I'd get a fire going in the grate, then I'd put the clothes horse with some shirts on it right in front of the fireplace. Next, I'd pour some beer on the hearth rug to make it look like Terry was so drunk he'd knocked the bottle over, making sure to put the empty bottle right by his hand. Then when the fire was really going, I'd push the clothes horse into it. That way it will look like a convincing accident.'

Again, he considered her words, then nodded his agreement.

And that was what they did, and when the fire in the grate was blazing fiercely and lighting up the room with its gruesome scene, Venetia pushed the wooden clothes horse into the fire. In no time, the flames had taken hold, and the shirt and underclothes were burning.

For a short while they stood and watched in fascinated horror before Venetia grabbed Lucien's arm and yanked him away. 'We have to get out of here,' she urged him.

That was when Terry opened his eyes.

Chapter Forty-Five

'Keith, you have to face this head on. Hilary is seriously unwell. She needs our help. We can't abandon her.'

'But as I said before, Nina, I gave her all the help I could. For God's sake, nobody tried more than I did! How many times did you say yourself that I must have had the patience of Job? Now you're accusing me of not doing enough, how does that work?'

'I'm not. But neither of us has truly appreciated just what she was going through and how badly it's affected the balance of her mind.'

'That may be so, but if we overlooked anything it was because we were going through the same process ourselves,' he said with a weary sigh of exasperation. 'You lost your husband, and I lost my son. We all had shit to deal with, we still do, but for some reason Hilary's shit is more important than ours!'

Keith was all too aware how defensively angry he was sounding, and he didn't like it. This wasn't him.

He'd always been Good ol' Keith who could be relied upon to lighten the mood.

Good ol' Keith who could put everyone at ease and smooth over any ruffled feathers.

Good ol' self-effacing-turn-the-cheek Keith who never had a bad word for anyone.

That's who he was! And right now, he wished he could be

that man. Because the man he had become while sitting here in Nina's beautifully ordered apartment and enduring what felt like a personal attack, wanted to shout back at her and say that Hilary was no longer his problem.

Hardening his heart this way was a defence mechanism, he understood that, he wasn't stupid. It was to protect himself from having to deal with any more misery. He'd borne enough and had done what anyone would probably do in his shoes: he'd walked away for the sake of his own wellbeing.

True he'd only walked away when he'd had somebody to walk to, but again, who wouldn't when that special somebody didn't constantly humiliate him or act as though he were to blame for everything?

He had no idea what the future held for him and Diane, but whatever it was, it sure as hell beat living with Hilary these past few years.

The only contact he'd had with Hilary recently was through his solicitor. Except you couldn't call it contact because she flatly refused to involve herself in the divorce process. He'd chosen to hold fire for now on the legal wranglings, it was a waste of money as it was costing him a pretty penny each time his solicitor fired off a letter or email, only for it to be ignored. He'd assumed she was being stubborn by maintaining radio silence and not responding to any of the communications, either from him or his solicitor, but having listened to what Nina had just said, and he had no reason to doubt it, he had to concede that Hilary's silence was down to her being mentally unbalanced, quite literally out of her mind.

When Nina had phoned to say that she had something important to discuss and could they meet, he'd hoped it was about her and Jakob. She'd already told him that Jakob was once again working at Lavelle's, and reluctant to ask what that might actually mean to her in personal terms, he'd left well alone. Her inscrutability was a defence shield, just as hardening his heart was for him, and so he'd trusted her to share with him when the time was right for her. A new relationship was, after all, a big step for her to take. For anyone to take.

Which was why, when he'd been on his way to see her, he'd felt so happy for her, that at last she was doing what was only right – she was moving on, just as he had – and had decided she was now ready to share that news with him.

He could not have been more wrong. Within minutes of him walking through the door, she'd told him about Hilary being caught shoplifting, and that she'd been stealing baby stuff for God knew how long and she was lucky the police hadn't been involved. Worse still, Nina now expected Good ol' Keith to wave a magic wand and make things right. How the hell did she think he could do that?

'Our grief is just as real and important as Hilary's,' Nina was now saying, 'but she's dug herself in so deep that unless we do something to help her, she'll stay there or sink even lower.'

'But what can we do?' he asked with tired annoyance, thinking that instead of being here he could have gone with Diane to her local church for that morning's Remembrance Sunday service. 'I tried every single one of those painfully dark days to help Hilary,' he added, 'and she always pushed me away. There was nothing I could do. Some days the way she treated me you'd think it was my fault our son died. Can you imagine how hurt I felt? Would it have killed her to show me a little kindness and understanding?'

'Keith,' Nina said firmly, 'this isn't about you or me, this is about Hilary. We're the lucky ones, as tough as it was, we've been able to cope. We've proved ourselves to be stronger than she is.'

He took umbrage at the word lucky. *'Lucky,'* he repeated irritably. 'My son is gone and so is my marriage, how is that lucky?'

'You've escaped a marriage that had probably been slowly dying for some years. Grief may well have given you the impetus to change your life. You now have a second chance at being happy.'

'Hold on a minute,' Keith said heatedly, 'who says my marriage was slowly dying?'

'Wasn't it?' she said, giving him an unnervingly long hard stare. It was a look he had never witnessed before from Nina and revealed a side to her he didn't recognise. Maybe in the same way he was revealing a side of himself to her which she didn't recognise, and quite possibly didn't like. He wanted not to care what she thought of him, but he did care. He cared a lot.

'I admit that things have been rocky since Hugh's death impacted our lives,' he said, 'but we jogged along well enough before.'

'Is "jogging along" enough?' she asked.

He swallowed, feeling like he was a butterfly being pinned to a board. 'It can't always be hearts and roses,' he said, 'marriage slips into a pattern of just being. It's what happens to couples who have been together for a long time. Eventually you would have come to understand that with Hugh.' Too late he realised the appalling crassness of what he'd said and immediately apologised. 'I'm sorry, that was completely inappropriate. Forgive me, please.'

'It's okay,' she said quietly, although he could see from the change in her expression as she stared out of the window, it wasn't okay. 'I get it,' she said, returning her gaze to him. 'I do. Marriages fall into a routine and a pattern of behaviour and roles played out. I see it with my own parents. But what I've never seen with them is either one of them demeaning the other, they support and encourage each other. That's what I envisioned I'd have with Hugh. If fate hadn't intervened.'

'I'm sure it would have been just as you say,' Keith said, desperate to make amends for his insensitivity.

'Not that I'm kidding myself,' she continued, 'that either of us would have been perfect, but I believe we would have always been . . . ' Her words fell away and she frowned.

'Yes,' he said, 'what would you have been?'

'I was going to say we would have always been honest with each other, but actually that's not true.'

'Isn't it?'

She shook her head. 'He kept from me that Hilary had given him the money for another round of IVF. Why did he keep that from me? Was he embarrassed? Did he feel guilty accepting the money? Did he think I'd be cross?'

'Chances are it was all of those things,' Keith said, glad that the spotlight was off him for a moment. 'Wouldn't you have been cross if he'd owned up to you about the money?'

She smiled. 'I would have been furious.'

'There you are, then. That's your answer.'

'So why take the money? Why put himself in that situation, knowing that it would annoy me?'

'Odds on it was to please his mother. You know how he always took the path of least resistance with her. He was like it as a small boy, he quickly figured out the best way to keep in her good books, or to cover his tracks when he'd done something wrong. He was also a people pleaser.'

'Just as you are,' said Nina. 'Which is why I know you'll do the right thing and help me to help Hilary. And what would Hugh think of us if we left her to go on suffering on her own?'

As hypothetical as it was, it was emotional blackmail pure and simple that Nina was throwing at him, but Keith couldn't deny that she was right, what the hell would Hugh think of him if he couldn't find it in his heart – even his hardened heart – to try and help Hilary?

But how?

Something Nina wasn't right about though, was her saying

his marriage to Hilary had been dying a long and slow death. That wasn't true. They'd had plenty of happy times, plenty of laughs and plenty of love. Yes, as the years had gone by Hilary had become more judgemental and critical as well as intolerant, but so had he. He'd just been better at hiding it than she had. He'd preferred to grumble in a humorous way, casting himself in the role of middle-aged man who was hopelessly out of his depth in this new-fangled world. It was a gift of a part for him and one that had amused him to play. Hilary had not been gifted such an easy role; she had been given the part of mother-in-law, a clichéd role that had not suited her one little bit.

Then they'd been cast as grieving parents, a role that neither of them should have ever been forced to play. It was wholly unnatural, divisive and cruel, and quite without mercy. Was it any wonder they were in the mess they were?

'What do you propose we do, then?' he asked Nina.

Chapter Forty-Six

Nina launched into explaining what she thought they should do. She could, of course, go ahead and do it all herself, but after the events of yesterday and seeing for herself the state Hilary was in, Nina was determined that Keith had to play his part. She had stayed until late last night with Hilary and cooked them supper – she'd unearthed a ready-made lasagna in the freezer – tidied the kitchen and loaded and unloaded the washing machine, as well as insisted that Hilary have a relaxing bath while Nina put fresh bedlinen on her bed. In Nina's experience, a bath followed by getting into a clean and perfectly made bed always made one feel better.

'Firstly,' she said, and fixing Keith with a steady gaze, 'we need to contact Hilary's sister Lindsay, as she's the most practical of the bunch. I'd suggest leaving the rest of her family out of it for now.'

Keith shook his head. 'I don't think for one minute Hilary is going to like Lindsay knowing what she's been up to. And what if Lindsay tells the rest of the family?'

'She won't do that, not when we stress the importance of keeping it strictly amongst ourselves. I thought perhaps you could speak to Lindsay.'

Keith nodded, but to Nina's eye he didn't look convinced. 'What then?' he asked.

'We encourage Hilary to seek professional help.'

'She won't do it,' he said emphatically. 'I repeatedly suggested that we both did that, and she flatly refused even to consider grief counselling.'

'That was then,' Nina said firmly, having anticipated this rebuttal from Keith. 'Now that Hilary knows her dirty little secret is out, her words not mine, she accepts that she can't go on as she is. Again, those were her words, not mine.'

'If she's reached that conclusion herself, why do I have to be involved?'

Nina was disappointed in her father-in-law's apparent readiness to absolve himself from the situation.

'Keith,' she said as patiently as she could, 'if you'd seen Hilary yesterday, you'd know how just desperate the situation is and that we have to support her, she can't do this alone.'

'Okay,' he said, 'so how do we convince Hilary to seek professional help?'

'We all sit down together and show her that we genuinely care about her and want to see her well again. We also need to give her something to care about and to think about, other than what she's lost. Because at the moment, that's all she can think of. She's lost everything that mattered to her, her son, the hope of a grandchild and . . . ' she paused, 'and you. We've all taken from her and now we need to give her something to make up for that.'

Keith looked puzzled. 'Such as?'

She told him what she had in mind and his immediate reaction was to dismiss the idea out of hand, saying there wasn't a chance in hell of Hilary going along with it. But ignoring his pessimism, Nina asked if he had anything better to suggest. He didn't. 'In that case,' she said, 'I'm going to do some research and make it happen.'

Over on the countertop where her mobile was charging, it buzzed and then buzzed again.

'Feel free to answer it,' Keith said. 'I don't mind.'

'It's okay,' she said, 'it can keep.' Some telepathic sense – or more likely just plain old-fashioned hope, the giddy kind that made you want to believe you were constantly in another person's thoughts – convinced her it was Jakob. If it was, she wasn't going to reply now, she wanted to do that when she was alone.

Something must have given her away as Keith said, 'Would that be Jakob by any chance?'

'Now why would you think that?' she said.

'Just a feeling,' he said blandly. 'And that you're blushing very prettily, and you suddenly look decidedly on edge. Not that it's any of my business,' he added.

Inwardly annoyed with herself for being so transparent, but wanting to show how at ease she was, she rose smoothly from her seat and went over to her mobile.

'You're right,' she said airily, 'it is Jakob.'

'Does he often contact you on a Sunday?' Keith enquired.

'You know how it is with work,' she said with a shrug, 'I'm never off duty.'

'Nor is Jakob by the looks of things,' remarked Keith with more than a hint of archness to his voice.

With her back to him, she put the phone down, but not before reading the message and looking at the accompanying photo. It was of Jakob, and he appeared to be immersed in a lake against a dramatic backdrop of snow-covered fir trees.

First proper snow in Tromsø and wishing you were here with me! he'd written.

Not on your life, she thought with a smile, thinking how icy cold that lake must be.

When she was sitting down again, Keith said, 'Are you going to tell me all about it, then?'

'About what?'

He tutted. 'You and Jakob, of course. I know your natural inclination is to keep things to yourself, and I respect that, but the thing is, Nina, I feel I owe it to Hugh to encourage you to move on with your life, whether that's taking a risk on finding love again, or just throwing yourself into having some fun.'

'It was always about the risk for Hugh,' she said with a faint smile. 'The riskier the better. But I'm not like him. That said, though,' she added cautiously, deciding to confirm what Keith clearly suspected, 'I have decided to take a risk and Jakob and I are' – she mentally took a deep breath – 'seeing each other; well, you know, we're in a relationship. Sort of.' *Why sort of?* she asked herself. Who was ever in a sort of relationship?

Keith's face lit up with a smile of pleasure. 'I'm so pleased for you,' he said. 'I've never forgotten how radiant you looked at Fabian's wedding when you were dancing with Jakob. You looked so happy. Obviously,' he added with a grimace, 'that was before it all went horribly wrong.'

Not wanting to dwell on the latter, and keen to stress how things were between her and Jakob, she said, 'For now we're at the very low-key-taking-it-steadily stage,' she said. 'More importantly, we haven't gone public yet. I need to find my way around being in a relationship again. Didn't you feel like that with Diane?'

'To be honest, we're both still finding our way. And that's perfectly normal, that's how every relationship works, isn't it? Every day is a new discovery. That's part of the fun.'

'You're right,' she said, 'that's how it should be. I'm afraid I spend far too much time analysing how I feel about Jakob and the logistics of a relationship with him, as well as the age gap. Whereas I should be letting myself enjoy the moment like I did when I danced with him.' She frowned. 'I never used to be like this.'

'But you'd never been widowed before. For what it's worth, I think you should forget about the age difference and focus on the fact that you like Jakob, and he likes you. What does it matter if a relationship with him comes unstuck, and for whatever reason; better to have tried than not. My advice is to throw yourself in at the deep end and see how it feels.'

Later, when Keith had gone, and she was changing into her running gear, Nina thought of what he'd said and although it probably wasn't the kind of thing that he'd been thinking of, Nina looked again at the photo of Jakob swimming in the freezing cold lake and tried to imagine throwing herself into doing that with him.

Hmmm . . .

She could think of other things she'd rather do with him, and it didn't involve any snow!

Amused at the thought, she smiled. And by the very fact that such a thought could amuse her, she knew that she was slowly moving in the right direction. Whether it was just her hormones getting the better of her, or the prolonged period of celibacy now yearning to be vanquished, her physical desire for Jakob was definitely hotting up.

It was the one thing she'd thought she would struggle to do, or even imagine doing, and that was to make love to a man who wasn't Hugh. But the physical need she now experienced for Jakob was so acute she knew that she was ready to take their relationship to the next level. She had feared he might push that side of things, but he hadn't. Maybe he'd held back out of respect for her need to go slowly, or perhaps because he was worried she would compare him to Hugh. She was trying more and more to see things from both sides, not just her own.

Looking again at the photo of Jakob, Nina thought of Cassie asking her if distance was making her heart grow fonder, and she had to admit that it was.

After adding a gilet to her running outfit, along with a short scarf which she wrapped around her neck, she took a selfie and sent it to Jakob with the words – *Wishing you were here!*

She then sent another.

I miss you. X

Chapter Forty-Seven

'You did what?' demanded Rosalyn.

The air in the kitchen had already been charged with a dangerously electric force, but now it was positively crackling, and Cassie felt like she was caught in the eye of a storm. But she held her nerve.

'I just explained to you what I did. I spoke to Finlay about what happened that night and he told me everything, that he threw Bon-Bon into the river.'

'You mean you *interrogated* my son while my back was turned,' Rosalyn shouted harshly, 'and put words into his mouth. Then you have the nerve, the absolute nerve, to twist whatever he might have innocently said into some kind of sick, malicious accusation? My God, I knew you resented me and could never forgive Drew for leaving you, but to harbour so much bitterness and jealousy that you would stoop to this is a whole other level of vindictive hatred. You're pathetic!'

Cassie had prepared herself for Rosalyn to be angry and go on the attack to refute what Cassie had heard with her own ears, but foolishly she hadn't expected the attack to be so personal and made with such virulence.

A long and very difficult week had passed since Finlay's admission to Cassie of what he had done, and she had felt weighed down by the burden of the knowledge she'd been given.

She had thought that by sharing what she knew with Ben and unintentionally with Emily, that the burden would be lightened, but the reverse had happened. For the last few nights, she'd had nightmares with her frantically searching for Bon-Bon and then hearing the sound of barking coming from the river. In the dream she would wade into the scarily dark water only to find herself being pulled under by slippery weeds while Finlay looked on from the bank. She would wake with a heart-thumping start and with Venetia's cry of anguish ringing in her ears, only to realise it was her own cry that she could hear, and it was Ben's comforting arms wrapped around her and not deadly weeds trying to drown her.

She became convinced that the only way to stop the nightmares was to talk to Rosalyn, to tell her what Finlay had done. To have the matter out in the open, the weight of the unwanted knowledge taken from her. This should be Rosalyn's problem, not hers.

Ben had warned her to be careful and said that perhaps he should be with her if she was going to broach the subject with Rosalyn, but Cassie had said it would be too confrontational for the two of them to tackle her, that it would be much better if she did it alone. Woman to woman. Mother to mother.

Emily had wanted nothing to do with it. Although in fairness, she had offered to take Finlay for a walk so that the boy wouldn't hear the conversation which Cassie had been determined to instigate. 'It's really none of your business,' Emily had said, 'so why can't you just let it go?'

'It's my business because Rosalyn and Finlay are living under my roof and it was my friend's dog that drowned,' Cassie had retaliated.

'Oh, so you're doing this for Venetia, are you, not a way to get back at my father?'

'Ems, that's a ridiculous thing to say. Surely if you care about Finlay, you'd want him to be helped because it's quite clear he has issues going on that need sorting. And even you must admit, it's weird what he's now drawing.'

'That's a low shot, Mum,' Emily had said, forever determined to defend her half-brother, 'it's obvious he's processing what happened that night.'

It might well be obvious but to Cassie it was totally unnerving. Finlay's artwork now included a lot of pictures of black stick-like trees and a black line representing a river and a black dog supposedly swimming.

Ignoring her daughter, Cassie had decided to tackle Rosalyn, as she'd known all along that she would. She'd approached the conversation when she'd been clearing away the lunch things and fortuitously Emily had taken Finlay outside to play. Rosalyn had been sitting on a stool at the island unit idly scrolling on her mobile, seemingly only too pleased for her son to be off her hands.

As casually as she could make it sound, Cassie had asked if Rosalyn had considered taking Finlay to a see a counsellor, one who specialised in helping children get over the death of a parent.

Barely looking up from her mobile, Rosalyn had said, 'Why? Why would he need to see someone when he has me to talk to?'

'Well, sometimes as mothers we're too close and can't see what's really going on.'

That was when Rosalyn had put down her mobile and looked at Cassie. 'Are you saying I'm not a good mother and that I don't know my son?'

'Not at all. Like I say, sometimes we're just too close.' *Tell her,* Cassie had thought. *Just get it over and done with and tell her.*

So she had.

As a result, Rosalyn was now on her feet and giving Cassie the benefit of her outrage.

'If anyone needs to see a counsellor,' she said, 'it's you! You're the one who's clearly not right in the head. You're heartless and pathetic, making things up about a little boy who's lost his father. God knows what a kind and decent man like Ben sees in a conniving bitch like you!'

Her blood suddenly fizzing with rage, a rage that was visceral, this was too much for Cassie, way too much, and her claws were out in a flash. A line had been crossed. She was a woman protecting the sanctity of her love for Ben, and his love for her. She was a warrior fighting for her man! *Hear her roar!*

'Yeah, and I bet you'd just love to make a play for him, wouldn't you?' Cassie snarled. 'You'd roll those tearful poor-little-me-eyes at him and offer yourself up on a plate. So back off, lady. And I think we can both safely agree that you've overstayed your welcome. It's time you and your son moved out! Go on, go and pack! I want you gone!'

Rosalyn opened her mouth to say something else, but wisely in Cassie's opinion, she decided against it. Snatching up her mobile, Rosalyn whirled round on her feet and flounced off, her Ugg boots squeaking on the polished floor, and leaving Cassie vibrating with fury.

And regret. She shouldn't have lost her temper. She'd promised Ben that she would be perfectly calm throughout the conversation, but she'd allowed Rosalyn's comments to get under her skin. It was as if Rosalyn had known her weak spot and had gone for it with a viciously sharp aim.

Her elbows resting on the cool marble of the island unit, Cassie slumped forward and pressed her head against the palms of her hands, which were hot and clammy, in direct contrast with her mouth which was bone-dry after the rush of adrenaline that had flooded through her.

Emily was never going to forgive her for what she'd just done. Ben would wonder how she could have been so hard on a widowed woman and her son. If only Rosalyn had stuck to the script Cassie had so carefully written in her head, the one in which Rosalyn, after the initial shock had worn off, would accept that Drew had been overly strict with his son and therefore the boy had developed a warped sense of right and wrong.

Ben's advice to be careful could not have been clearer. 'Put yourself in Rosalyn's shoes and imagine how you would react in the same situation. Think how far you would go to protect Emily from any criticism.'

His wise words dropped like bricks from a great height as she contemplated the mess she'd made of things. Because it wasn't any old criticism Cassie had tossed into the conversation; indirectly she'd implied that Finlay needed help because the abusive actions of his father had turned him into a serial killer in the making! How else could Rosalyn interpret what she'd said?

Lifting her head, she moved away from the island unit and went and stood at the full-length window that overlooked the expanse of lawn, out to where Emily, down by the riverbank, was talking to Venetia while Finlay ran around them waving a large stick in the air.

Cassie hadn't seen or spoken to Venetia since the day they'd buried Bon-Bon. She had cowardly avoided Venetia, scared that her friend might ask if she had got to the bottom of what had happened that dreadful night. She had sent an occasional text, just to check in with Venetia, but the replies had been minimal, as though Venetia didn't want to be bothered.

Yet there she was taking advantage of the good weather and chatting to Emily, the weak mid-November sun shining down on them. What if Venetia was asking Emily if Finlay had said anything to her about that disastrous night?

She was just contemplating what Emily might say, when there came an alarming crashing sound, followed by another and then a loud, strangled cry.

There was no doubt as to where the noise was coming from, and after creeping quietly along the hallway, and hardly daring to think what she might find the other side of it, Cassie pushed against the door that was ajar.

There was an opened suitcase on the double bed and clothes piled up on it; at the foot of the bed was Rosalyn. She was on her knees and surrounded by splintered glass and broken photo frames that contained pictures of her and Drew. She must have hurled the frames with some considerable force as there were indentations in the wall in front of her.

Trying not to be annoyed about the damage to the wall, Cassie stepped into the room. 'Rosalyn,' she said. 'What's going on?' But her voice went unheeded, and Rosalyn let out another disturbing shriek.

'Rosalyn,' she said more firmly this time, going over to put a hand on the woman's shoulder.

Rosalyn started and after letting out one last shuddery cry, she fell quiet and looked dazedly about her as though suddenly aware of her surroundings and the lethally sharp glass on the carpet.

'Come with me,' Cassie said, and like a docile child now, Rosalyn allowed herself to be led out of her bedroom, along the hallway and back to the kitchen.

Cassie settled her on a stool and sat on the other side of the island, the better to be able to observe Rosalyn. She had no intention of apologising for what she'd said earlier, even if it was what had tipped Rosalyn over the edge, and so she waited for the other woman to speak.

A lengthy silence ensued and perceiving a battle of wills was in play, Cassie waited some more, her gaze never leaving Rosalyn's face.

Eventually Rosalyn gave in. 'I'm sorry for all the drama.'

Drama, thought Cassie, was that what it had been? 'Was it something I said,' she enquired, somewhat ingenuously, 'that triggered the *drama?*'

Rosalyn nodded and pursed her lips. Well, as pursed as they could be, given how plumped they were with filler. *Bad Cassie!* Cassie chided herself. *Not the time for petty judgeyness!*

'I lost it because I'm afraid it's true,' Rosalyn murmured.

'What's true?'

Rosalyn now met Cassie's stare with one as equally direct. 'Drew was often much too hard on Finlay and punished him in ways he never should have. So there's every chance that he has caused behavioural problems in our son.'

'Why didn't you stop Drew?'

Rosalyn blinked. 'I was too scared to do that. I know I should have but if I ever disagreed with Drew, it only made things worse. It was stress at work that made him do what he did. He was always worried about money. About providing for us as a family in the way he wanted.'

'I'm sorry,' said Cassie, 'but that's really not much of an excuse.'

'Maybe not. But that was how it was. My job was to keep the peace. To keep our lives running as smoothly as possible.'

'What happened if you didn't?'

Her hands fiddled with the cuff of her right sleeve. 'Then he'd be angry and take it out on me,' she murmured. 'He would always say sorry afterwards and then everything would be okay for a while.'

'Until the next time?' asked Cassie.

Rosalyn nodded.

'Are you saying he hurt you physically?'

'Only when he was very angry.'

'Why the hell did you stay with him?'

Rosalyn looked at her as though Cassie had just asked the stupidest of questions. 'Because I loved him. Just as you did.'

Cassie was taken aback at that. She had loved Drew, of course she had, but would she have turned herself into a doormat, or worse, a punchbag, just to keep him? It was a sickening thought, and she knew she had no moral high ground on which to stand, not when she had put up with Drew cheating on her. How many times had he promised he'd never do it again, that she was the only one he loved?

Why were women so weak when it came to a certain type of man? It was a question she imagined Emily, with all her youthful black and white certainty, would ask.

As though picking up on her thoughts about Emily, Rosalyn said, 'Drew behaved better when Emily came to visit us. It was like he was presenting his best self when she was around. Only once or twice did the mask slip, but never in front of her. It was why I grew to be so fond of her so quickly. Life was simply better with Emily in our lives. Particularly mine. It still is.' She fiddled with the cuff on her left sleeve now. Then: 'I thought with Drew gone, Finlay and I could make a fresh start, but everything's changed now after what happened to your neighbour's dog. I'm sick with worry about Finlay, that Drew taught him to be just like him; an abusive monster.'

'It needn't,' said Cassie. 'You can undo the harm if you seek help for your son.'

'The thing is; this isn't the first time something unpleasant has happened. There was an incident at nursery not so long ago.'

'Such as?'

Rosalyn shook her head. 'I'd rather not say. Are you going to tell your neighbour what Finlay told you?'

'I'm not sure it would be of any benefit to Venetia to know something so awful.'

'Does Emily know? And Ben?'

'Yes,' replied Cassie. There was no point in saying otherwise. 'Emily refuses to believe it though,' she added, 'and hates me for believing that Finlay could have done such a terrible thing, or that her father could punish his son in the way Finlay said. She prefers to believe that I'm making it up and exacting some kind of sick revenge on her father.'

'Just as I accused you. I'm sorry I said that. And I'm sorry what I said about Ben. It was easier to lash out and remain in denial than to accept the truth.'

'That's often the way it is,' Cassie said softly. 'But something must have changed for you, because you went back to your room and—'

'And I lost it,' Rosalyn finished for her. 'I was packing, and I picked up the photographs which I'd put on the bedside table, and I couldn't stomach the sight of them. The photos were taken on our honeymoon, and I remember being so blissfully happy, but it wasn't long before it was harder to reproduce that expression of carefree happiness on my face whenever we posed for a photo of us. Sometimes, if Drew thought I didn't look happy enough in a photograph with him he would be angry with me. The more I tried to look happy, the worse I looked.'

'You looked happy enough in your Instagram photos with him,' Cassie said.

Rosalyn sighed. 'Instagram isn't real, you surely know that. None of what I posted was genuinely me. But I did it to please Drew, he liked the idea of our perfect life being out there in the world for people to view and like. He was desperate for approval and admiration. The hours I spent on doing that and all the time I knew it was fake. Nothing about our life was real. You had a lucky escape all those years ago.'

Didn't I just, thought Cassie.

There was nothing else they could say for at that moment the doorbell rang loudly in short staccato bursts, announcing that Emily and Finlay were back.

Chapter Forty-Eight

Later that evening, after Rosalyn had put Finlay to bed, they gathered around the island unit in the kitchen. With the pendant lights softly glowing above their heads, there was a stage-like atmosphere to the space and Cassie felt as if they were actors in a play and were about to deliver their lines. The cast consisted of the ex-wife, the daughter, the husband-to-be, and the widowed wife. There was a character missing, of course, and that was the dead husband, Drew. He was the reason they were here. Everything always seemed to lead back to him.

In front of them were glasses and a selection of drinks – wine, fizzy water and beer which Ben was offering round. There hadn't been time to cook supper, but Cassie had set out an assortment of snacks – olives, pistachios, salted almonds, and chilli-flavoured crisps with a soured cream dip.

It was Rosalyn who had wanted to do this. In fact, she'd insisted on it. She'd claimed it would be better to get everything out in the open, and that included telling Emily the truth about her father. Cassie had been one hundred per cent opposed to doing it this way, believing it to be unfair to Emily being put on the spot like this. It was all very well for Rosalyn to say she needed to speak her truth – *such an over-used expression!* – so she could take the first real honest steps of her new life, but did it have to be at the expense of Emily's feelings?

'Wouldn't it be better for you to talk to Emily on your own?' Cassie had asked. 'So you can break things to her gently? Ever since Drew came back into her life, she's so badly wanted to believe in him.'

'No,' Rosalyn had replied with surprising rigidity. 'I'm tired of being pushed around and told how I should do things. That's all in the past. From now on, I do things my way.'

It had been a difficult day as it was and not wanting to make the situation any more stressful, Cassie had reluctantly agreed to do as Rosalyn had requested. She couldn't deny that a small part of her was relieved that Rosalyn hadn't wanted Cassie to be the one to shatter what remained of Emily's newfound belief in her father.

Not so long ago, and in the hope that their relationship would have returned to how it used to be, Cassie would have been only too eager for Emily to be disabused of the notion that Drew was a changed man, that he'd never actually been as bad as Cassie had made out. She might even have taken pleasure in doing that. Somehow that didn't sit comfortably with her now.

But she wouldn't have gone about it like this, especially as Drew now appeared to have become a far worse man than when he'd abandoned Cassie and Emily. Learning the truth that he'd been abusive and manipulative was going to be painful for Emily. Did she really need to know that? But would it be right to keep her in ignorance of the truth?

Truth had always been so important to Cassie; she had never wanted her relationship with her daughter to be tainted with lies. Which was why it hurt so much that Emily had recently accused her of making things up about Drew.

Ben had agreed with Cassie that it was better to be honest with Emily. 'It would be treating her like a child if you pretend your discussion with Rosalyn never happened and she later found out about it.'

This conversation with Ben had taken place when he'd been driving home. Not wanting to be overheard, Cassie had gone for a walk in the chilly darkness to call him and to tell him all that Rosalyn had told her. She'd stayed out there in the cold talking with him until the headlamps of his car appeared on the long driveway. Then going round to the courtyard, she'd watched him park and then hugged him tight when he'd stepped out of the car.

Burying her face into his chest and thinking of Rosalyn's words earlier – *You had a lucky escape all those years ago* – she'd said, 'I'm so very lucky, Rosalyn's story could have been mine.'

Yet now as they stood together in this oddly stage-managed ensemble, a niggling doubt had wormed its way into Cassie's mind, and she couldn't help but feel that something was off. But what exactly? Was it no more than her maternal need to protect her daughter?

Or was it less noble than that? Was it a combination of Cassie's age-old insecurities and her deeply rooted antipathy towards Rosalyn that was causing her to be irritated by the younger woman's apparent vehemence to control the narrative?

Because by rights Cassie should feel some kind of sisterhood sympathy for Rosalyn, but she didn't. So perhaps that was what was giving Cassie a sense that was something was 'off'. It was shame that she felt. Shame that she didn't have it in her heart to feel genuinely sorry for Rosalyn. Not that she thought Rosalyn deserved what she'd got from Drew. Absolutely not. No one deserved to be abused under any circumstances.

But what if . . . niggled the doubt burrowing deeper still into her mind . . . what if it wasn't true what Rosalyn had said?

What if being the abused wife was just another persona she had adopted in what now looked like a series of personas? There was no doubt that since her arrival, Rosalyn had displayed a variety of moods and guises.

Firstly, there had been the anguished widow barely surfacing from her bed and then when she had, she'd shuffled around in her dressing gown like an old woman incapable of doing anything.

Next, she had morphed into the attractively made-up young woman cheerfully and purposefully cooking Ben's favourite meals.

After that had come the screaming banshee shrieking at Emily when Finlay had gone missing. Which may or may not have been understandable.

Then this afternoon she had been the malevolently confrontational woman accusing Cassie of hating her, followed soon after by the out-of-control woman hurling photograph frames at the wall.

And now she was a woman who was wholly in control of not only herself, but the rest of them, dictating terms and expecting everyone to fall in line with what she wanted.

She really did seem to be extraordinarily adept at changing according to the situation, just like a chameleon.

And there was something else that had occurred to Cassie. There had not been a single tear shed during that explosion of emotion in the guest bedroom this afternoon, just a lot of shouting and smashing. It seemed a bit performative when Cassie really thought about it.

But hadn't all of it been performative, including how they'd been made to act around Rosalyn so as not to upset or offend her. All that tiptoeing around the grieving widow that Cassie had been reduced to. All that gritting her teeth at the mess Finlay created. Ben cancelling the party he'd wanted to arrange for Cassie's fortieth, and worse still putting on hold their wedding plans. All to avoid upsetting Rosalyn. Had they been played for mugs?

Then there was Emily who had carried out the lion's share of looking after Finlay, while his mother did what precisely? Not a lot as far as Cassie could tell. Or had she been working on this latest role, that of abused wife?

But why? To garner yet more sympathy? Was she thinking of how many more likes this would gain her on her social media accounts?

'I'm getting seriously weird vibes from you guys,' said Emily, breaking the silence while helping herself to a handful of pistachios. 'What's going on?'

Good question, thought Cassie as Rosalyn looked up from the glass of wine in her hand and met Cassie's gaze across the island unit. Her eyes were narrowed ever so slightly as if seeking Cassie's permission to continue.

No! Cassie wanted to say. *No, No, a million times NO!*

But before she could think of a way to stop Rosalyn from going ahead, it was too late.

'Emily, there's something I need to tell you,' Rosalyn began, her voice cool and steady, her gaze now switching to Emily. 'It's not going to be easy for you to hear this, but I want you to know that everything I'm about to say is true. I wish it wasn't, and I'm only doing this because I value our friendship and everything you've done for me. For Finlay too. You've been such a fantastic big sister to him, and I never want that to change. But your mum's been right all along, your dad wasn't a good man. He was an abusive bully. He was controlling, coercive and frequently violent towards me. And Finlay.'

Chapter Forty-Nine

Venetia wished she had never given in to the whim of returning to Hope Hall in the foolish belief it would bring her closure and peace of mind. If she'd only stayed where she was, her beloved Bon-Bon would still be alive and she wouldn't be cursing herself and that wretched boy, Finlay.

She didn't care what the child's mother said, or how vociferous her denials were, Venetia knew in her bones that Bon-Bon was dead because of something that boy did. And the sheer nerve of the woman shouting at Venetia the way she had and dismissing Bon-Bon's death as being of little importance compared to losing a child. How dare she say that Bon-Bon could be easily replaced! To Venetia, a life was a life!

All life, so Lady Constance used to say, was sacred and equal in the sight of God.

'Including nits?' Venetia had asked during a Religious Instruction class which Lady Constance was in charge of. They'd just had a few weeks when all the children were lousy with nits and poor Edie Buckle was beside herself while waging war on the beasts and eggs that infested their heads.

'Perhaps we could make an exception in the case of nits,' Lady Constance had said with a smile.

'How about fleas?' someone else had asked.

'And rats?' piped up another.

And what about bullies like Terry Sands? Venetia had thought.

Closing her eyes for the briefest of moments, Venetia cast that memory from her mind, and thinking how quiet the apartment was, she looked around the sitting room wondering where Bon-Bon had got to. Her body responded before her brain did and feeling as though she had been punched in the chest and the air knocked out of her, she reached for the back of an armchair to steady herself and then sat down heavily, a tremble running through her.

It was not the first time something like this had happened since Bon-Bon had died, but the pain of it didn't lessen with each occurrence. She knew that it was going to take time to break herself of the many habits and rituals that had developed between her and Bon-Bon. Like the way he'd see her tote bag and immediately hop into it because he knew they were going out. Sometimes he even went in search of her bag and dragged it towards the door because he'd decided it was time to go somewhere. She missed the way he'd comically pricked up his ears when she was talking to him as though he were hanging onto her every word. She missed how he had loved to sit on her lap, and would sometimes jealously nudge the book or newspaper she was reading out of her hands so she would give him her full attention. She missed the way he'd circle round and round in his basket, arranging himself and his blanket until all was just right before settling down to sleep. She especially missed his presence on her bed at night. Oh yes, she'd been one of those dog owners who had proclaimed at the outset that no dog, no matter how sweet, would ever sleep on her bed. That rule had soon fallen by the wayside and now more than anything she wished she could still be woken in the morning by a small black nose nudging at her cheek.

Seized with a wave of tearful emotion, she went over to the drinks cabinet and with a shaking hand, poured herself a tumbler of whisky. She was just about to toss it back in one large restorative gulp when there was a knock at the door. She debated whether to answer it. But then, and following what she'd overheard earlier, or imagined she'd heard, she wondered if it was Cassie wanting to explain and apologise for the noise.

Venetia had fallen asleep in the armchair that afternoon – sleeping so badly at night these days a daytime nap often crept up on her. This time she had been woken by strange noises coming from Cassie's apartment above hers. She couldn't be sure, the walls and floors were so thick and solid, but it sounded like something being thrown. Then there had been a cry, or possibly a scream. But equally it could have been a piece of furniture being moved and emitting some sort of squeal of resistance, like the castor of a chair or sofa. It had fleetingly crossed Venetia's mind to text Cassie to see if everything was all right, in case it had been a cry she had heard, but she really didn't want to be that kind of neighbour, the type who poked her nose into other people's business.

There was another knock at the door and downing the whisky in one long swallow, she went to see who it was.

It was Nina. 'I shan't mind if you tell me to go away,' she said, 'but I wondered if you might like some company and something to eat. That's if you haven't eaten already.'

'I'm not sure I'd be the best of company right now,' Venetia said.

'You don't have to be. And I understand that you might prefer to be alone. I'd have hated anyone turning up unannounced like this on my doorstep when Hugh died, so send me packing and I won't take offence, I just wanted you to know that—'

'It's fine,' Venetia interrupted her, not wanting to hear the words *I was thinking of you* one more time. 'I haven't eaten,' she said. In fact, she couldn't remember if she had eaten anything that day.

'How does poached salmon with lemon rice followed by Waitrose's finest frangipane tart sound?' Nina asked.

'It sounds delicious,' replied Venetia and meaning it. 'But are you sure you have enough for two?'

'More than enough.'

There was something irresistibly soothing about being in Nina's company, and her apartment. As Venetia had noted before when she'd been here previously, there was no clutter, and no extravagance of design on show, just an unpretentious palette of soft hues of sand and cream with a hint of silver here and there. On the walls there were, as you'd expect, a collection of beautiful paintings, a mixture of watercolours, acrylic and oil that included bucolic landscapes, seascapes and still lifes. Nothing jarred on the eye, or the senses, and Venetia imagined that nothing in the apartment had been placed there by chance, and yet the artful simplicity of it all combined to create a beautiful oasis of calm. It had an oddly cleansing effect on Venetia, as though allowing her permission to take a moment to hit the reset button and clear her mind of all its turbulent disorder.

Then there was Nina herself who looked so right in this oasis of tranquillity. There was nothing about her that jarred either. Softly spoken and dressed in what modern parlance referred to as lounge knitwear – loose-fitting silvery-grey trousers and a matching hoodie top, probably made of cashmere – there was a pleasing economy to her flowing movements as she steadily went about the business of preparing their meal, rhythmically chopping, mixing, stirring, and seasoning. In what seemed like no time at all, she was soon placing two appetising plates of food on the table and inviting Venetia to sit down.

Their wineglasses filled from a bottle of chilled Sancerre, Venetia said, 'Thank you for inviting me to join you. Much to my surprise, I feel better already for being here with you.'

Nina smiled. 'I'm glad you agreed to come. But please don't feel under any obligation to say yes another time. In no way does this set a precedent.'

'I appreciate your thoughtfulness,' responded Venetia. Then: 'When we were coming up the stairs you mentioned that you wanted my advice. Was that true, or was it a ruse to lure me here?'

'It was true,' said Nina. 'I wouldn't dream of insulting your intelligence by lying to you. However well meant,' she added.

'So how can I help you?' asked Venetia after she'd eaten a few mouthfuls of the salmon and lemon rice and declared it the best meal she'd eaten in days.

'I have a situation which requires careful handling, very careful handling and I'm hoping you might be able to offer some advice.'

'Is this something to do with you and Jakob?'

A faint blush instantly adorned Nina's beautiful face – she really did have the loveliest of cheekbones – and she shook her head. 'No, it's nothing to do with Jakob.'

Regretting the assumption she'd made, Venetia was annoyed with herself. 'I'm sorry for jumping in like that, only I know how nervous you were about taking things further with him. Forgive me, please.'

'You have nothing to apologise for. I'm happy to say all is well in that department of my life.' The blush on her face intensified. 'Although the age gap is never far from my thoughts, I can't deny that.'

'But if the gap was the other way round, you probably wouldn't give it a second thought, would you?'

'I know what you're saying, but what troubles me is when I think of the long term and how the gap might feel then.'

'Is anyone talking about long term?'

'No,' Nina said with a frown, 'but I don't want to waste time investing myself emotionally in something that might not go the distance.'

'Good grief, do you think your twenty-year-old self would have thought like that? That young girl would have just looked forward to the next date and that would have been enough. Wasn't that how it was when you met Hugh, you simply put one foot in front of the other and took each day as it came? Can't you do that now? Because take it from me, don't let an opportunity to be happy pass you by or deny you the chance of an adventure. Life is full of toss-of-the-coin moments. And regrets.'

'You should know me well enough by now that toss-of-the-coin moments are really not my thing, I always err on the side of caution.'

'But you took a risk on Hugh, dare I suggest?'

With a small moue of bemusement, Nina said, 'I often wondered what he saw in me as I was the complete opposite to him; he was such a daredevil and a serial risk-taker.'

'Maybe you were his greatest risk and challenge, the one that really gave him the biggest thrill. Did you fall in love with him straight away?'

'No, anything but,' Nina said, her face brightening with a smile. 'I thought he was arrogant and had far too big an opinion of himself!'

Venetia smiled too. 'I knew somebody like that a long, long time ago. Somebody I grew to love very much.'

'Did he love you in return?'

'Yes,' she answered in a faraway voice. 'He did. Sometimes I wished he hadn't because then . . . ' She swallowed, not sure she should continue, not sure that her emotions were strong enough right now to recall the loss she'd felt all those years ago. First love, as they say, is the love you never forget or get over. She sipped her wine before going on. 'Because then he wouldn't have run away and in so doing broken my heart.'

'Was this Lucien who you mentioned to me before, your special friend when you were here as a child?'

'Yes,' said Venetia softly.

'Why did he run away?'

Because, Venetia said silently in her head, *we both did a terrible thing and by him disappearing it made it look as though only he was guilty.*

'It's a long story,' she murmured.

'I'd like to hear that story,' Nina said in a tone that Venetia found beguilingly persuasive, 'if you're happy to share it with me.'

Chapter Fifty

May 1960

Venetia stared in petrified horror at Terry Sands, his open eyes shining glassily in the fiery orange light of the flames.

'He's alive!' she gasped, clutching Lucien's arm to drag him away, not just because the fierce heat of the fire was now blazing dangerously close to them – already the exposed skin on her hands and face felt like it was being scorched – but because she was terrified Terry might rear up and grab them.

But as though turned to stone, Lucien didn't react. His expression was mask-like as he stared at Terry lying on the floor, the flames now licking around the man's body. Venetia knew they had to do something, and fast. They could either run like the devil and leave Terry to burn to death or . . . or they could save him and face the awful consequences.

The fire was spreading. Flames were devouring anything in its path, the hearth rug, the fabric of the armchair and the flimsy curtains at the window. And with smoke rapidly filling the room, Venetia made the only decision she could. Using all her strength, and noticing that Terry's eyelids had closed again, she gripped his ankles and began hauling him out of the room. Lucien still hadn't moved, and she screamed at him to help her, but it was as if he couldn't hear or even see her. When she'd managed to drag Terry as far as the relative safety of the hall, she went back into the smoke-filled room and yanked Lucien by his arm. Only then did he seem to realise where they were or what was happening and as if in response, his chest heaved with a series of debilitating wracking coughs that had him bent double.

'We have to get out of here!' she yelled at him, spluttering as flames and thick choking smoke made it virtually impossible to see, but thankfully he did what she said. In the hall he seemed to come to his senses and helped her to drag Terry outside, down the garden path and beyond the gate where there was no danger of the fire reaching them. Terry's body was such a heavy dead weight it took them an age to cover the distance. His eyes had remained shut while they'd wrestled with his body, and there'd been no flicker of life from him. Frightened to do it, but needing to know, Venetia dropped to her knees and put her fingers to his wrist.

'Is he alive?' wheezed Lucien.

'I can't find a pulse,' she said, shaking her head, then putting the palm of her hand on his chest to feel for a heartbeat.

Lucien got down onto the ground and just as she had, he pressed his fingers to Terry's other wrist. 'Nothing,' he said.

They looked at each other. 'It's best this way,' Venetia said.

'Did I imagine his eyes opening?' Lucien asked.

'No,' she murmured, 'I saw them open too. It must have been what they call death throes, a last—'

Before she could finish, there came a succession of loud splintering sounds followed by a crash as the roof gave way and the cottage began to disintegrate. In the fading light of the evening, and now that the cottage was entirely engulfed in flames, the sky glowed as with a blazing setting sun.

'We should call for help,' said Venetia, her throat scratchy from the smoke.

'Too late,' said Lucien hoarsely, 'it's on its way.'

He was right. Running towards them were Miss Selby and Mr Grafton.

'Leave the talking to me,' she instructed Lucien. 'Don't say a word.'

'What the hell's happened?' demanded Mr Grafton.

Ignoring his question and deliberately sounding like she was about to burst into tears, Venetia said, 'We did our best, but we were too late.' She coughed for extra effect and immediately regretted it; her throat felt like it had been rubbed with sandpaper. 'The smoke,' she managed to say, 'the flames . . . it was too much . . . we were too late.'

At that Mr Grafton and Miss Selby turned away from the burning cottage and saw Terry's body on the ground behind Venetia and Lucien.

Miss Selby let out a shrill cry and staggered against Mr Grafton. 'He's not dead, is he?'

Maybe it was shock she was now experiencing, but Venetia began to shake and in a genuinely choked voice she said, 'He was on the floor inside when we found him . . . there was an empty bottle by his hand and the fire . . . there were flames everywhere . . . it was so . . . so scary and so very hot.'

'God! This is the last bloody thing we need!' Mr Grafton said furiously, pushing a hand through his hair. 'A fire and a death on top of everything else!' He suddenly fixed his eyes on Lucien. 'What were you two doing here in the first place? You should have been in your dorms!'

'We know it was wrong, but we just wanted to go for a walk,' said Venetia, 'and then we saw the fire.'

'Can he not speak for himself?' Mr Grafton said.

'It's his chest,' Venetia said, 'the smoke has made his asthma worse.'

'Never mind all that,' said Miss Selby, taking charge, 'we need to call the fire brigade, and for an ambulance to come, the police too.'

'Lucien needs to go and see matron,' insisted Venetia, 'his

chest is bad from all that smoke.' He was wheezing even more now.

'Both of you should go,' said Miss Selby. 'You,' she said to Mr Grafton, 'stay here with Terry while I go and make the necessary telephone calls.'

'Why do I have to stay with the body?' said Mr Grafton.

'Because I'm Lady Constance's deputy and I've asked you to,' snapped Miss Selby. 'Come on you two,' she said, looking at Venetia and Lucien. 'Go and see Mrs Buckle and then I expect the police will want to talk to you.'

'Heavens to Betsy, just look at the state of the pair of you!' cried Edie when they knocked on her inner sanctum. 'What have you got yourselves into now?' But then hearing the wheezing and rattling coming from Lucien's chest, she frowned and guided him towards a chair. Instructing Venetia to go and wash and then make some hot sweet tea in the small kitchen, Edie focused her attention on Lucien.

It was when Venetia went to turn on the taps at the sink in the small kitchen, she saw that her hands were smeared with blood: Terry's blood. It must have come from his head when he'd hit it on the hearth. She scrubbed her hands, then scrubbed them some more. She looked in the small mirror Edie kept on the wall in the kitchen and saw that her hair and face were covered with black smuts, as well as more blood where she must have put her hands to her face at some point.

Bile rose up to her already stinging throat and dipping her head low, she tried to wash her face, cupping her hands under the tap and then rubbing her cheeks hard with soap. But as hard as she scrubbed her face, she doubted she would ever feel like she had entirely washed away the nightmarish events of that day. It would be the same for Lucien, she suspected. She just hoped that he wouldn't do anything silly, like admit to pushing Terry.

Remembering that Edie had told her to make some hot sweet tea, she dried her face and filled the small whistling kettle, then found some mugs, tea, milk and sugar, and did it all with shaking hands and her stomach churning. She couldn't stop thinking about Terry and that horrifying moment when his eyes had opened. Had it been a final death throes spasm or had he been coming round from being unconscious all that time? And what if they'd just made another mistake when trying to find his pulse, and he was now fully conscious and telling Mr Grafton the truth of what had happened?

Terry was officially declared dead later that night, when his body was taken away. They were told that there would be a postmortem carried out and Edie briefly explained to Venetia what that meant.

'It's to find out what the cause of death was. It's just a formality.'

'Will we have to answer more questions?' Venetia asked anxiously.

She was sitting up in bed in the sick room; the other beds were unoccupied and she was glad of that, it meant she had Edie to herself. Lucien's already weakened chest had been so severely affected by the smoke he had been taken to hospital in the ambulance Miss Selby had called for. They had wanted Venetia to go as well, so she could be properly checked over, but Venetia had said she was fine and would be happier staying at the Hall where Edie could keep an eye on her. She hadn't felt fine, but she hadn't been about to admit that. Poor Lucien had stood no chance in arguing that he was OK, it was clear to everyone that he was in a bad way and would likely stay in hospital for some days. She had been tempted to go so she could be near him, but had decided it would be better for her to stay behind so she would hear what was being said about Terry's death.

'You might have to answer a few more questions, maybe make a statement as well,' Edie answered her. 'I'm no expert, of course, but I should think there'll be an inquest, the result of which will probably be that it was a terrible accident.'

'An accident,' repeated Venetia at length, 'because he drank too much and . . . and somehow knocked the clothes horse into the fire. That kind of accident?'

'Yes,' said Edie. 'A simple accident. Just one of those things.'

'So a *tragic* accident,' Venetia further suggested.

'Well, perhaps not so tragic,' said Edie, patting Venetia's hand. 'He wasn't a nice man, was he?' The pressure on Venetia's hand increased. 'He'd made life very difficult for Lucien, and for you too. Maybe,' Edie said slowly and gazing straight into Venetia's eyes, 'it's a blessing he's no longer around.'

Venetia swallowed and then winced. Her throat felt even more sore than it had earlier. Previously it had felt like it had been rubbed raw with sandpaper, now she'd swear a cheese grater had been taken to it. 'I don't know whether it's right to say it's a blessing,' she murmured, dropping her eyes from Edie's all-seeing gaze, 'but it's certainly going to be better without him. He was a bully. A nasty bully.'

'I know he was,' Edie soothed, 'you don't need to tell me that. I know his type. I came across plenty like him during the war in London. When my neighbours and I were bombed out, there was this ARP warden who loved the power the uniform and tin hat gave him. He used to strut about like he owned the place. We none of us trusted him as far as we could throw him, and we were proved right when we discovered he was helping himself to stuff from bombed-out houses and selling it. He was caught red-handed one day and given a lesson by a couple of lads home on leave that he wouldn't have forgotten in a hurry.'

Venetia wanted to believe that what Edie had shared with her was just another of her wartime stories, but she suspected there was more to it than that. Should she confess to Edie, tell her everything that had happened, including what Terry had done to Lucien that afternoon, which would be breaking the promise she'd given to Lucien that she would never tell anyone what she'd witnessed? But if Edie knew everything, would she then protect them from the police?

It was Mr Grafton who worried Venetia most. It had been the way he'd looked at her and Lucien, like he hadn't believed a word of what Venetia had said about trying to rescue Terry.

She then remembered what Mr Grafton had said – *'God, this is the last bloody thing we need! A fire and a death on top of everything else!'* What else was going on then, that was so bad?

'Edie,' she said, 'is everything all right here at Hope Hall?'

'Whatever do you mean?'

She told Edie what Mr Grafton had said.

The woman tilted her head to one side as if giving the matter her serious consideration. 'How interesting,' she responded, 'and it rather confirms what I've been thinking for some time. But now,' she said, and rising from her chair, 'I think it's high time you went to sleep. If you need me, I'll be in my room.'

She waited for Venetia to lie down and then she kissed Venetia on her forehead. 'Sleep well and don't worry about anything,' she said softly, 'it's all going to be all right for you and Lucien, I'll make sure of that.'

But it wasn't all right. A few days later Edie broke the news to her that Lucien had gone missing. He'd left his hospital bed, and no one had seen him since. This coincided with the return of Lady Constance and her husband, back from their extended honeymoon. And that was when everything went from bad to worse.

Chapter Fifty-One

'But why did Lucien run away like that?' asked Nina. She had long since finished eating and her wineglass was empty, and while Venetia had been talking, the younger woman had listened intently. She now had her elbows resting on the table and was leaning forwards as though all the better to hear what Venetia had to say.

Of course, what Venetia had shared with Nina had lacked many of the crucial details of what had really happened, and so it came as no surprise to Venetia that Nina would ask the question she had.

'It was the shock,' Venetia lied. 'Seeing a man dead like that, Lucien just couldn't handle it. He'd always been such a sensitive soul. There was guilt too, Terry Sands had bullied him mercilessly, and Lucien had often wished the brute was dead, and then unexpectedly Terry was very much dead. I can quite understand why Lucien reacted the way he did.'

'But you didn't react in the same way,' said Nina.

'No. But then Terry didn't target me as much as he did Lucien. Bullies do that, they perceive vulnerability, and they go for it, again and again. I never showed Terry that I had a weakness.'

'Other than your love and loyalty for Lucien,' remarked Nina, 'doubtless Terry saw that straight away.'

'Yes,' Venetia said softly, thinking how insightful that was of Nina. 'Love is always easy to spot. Its absence too.'

'And did you never hear from Lucien again? Not even a letter?'

'That was the hardest part,' Venetia replied, her gaze drifting away from Nina's face and settling on a beautiful painting above a pale wood console table. For a moment she lost herself in the delicate Victorian watercolour that featured two young girls carrying a basket of apples through an orchard, the sunlight filtering through the leaves on the tree branches and illuminating the whiteness of the girls' aprons and bonnets. 'The daily hope and endless waiting for Lucien to get in touch,' she said, returning her gaze to Nina's, 'but he never did.'

'That must have hurt.'

Venetia sighed. 'It worried me more than pained me. I just wanted to know that he was all right, that he was safe.'

'From what you've said, it sounds like you were always looking out for him.'

'It's true, I was, from his very first day here at Hope Hall when Lady Constance asked me to show him the ropes. There was just something about Lucien that made me want to protect him. He'd have hated knowing that, of course. He was very proud and could be quite arrogant at times. But it was just a defence mechanism on his part.'

'We all do that to a degree, don't we? We present a front to the world and hide our vulnerable selves behind it.'

'Are you thinking of anyone in particular?' asked Venetia, wondering if Nina was referring to herself.

'My mother-in-law,' Nina said. 'When I first knew Hilary, she was always opinionated and overbearing as well as dogmatic, but when Hugh died everything escalated until finally she spiralled out of control and had no one to turn to. She'd pushed everyone away.'

'You mean literally, no one?'

'No one except for me, so it seems.'

For the next few minutes, it was Venetia's turn to listen and when Nina fell quiet, Venetia said, 'The poor woman, to be so bereft and alone in the world that her only way to find comfort was to steal baby clothes to assuage her grief. That is so very, very sad.'

'It is,' agreed Nina. 'The way Hilary sees her life now, she has nothing left of any worth. She has nothing to look forward to, especially after I ended her hope of one day becoming a grandmother to Hugh's child. She also has nothing with which to occupy herself. Other than brood on what will never be. Her friends have dropped her. Or more likely, she's dropped them because they've run out of patience and just want her to get on with her life.'

'She sounds depressed,' said Venetia.

'I'm no expert, but I would agree with you. This,' Nina then went on, 'is what I wanted your advice for.'

Venetia was thrown. 'Sorry,' she said, pushing her empty plate away from her, 'but I wouldn't know how to help somebody with depression.'

'No, it's not that kind of advice I'm interested in. And look, I'm very conscious that this might be insensitive of me, and I certainly don't mean it to be, but I can't help but think that Hilary needs something to look after, something to nurture and love, so I've been thinking about encouraging her to have a dog. I know she isn't a cat person, she made that very clear some years ago when a neighbour's cat persisted in using her garden as a toilet.'

'A dog is a big responsibility,' Venetia said carefully, 'do you think Hilary would be capable of taking one on?'

'I really believe that having something to love and cherish is just what she needs. Hugh once told me that when his mother was a child, she'd begged her parents for a dog, and they wouldn't let her have one.'

'Did she ever fulfil her wish as an adult?'

Nina shook her head. 'No, she never did. But then I think Hugh fulfilled all her wishes and a lot more besides.'

'And now that she has nothing, a dog might fill the void, is that what you're thinking?' Venetia's words came out more tersely than she'd intended.

'Would that be so very wrong?' asked Nina, her brows drawn together in a small frown.

Venetia shook her head. 'I'm sorry, I didn't mean to sound so crabby, especially as I did the very same thing after my last husband died. I didn't want to be on my own, so I found Bon-Bon at a rescue centre. He was an abandoned puppy and Bon-Bon wasn't his name, but the moment I looked at him, with his adorable face, that was who he became for me, my tiny bundle of perfectly wrapped sweetness.' Her lips suddenly wobbled at the memory of meeting her precious little companion for the first time and she pressed her hand to her mouth. 'Goodness,' she said, 'just look at me, I've turned into such a sentimental mess.'

'I'm sorry for upsetting you.'

'Don't be silly, you did nothing wrong. And to answer your original question, I think it's a good idea, but you'll need to go about it the right way. Rescue centres these days are very strict on who can and cannot have one of their dogs, and rightly so. If buying from a breeder, you need to do your homework and find a reputable breeder. There are a lot of dodgy ones out there.'

Nina nodded. 'I confess I did have this daft picture in my head of surprising Hilary with a cute puppy and melting her heart on the spot and everybody living happily ever after.'

'That could still happen, but Hilary has to be the one to choose the dog, whether it's a puppy or a full-grown dog.'

'But ostensibly you think it's not a bad idea and that I should pursue it?'

'Definitely. If you like, I could help you.'

'That would be wonderful, so long as it won't be too upsetting for you. But firstly, I need to broach the idea with Hilary. And before that, I'm going to make us some coffee. I'm pretty sure I have some chocolate mints too.'

'Perfect. You do that while I stack the dishwasher for you.'

'There's no need. Why don't you move to the couch and make yourself more comfortable, and then perhaps you'll tell me what happened when Lady Constance returned from her honeymoon?'

'Let's save that for another time,' said Venetia, with forced brightness. She suddenly felt like she'd had quite enough of the past for one night.

Chapter Fifty-Two

'Are you frickin' kidding me, Mum?'

'I've never been more serious,' Cassie answered her daughter. 'There's something about it all that just doesn't sit right with me.'

Emily rolled her eyes. 'You mean Rosalyn doesn't sit right with you. From the moment you knew of her existence you've had it in for her!'

'That's an outrageous thing to say and simply not true!' Cassie remonstrated, although of course it was completely true. Ever since Emily had gone to Dubai to stay with Drew and had reported back about what a great time she was having with her father and Rosalyn, Cassie had tortured herself with daily observations of not only Emily's Instagram and TikTok accounts, but Rosalyn's. Every single one of Rosalyn's posts had thoroughly rubbed Cassie up the wrong way. 'This has nothing to do with my feelings about Rosalyn,' she added in a more subdued voice, conscious of their surroundings. 'It's about instinct. Something feels off to me. Don't you feel it too? Just a little?'

Using a long-handled teaspoon, Emily prodded at the surface of her oat milk latte, obliterating the cute heart the hot Italian barista had put on it. 'I don't know what I feel,' she said morosely.

Cassie had taken the afternoon off from work and she and Emily were having what she hoped would be some much-needed quality mother-and-daughter time together in town. Cassie had dressed it up as doing some early Christmas shopping, but in reality she had wanted time alone with Emily.

It was just over a week since Rosalyn had shared her revelations about Drew and for some reason it had galvanised her. Within no time she'd decided on a school for Finlay and applied for a place and was now actively looking for somewhere to rent within the catchment area, as well as job-hunting. Before going to Dubai with Drew she'd managed a beauty salon and was looking for something similar. The change – *yet another change* – in her was extraordinary. But weird too. She seemed unnaturally upbeat. It made Cassie suspicious, and she now doubted that the grief Rosalyn had previously displayed had been genuine: it had been nothing but an act to cultivate sympathy.

Admittedly Cassie had a suspicious nature, but piecing everything together she had reached the only conclusion that made sense: Rosalyn was a narcissist. Having listened to plenty of podcasts about narcissists, in particular the dangerous sort, Cassie reckoned Rosalyn displayed many of the tell-tale traits. Like the constant need for attention and the desire to be at the centre of things. Then there was the inability to think or care about others and being overly sensitive to any perceived criticism. There was also the aspect of alienating people, cutting herself off from anyone who disagreed with her. Was this why Rosalyn hadn't had a rush of friends to help and support her after Drew's death? Had they all been dropped?

Then there was the story she'd told about her parents. Cassie had never been able to get her head around the idea that Rosalyn's mother and father wouldn't have wanted to patch up whatever differences they'd had with their daughter so they could get to know their grandson. But according to what Rosalyn had now shared, it was Drew's coercive behaviour that had isolated her from her parents. But what if that was a lie and it had been Rosalyn who had pushed them away because they could see through her act? Because if Drew really was to blame, why hadn't Rosalyn contacted them now that he was dead?

None of these suspicions had Cassie dared discuss with Emily. She'd discussed them with Ben and as ever he'd cautioned her to stand back and just let Rosalyn get on with organising her new life. He'd admitted that he'd be hugely relieved when Rosalyn and Finlay were gone so they could focus on arranging their wedding. They still hadn't set a date.

'But where does Emily fit into that new life Rosalyn is suddenly so eager to arrange?' Cassie had asked Ben.

'That's not really our problem,' he'd said.

'It is if Emily ends up hurt.'

'Then we'll be there to pick up the pieces. Like we always have been.'

But of course, Cassie was incapable of standing back. She wanted to avoid there being any pieces to pick up; she wanted to protect Emily from being hurt in the first place.

In contrast to Rosalyn's sudden burst of energy, and the constant breezing in and out of the apartment with Finlay, it seemed that Emily's energy had been depleted. She spent much of her time avoiding Cassie, and when she offered to help Rosalyn with looking for somewhere to live, Rosalyn said she had it all in hand and she'd taken up enough of Emily's time already.

Poor Emily, thought Cassie as she observed her daughter's downcast face, she had to feel rejected after everything she'd done to help. She was also having to come to terms with everything Rosalyn had said about Drew, shattering in one fell swoop the version of her father she'd come to believe and had perhaps begun to love. So far, and despite Cassie's attempts to encourage Emily to discuss it with her, she had refused to do so.

Which was why they were here in town having coffee and cake together. Obviously, Cassie was meddling, but that's what a good mother did. Meddling was one hundred per cent part of the job description. It was how you protected your daughter.

'I just don't get you,' Emily said, looking up from her latte, 'I'd have thought, given how much you hated him, you'd be only too happy to discover my father was an abusive husband.'

Ignoring the jibe, Cassie said, 'I know you're very fond of Rosalyn, but what if she's made stuff up? What evidence do we really have that your father did any of those things she claimed he did?'

'Yeah right, wasn't that what MeToo was all about, women coming forward and actually being believed?'

'Absolutely. But hand on heart, Ems, I never once experienced any kind of coercive behaviour when I was with Drew.'

'You said he lied to you. You said he tried to make you believe you were imagining that he was seeing other women. Isn't that coercive behaviour?'

'Well, yes, but . . . but look, he was no saint, and he often lied to cover his tracks when he was with another woman, but I never felt threatened by him. That's quite a different matter.'

'Maybe he changed,' Emily said flatly.

How many times had she said that in defence of her father when Cassie had been so tempted to say that leopards couldn't change their spots. Now Emily was using it to condemn her father.

'Women generally have an instinct,' Cassie said warily, 'did you ever feel uncomfortable around your dad? Did you ever witness him saying or doing something which you thought was out of order?'

'No,' Emily said. 'But abusive men are calculating, aren't they?'

Cassie tried another tack. 'You must admit that it does seem odd that Rosalyn is now sharing online on all her platforms how coercive Drew was and that she hated living the lie she'd put across to her followers.'

Odd was putting it mildly. Cassie had been disgusted watching Rosalyn's posts. There she was with her flawless make-up and her eyes enlarged with false eyelashes and smudgy eyeliner, pouring out her heart in a breathless little girl's voice. *'You need to know it wasn't what I wanted to post, but he made me do it. He wanted everyone to see what a perfect dream life we had. And all the time it was a nightmare, and I couldn't tell anyone. I hope you can forgive me for lying to you.'*

The support that followed her posts was instant and quickly grew and with each new post of Rosalyn claiming she'd been gaslit or forced to do things she didn't want to do, Cassie was ever more convinced that Rosalyn was lying, and playing yet another role. Never would Cassie have imagined that she would want to defend her ex-husband, but a dead man unable to defend himself just didn't seem right.

Not all the online replies were positive. Men, probably pathetic and angry incels, had been quick to weigh in, telling Rosalyn she undoubtedly deserved what she'd got, that she was just another freeloading bitch who'd had it coming.

Such was the volume of responses to the posts, Cassie had wasted hours scrolling through the comments, but it was a needle-in-a-haystack task. What she was searching for was someone who knew Drew personally and who was prepared to call Rosalyn out for lying.

In answer to Cassie's question, and after finishing her latte, Emily said, 'It's not that odd what Rosalyn's doing; people are used to living their lives online, it's as natural as breathing. It's not like it was back in your day.'

Cassie smiled. 'Make me feel a hundred and ten, why don't you, and here I am convincing myself that forty is the new thirty!'

Emily smiled faintly too. It was the first time Cassie had seen her look anything but completely miserable in the last nine days. 'You're okay, Mum, don't stress it.'

'I'll take that as a compliment, thanks.'

For a few moments Emily stared out of the window and Cassie followed the direction of her gaze. Directly opposite the coffee shop was King's College and through a parting in the gunmetal-grey sky, a shaft of brilliantly radiant light shone like a laser beam on the magnificent old building, giving it an unworldly appearance. 'If Rosalyn is lying,' Emily said, turning to look at Cassie, 'or exaggerating, how do you explain what Finlay said about Dad throwing him in the swimming pool to punish him?'

'I don't know, not for sure,' Cassie said, 'but when I think back to what Finlay told me, he didn't actually say the words "Daddy threw me in the pool". He said something about it being a secret and that Daddy would be cross if he told anyone.'

'Wait, you're now saying you misinterpreted what Finlay said?'

Cassie shook her head. 'Not exactly. But look at it this way, a child can be very easily manipulated. What if it had been a game Drew was playing with Finlay and then Rosalyn twisted it round to make it seem like it was a punishment that Drew had carried out? Cleverly done, a small child can be convinced black is white and white is black. And, what if it was Rosalyn who threw Finlay into the swimming pool as a punishment and told him he mustn't ever tell Daddy about it because Daddy would be cross, not with Finlay, but with her?'

Frowning, Emily said, 'I can't believe you of all people would be standing up for a man you've hated ever since I was a baby.'

'I can't believe it either,' responded Cassie. And because Emily seemed receptive, she told her about her theory that maybe Rosalyn had a narcissistic personality disorder.

The frown deepening on her face, Emily said, 'Why are you so bothered about disproving Rosalyn? Why would you care?'

'I care because Drew was your father, and he mattered to you.'

Emily picked up her napkin and began tearing bits off it.

Cassie watched her. 'Ems,' she said, 'can you think of anyone back in Dubai who knew your father well and who might be prepared to dispute Rosalyn's claims?'

'Not really. But what I could do, seeing as I have so much free time now that Rosalyn doesn't seem to need me, is check out her socials to see if anyone is sticking up for Dad.'

'I tried doing that, but I've been so busy with creating a new website and helping Nina at the gallery, I didn't have the time to scroll through all the comments. There are thousands of them.'

Emily tossed aside the last remaining piece of the napkin as though she'd lost interest in it. 'Well, like I say,' she said with a shrug, 'I do have time on my hands now. Which leads me on to something I wanted to tell you. And whatever you do, please don't say, *"I told you so"* or that you knew all along I'd regret chucking it in, but I think I'd like to go back to uni next year, to finish off my degree. Meanwhile I'll get a job to help fund myself, but can I stay on with you and Ben until, you know, I'm properly sorted?'

Nothing could have pleased Cassie more. But knowing it was always better to play it cool, especially in public, she resisted throwing her arms around her daughter and said, 'Of course, Ems. And you know what,' she added with the happiest of smiles, 'you can help me plan the wedding.'

'Oh, great, it'll be 24/7 brain-numbing wedding talk, will it?'

And just like that, Cassie knew she had her daughter back. Her wonderfully sharp-tongued, sassy Emily, with all her mocking sarcasm and eye-rolling condescension. *Welcome back, Ems!*

Chapter Fifty-Three

With growing excitement Nina headed towards the arrivals hall.

Her plan to surprise Jakob at Stansted Airport had almost gone awry when the delivery of the paintings for the upcoming exhibition she was holding turned up several days earlier than planned at the gallery. Cassie had taken the day off to spend time with Emily and so Nina had helped the delivery man offload the carefully wrapped canvases and placed them with equal care on the floor where space permitted in the gallery before setting the alarm, locking up, and dashing to her car and then driving as fast as she dared to the airport.

Now here she was, anxiously awaiting Jakob's arrival. The screen directly in front of her showed that his plane from Oslo had landed five minutes ago. She was absurdly excited about surprising him this way. She just hoped that in the mêlée of the busy arrivals hall she wouldn't miss him. There seemed to be a lot of flights which were showing either as just landed, as the one from Oslo had, or were about to.

They'd spoken last night when he'd confirmed that he was definitely on his way back to Cambridge after extending his stay to check out some artwork he hoped she would find suitable for Lavelle's, but she hadn't said anything about meeting him at the airport. At that point she hadn't planned to. But then first thing that morning when she'd been in the shower, she'd decided to surprise him.

It had been quite a pivotal moment, climactic, you could say. There'd she'd been, going about the business of showering and thinking of work when, and from nowhere, a powerful pulse of desire had shot through her as the jets of hot water had played over her skin. For a delicious moment, her eyes closed, and her breath held, she'd imagined Jakob in the shower with her and how it might feel to have his naked body pressed against hers, their hands and mouths exploring each other.

The potency of the sensation had stayed with her while she'd dressed and then driven to work. It had been like a warm glow deep within her, and the feeling was with her still, except it was so strong now she felt almost feverish with desire for Jakob.

Her widowed self wanted to be shocked at the betrayal she was committing, that she could feel this way for a man other than Hugh. Yet her new self, the woman who wanted to love again and be loved in return, was now truly awakened with the need for the ache of desire she was experiencing to be satiated.

When she'd arrived at the gallery that morning, she'd texted Jakob to say that instead of going out for dinner as he'd suggested, she would cook for them at her place.

Are you sure? he'd replied immediately, as if he'd been waiting for her to message him.

Very sure, she'd responded.

She'd watched the three dots dancing on the screen of her mobile as he'd typed. *What time and can I bring anything?*

7.00. Just yourself.

A smiling emoji had then appeared.

It was later that she wondered about his response *Are you sure?* And her reply *Very sure.* Not for a minute did she think either of them had been referring to her cooking dinner.

*

The appearance of a flurry of travellers heightened her anticipation at seeing Jakob. She was looking forward to seeing the surprise on his face when he caught sight of her.

Most of those now dispersing into the arrivals hall and carrying only hand luggage had the look of purposeful business travellers and convinced her that they'd been on the Oslo flight and not the one from Tenerife that had landed a few minutes afterwards.

The conviction set off an explosion of what felt like turbocharged butterflies in her stomach, followed by a strange buzzing sensation. It took her a few seconds to realise that it was her mobile vibrating. She fished the device out of her bag and saw that it was Saul Bernice. No way did she want to speak to him and risk missing Jakob's arrival, but she hated to be unprofessional. Saul probably just wanted to know that his pictures for the exhibition had been safely delivered. He was always very taciturn to the point of rudeness, so she risked taking the call in the hope he wouldn't keep her too long.

'Hello, Saul,' she said.

'I wanted to check that the delivery was made without any problems,' he said curtly and without preamble.

'Yes, I personally helped the delivery man, everything's now in the gallery.'

'And there's no damage to any of the paintings?'

'I can't vouch for that as I had to rush out,' she explained, 'but I'll let you know as soon as I've had a chance to . . . '

Her words trailed off as she spotted Jakob in his familiar black puffa jacket, and she was just about to raise her hand to him when she noticed the beautiful, and very young, blonde girl at his side. Their faces bright and cheerful, they were chatting and laughing while together they pushed a trolley loaded with a set of smart Louis Vuitton luggage, as well as a medium-sized charcoal-coloured suitcase, presumably Jakob's, which just at that moment slid off the trolley.

Watching Jakob bend to put the case back on the trolley, his handsome face so animated and smiling, Nina wondered who the pretty blonde girl was. A fellow passenger perhaps whom he'd offered to help, which would be so typical of him.

'Are you still there, Nina?'

'I'm sorry, Saul,' she murmured, her eyes still on Jakob and the attractive girl, 'but now isn't a good time. I'll ring you in the morning.'

Before he could say anything else, she ended the call, slipped the phone back inside her bag and went over to surprise Jakob.

His reaction at seeing her went far beyond anything she'd expected. Grinning wildly, he threw his arms around her, then lifted her off her feet and spun her round as though she were a child of six. Which was ridiculous, she was a forty-three-year-old woman!

When he put her down, he kissed her on the mouth and then as if remembering the blonde girl standing behind him with the trolley and who now wore a bemused expression on her face, he said, 'Nina, this is my sister, Amalie, who has done nothing but complain the whole way here.'

The girl wobbled her head and rolled her eyes, and then held out her hand to Nina. 'Hey,' she said, 'the worst brother in the world has told me so much about you, but it's good finally to meet you in person. He kept saying you were beautiful, and now I can see with my own eyes that for once he was not exaggerating.'

Her English was excellent, just like Jakob's, though hers had more of what Nina perceived as a Scandi tone to it. She looked first at Jakob and then back to the girl, taking the two of them in. 'You really don't look at all alike, do you?' she said.

The girl laughed. 'Thank God for that! And I might add that as well as all the looks, I was given the brains too.'

Jakob smiled at Nina. 'But modesty, I'm afraid, was not gifted upon her.'

Nina smiled. 'It's lovely to meet you, Amalie. I think we have some catching-up to do. I want you to tell me everything you think I should know about your brother.'

'Oh, trust me, I plan to!'

Jakob groaned and grabbing hold of Nina's hand, he said, 'You mustn't listen to a word of what my little sister says, she is not to be believed! Trust me on that.'

Chapter Fifty-Four

The drive to Cambridge from Stansted had passed in something of a blur with Jakob's sister chattering nonstop for most of the way. When she'd managed to get a word in edgewise, Nina had invited Amalie to join them for dinner, but Jakob wouldn't hear of it.

'No, no, Amalie has already planned to amuse herself this evening,' he'd said, turning round to look at his sister in the back of the car, 'isn't that so, Amalie?'

Laughing, she had said, 'Don't worry, Jakob, I have no intention of spoiling your evening. And think yourself lucky I'm only staying a couple of days with you!'

'That's a short visit,' Nina had remarked, thinking of all the luggage they'd stowed in the boot of her car.

'I'm flying to New York the day after tomorrow,' she'd explained, 'to stay with friends.'

After they'd dropped his sister off at Jakob's house in Cambridge, Nina drove on to Hope Hall.

Inside the apartment, and while Jakob went to freshen up in the cloakroom, Nina fussed with switching on lamps, drawing curtains and ordering herself to calm down. She had been fine before. More than fine. She'd been longing for Jakob to be here with her, aching for his touch and to feel her body responding to his in ways that had made her head swim.

Taking a deep steadying breath and whipping round to go over to the kitchen and open the bottle of white wine in the fridge, she promptly found herself smack in front of Jakob, all but headbutting his chin. She let out a startled cry.

'Sorry,' he said, raising his hands as though in surrender, 'I didn't mean to alarm you.'

'You didn't. Well, okay, you did. It's just that—'

'That you're jumpy as hell,' he finished for her, and smiling, 'is that it?'

Nina smiled too. 'It's absurd,' she said, 'but for some reason, now that you're here, I'm behaving like a silly teenager on a first date.'

'Would it help to admit that that is just how I feel?'

'In that case, what we both need is a glass of wine.'

'Good plan, then I can try and explain exactly why I'm finding this situation so awkward.'

She pressed her hands against his chest, suddenly not wanting to move away from him. 'What situation?' she asked.

'You. Me. Us. Here. And what I've wanted to do with you since I first knew you.'

'And the awkward part?'

'Wine first,' he said firmly.

The wine opened and poured, they sat on the sofa, Nina having already kicked off her shoes, her feet tucked under her as she leant towards Jakob and touched her glass against his.

'The thing is,' he said, after he'd taken several large swallows of wine, 'and I know I've touched on this before, but I need to say it again, so humour me, please. I know I have a hell of an act to follow. You and Hugh were happily married for some years, and you probably still love him. Because why wouldn't you? So here I am, a very poor substitute. I'm not Hugh. And I never will be. I can only be me. What if I disappoint you because in your heart it's Hugh you still want and not me? What if it's Hugh you picture when we make love? And does all that make me sound totally paranoid?'

At the candour of his admission, and the seriousness of the expression on his handsome face, his crystal-blue eyes shining intensely in the lamplight, Nina's heart ached for him. But how could she reassure him when she didn't know for sure whether there could be an element of truth in what he'd just said? What if she did picture Hugh at the crucial moment of their love making? All she could be sure of was that unless they tried, they would never know.

In the silence that had settled on them, and as Jakob took another long swallow of his wine then put the glass on the table in front of him, she said, 'I've never compared you to Hugh, although I do appreciate that you might think I would. And in no way are you a poor substitute, that thought has never crossed my mind; in that respect, you couldn't be more wrong.' She frowned and placed a hand on his leg. 'I hate knowing that you've been worrying in this way. I wish you'd said something before.'

'It wasn't easy to admit what I was feeling even to myself. So,' he went on, after a pause and covering her hand on his leg with his own, 'tell me what is making you so anxious?'

'I'm not sure it's just one thing,' she replied, placing her wineglass on the table alongside his, 'but perhaps it's the level of expectation on both sides that is the problem. Then, of course, never far from my thoughts is that I'm older than you.'

'I thought we'd dealt with that.'

'Yes, but . . . ' she forced herself to say the words, 'but my body is not what it once was and—'

'Hey, take it from me,' he cut in, swinging round to face her, 'your body is perfect.'

'But you haven't seen—'

'No buts,' he said, 'absolutely no buts. And you know what?'

'What?'

'It's time we spent less time thinking and worrying and more time *doing*.' As if to show what he meant, he placed his hands either side of her neck, his thumbs grazing her jaw, his steadfast gaze staring deep into hers, and drawing her to him, he kissed her on the mouth. His lips were light and tender at first, then became more urgent and passionate, sending a rush of molten-hot desire streaming through her. But just as she was revealing the depth of her feelings for him, he pulled away and locked eyes with her.

'What's wrong?' she asked, worried.

'Nothing,' he said, 'and don't laugh, but I suddenly experienced a flashback to that wild night at the wedding party when we were dancing together.'

Her senses still reeling from the effect of his kiss, she groaned. 'Please don't remind me of that dreadful night,' she said.

'It wasn't all dreadful,' he said with a smile. 'I remember some very nice parts of the evening, especially when you kissed me.'

'Not true, *you* kissed me!'

He was grinning now. 'I don't remember it that way. I remember very well your lips touching mine and the night exploding.'

'I think you'll find that was when Hilary launched herself at me.'

'No, no, that came later. How is the poor woman now?'

At this rapid one-hundred-and-eighty-degree turnabout in the conversation, they simultaneously reached for their wineglasses and Nina told him about putting her idea to Hilary that maybe she should consider having a dog, a rescue dog perhaps. Just as Nina had expected, Hilary had been aghast.

'You think a dog can replace Hugh and the grandchild I dreamt of having?' Hilary had said. 'Is that what you honestly think will fill the horrendous void in my life?'

'Not entirely,' Nina had answered, 'but a dog would be marvellous company for you, and think of the lovely walks you could do together, and you'd meet lots of other dog walkers.'

The idea summarily dismissed out of hand, Nina didn't mention it again, but, and as she'd hoped might happen, Hilary rang her one evening to say that she'd been thinking it over.

'I'm not totally sold on the idea,' Hilary had said, 'and I definitely don't want some large-pawed beast digging up my garden or barking for hours on end, but I am prepared to consider it and I wondered if you might come with me tomorrow to meet a breeder who has bichon frisé puppies for sale. I've done all the checks online about the woman and she is a registered breeder with the Kennel Club.'

Impressed that Hilary had done her research, the next day Nina drove her mother-in-law to meet the breeder in Saffron Walden and it was during the drive that Hilary shared with Nina that when she'd been a child she had desperately wanted a dog, but her parents wouldn't let her have one. Nina said nothing about Hugh having told her this.

'And did that meeting go well,' asked Jakob. 'Is Hilary going to have a puppy?'

'It was never in doubt from the minute we arrived,' Nina said. 'It was extraordinary the change that came over her when she saw the puppy that was still for sale. Honestly, I'd never seen that soft side of her as she cradled the small bundle of white fluff. She was a woman transformed, talking away to the dog as though they were old friends. I took a photo to capture the moment for her, because it was just priceless. If I hadn't seen it with my own eyes, I wouldn't have believed it.'

While driving home afterwards, and having seen that new side to Hilary, it had made Nina wonder if she'd previously misjudged the woman, that she might have been a wonderfully loving grandmother if she'd had the chance. Well, it was too late now, that ship had well and truly sailed.

'It was a good idea of yours for her to have a dog,' Jakob said, 'when will she have the puppy?'

'Shortly before Christmas, when it's old enough to leave its mother. It's the perfect breed for Hilary as it requires a lot of companionship and that's exactly what she needs. I'm not saying it's going to cure all her problems, but it will give her something to love, and a sense of purpose.'

'And talking of companionship,' asked Jakob with a tilt of his head, 'how much of my company do you think you'll require?'

Nina laughed happily. 'Plenty,' she said, then glancing at her watch and seeing how late it was, she added: 'I should do something about supper, or we'll never get around to eating.' She was on her feet when Jakob reached for her hand.

'I have a much better idea,' he said, smoothly pulling her back down to him. 'Let's forget about eating, unless you're hungry, of course.'

Sinking into his embrace and the warmth of his mouth against hers once more, the thought of food suddenly couldn't interest her less.

Chapter Fifty-Five

When Keith had shared with Diane what Nina had told him and how hurt he'd been by the severity of her criticism of him, he had hoped for Diane's support. But it hadn't been forthcoming, certainly not in the way he'd anticipated or hoped for.

'Nina's right, you can't abandon Hilary, you've both been through too much together to walk away without helping her when she's in such profound pain. I'm shocked that you would even think of doing that.' Nina had warned him that Diane wouldn't think well of him if he abandoned Hilary by refusing to help her.

Just as he had with Nina, and not without a degree of exasperation, he'd said, 'But what about *my* pain? Why does Hilary's grief always have to trump mine?'

'The strong should always help the weak,' Diane had replied, her voice mild but tinged with what he'd perceived as admonishment, as if he were a naughty child.

He'd found her comment particularly galling. Why did she think he was stronger than Hilary? For that matter, there was nothing weak about Hilary! He'd tried saying this, but Diane had shaken her head and told him he was taking her too literally.

'I'm not talking about a physical state of being,' she'd said, 'I'm talking about the inner person, the soul. Perhaps your wife has never been as mentally strong as you thought she was. It's possible she was always trying to be the woman she believed you wanted her to be. Have you ever thought that the two of you have never really been honest with each other?'

He'd sensed a change in Diane in the last month or so. He blamed it on her attending a spiritualist church, because ever since she'd started going, he hadn't felt as in step with her as he had before. For a start, he couldn't understand her sudden interest in spiritualism, the whole concept was bunkum as far as he was concerned. Surely she was far too grounded and sensible to believe a word of it? Everyone knew that the psychic world was a con that took advantage of the vulnerable, who were desperate to feel closer to those they'd lost.

After seeing a poster at the local library advertising a talk to be given by a supposedly well-known medium, Diane had announced that she wanted them both to go. He'd initially thought she was joking and said he couldn't think of anything he'd like less.

'You might at least have an open mind on the subject,' she'd said. 'A closed mind is as good as an empty mind.'

It had been the first time they'd really disagreed on anything, but he'd stuck to his guns and refused to go with her. When she came home after the talk, he'd felt duty bound to encourage her to tell him all about it, if only to hear her admit that it had been a load of old hokum. 'I'll tell you about it if you're genuinely interested,' she'd said.

He'd lied and urged her to share what had gone on. She spoke cautiously at first and then she warmed to her subject and said how amazing it was when the medium started receiving messages to pass on to various people in the audience.

'The woman knew so much about them and about the loved one they'd lost and how they died. It was very moving.'

Of course it was, it was a stage show acted out by a grasping charlatan! Keith had wanted to say. But wisely, he'd held his tongue and had merely nodded and made what he hoped were supportive comments.

Since that evening, Diane had begun reading something called *The Seven Principles* and signed up for a workshop and lecture on healing, as well as attending Divine Services at the spiritualist church where the talk had been held. Every time she came home, she pressed Keith to go with her the next time.

'It's really nothing like you think it is, you're falling into the trap of imagining something out of a television programme with people being tricked,' she'd explained. 'There are hymns and prayers at the Divine Service, just like in an ordinary church service. There's a healing part to the service and time for when a medium connects with the departed in spirit and shares their messages. Next Sunday I'm going to ask if the medium can connect with my daughter, Fiona.' Reluctantly, and because Keith didn't want to see her made a fool of, or be hurt, he agreed to go with her.

But now, as Diane parked her car and pointed across the road to where they were going, Keith felt his worst fears rise to the surface of his dread. Their destination looked unlike any church he'd ever been to before. It was a brutal seventies-built eyesore, squat and ugly and with a flat roof. One of the windows was boarded up and there were daubs of graffiti on it. On a bitterly cold December afternoon, with what little light there had been that gloomy day, the so-called church could not have looked less inviting.

They were greeted by two young women wearing beanie hats and an excessive amount of metalwork pierced into their lips, noses, eyebrows and ears. They smiled brightly at Diane, saying it was good to see her again.

'And this must be your friend, Keith, who you've been telling us about,' the taller of the girls said. 'Welcome, Keith,' she added, increasing the wattage of her smile and revealing what looked like a bit of spinach stuck between two of her teeth. 'It's so lovely that Diane persuaded you to come. We're sure you'll feel right at home with us.'

Nothing could have been further from the truth. This was so far out of his comfort zone, he might just as well have been transported to Mars.

The service was led by a tall, thin man about the same age as Keith dressed in an ill-fitting suit, the trousers of which were too short. The bright strip lighting in the low-ceilinged room reflected off the man's shiny balding head, giving him an alien-like quality. Or perhaps others saw it differently: aura-like. He was exceptionally quiet spoken which had the effect of making his audience lean forward as though afraid to miss what he was saying. There was no show to the man, no flamboyance or obvious quackery; in fact he was disappointingly mundane.

But then everything changed when the bald man sat down, sending his trouser hems up around his calves, revealing white hairless legs, and it was the turn of the visiting medium to take to the dais. She was of a statuesque build and was wearing a shapeless dress of vivid purple. Her thick hair had a matching purple tint to it and was coiled on the top of her head like a large cottage loaf. From the moment she made herself comfortable in the chair on the dais, closed her eyes and held out her hands as if in an act of supplication, her presence commanded total silence, and a zealous hush fell on the room.

And so it began, the part that Keith had dreaded but which Diane had so looked forward to. He sensed her sitting up straighter beside him, all eager hope and anticipation. He didn't dare turn his head to look at her for fear of showing the dismay and disbelief on his face.

Keeping his gaze on the statuesque woman who now seemed to be in a trance – her eyes were open, but her expression was entirely blank – he wondered how the hell he'd got here. This wasn't him. He wasn't some poor deluded sap who needed to believe in the afterlife to comfort himself. What's more, he hadn't thought Diane was the sort to need this kind of false hope. He felt disappointed that her seemingly rock-sure ability to bear the death of her own child was in fact far shakier than he'd believed. For some reason he felt let down, cheated.

He'd thought her too intelligent and secure in her acceptance of losing her daughter, but seeing her like this and realising he'd fooled himself into thinking she was the answer to his own grief, he knew with gut-wrenching conviction that this was the beginning of the end of his relationship with her.

Whatever they'd had, or thought they'd had, he couldn't conceive of being part of her life if it included this . . . this world of supernatural jiggery-pokery. What next, Ouija boards and tarot cards? The spirit world being peddled here didn't exist, it was nothing but a cheap parlour trick that gave the vulnerable and the gullible false hope. And to his mind, there was nothing worse than false hope. Why couldn't these people accept that death was the end? There was nothing beyond it. It was what he'd always believed. And as much as he'd loved his son, he knew that Hugh was gone, and no amount of wishful thinking, or tapping into 'the other side' would ever change that.

He suddenly longed for the certainty of his old life. It might not have been perfect but at least he'd known exactly where he'd stood. What he'd give to turn back the clock to when he and Hilary had rubbed along well enough together . . . to that time before Hugh's death had imploded their lives.

Thinking of those relatively halcyon days, he was hit with a wall of shame. Despite Nina's urging that he involve himself with helping Hilary, he had selfishly, not to say childishly, dug in his heels. She wasn't his responsibility! To his further shame he hadn't even bothered to contact her sister, Lindsay. What kind of man had he become that he could be so self-centred and heartless?

He decided, just as soon as this nightmare was over, he'd ring Lindsay. What was more, he would go and see Hilary. He would apologise and do his best to help her just as Nina had asked him to.

At the sharp nudge in his ribs, he turned to look at Diane.

'It's Hugh,' she whispered, 'the medium's received a message for you from Hugh.'

Chapter Fifty-Six

A good night's sleep had eluded Venetia ever since losing Bon-Bon. This morning, and with an unpleasantly fuzzy head, she had been awake long before the first signs of the wintry dawn had appeared.

Now, as she finished her third cup of coffee and stood at the window of the sitting room, she looked out at the dense ribbons of eerily opaque mist snaking their way over the river. Despite the quantity of strong coffee she had consumed, it hadn't cleared the fog from her head, so she decided to go for a walk to see if that would do the trick. She was also aware that she needed the exercise. A disagreeable lethargy had come over her and she was conscious she was in danger of vegetating, of letting herself go. It was ages since she'd had her hair and nails done and if she wasn't careful, she was in danger of turning into one of those ancient old hags she'd vowed never to become. Something had to be done.

It was the worst kind of cold outside, the sort of bitter damp cold that seeped right through to the bone. Jamming her hat further down over her head, she tightened the woollen scarf around her neck and set off with a resolute and purposeful step across the soggy long grass towards the river where the mist still hung over the torpid surface of the water. The drab December sky was low and the air, still and dank, smelt of decay. From the woods over to her left came the ugly call of crows, their sound magnified in the inertness of the morning as they circled above the naked limbs of the trees.

How would Ronnie adapt to this after the blue skies and sunny warmth of his life in Majorca? she wondered. The last she'd heard from him, just a few days ago, was that the final stages of selling the hotel were within sight. He claimed he was looking forward to retirement and taking it easy for the first time in his life.

'It's been a long time in coming,' he'd said on the phone. 'Stupidly, and maybe something to do with vanity, I believed I could keep going for ever, that retirement wasn't for me, that the moment it happened it would sound the death knell.'

'We always keep going with something when we enjoy it,' she'd replied, 'but the minute it stops being fun, that's the time for a change of plan.'

The thought had crossed her mind more than once in the last few weeks that maybe she needed a change of plan for herself. Moving here to Hope Hall had not brought her the satisfying sense of completion she had thought it would. She knew that in all probability that was because of the needlessly tragic way her darling Bon-Bon had died, but even so she couldn't shake off the feeling that she had made a mistake. A terrible mistake.

By the time she'd been walking for almost an hour the mist had lifted from the river, and there was a glimpse of an ethereal white ball of light breaking through the murkiness of the sky. After watching the progress of a heron flying languidly off into the distance, she turned around to go home.

Home. In her heart, Hope Hall had always been her home. A place where she had known love and given love, where her dreams for the future had been forged in the very fabric of the building. It had been her world, and everyone in it had been her family.

With the Hall now in front of her, she looked up at the extraordinarily imposing building, a sight that had never failed to fill her with myriad emotions. *Lucky* and *proud* had been two of her early childhood feelings whenever she had taken the time to stand and gaze at the Hall. She had felt so very lucky to call the place home, and proud too that she was a part of its history. That was something that Lady Constance had tried to instil in them, to be proud of their beginnings in life and not be ashamed of growing up in a children's home.

Venetia couldn't speak for all the other children who had spent their childhood here, but she had never felt ashamed of her background. Even after everything that had happened here.

Chapter Fifty-Seven

June 1960

Nobody cared about Lucien disappearing.

The medical staff at the hospital had apparently been glad to see the back of him because he'd been so rude. The police certainly weren't bothered, to them he was just another runaway who'd decided he'd had enough of institutions. In their eyes, Lucien was old enough to make his way in the world.

Mr Grafton and Miss Selby weren't interested either, they were too busy covering themselves in readiness for Lady Constance's arrival home with her husband, Mr Butler. It was only Edie who cared about Lucien but as she and Venetia had no way of knowing where he could have gone, searching for him would be a Herculean task.

Terry's death and the burning down of the cottage at Hope Hall had held barely any interest for the local newspaper, giving it no more than a column inch. The paper was far more concerned with a scandal that had broken about the Master of one of the Cambridge Colleges who had been revealed to be a Russian spy.

Edie had promised Venetia that she fully intended to complain to Lady Constance on her return about the way Mr Grafton and Miss Selby had treated Lucien, how they'd believed Terry's word over his and how he'd been forced to apologise for something he hadn't done. Venetia hadn't had the courage to tell Edie the awful thing that Terry had made poor Lucien do, she wasn't sure that Edie would even understand, and besides Venetia had promised her friend never to tell anyone.

'I can't see that speaking to Lady Constance will do any good,' Venetia had said miserably. 'Mr Grafton will claim he was right, he might even say Lucien had confessed to him that he had taken the money which was why he then made him apologise. And that's why he's run away, because of the shame of being caught out.'

'He won't say anything of the sort,' Edie had said, 'because I shall make Mr Grafton tell the truth.'

'How?'

'I have my ways,' the woman had said mysteriously. 'You just have to trust me.'

It was some years later that Edie had admitted to Venetia that her way of making Mr Grafton and Miss Selby tell the truth was because not only had she observed the two of them snooping through Lady Constance's private things in her office, but she had also caught them having sex in one of the store cupboards. Understandably Miss Selby had been mortified and had begged Edie not to say anything to anyone, especially not Lady Constance. Hearing this from Edie, Venetia had finally understood why Mr Grafton had said what he had the night of the fire – *This is the last bloody thing we need.*

When Lady Constance had finally arrived home from her extended honeymoon with Mr Butler, everyone was shocked at the news that followed: she was desperately ill and had been given just months to live. She'd thought her lack of energy was due to all the travelling and sightseeing she and her husband had been doing, combined with a chest infection which had stubbornly refused to budge. It was only after she'd begun coughing up blood that Mr Butler had insisted she see a doctor at a hospital in Florence and she was then told that she had an aggressive form of lung cancer and it was beyond treatment. The advice was that she should travel home as soon as possible.

Venetia was devastated at the news, and by the sight of Lady Constance, who looked a shadow of her former self. She died in July of that year and her funeral was held at Farleigh Fen Church. The older children from the Hall were allowed to attend and Venetia sat with Edie, both holding back the tears as Mr Butler gave the eulogy. Standing at the lectern, his voice shaking with emotion, he'd looked utterly broken.

More bad news followed in the days after the funeral when Mr Butler announced in morning assembly that Hope Hall would have to be sold. Edie explained to Venetia that it was to do with death duties and that by the time these had been paid there would be hardly anything left to keep the place going.

'But it's our home,' Venetia had cried, 'it can't be closed! What about all the children here, where are they supposed to go? And you, Edie, this is your home too, what will you do?'

'You mustn't worry about me,' the woman had assured her. 'I have my savings, and I'm sure I can find another job without too much difficulty. And anyway, it won't be long before I'll have to retire. I shall find a cosy little flat in Cambridge to rent and live very quietly.'

'Take me with you!' Venetia had begged. 'I promise I won't be any trouble and then I can look after you, you know, when you're old, or if you get ill like Lady Constance.'

'Now don't you go fretting yourself about me, dear girl, I'm as fit as a fiddle, nothing's going to happen to me.'

'That's what Lady Constance probably thought and look what happened to her!' Venetia had said wretchedly.

In the end, and after Venetia kept up a steady stream of promises that she wouldn't be any trouble to Edie and that she'd get a job and help pay her way, the woman gave in.

Venetia had thought Lucien's running away and then Lady

Constance's death were the saddest things she would ever have to deal with, but leaving Hope Hall, her home since she was a baby, and even though she had a new home to go to with Edie, was just as painful. Never again would she sleep in the dormitory with the girls she'd known for so many years. Never again would she spend a quiet few hours reading in the library. And never again would she play in the idyllic grounds, walk along the river, or hide out in the woods with Lucien, her best friend and soulmate.

'That was your old life,' Edie said when they set up home together in a small flat, not in Cambridge as originally planned, but in London where Edie had a job in a home looking after disabled children. 'Now begins your new life.'

Chapter Fifty-Eight

Still lazing around in her warmest fleecy pyjamas, Cassie wondered at the energy some of her neighbours were exhibiting for a Sunday morning, especially on such a drearily cold day.

First, she'd spotted Venetia tramping about the grounds and now, clad in running gear and hats and scarves, Nina and Jakob were sprinting energetically along the riverbank. Their pace, Cassie observed as she stood at the kitchen window, was perfectly matched, even the pom-poms on their hats bounced in time on the top of their heads.

And don't go reading anything into that, she imagined Nina saying to her.

Jakob had become a regular fixture at Hope Hall since his return from Oslo and even Ben had commented on how happy and more animated Nina now looked. To Cassie's eye, Nina positively glowed with a radiance that spoke volumes of a woman currently enjoying the delights of a fabulous new sex life. And good for her!

Moving over to the coffee machine, she set it going and then opened the fridge. Never mind flogging herself half to death by doing a virtuous early morning run in the freezing cold, what she needed to set herself up for the day was a big greasy bacon sandwich, and to hell with the calories or whatever else would put her into an early grave! When the others were up, she'd make them one too. It was the least she could do for her wonderfully ingenious daughter.

Emily had disputed that she'd been ingenious. According to her, any fool could have done what she had. All it had taken was time and a bit of stealth and guile. But thanks to her efforts, they could now expose Rosalyn for the lying narcissist she really was. Cassie just wished they'd known the truth before, because then she would have had the perfect right to boot Rosalyn out of the apartment weeks ago. And if she had done that, the Devil Child wouldn't have drowned poor Bon-Bon. Okay, calling Finlay a devil child might be slightly unfair, but there was no getting away from the fact that if it wasn't for the boy's actions, Venetia's beautiful little dog would still be alive.

Ever since their chat at the coffee shop in town, when Cassie had shared with her daughter that she didn't believe a word of what Rosalyn had told them about Drew abusing her, Emily had applied herself with all the meticulous precision of a forensic scientist to scrutinising Rosalyn's social media accounts. It was a few days into the process when she admitted that she'd really struggled to believe the awful things that Rosalyn had accused Drew of and that she had been torn between wanting to support Rosalyn and wanting to defend the man she'd come to know as her dad.

'He's not alive, so he can't defend himself,' she'd said to Cassie, 'so I have to find a way to know the truth. Even if it means I discover Rosalyn was right and he was abusive. I have to know.'

After an eternity of scrolling through the endless responses to Rosalyn's social media posts, yesterday Emily had finally found the missing link to the truth. After an exchange of private messages, she had FaceTimed the woman in Dubai, a woman who had a very different version of Rosalyn and Drew's marriage. And today, all of Rosalyn's lies were going to come crashing down on her.

Emily had wanted to be the one to confront Rosalyn and to do it alone. 'You have to let me do this,' she had said last night. 'I got us into this mess, so it's my job to finish it.'

Cassie couldn't be prouder of her daughter, but she and Ben had agreed that Cassie should be with Emily when the conversation took place. After all, with a narcissist in their midst anything was possible.

Much to their collective relief, Rosalyn and Finlay had moved out three days ago, and this morning they were returning to collect the last of their things. The plan was for Ben to occupy Finlay with some game or other while Emily and Cassie tackled Rosalyn with what they now knew.

It was gone midday when Rosalyn showed up, bringing with her an act of airy self-importance, as though she were doing them a big favour by bestowing her presence upon them.

Seeing the two large suitcases which Ben had put ready for her, she had the cheek to say, 'Ben, while I say goodbye to Cassie and Emily, would you be a total sweetheart and take the cases down for me?' She nonchalantly tossed him a bunch of keys like he was her lackey. 'You can't miss it,' she added with a flutter of false eyelashes, 'it's a silver BMW.'

'Sure,' he said, smoothly, and in a skilful manoeuvre he commandeered Finlay to show him where the car was and the two of them disappeared out of the apartment.

'Well then,' said Cassie with a dose of hearty false cheer – *Rosalyn wasn't the only one who could put on a masterly performance!* 'This is it, then, a final parting of the ways.'

Rosalyn's newly plumped-up lips twitched with what might have been a smile, or there again, it might have been a smirk, but since her facial expressions looked like they'd been Botoxed to a standstill, it was anybody's guess.

'I so wish our paths had crossed in happier times,' she said in an irritatingly girlish voice, 'but I'm sure you'll agree with me that we've been on quite a journey together.'

Cassie cringed and Emily let rip with a loud snort. 'Some have journeyed further than others,' she said, her tone unmistakably barbed.

Rosalyn's eyes narrowed a fraction. 'Sorry, Ems, what did you say?'

'I mean that you checked out of the real world a long time ago and swapped it for a parallel universe in which you lie to suit your own selfish needs. You're a malicious fraud, Rosalyn! You wouldn't know real love or genuine friendship if it slapped you round the face. You're a user and you've certainly used me.'

As much as it was able, Rosalyn's face registered shock. 'Ems, have you completely lost your mind? Or,' she swung round to glower at Cassie, 'has your mother been filling your head with her spiteful bitching about me? God, you just can't help yourself, Cassie, can you?'

'Don't you dare talk about my mother that way,' Emily said before Cassie had a chance to respond. 'And don't ever call me Ems again. You don't have the right to do that!'

Her attention back on Emily, Rosalyn pointed a finger at her. 'And you don't have the right to talk to me the way you are. In fact, I'm going to leave right now before you cause me any more distress. I put up with abuse from your dad and I'm not going to take it from either of you.'

'Yeah,' said Emily, 'let's talk about that abuse, shall we? Or rather, the *non-existent* abuse. You made it all up about my dad. And for what? To cast yourself in the role of victim and to gain a few more likes on your socials?'

Looking a lot less sure of herself now, Rosalyn readjusted the Coach bag on her shoulder. 'I don't know what's got into you, Emily,' she said. 'But I feel sorry for you that you can't accept the truth about your dad. But maybe that's understandable. You're in denial and want to believe in the man you wanted Drew to be. That's only natural. And I forgive you.'

'You can shove your fake forgiveness!' Emily fired back. 'The only one in denial is you. Because here are the facts. My dad was planning to leave you. He'd been having an affair for more than a year. Not only that, he'd also discovered Finlay wasn't even his. You'd passed the child off as my dad's. You must have been so happy when he died, suddenly all your problems were instantly solved, weren't they? His death meant that you copped the jackpot, instead of only half of his money if he divorced you.'

Rosalyn swallowed. 'Where on earth has this nonsense come from?' she demanded, her eyes switching between Emily and Cassie.

'From the woman my dad was leaving you for,' Emily said. 'I found her on your TikTok account. I had a long and very interesting chat with her last night. She's furious that you've said the things you have about the man she loved. You tried blocking her after she publicly called you out for your lying, you even set your followers on her, but the thing about social media is that nothing ever disappears. There's always a way to find something if you know how to go about it.'

For the longest moment, Rosalyn didn't speak, and it was all Cassie could do not to fill in the silence by applauding Emily for bossing it the way she had.

'Well, la-di-da,' Rosalyn said at length, 'who do you think you are, Coleen-bloody-Rooney?'

'I wish I could take the full credit for uncovering your endless lies,' Emily said, moving nearer to Cassie and putting an arm around her, 'but really that honour should go to my mum. She'd figured you out ages ago. I just wish I'd trusted her judgement from the outset. You see, that's the thing about a mother who truly loves her child, she genuinely only wants the best for them. Something you've yet to learn because you don't know the first thing about being a good mother. I pity Finlay and the harm you've caused him with your twisted idea of parenting. My dad never punished that boy the way you claimed he did, it was you!'

'Well, as interesting as this is,' Rosalyn said with a sigh and adopting an air of boredom, 'I have the rest of my life to get on with. So, I'll say goodbye. I see no reason why our paths should cross again.' She turned away from them to make her way back towards the hallway.

'Don't you want to know who Emily spoke to last night?' asked Cassie, strangely fascinated at the way Rosalyn could affect such indifference to what she'd just been accused of.

'I don't need to,' she responded. 'Bianca's always been jealous of me. Just like you, Cassie. She was Drew's assistant in Dubai and tried her luck numerous times with him. Anything that comes out of her mouth is a lie!'

'You'd certainly know all about that,' said Cassie. 'I've never known anyone to lie as much as you do.'

Rosalyn shrugged. 'Don't make me laugh, everyone lies every single day, whether it's to the people they care about or those they despise. Of course, the easiest lies to tell are the ones to the people who love us. They'll believe anything. Just like you did, Emily. You lapped up the idea of having another family, of having a little brother to love. Perhaps you need to ask yourself why that was, why you were so keen to be part of a make-believe new family. Was your existing one not enough for you?'

Cassie saw Emily falter and swiftly stepped in. 'You despised us from the day you arrived here, didn't you?' she said to Rosalyn. 'You saw what Emily, Ben and I had, and if you'd had the chance, you'd have happily destroyed it.'

'Why not?' Rosalyn replied with another careless shrug. 'It would have been fun. And so, *so* satisfying. After all, a girl has to make her way in the world, doesn't she? And Cassie, you certainly landed on your feet when Ben came into your life. You too, Emily. A cushy option all round, I'd say.'

'*Bitch!*' cried Emily. Her voice had risen, and she suddenly looked close to tears.

'Touched a nerve, have I?' said Rosalyn.

'It wasn't true what she said,' Emily explained a short while later when it was just the three of them in the apartment, as she, Ben and Cassie stood at the window and watched the silver BMW drive away down the long driveway. 'I didn't go to Dubai because you weren't enough of a family for me. It was just Dad I wanted to meet. I was curious. I wanted to see for myself which bits of him, if any, I'd inherited and whether I'd even like him. Because you're supposed to feel something, aren't you? Feel some kind of connection because of the genes. Does that make sense?'

'Yes, of course it does,' said Cassie. 'And there was nothing wrong in you wanting to explore what your father was like and wanting to be a part of his life.'

'Even though you absolutely hated me going to stay with him?' murmured Emily, turning away from the window. There was no trace of reproach in her voice, only sad regret which tugged at Cassie's heart.

'I didn't want you to get hurt,' Cassie said.

Emily shook her head despondently. 'I messed up badly, didn't I?'

'No,' said Ben firmly, putting an arm around her. 'You didn't. You must never ever think that. It was circumstances and the subsequent actions of a sick woman who messed things up. If your father hadn't been involved in a fatal car accident, this story would have had a very different ending.'

Emily smiled wanly. 'You always say the right things.'

'And that's why we love him to the moon and back, isn't it?' said Cassie brightly, desperate to lift the mood. However she had imagined the confrontation turning out with Rosalyn, she hadn't foreseen Emily coming under attack the way she had. There had been no sense of victory or triumph in exposing the woman for the fraud and liar that she was, but maybe that was only right because sometimes in life there were simply no winners. Just survivors.

Chapter Fifty-Nine

Keith had arrived at The Maples just over an hour ago. The purpose of his visit was to make himself useful to Hilary, and in a very practical way. To that end he'd arranged for a log delivery, something he'd always done before winter set in, and he had duly arrived at the same time.

As plans went, it had been a huge gamble. Hilary could have accused him of being high-handed and sent him away, which she'd had a perfect right to do. He had not behaved well towards her. He hadn't behaved well towards Diane either, but Diane wasn't his problem right now. His focus had to be on his wife.

When Hilary had opened the door to him – he hadn't used his key to let himself in, he didn't feel he had any business doing that – she had stared back at him with the severest of expressions on her face. She'd then tilted her head to look over his shoulder and had seen the delivery man dropping off the logs on the drive.

'I didn't order any logs,' she'd said. She'd sounded confused rather than affronted.

'No,' he'd replied, 'but I thought it might be a good idea with the weather now turning so cold. If you'll let me, I'll barrow them round to the back garden and put them in the log store for you.'

'Why?' she'd asked, still looking at him severely.

'Because that's where they always go.'

'I'm not stupid, Keith,' she'd said stiffly, and folding her arms across her chest. 'I know where they go, I'm just asking why you would want to go to the trouble of doing that. Or,' she'd gone on, her voice taking on a more suspicious tone, 'did Nina put you up to coming here?'

'I came because I wanted to talk to you. But first, I'll deal with the logs, if that's all right with you?'

'Hmm . . . ' she'd said.

Which he'd taken as near to an affirmative answer as he was likely to receive from her.

Now, and with one last pile of logs to stack neatly in place, he removed his jacket. He'd worked up quite a sweat while applying himself to the task and he'd found that he'd enjoyed the physical labour of it. The satisfaction too of making sure everything was placed in neat tidy rows had given him a sense of a job well done.

This was something he hadn't experienced in a while, he thought, the single-minded focus of committing both mind and body to the simplicity of a strenuous and mundane chore. He pondered if there wasn't an element of *putting his house in order* as he'd gone about the job.

All the while he'd been working in the garden, catching snatches of birdsong and reliving happier times of family life here, he'd been conscious that from inside the house Hilary might have been watching him. Possibly she was wondering what he wanted to say to her. He wondered much the same thing. How to begin? How to explain even a fraction of the emotions he'd gone through?

The raging anger.

The gut-wrenching pain.

The absolute bewilderment.

The very profound sense of regret.

All of it had combined into a roiling explosive mess and erupted because of going to that awful spiritualist church. It had left him badly shaken, hollowed out and he doubted Diane would ever forgive him for some of the things he'd said. Having completely lost control of himself that evening, he now possessed a better understanding of what Hilary had experienced when she'd lost control at Tigs and Fabian's wedding.

'I thought you might like a mug of tea.'

Surprised at the sound of Hilary's voice, he stopped what he was doing. 'Thank you,' he said, taking the mug from her and hoping it was a peace offering, a sign that she might be prepared to talk to him. Until this moment she'd given no indication that she would.

'I see you've stacked the logs in your customary orderly fashion,' she observed.

'Some things never change,' he said.

'Perhaps not,' she murmured, turning to gaze down the length of the garden.

There was an unreadable faraway look in her eyes and after sipping his tea, he said, 'It's freezing out here, don't get cold, will you?'

Ignoring him, she said, 'Did Nina tell you I'm getting a dog?'

'Yes,' he said. 'Sounds like a great idea to me.'

She wheeled round. 'I don't need your approval.'

He felt the sting of her rebuke. 'No, of course you don't, and I didn't mean to sound like I was giving it. I just meant that—'

She waved his words away with a sigh. 'I know what you meant. I was being . . .

'Being what?' he prompted when she didn't go on.

'My usual combative self,' she replied. 'As you just said, some things never change.'

Seeing an opening, Keith said, 'When I've finished here, can we have that chat, please? I'd really like to.'

With a small nod, she left him to it. He drank some more of his tea, placed the mug on the ground out of harm's way, bent down to gather up more of the logs and then gasped as a sharp pain ripped through his lower back. Holding his breath, he very tentatively tried to straighten up. But at the slightest movement, the pain ripped through him again and keeping as still as he could, he considered his options. Call for help in the hope Hilary would hear him or get down on his hands and knees and crawl into the house because there was no way he could stand upright.

It was ages since his back had given him any problems; the odd occasional twinge, but he knew this pain was on a whole other level. *Slowly does it*, he told himself as he lowered himself to the frigid ground. Then once he was in position, on all fours, he began the excruciatingly slow trek towards the back door. At one point, and now shivering with cold without his jacket, he didn't know whether to laugh or cry at the absurdity of the situation.

He was just a few yards from the door when it cracked open and there was Hilary. Never had he been more pleased to see her!

'My back,' he groaned, 'it's gone. Like that time I was clearing the drive of the snow and slipped a disc.'

'How can I help?' she asked, bending down to him.

'I'm not sure, perhaps I'll just keep crawling until I'm inside and then we'll figure something out.'

Later, by the fire in the sitting room, he was dosed up on painkillers and a large medicinal glass of whisky and was resting in his favourite old leather reclining chair – the chair Hilary had frequently tried to get rid of because it was so shabby. So long as he didn't move, he felt pleasantly detached, his mind and body drifting on a wave of fuzzy warmth.

He was so comfortably drifting he didn't realise he'd fallen asleep, not until he was woken by the sound of ringing. Opening his eyes, he looked around him in the half-light, momentarily disorientated by the familiarity of his surroundings yet not understanding how he was there.

Eventually, and after trying to move and experiencing a sharp stab of pain in his back, he joined up the dots and remembered the hows and the whys. He checked his watch. It was gone four and by his reckoning he must have slept for over three hours.

The ringing had stopped now, and he could hear Hilary talking indistinctly to someone. As the one-sided conversation went on, he was suddenly conscious that he was going to have to move, and soon.

Pushing aside the blanket that covered him, he cautiously leant forwards in the chair, gritting his teeth against the pain. Mind over matter, he said under his breath as he leant forwards and prepared to haul himself to his feet.

Once upright and doing his best to ignore what felt like a knife being jabbed into the base of his spine, he put one foot in front of the other and slowly moved towards the door. He'd made it as far as the hall when, and with the pain causing sweat to break out all over him and nausea to churn in the pit of his stomach, he had to stop and lean against the wall to rest. He had the awful thought that he wasn't going to make it to the loo in time and was about to push through the pain and cover the final distance to the downstairs cloakroom when, once more, Hilary appeared.

'Oh,' she said, 'you're awake. How are you feeling? No, no need to answer that, you look dreadful.'

'Thanks,' he said, with a half-hearted attempt at a smile. Then: 'I need the loo and with some urgency.'

'Here,' she said, offering her arm, 'lean on me.'

'If you could just help me to the door,' he said, gratefully leaning on her arm, 'you don't have to do more than that.'

'It wouldn't be the first time,' she said, matter-of-factly.

Yes, he thought when he was safely installed in the cloakroom, but that was when they were a happily married couple, when they shared everything and did whatever they could to help the other.

She was waiting for him in the hall when he emerged from the cloakroom. She held out her arm again and once more he leant on it. 'I'm sorry for putting you to all this trouble, it wasn't what I'd planned when I came here today.'

'I should hope not. By the way, have you phoned your . . . your girlfriend to tell her what's happened?'

'No,' he said, wondering how much it had cost her to use the word girlfriend.

'Shouldn't you?'

'No,' he said again. 'We had a falling-out.'

'Oh,' she said flatly.

'That's not why I'm here,' he felt compelled to say. Although that wasn't altogether true. But he didn't want Hilary to jump to the wrong conclusion.

'In that case,' she said, 'I'd suggest you go and sit in your ghastly old chair while I make us something to eat. I have a chicken and mushroom pie which will stretch to two without too much difficulty. Are you ready for some more painkillers?'

He was so weakened by the agony he was in, he felt pathetically weepy at her kindness, which he certainly didn't deserve.

She helped to settle him, put some more logs on the fire, switched on lamps, drew the curtains and then after placing a glass of water and a packet of tablets within easy reach, she left him alone. She seemed to him to be the woman she once was, the woman she'd been before Hugh's death – capable and caring and quite unlike the shattered woman Nina had described and whom he'd expected to encounter today, the wreck of a woman he'd come to help. What a joke that was; he was the one who was a wreck and in need of help!

They ate in the sitting room, off trays, and the conversation was mostly about the puppy which Hilary would be collecting in a few days.

'No doubt you know that it was actually Nina's idea for me to have a dog,' she explained, 'and at first, I resented her suggesting it. Again, you probably know that too, but now that it's all happening, I can't remember when I felt so excited about something. Can you believe I'm even using a word like excited?'

'It sounds good, Hilary,' he said and meant it. 'I'm pleased for you. And how are you in general? I know about the incident in John Lewis and that—'

'Please don't say any more!' she interrupted him. 'It's enough that you know about it.'

Knowing that he had to tread carefully, he said, 'Have you spoken to anyone about what you did and why?'

'Not specifically about my compulsion to steal baby clothes, if that's what you're asking. I know why I did it. It's obvious. The shame of being caught, and of Nina also knowing about it, was enough to bring me to my senses. I won't relapse. I know I won't. What's more, I've given all the things I took to a charity.'

'Do you think that turning to Nina was in some way a cry for help?' he suggested.

'As dramatic as you make it sound,' Hilary answered with a small sniff, 'I suppose that's what it was. In my panic after I was caught and was being questioned, Nina, with her calm composure, was the only one who I trusted not to overreact. Also, her opinion of me was at rock bottom already, so it couldn't get any worse, could it? She was extremely good with me. There was no judgement from her, only practical help.'

'Hugh would have been proud of her.'

'Yes,' Hilary said softly. Then putting her tray and empty plate on the coffee table in front of them, and taking his tray from him as well, she said, 'And it's because of Nina that I found the courage to join a support group for parents who are grieving for the death of a child. It's not online like the group you joined, but we actually sit in a circle and take it in turns to speak. That's if we want to. I don't always, it's enough just to listen sometimes. I have to say, the common denominating factor amongst us, is how angry we all feel. Someone joked that we should rename it as an anger management group and maybe we should take up boxing classes.'

Keith smiled his understanding and was about to say that he wouldn't mind joining that himself, when she said, 'Well then, I suppose you're here to talk about the divorce, aren't you? So shall we get down to it?'

Taken aback, he swallowed and marshalled his thoughts. Divorce wasn't the first thing he wanted to bring up; there was something else he needed to say before that. Originally, he had been in two minds about telling Hilary about his visit to the spiritualist church with Diane, but since it had been such an important turning point for him, he wanted Hilary to know about it.

'Firstly,' he began, 'I want to apologise for walking out on you the way I did. It was brutal how I did it and cowardly that I blamed you for pushing me away, and at a time when you needed me most.'

'It's true, I did push you away, but then you had someone to go to, so I didn't need to push too hard, did I? Would you have gone if there hadn't been anyone?'

Her extreme reasonableness and the unwavering manner of her gaze was quite unnerving. 'It's a fair question,' he said, 'and probably the honest answer is no.'

'Apology accepted,' she said briskly, sounding as if she were moving on to the next point on the agenda of their meeting. 'And it seems only fair that I should apologise for my own part in the breakdown of our relationship. That's something I've learnt at the group, how many relationships unravel following the death of a child, no matter the age of that child. You'd think it would bring couples closer together, wouldn't you, that we'd be united in grief? But then you know all this already, don't you? That was how you were able to move on.'

He sighed. 'I wish that were true,' he said. 'That was my mistake, thinking that I had come to terms with losing Hugh, or at least believing that I had managed my grief. I've since realised I'd merely suppressed it and then a few days ago, it all came spewing out.'

And as much as he'd rather forget the incident had ever happened, he told Hilary about Diane's unexpected interest in spiritualism and how he'd been talked into accompanying her to the church she had become so taken with.

'I didn't believe in any of it,' he explained, 'I've never had any time for that kind of thing, you know that, but I went to please Diane. To keep the peace.'

Hilary rolled her eyes at that. 'It always annoyed me when you did that, did something for the sake of keeping the peace, it was as if you were martyring yourself. So what happened when you went to this spiritualist church?'

He blinked and went on. 'The church had a visiting medium and my mind had wandered while the woman was supposedly in some kind of trance and then suddenly Diane was whispering that the medium had a message for me from Hugh.'

Hilary stiffened at that, and her expression intensified. 'And?' she said sharply.

'And apparently Hugh was happy, and I wasn't to worry about him or be sad. He wanted me to know that he'd been prepared for his death, and it came as a merciful release, and I was to get on with enjoying my life, that I had to look to the future. Death wasn't the end, he wanted me to know, only the start of a new and better journey.'

Visibly distressed and a hand now covering her mouth, Hilary said, 'What rubbish! Hugh wouldn't speak like that. He didn't want to die when he had everything to live for! He wasn't prepared! He wanted to live!' Her voice shook and tears filled her eyes.

If he'd been able to, Keith would have leant forwards and reached for her hand, but as it was, he said, 'That's basically how I reacted. But not so politely. I was on my feet and raging like a man possessed. I completely lost it. I accused the medium of deceiving vulnerable people, of lying and telling people what they wanted to hear. Then I turned on Diane. I accused her of being complicit in the con, of forcing me to go to that awful place just to convince me that I should get on with enjoying my life with her.'

He paused and took a shuddery breath. 'I shouted at her, right there, in front of everyone. She was crying and I didn't care. I just kept on yelling at her. Someone tried to stop me and I . . . I think I must have shoved him harder than I meant to because he went over and while everyone fussed over him, I escaped.'

After a lengthy silence, Hilary spoke. 'What made you react the way you did?' she asked.

'It was hearing a stranger talking about Hugh and using him in that cheap manipulative way. I just couldn't bear it.' His voice cracked. 'It broke me. It broke my heart.'

Another silence passed between them while he stared wretchedly into the fire.

'Was there a moment when you wanted to believe it was Hugh?'

Surprised at the question, Keith looked at Hilary. *'No!'*

'Are you sure?'

He hesitated before answering. 'On one level, maybe, that's what these charlatans rely on, a desperate need for the void to be filled. But to my mind, to believe would be an act of delusion, an act of self-harm.'

'Yet presumably it gave Diane some sort of comfort?'

'That's what I found so hard to accept, that she could be taken in so easily.'

'What happened after you'd escaped?'

He rubbed a hand over his face, recalling the humiliation. 'I had to wait outside for Diane to appear. She'd driven us there and I had no way of getting back to her place to pack up my things. I wouldn't have blamed her if she'd refused to let me get in the car with her. But she did.'

'I would have left you there to sort yourself out,' Hilary muttered.

He smiled faintly. 'Yes,' he said, 'I believe you would have.'

'Is it over between the two of you?'

He nodded.

'Where are you staying now?'

'Would you believe, I'm just up the road at Madingley Hall?'

'A home from home for you,' she said, rising to her feet and putting a log on the fire, followed by another. 'You used to be there all the time before you retired.'

'Yes,' he said, thinking of all the conferences he'd attended there during his many years working for ARJ IT Developments PLC, the multinational consulting company based at the Business Park in Cambridge. He'd always enjoyed his job and had given it his all. He had never really thought of what life would be like once he retired, but then retirement had coincided with Hugh's death, and he knew that he'd lost a huge part of himself when those two things had collided and crashed into him. He'd never spoken at the time how he'd felt about his work life coming to an end; how could he when it was so puny and insignificant compared to losing his son?

'I'm going to put the kettle on for a cup of tea, would you like one?' Hilary asked, breaking into his thoughts. 'Or would you prefer another whisky?'

'Tea would be great,' he said, once more overwhelmed with gratitude at her kindness.

She stacked their plates onto one of the trays and carried it to the door but then looked back at him. 'Tomorrow we should discuss what's going to happen next. For now, I would suggest you stay here for the night as I don't see you returning to Madingley Hall in the state you're in.'

'Are you sure that's okay?' he asked.

'I wouldn't have suggested it if I wasn't sure.'

'Thank you,' he murmured.

'Then in the morning, we'll consider your position.'

Somehow, she made the words *your position* sound both hopeful and hopeless.

Chapter Sixty

Nina was always anxious before an exhibition at the gallery. There was so much that could go wrong. What if the bitterly cold weather and the threat of snow put people off from coming? What if *nobody* came? What if the drinks and canapés ran out? What if those who did come hated what they saw? What if there was not a single red sold sticker to be seen by the end of the evening? What if the artist drank too much and got horribly drunk and started insulting guests? That had happened on one memorable occasion when her parents still owned the gallery.

Artists were, her father had claimed, some of the most egocentric and fragile people on the planet, and right now as Nina watched Saul Bernice prowling like a caged tiger around the gallery while checking his work before curtain-up on his first ever exhibition, she hoped for all their sakes the evening proved to be a success. From the minute he'd arrived, he'd started complaining. The lighting wasn't right, the order of the paintings on display wasn't as he'd stipulated (although they absolutely were, both Nina and Jakob had made doubly sure of that), and he disapproved of the Christmas tree in the window and the fussy decorations they'd put up. The biggest crime they'd committed had been not to provide enough space between the paintings, which earned Nina a lecture about the necessity of there being plenty of *ma* to better showcase his work. She had patiently explained that she knew all about the Japanese concept of negative space, but given the space available in the gallery, compromises had to be made.

It was times like this that she questioned whether it was a good idea to hold exhibitions, there was so much work and angst involved. Give her dead artists any day!

Yet for all that, Saul Bernice's work – paintings that were always signed as *Saul N. Bernice* – was most certainly exhibition-worthy and deserved to be seen and enjoyed. He favoured oil mostly and while his landscapes and seascapes, often bleak and imposing, were dramatically eye-catching, it was his still life pictures that had the greatest appeal for Nina. There was an intimacy about the interior scenes, rich in detail but somehow sparsely painted, the brushstrokes seemingly casually applied as though in an idle moment of nothing better to do.

It was a wonder to Nina that his work wasn't better known, but if all went well tonight, she might be responsible for changing that for him. Not that he gave the slightest indication of wanting to make a name for himself. Quite the reverse. When she'd initially approached him about showing his paintings, he'd furrowed his bushy eyebrows from beneath which he had given her a haughty stare as though it were quite beneath him to share his work. Perhaps it was his very resistance to the idea of an exhibition that compelled her to make it happen and she'd employed all her charm and persuasion to that end.

She'd first come across a painting of his while browsing an online catalogue for an auction house in Bury St Edmunds. The still life had caught her eye, and she'd contacted the auctioneer to enquire about its provenance. Nothing was much known about it, other than the owner had been an elderly man now deceased, and the family was selling off the contents of his home. Whatever it was that Nina had seen in the painting, nobody else had and hers was the only bid on the day of the auction. After having it reframed, it had since hung on the wall in her hallway at Hope

Hall. Meanwhile, and with patient and determined diligence after spotting another of his paintings for sale in an auction, she had tracked down the artist to his ramshackle studio in Bawdsey with its bleak view out towards the North Sea.

'The caterers seem to have everything organised in the kitchen,' Jakob said, appearing at Nina's side and slipping a hand around her waist. Whenever he did this, it had the spontaneous effect of her body subtly leaning in towards his as though she were magnetically drawn to him. Had they been alone she would have undoubtedly turned her face up to his and kissed him, but with Saul stalking his way round the exhibition space and grunting his displeasure every few steps as he straightened a picture here or tutted at some perceived inadequacy on the part of the gallery, she merely smiled at Jakob and said, 'I think it's time for a glass of wine.'

'I'm on it,' he said.

Leaving Jakob to do the honours, Nina went over to Saul to ask if he would like a drink. One of her many jobs for the evening was to ensure that he was at ease and knew that he was very much the star around which everyone was there to gather and applaud. Of course, she had to do much the same for those who had been invited as without them the evening would be a mortifying disaster.

Saul's response to her offer of a glass of wine was a vigorous shake of his wildly shaggy head of hair which from the very first moment she'd met him had made her think of an enormous Newfoundland dog. There was the same kind of hefty bulk to him too, that and a crumpled face and a stooping lumbering demeanour.

'If not wine, what about a soft drink?' she tried pleasantly.

'Coffee,' he said gruffly, barely glancing at her. 'If it's no trouble. Black. No sugar.'

'No trouble at all,' she said with a smile. With his crumpled face and stooping demeanour, he really was a crusty old devil!

*

Her neighbours from St Anne's Court, Jeremy and Philip, were first to arrive and were quick to get the party started, insisting that Saul show off his paintings to them. To Nina's amazement, he obliged without protest.

From then on, and in what seemed like no time at all, the gallery was soon thrumming with the eager chatter and laughter of invited guests, many of whom knew each other and were delighted at the chance of a catch-up gossip. And while the caterers did an excellent job of circulating with trays of tasty canapés and topping up glasses, and Nina carried out the job of meeting and greeting, Jakob was busy talking up the paintings, occasionally managing to include Saul in the conversations he was having. Already there were a pleasing number of red stickers placed alongside the pictures.

Every now and then and in a classic case of eyes meeting across a crowded room, Nina and Jakob would look at each other and an exquisitely intimate moment would pass between them during which her heart would lurch and tumble, her breath would catch, and her mind would wander from the person she was talking to.

Jeremy and Philip had been absurdly pleased when they'd learnt that Jakob had not only returned to work at Lavelle's but that he and Nina were more than mere work colleagues. They'd high-fived each other at the news and behaved as though they were responsible in some way. Then they'd wanted all the details.

'Don't leave anything out!' Philip had begged.

'Not a delicious word!' Jeremy had implored.

Naturally, and much to their annoyance, Nina had given them nothing. Jakob had proved to be the soul of discretion too. 'A gentleman never tells,' he'd informed the two men when they pressed him. 'Especially a Norwegian gentleman.'

It was still very early days into their relationship, and they were enjoying what might be considered as the 'honeymoon' phase, the sweet spot when all was fun and exciting, and sex was . . . Well, sex was the marvellous gift that kept on giving! But for all that, Nina was constantly on the lookout for something to go wrong, like discovering they really weren't as compatible as they'd thought they were. Or discovering Jakob had a habit which she could never live with – like cutting his toenails in bed, or a fondness for recreational drug use. Neither of which he did! But so far there were no red flags or deal-breakers, no aspect of his behaviour that annoyed her.

Of course, in turn that meant she was constantly aware of her own habits. Was she too tidy, too exacting and too set in her ways? Was she too organised and too analytical? All these she viewed as strengths to her character, but could they be irritants? More than once, Hugh had urged her to be more impulsive, to take more risks, but she never had. Not until Jakob.

She had raised her concerns with Jakob, and he had laughed.

'Nina, I've worked with you all this time,' he'd said, 'I know just how exacting and organised you are, and surely you know that I'm the same. It's why we're so compatible.'

He was right, they did seem eminently compatible, in spite of the age difference – something she had to force herself not to dwell on – and they agreed on most things. Although she drew the line at pickled herring for breakfast!

One important thing they had agreed on was that they wouldn't rush things, so for now, Jakob only stayed a few nights with her at Hope Hall, and occasionally she stayed at his house in Cambridge, which she'd discovered was as immaculately tidy as her own home now that his lodgers had moved out. There was no talk between them of what might happen next, for now they were happy getting to know themselves in the role of a couple and what that meant to them both. Which sounded like they were being boringly practical, but there was nothing boring about her life now with Jakob in it. Every day for Nina was an adventure in exploring new ways to be and it filled her with a lightness of heart and spirit. It really was possible to be happy again, she now knew. Widowhood was not the end.

Out of the corner of her eye, she saw the door of the gallery open and in came Cassie and Ben with Venetia and Ronnie following behind. Weaving her way through the guests, Nina went to greet them.

'Thank you for coming,' she said, 'especially on such a chilly night.' She could feel and smell the sharp icy cold of the evening which they'd brought in with them on their coats.

'Don't be silly,' said Cassie, 'we wouldn't have missed this for anything. How's it going? You look like you have quite a mob here.'

'I had them at free wine and nibbles,' Nina said with a laugh.

'That'll do it every time,' said Ben. 'Never fails.'

'But are they buying any pictures?' asked Venetia, glancing around the gallery.

'Yes,' said Nina, lowering her voice. 'Jakob's been busy with the red stickers. I can't tell you how relieved I am. Anyway, let's find you something to drink and then you can have a browse, see if there's anything that takes your fancy.'

'Oh, here we go, here's the hard sell,' said Ronnie with a chuckle, 'time now to empty our wallets!'

'Behave yourself,' Venetia warned him, 'you're mixing with the great and the good of Cambridge now, not the hoi polloi of Majorca!'

Nina smiled, genuinely happy that her friends had come, and while trying to catch the attention of a waitress, she said, 'No Emily, then?'

'No, she had a better offer,' said Cassie. 'Remember that hot barista in the coffee shop I told you about, the one who put a cute heart in her latte?'

'Yes, I remember you mentioning him. Didn't you also say that she applied for a job at that place?'

'She did. She started work there a few days ago and was asked out today by Franco-the-Hot-Barista-from-Vicenza.'

'Who's from Vicenza?'

The question came from Jakob who, and with perfect timing had materialised with a tray of drinks which he immediately began handing out.

'The guy with whom Emily is on a date tonight,' said Cassie. 'But never mind all that, let me at this wine and then I'm going to look at the paintings.'

'I'll come with you,' said Venetia.

'That leaves you and me to do a reconnoitre, Ronnie,' said Ben. 'Shall we?'

'Lead on, lead on!'

Nina watched them go and was about to ask Jakob if he knew how Saul was coping, and if there was any chance that he might actually be pleased with the reaction to his pictures, when once more the door opened. This time it was Keith and Hilary who came in. Nina had invited them ages ago, as she always had when she held an exhibition, but she hadn't expected either of them to come. And certainly not together.

Aware that Jakob had discreetly melted away, she welcomed her in-laws.

'This is a lovely surprise,' she said, noting that Hilary was looking infinitely better than a few weeks ago. She was smartly dressed in a camel-coloured full-length coat, make-up applied, and her hair washed and nicely styled. The transformation was extraordinary. As was the change in Keith. But not in a good way. He seemed drawn and haggard, his shoulders hunched, perhaps from the cold, but nonetheless she thought she perceived a trace of the familiar old twinkling light in his eyes. A twinkle that had not been there the last time they'd met, when she'd harangued him about stepping up and helping Hilary.

'We've never missed one of your exhibitions,' Hilary said, 'so of course we thought we'd come along and support you, as we've always done.'

'But weren't you collecting your puppy this week?' Nina said.

'We're doing that tomorrow,' Hilary replied, her face brightening with a smile. 'I have everything ready,' she went on. 'I'm so looking forward to bringing him home. You'll have to come and see him. He's so sweet, a gorgeous little bundle of fluffy joy.'

'I've seen plenty of photos, and I can vouch for the high cute factor,' Keith joined in.

There was a lot to unpack in what Nina was hearing and quite apart from Hilary sounding girlishly excited, there was Keith's apparent inclusion in what was going on. Were they reconciled? And what of Keith's relationship with Diane? But now wasn't the time to delve into all that. So instead, she said, 'Do you have a name for the puppy?'

'I'm calling him Teddy,' Hilary said, 'because that's exactly what he looks like.'

'It sounds perfect,' said Nina. 'Now then, what can I offer you to drink?'

'I hate to be a party pooper, but would it be possible for me to sit down, please?' asked Keith.

Nina looked at him concerned. 'Are you feeling unwell?'

'Can you believe it,' Hilary said, 'he hurt his back earlier in the week playing the hero when he came to stack a delivery of logs for me.'

It was such a typically Hilary thing to say, and it made Nina smile.

'Oh, so you think me being in agony is funny, do you?' remarked Keith in his old good-humoured way.

'Not at all,' Nina said, pleased that he had tried to help, even if it had gone painfully wrong for him. It explained why he looked so drawn. 'I'm just picturing you in your Superman cape.'

'Now you're making fun of me.'

'Maybe just a tiny bit. Come with me and I'll find you a nice comfortable chair, and a drink.'

She had rounded up some glasses of wine and had Keith seated when she heard a sudden noise that cut through the buzzing hubbub of people enjoying themselves. She scanned the gallery, seeking out the source of what had sounded like somebody in distress. Her gaze eventually settled on the farthest corner from her.

She wasn't the only one whose attention had been attracted by the noise. Amongst others, Jakob was also staring in the same direction as Nina and in unison, they both began moving towards the focus of the commotion. Once there, they found Venetia on the floor with Cassie kneeling on one side of her and on the other side, of all people, was Saul.

Instructing everyone to stand back and make room, and sending Jakob off to fetch a chair while wondering if she should call for an ambulance, Nina was relieved to see Venetia open her eyes. Clearly dazed, and the colour drained from her face, Venetia looked up at Nina, then Cassie, and then, turning her head to look into Saul's face, she gave a small gasp.

'It is you, isn't it?' she murmured.

'I'm afraid it is,' he said, his voice low and shaky.

'In that case,' Venetia said, easing herself into a sitting position, 'you have some explaining to do.'

As well as finding a chair, Jakob returned with a glass of water and at her own insistence, Venetia was soon declaring herself perfectly fit and well and telling everyone to stop fussing.

'I fainted, that was all. And don't you dare think of calling an ambulance!' This was aimed at Ronnie, who had now joined them with Ben and had his mobile in his hand and an agitated expression on his face.

'But what made you faint?' he wanted to know. 'Nobody faints without there being a reason. And usually it's a bad reason.'

When Venetia didn't answer, it was Cassie who spoke. She pointed an accusing finger at Saul, and said, 'Ask him. He knows why Venetia fainted; it was because she was so shocked at seeing him.'

With all eyes now on Saul, he said, 'I'm an old friend from way back.'

'You were a bit more than that,' Cassie said sharply. 'I heard what she called you when she recognised you, and it wasn't Saul!'

'Cassie, darling,' said Venetia, 'I expect he's as shocked to see me as I am at seeing him after all this time. After all, it is more than sixty years since we last saw each other. I'm just sorry I overreacted by fainting. It was most undignified of me.'

'Is Saul your childhood friend, Lucien?' asked Nina in astonished disbelief.

Venetia looked up at the grizzled man standing next to her and when he gave a small nod as though giving her permission to go ahead, she nodded in turn. 'Yes, Nina,' she said, 'he's the very dear friend I told you about.'

'The one who ran off and never had the decency to let you know where he was or that he was okay?' said Cassie.

'Cassie, my dear, you sound so cross, please don't be. Not when there's so much to be happy about.'

'But I am cross,' Cassie said, heatedly, 'because when you fainted, I thought you'd died! And I think you'll agree, that was pretty upsetting!'

'But it wasn't his fault.'

'It was his fault for running out on you all those years ago.'

Nina realised that the anger Cassie was displaying echoed the way she had reacted when Nina had told her all that Venetia had shared with her about Lucien, how he'd disappeared and left

Venetia broken-hearted as a sixteen-year-old girl. Understandably, abandonment to Cassie was practically the worst thing that anyone could do to another person.

Stepping forward, Ben put a solicitous arm around Cassie. 'I think maybe we should let Venetia and Saul, or whatever his name is, have a few minutes alone together, don't you?'

Reluctantly, they did just that, but not without casting curious backward glances. Nina and Jakob were immediately approached by several guests keen to make a purchase and it was when the necessary paperwork had been completed that Nina felt a tap on her shoulder. It was Cassie.

'Come quick,' she whispered, 'they're leaving!'

'Who's leaving?'

'Venetia and Lucien!'

They hurriedly made their way over to the gallery door, just in time to see snow softly falling in the darkness and Venetia and her childhood friend, Lucien, walking away down the cobbled street of St Anne's Court.

'Look!' hissed Cassie. 'She's resting her arm on his! Oh, it's just so romantic!'

'That wasn't what you thought a few minutes ago,' said Nina.

'Well no, then I was still recovering from the shock of thinking Venetia had died. But,' she went on, craning her neck yet further to get a better view, 'this could be the start of their happy ever after.'

Chapter Sixty-One

There was so much to say but it was far too cold to wander the streets of Cambridge so they could talk and with fat flakes of snow falling determinedly and settling thickly on the ground, they went into the nearest restaurant, even though Venetia doubted she would be able to eat a thing.

They were shown to a table by an excessively cheerful young waitress who gave them over-sized laminated menus and pointed to the specials of the day on the blackboard. 'Anything to drink?' she asked chirpily.

'Brandy for me,' answered Venetia, 'I need it for the—' she was going to say shock, but changed her mind. 'For the cold,' she said.

'I'll have the same,' muttered Lucien.

'With ice?' the girl asked.

'Certainly not,' Lucien said, his bushy eyebrows raised as if in disgust.

When they were alone, Venetia said, 'That girl probably isn't much older than the age we were when we last saw one another.'

'I can't tell how old anyone is these days; I just know that I'm as old as Methuselah and ready for the scrapheap.'

'We're the same age, and if you don't mind, I don't consider myself ready for the scrapheap.' Venetia's voice was light and playful.

He rattled his throat. 'Maybe you've been lucky in life.'

'Have you not had a happy life, then?' she asked.

He shrugged. 'What does happy even mean?'

She studied his craggy, weatherbeaten face and felt a great surge of tender nostalgia for her old friend. Despite the many years that had passed, and which had undeniably left their mark on him, she could still discern the boy within, the proud boy she had loved so much and wanted to protect so badly. 'What a question, Lucien!' she remarked. 'Are you saying you've never known what it is to be happy?'

'Again, it all depends on your definition of happiness.'

How sad, she thought, sensing that maybe, even with all its many ups and downs, her life had been a lot happier than his.

'But I must say, luxury apartments or not, I was surprised when you said earlier that you'd moved back to Hope Hall. Of all the places in the world you could have gone! Why the hell there?' Not giving her a chance to reply, he rumbled on throatily. 'And as for recognising me the way you did, I still don't know how you did that.'

'Presumably in the same way you eventually recognised me,' she said, 'a sixth sense of just knowing one another. I swear I felt something, a tingling up and down my spine before I'd really looked at you, as though my subconscious had already figured it out.'

'But was there something in particular that made you know it was me?'

'It was when I overheard you speaking to that woman who was admiring your painting, it was the gruff offhand way you spoke to her, it took me right back to being a child with you at Hope Hall.'

'For me,' he said, 'it was your eyes which I recognised first. They were always so sharp and alert. You never missed anything and clearly you didn't this evening.'

Their waitress appeared then with their drinks. Setting them on the table, she asked in her bright chirpy voice if they'd chosen what they wanted to eat.

'I can recommend the medallions of pork with apple,' she said, 'and the lamb shanks are good too.'

Lucien looked askance at Venetia.

'I'm sorry,' she said to the waitress, 'we haven't had a chance to look at the menu yet. We've been too busy talking.'

'No problem, I can come back in a few minutes.'

'I only need something very small,' Venetia said, thinking that perhaps it would be easier to get the decision over and done with. 'A starter would be fine for me.' She ran her gaze over the menu. 'I'll have the lentil and sweet potato soup.'

Lucien ordered the lamb shank and a side order of chips and when the waitress had gone, he said, 'I haven't eaten all day, I'm starving.'

Venetia smiled. 'That's fine, no explanation needed.'

'That wasn't what you said back at the gallery after you'd fainted, you said I had a lot of explaining to do.'

'And so you do. But first, raise your glass.

He did as she said.

'Here's to old friends.'

'Old friends,' he echoed.

They each took a sip of their brandy.

'Come on then,' he said, lowering his glass, 'let's start the full interrogation process, shall we?'

'Very well,' she said. 'Why didn't you ever try to contact me?'

'Ah,' he said, 'the sixty-five million dollar question. I did contact you in the months after I left Hope Hall. A thousand times at the very least. But only in my head.'

'Why was that?'

'Shame. Fear. Guilt. Self-loathing. You name it. All I knew was that I needed to cut the tie with Hope Hall, and I'm sorry but that meant you as well.'

She nodded. 'Self-preservation. I understand. But one small letter would have made all the difference, just so that I knew you were alive and that you were well. That was all I needed. Every day I lived in hope of hearing from you.'

'I was alive, but as for being well, that might have been a stretch. For a long time, I was in a pretty dark place. Running away does that to you.'

She thought of the disturbingly opaque and austere painting of a moonlit forest she and Cassie had been looking at before she'd realised she was not only standing next to the artist, but that there was something strangely familiar about him. And then the axis of the world had tilted and uttering his name in shocked amazement – the name she had known for nearly all her life – she had slowly slipped to the floor.

'Where did you go when you disappeared?' she asked.

'London. Obviously. It was where all runaway kids went; it was the easiest place in which to lose myself and start a new life.'

'That's what Edie Buckle and I did; we moved to London when Hope Hall had to close.'

'You did? Just think,' he said reflectively, 'our paths could have crossed! Where did you live?'

'I'll tell you about that later. For now, I want to know all about you. How did you cope in London on your own? You were so young. Was there anyone to look out for you?' She thought what a slight boy he'd been, his chest weakened with asthma and his eyesight so dependent on spectacles.

'I had to grow up fast,' he said. 'I slept rough to begin with and then I managed to get a job in the East End working in the docks. Next, I found somewhere to doss down.'

'But you wanted to do so much more than that. You wanted to be a doctor.'

He took a mouthful of his brandy. 'Rarely can we have what we dream of. Did you end up doing what you thought you would?'

'No. But I enjoyed the work I did, and I made a success of it for myself. Just as you have with your art,' she added, worried that she sounded as if she were boasting.

'I wouldn't call my art a success, I merely dabble for my own amusement. I started painting when I moved to Suffolk to be by the sea. I still suffer with asthma and the sea air suits me.'

'You no longer wear glasses,' she pointed out.

'Laser surgery sorted that.'

'Did you stay in London for very long?'

'No, I moved around getting cash-in-hand work wherever I could.' There was a slight softening in his expression. 'I spent one summer hop-picking in Kent. I would have returned the following year, but the farm had done away with cheap labour and mechanised things. It was the end of an era.' His expression altered again, resumed its earlier hard edge. 'I kept moving because there was always a part of me that believed one day there would be a knock on the door and I would be accused of killing Terry Sands.'

'But you didn't kill him,' she said. 'It was an accident.'

He gave her a long studied look. 'Is that what you've told yourself all these years?'

She was momentarily shocked at his contemptuous tone. 'It *was* an accident,' she repeated, this time more resolutely. 'And we were only children.'

'But I planned to kill, I went to that cottage with murder in my mind.'

It was hard to hear him say those words so boldly and with such conviction. 'But you didn't actually do it, did you?' she said. 'Yes, you pushed him, but I would have done the same. Anyone would have.'

'I wanted to leave him there to go up in flames, but you didn't. So don't try and tell me you would have done the same as I did. You wouldn't have. You didn't!'

His tone was suddenly so aggressive and made her feel disagreeably under attack. 'That's a futile line of argument, because we're all capable of murder given the right circumstances.'

'So you admit it, I did murder Terry Sands?'

'I said no such thing!'

Once more their cheerful waitress appeared and gaily presented Venetia with her soup and Lucien his lamb shank. The juxtaposition of the girl's eternally sunny demeanour was quite at odds with the sombre mood that had now descended on them, and oblivious to it, she expressed her hope that they would enjoy their meal. Venetia picked up her spoon with a smile, feeling she owed the girl that much at least and thanked her.

'Whatever you think now, whatever you've convinced yourself of,' Venetia said, after a lengthy pause and while they both ate, 'you did help me drag Terry out of the burning cottage.'

'I did it for you, Venetia. Not for me.'

She frowned. 'It doesn't matter what your motive was, your heart was in the right place. You knew what was the right thing to do.'

He scoffed at her. 'You always did want to believe in the myth of good overcoming bad. It's like believing in fairies. Or God!'

Annoyance flared within her, and Venetia suddenly found, quite uncharitably, that she didn't much care for the man Lucien had become. He seemed so arrogant, and so sneeringly determined to be miserable. But then hadn't he so often been that way as a boy?

Hoping to manoeuvre him back onto safer ground, she said, 'When did you become Saul Bernice? And why that name? What's the significance? Or maybe there isn't any and you plucked the name out of the ether.'

He put down his knife and fork and reached for his brandy glass, draining what was left in it in one swallow. 'You disappoint me. I would have thought you'd have worked it out by now.'

'Worked what out?'

'The name. It's an anagram of Lucien Barnes.'

Mentally she tried to match up the letters and eventually said, 'It doesn't work.'

He smiled, scrunching up his eyes within the folds of the deep lines around them. 'That's why I always sign my pictures as Saul N. Bernice. I needed to use up the extra N from my real name.' He seemed exceptionally pleased with himself.

'When did you change your name?'

He resumed eating. 'After my eighteenth birthday,' he replied between mouthfuls. 'I decided it was time to sort out the necessary paperwork that would enable me to move further afield. So I adopted a new identity. You'd be amazed how easy it is to do that, if you have the money and can find the right people.'

'Where did you go?'

'France, Spain, Morocco, Ireland, then back to England before finally settling in Suffolk. I went wherever the wind took me.'

'What about marriage?'

'I tried it once but not surprisingly it didn't work out.'

'Children?'

He shook his head of shaggy hair. 'No. You?'

'Three marriages but no children. It wasn't to be.'

'I always imagined you with a large family,' he said, leaning back in his chair. 'Lots of obnoxiously noisy children running amok. Grandchildren too. I pictured you wanting to recreate what you believed Lady Constance had given us at Hope Hall. And I suppose in part you have tried to hang on to that life by moving back there, haven't you?'

Something jibbed in the way he was speaking to her. He was patronising her, wasn't he? 'What do you mean by *believed?*' she demanded.

'You know, that whole happy family vibe. None of it was real back then. We weren't a family. How could we be? We were all so disparate. We were just commodities to a posh woman who wanted to think she was doing good in the world. We were nothing but toys to her, accessories in a pathetic fantasy she wanted to live out.'

This was too much for Venetia. *'No!'* she protested. 'That's not true, Lady Constance genuinely cared about us, she really did! I don't know how you could twist the past the way you are.'

'I'm not twisting anything. I'm just telling you how it was.'

'No you're not. You're just a sad, bitter old man and I won't have you destroy my childhood! And to think I'd thought about you all these years, wondering where you were and how you were, and always hoping for the best for you!'

He flung his knife and fork down, causing a couple on the nearest table to glance over. Although in all probability they had already been having a good gawp at them during Venetia's outburst.

'More fool you!' he retorted. 'And I suppose you thought this little reunion would result in a stupid happy ending for us, didn't you?'

What precisely it was she had expected or hoped for when at the gallery Lucien had agreed to go somewhere so they could talk properly, it wasn't this. Walking alongside him while resting her arm on his to avoid slipping over in the snow, her heart had been bursting with the wonder of the moment, of finally being able to bring her life full circle.

Fighting against the tears that were threatening to fill her eyes, she stood up and pulled on her coat which had been on the back of her chair and in so doing knocked against the table, sending her brandy glass crashing to the floor. 'Enjoy the rest of your meal,' she said. 'And the rest of your miserable life.'

Chapter Sixty-Two

A week after the exhibition at Lavelle's gallery and Venetia's disastrous encounter with Lucien, a large square package arrived at Hope Hall for her. It had been left in the communal hallway downstairs and a neighbour, having seen Venetia's name scrawled across it, brought it up to her apartment.

She was now removing the wrapping and wondering what on earth it could be. Whoever had wrapped it had gone to a lot of trouble to ensure its safe arrival. There was no end of sticky tape, cardboard and paper to deal with.

When she at last had the final layer of wrapping removed and realised it was a painting she had in her hands, she let out a gasp of shock. For there was her childhood self! It simply wasn't possible, yet it was. It was her as a young girl sitting under a tree while staring off into the distance, her face slightly upturned, catching the dappled sunlight. There was something almost noble about her expression, a quality she surely couldn't have possessed at so tender an age. Her eyes moved from her face on the canvas to the lower corners searching for where the artist had signed his name. There was no name, but then she didn't need to see one to know who had painted the picture. But why? And when?

She turned the picture over and saw an envelope stuck to the back of it. Carefully putting the picture flat on the floor, and with her heart racing, she opened the envelope and pulled out a folded piece of paper.

> *Dear Venetia,*
>
> *Your first reaction might be to hurl this daub of mine from the roof of Hope Hall and send it crashing to the ground, and I wouldn't blame you if you did.*
>
> *I painted the portrait of you many years ago, when I decided I might have sufficient talent to do your memory justice. In my mind's eye this was how I thought of you, and I'd say it's a fair likeness. But don't go thinking it's a peace offering or some kind of olive branch. Or even an apology. It's not. It's just a painting. One I'd like you to have.*
>
> *I believe we said all we needed to say last week in Cambridge, and I have no desire to rake over any more old memories, or imagine we could be friends. I'm not the person you remembered, and I see no reason to inflict that on you, or anyone else for that matter.*
>
> *Live the rest of your life just as you want to live it, and if our time together at Hope Hall means anything to you, please leave me to live mine how I want to live it. Alone.*
>
> *Lucien.*

She turned the piece of paper over, half hoping he might have written a P.S. But there was nothing. Just a blank page. She read the letter through one more time, thinking how very final that full stop was after Lucien's name.

She put the letter down and returned her attention to the painting. Propping it up in an armchair, she studied it in more detail. The background was so rough it was hardly there, but she – the young girl with her long plaits and a sunny yellow dress which she remembered so well and was her best dress for special occasions – was very much the focus of the picture. It was uncanny how perfectly Lucien had captured her. How had he done that? Had he kept a photo of her, or had he had her image etched into his memory? Either way, she knew that to have painted the picture, she had meant something to him, and that was all that mattered.

However he had come to paint this portrait of her, she knew she would treasure it. Lucien might have dismissed it as being just a picture, but he had to have known that to her it would be so much more. And because their time together as children had meant the world to her, she would respect his wishes. Besides, if he wanted to find her, he knew where to look.

It then occurred to her that maybe he'd delivered the picture himself. Perhaps curiosity had got the better of him and he'd come for a look at Hope Hall to see it once more with his own eyes. Or was she being insensitive, that he could never come here because the place held the darkest of memories for him which he'd never been able to let go of? Certainly, from what she'd seen of his work that night at the exhibition, there was very much a dark and a light side to him.

But thanks to this beautiful painting he'd given her, all the anger and heartbreaking disappointment she had felt after their painful encounter was gone from her. Despite his protestations about the picture being just a picture, she knew it was his way of saying sorry.

Apology accepted, my dearest old friend, she murmured. *Apology accepted.*

Chapter Sixty-Three

Epilogue

March could not have given them a more enchanting day. The sun shone from a cloudless cornflower-blue sky, and it was pleasingly warm for early spring. Everywhere Cassie looked, she saw happy faces, but none was happier than her own. She couldn't stop smiling and didn't think she ever would. She was now officially Mrs Cassandra Henshaw-Pearson. Which everyone said had a perfect ring to it.

The wedding ceremony had taken place at Farleigh Fen Church and Cassie's father had walked her down the aisle with Emily following behind as her one and only bridesmaid. There had been disappointment amongst the ranks of nieces from both sides of their families, but Cassie and Ben had held the line, claiming that it was to be as unfussy a wedding as possible.

The reception, which was in full flow now, was at Hope Hall, and as she and Ben had said, where else would mean so much to them, or look more stunning for their photographs? With permission granted, a marquee had been erected and yesterday the interior had been kitted out with tables and chairs. Having decided on a traditional country-style wedding, Cassie had wanted the marquee to have the feel of a village fête tea tent rather than anything too swanky and overdressed. Bunting had been strung up and tables were simply decorated with jam jars filled with daffodils, tulips, anemones, muscari, primroses and small twiggy branches of Salix with their pretty golden catkins. Along with family, friends and work colleagues, all their neighbours at Hope Hall had been invited, including the Enforcers who had recently handed over the running of the residents' committee to other neighbours, one of whom, now that Hope Hall was his primary residence, was Ronnie. Cheryl and Joanna seemed a lot more chilled these days.

The caterers had set up two impressive barbecues and from lavish serving bowls the size of cauldrons, there was every imaginable salad available. Like many brides, Cassie had been so involved with planning the wedding, the stress of it had done wonders in minimising her appetite and she'd had no trouble fitting into the beautiful dress she and her mother had found. Made of ivory-coloured lace tulle, it had a cute 1950s feel to it. A-line in shape with a V-neck, long sleeves and a velvet ribbon around the waist, it was full-skirted and came to just below her knees.

Ben's outfit of a cream linen suit with a floral waistcoat, white shirt and caramel-coloured silk tie complimented her dress perfectly, but then she had dropped plenty of hints to him as to what he should wear!

From where she was standing with her parents and sister, Cassie was watching Ben as he and his brother, along with Jodie's husband, having got rid of their jackets, were now playing a boisterous game of croquet with all the nephews and nieces. It wasn't just the children enjoying the array of games on offer; some of Ben's work colleagues were playing splat-the-rat, and the coconut shy and hook-the-duck were proving popular with everyone.

'Do you suppose any of them know what they're supposed to be doing?' commented Cassie's sister, as they watched the children running around with wooden mallets held aloft.

'I doubt it,' answered their mother, 'but I vote we leave them to it because I spy desserts now being served.'

'Good call, Mum,' said Cassie, looking over to where an eager queue of guests was already forming in front of two long tables laden with a selection of mouthwatering desserts. 'Go and help yourselves, I'm going to do some more circulating.'

'Do you want us to save you something?' asked her father.

'I'll take my chances,' she said with a smile. 'Besides, it looks like there's plenty to go round.'

Stepping into the marquee and breathing in the milky-sweet smell of crushed grass and spring flowers, Cassie found Venetia and Ronnie sitting at a table with Nina and Jakob. It was the first time that day that she'd had a real chance to chat with them.

'Here she is!' boomed Ronnie, getting to his feet and greeting her with a hug, 'the belle of the ball! Go on, give us a twirl in that lovely dress.'

'Ronnie, you always say the sweetest things,' she said, unable to resist spinning round for him and then performing a curtsey. 'Mind if I join you for a while?' she added. 'My feet are killing me in these wretched heels. I'll be so glad to take them off.'

'The cry of every bride there's ever been,' said Venetia, 'I know that's just how I felt.'

Ronnie laughed. 'Says the woman who's been married three times.'

'Says the man who's not far behind with his two marriages.'

Laughing, Cassie sat in the chair which Jakob had pulled out for her.

'Are you enjoying your big day?' asked Nina.

'I am,' Cassie said with a heartfelt sigh of pleasure. 'Everything's gone like clockwork.'

'And so it should with the amount of planning you put into it.'

'It wasn't just me; Ben and Emily played their part too. Talking of Emily,' she said, looking around them, 'have you seen her?'

'She was with Franco, the last I saw her,' said Jakob. 'They were walking along the riverbank.'

'Is it serious between them?' asked Ronnie.

'As serious as anything is at that young age,' said Cassie with a shrug. 'For now, it works well between them. They're having fun, working hard and sharing somewhere to live, but they're both planning quite different futures. Franco wants to go back to study in Italy in the autumn and Emily plans to study here.' All of which suited Cassie perfectly; she didn't want her daughter throwing away a second chance of getting her degree.

To her relief, Emily had bounced back relatively well from the Rosalyn Saga. Having revealed how devious and manipulative Rosalyn had been, it had somehow released in Emily the capacity to grieve, and in her own private way, the loss of her father whom she had only just begun to know. For several months after Emily had outed her as a narcissistic liar, Rosalyn hadn't posted anything online, but a few weeks ago, and Cassie hated herself for still checking, she noticed Rosalyn had posted a video of herself on TikTok. *'I'm back!'* she'd announced into the camera, *'and I just want to thank you all for your messages of love and concern, and for wondering where I was and if I was okay.'* She'd rattled on ad nauseum about taking time out from social media to look after her mental health and how suddenly the universe was teaching her so much and she was manifesting a new and better life for herself now that she had been led to live in Manchester. There was no mention of her son. It was me, me, me.

But today of all days was not the day Cassie wanted to waste any time thinking about Rosalyn. All that mattered was that she was out of their lives for good, especially Emily's.

'If anyone's interested,' she said brightly, 'puds are now being served.'

'So I see,' said Ronnie, observing guests drifting back into the marquee with dessert plates generously loaded.

'Why don't you boys go and join the queue and bring something back for us all?' suggested Cassie. She fancied some girl time with Nina and Venetia – her Hope Hall Besties, as she thought of them.

Ronnie and Jakob duly obliged and when they'd gone, Nina said, 'Ronnie was right when he said you're the belle of the ball, Cassie, you look absolutely beautiful.'

'Radiantly beautiful,' agreed Venetia.

'You both look lovely too,' Cassie said. 'And how sensible the two of you were to opt for trouser suits and trainers.'

Nina laughed. 'We discussed it together and decided comfort was what we wanted.'

'And we didn't want to outshine the bride, did we?'

'Oh, Venetia,' Cassie said, 'how disingenuous of you, you will always outshine us all. You're the epitome of elegance. I just hope I look half as gorgeous when I'm your age.'

At the mention of age, Cassie exchanged a furtive look with Nina. In a few weeks it would be Venetia's eightieth birthday and with Ronnie's help, Cassie and Nina had planned a surprise party for her. As far as they knew, Venetia didn't have a clue what they were up to.

In the days after the evening of the gallery exhibition in December, Venetia had been overwhelmed with melancholy, almost as bad as when Bon-Bon had died. They had all tried to comfort her, but it was Ronnie who had really been the one to help her the most. He was such a dear friend. When Venetia had told them how nasty Lucien had been to her in the restaurant, none of them could believe or understand why he had been so needlessly cruel. But then he'd given Venetia a painting – a stunning portrait of her as a child – and seeing how much pleasure it gave Venetia, they'd all found themselves feeling less angry with him.

Of course, Nina had had to deal with Lucien about the sale of his paintings, but at Venetia's express wish, Nina had kept matters strictly on a business footing, there were to be no questions, no interrogation of him. In contrast Ronnie had wanted to give the swine a damned good talking to, *mano a mano*. Instead, Venetia had given Ronnie a damned good talking to and made it clear that he was to keep well out of it, that everything was resolved, and that was the end of it.

'Now tell me, you two,' Cassie said, leaning forwards and planting her elbows firmly on the table, 'where is Ben taking me for our honeymoon?'

Nina smiled. 'Nice try, Cassie, but you won't get it out of either of us. Our lips are firmly sealed. We promised Ben.'

'And there was I thinking you were my besties,' Cassie said with a pout.

'We are, dear girl,' said Venetia, 'and that is why we are not going to spoil the surprise Ben has put so much thought into for you.'

'Can't you give me a clue, then? Just a small one. *Pleeease!*'

Laughing, both Nina and Venetia shook their heads.

The surprise, when it came, had everyone staring up at the sky in amazement and then they were all holding onto hats, fascinators and hair as the helicopter came closer and closer and then landed on the grass a safe distance from the marquee.

When the rotating blades had come to a stop and all was quiet and the pilot appeared, Ben turned to Cassie. 'Mrs Henshaw-Pearson, your carriage awaits.'

Nina had been so looking forward to this moment and seeing the expression on her friend's face. It didn't disappoint.

Open-mouthed, Cassie gaped at Ben. 'You're joking!' she cried.

'No. It's really happening.'

'But where are we going?'

'I'll tell you when we're up and away.'

'But . . . ' Cassie looked at everyone who had now gathered around them, including Nina and Jakob. 'But we can't just leave our guests.'

'Oh, yes you can,' said her father. 'It's all arranged.'

Cassie spun round to look at him. 'You knew about this, Dad? Why on earth didn't you tell me?'

'Because it was a secret!' chorused her mother and sister together.

A secret that had been miraculously kept by those who had been in on it, thought Nina. Whether Cassie had sensed that Nina knew something, she had tried repeatedly to get some grain of information out of her, but not a word did Nina say. She hadn't even told Jakob. Which had been the hardest part as she'd longed to tell him about it, but she'd been worried that Cassie might be sneaky and somehow get it out of Jakob or get him accidentally to drop some hint or other.

After hugging his parents goodbye and exchanging matey back-slapping and fist-bumping with friends, Ben rejoined Cassie. 'We'd better not keep the pilot waiting,' he said. Then: 'And right on time, here's our luggage.'

Cassie turned to see Emily and Franco coming towards them, each of them with a medium-sized case and a suit carrier.

'I helped Ben pack your outfits,' Emily told her mother, 'so blame me not him if I've got anything wrong.'

'Oh, Ems, I don't know what to say.'

Emily laughed. 'Well, that'll be a first then! Now go and enjoy yourselves. Text me when you've arrived. And stop worrying about where you're going, you're going to love it, I promise you.'

Cassie hugged Emily tightly and then after hugging and kissing the rest of her family, and then Nina and Venetia, and probably before she began hugging everyone else, Ben insisted it was time to go.

Once again hair and headwear were firmly held in place as

the blades began spinning with a rhythmic *thwap, thwap* and the helicopter slowly lifted off the ground. Within seconds, it was high above them, and they were all madly waving, even when it was just a distant speck in the cloudless late afternoon sky.

Awake and unable to sleep, Nina slid silently out of bed, not wanting to disturb Jakob. He always slept so well, like a man who didn't have a care in the world. There was something wonderfully uncomplicated about him, which she envied. She was, she supposed, one of those people who saw obstacles, whereas Jakob saw only opportunities. It had taken her a while to get used to the idea of him being in her bed, but now it felt right and when he wasn't there, she felt his absence keenly.

He now had space in the wardrobes in the guest room where he kept a selection of his clothes and in the bathroom, there was a shelf set aside for him and a hook on the back of the door where he hung the bathrobe she had given him for Christmas. His Christmas present to her had been a striking necklace made by a jeweller friend in Oslo. She had worn it today for Cassie and Ben's wedding and had received several compliments about it.

In the kitchen, and with only the under lights switched on, she made herself a cup of mint tea and took it over to the window seat. It was just after three o'clock and parting the curtains, she looked outside. In the soft moonlight the white marquee, which would be taken down tomorrow, was clearly visible. It had been a wonderful wedding and the helicopter whisking Ben and Cassie off to the Burgh Island Hotel for their honeymoon, the place where Ben had proposed to Cassie, was an inspired touch on his part. Emily had been right when she'd said she knew Cassie would love where Ben was taking her.

Still staring out of the window, Nina watched a fox trotting with singular intent across the grass. She soon lost sight of it in the shadows, and she thought of Hilary's adorable puppy, Teddy, and the way he trotted along at her feet when he was on his lead. He was the sweetest of little dogs and had given Hilary the most wonderful of gifts: something to look forward to each day, and something to love and cherish.

Keith had returned to The Maples and for now he and Hilary were trying to put the past behind them as well as forgive each other for all the mistakes they'd made, and the way they'd treated one another. Nina was glad. She wanted them to be happy, it would have been what Hugh wanted. He would have hated the thought of his death tearing them apart. She had said this very thing when she'd gone to see them a short while ago, for their traditional Monday evening get-together. They'd totally surprised her by suggesting the next time she visited she might like to bring Jakob with her. As astounded as she was by the suggestion, she was grateful that Hilary had at last truly accepted that Nina was entitled to enjoy life again, and in her own way.

Thinking of this, she thought of what had been in her mind and keeping her awake, long after Jakob had fallen asleep. For some weeks now the nebulous idea of a future with Jakob had been hovering on the periphery of her thoughts. Some days it felt almost within her grasp and other days it slipped from her. Today though, spending it with Jakob and having such fun together as a couple, it had seemed a very real and tangible possibility. Even so, the cautious side of her that always flagged up a potential obstacle was convinced it was too soon to discuss what she had in mind with Jakob. She needed more time to be sure it was the right thing to propose, that it would be something he would want, and something she wouldn't regret.

Her parents had hinted at it when they flew over to spend Christmas with her and Jakob – they had both taken to him straight away – and ever since, she had been pondering what they'd said. Having Jakob as a partner at Lavelle's would be great for the business but more importantly, she didn't want him working *for* her; she wanted him to work *with* her, that way their relationship would have a more balanced feel to it. But would he want to commit himself that much? The only way she would ever know the answer was if she was brave enough to risk asking him the question.

'Can't you sleep?'

She turned round from the window to see Jakob. With his hair all tousled from sleep, and wearing just a pair of boxers and a T-shirt, he came towards her.

'I was thinking,' she said, putting her empty mug down and rising from the window seat.

'Of anything in particular?'

'The future.'

He took hold of her hands and held them firmly. 'That sounds important.'

'Yes,' she said softly. 'It is.'

'In a good way?'

She smiled. 'I hope so.'

'In that case,' he said, leaning into her and grazing his lips against her cheek, 'come back to bed and tell me all about it.'

The morning after the wedding, Venetia returned to Farleigh Fen village church. There hadn't been time yesterday to do what she'd wanted to do, but today she had plenty of time and had brought some flowers. Cassie had said guests were to help themselves to the table decorations, and one of those jam jars of pretty spring flowers now adorned Lady Constance's grave.

The grave had one of the largest tombstones in the churchyard, as befitted Lady Constance's life, and Venetia had located it without too much difficulty. She had only been here once before, on the day of Lady Constance's funeral, yet her memory had served her well. She felt guilty that she had never bothered to visit before now, and it didn't look like anybody else had cared for the grave in many a long year. It was possible there was no one left of the woman's family who would care enough to tend it. There was no sign of Lady Constance's husband having been buried nearby, but then Venetia had no idea what had happened to him once the children's home had closed.

She thought of all the lives connected to Hope Hall, before, during and after its time as a children's home, and she felt privileged to have been a part of its history. Glad too that she had decided on a whim to make it her home again.

Following Bon-Bon's death she had seriously considered moving away, believing it to be a mistake to have come back. But during Christmas and New Year, which she had spent mostly with Ronnie, she had shaken off any regrets about living here.

As for Lucien, and his offensive comments about Lady Constance and what she had achieved at Hope Hall, Venetia had disregarded them. He had his own reasons for saying what he had, but she knew in her heart that he was wrong: Lady Constance had been a force for good.

There had been no further word from Lucien and Venetia had stuck to his wish that he didn't want any further contact between them. It was enough for her to know that he still existed in the world and, of course, there was the beautiful gift he'd given her. The portrait of her meant more than any word from him ever could. Every time she looked at it, it brought back so many happy memories and filled her with pleasure.

Hope Hall had given her so very much as a child, a home and a family, and now as she approached her eightieth birthday, it had given her a home and a wonderful new family all over again. A family that loved and cared for her, just as she loved and cared for them. She was indeed lucky.

Before turning to go, and while listening to the cheerful song of a blackbird, she looked one more time at the Henry Wadswoth Longfellow inscription on Lady Constance's headstone.

> Look not mournfully into the past.
> It comes not back again.
> Wisely improve the present.
> It is thine.
> Go forth to meet the shadowy future, without fear . . .

And that, she thought, as she drove home to Hope Hall to have lunch with Ronnie and Nina and Jakob, was the best advice anyone could be given in life.

Acknowledgements

Amazingly this is my twenty-seventh novel and ever since my first novel was published back in 1996, my super-star agent Jonathan Lloyd has been with me every step of the way. Thank you doesn't come close!

If my memory serves me right, this is my sixteenth novel with my brilliant editor, Kate Mills. Huge thanks to you, Kate, for always keeping me on the straight and narrow! Thanks also to Lisa Milton and the excellent team at HQ – team work makes the dream work every time.

Lastly, a special thank you to a certain Mr Fix it called Trevor who has helped me create what I hope will be my own forever home. For the record, and to all my friends who doubt me, I'm definitely not moving again, this is it!

P.S. I should point out that while I've featured Cambridge in *The Forever Home*, St Anne's Court doesn't actually exist, just in case anyone goes looking for it.

ONE PLACE. MANY STORIES

Bold, innovative and
empowering publishing.

FOLLOW US ON:

@HQStories

What's MultiColoured?

What colours are the paints?

Which button is the odd one out?

PAINTS

RAINBOW

BUTTERFLY

BUTTONS

What's Black?

Can you get through the the spiderweb maze?

BATS

SPIDER

How many legs does a spider have?

HAT

What colours are the bats' bellies?

CAT

CAULDRON

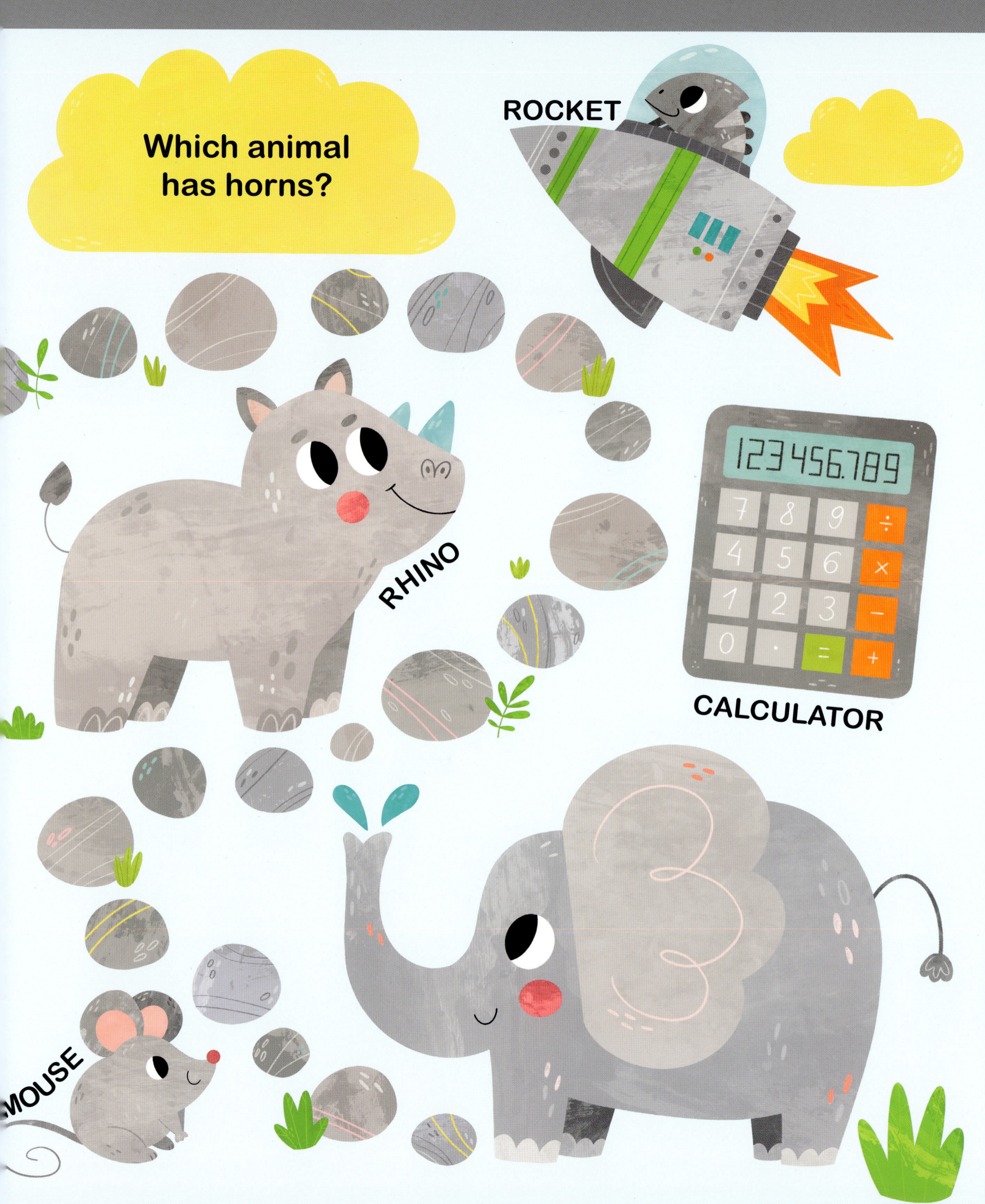

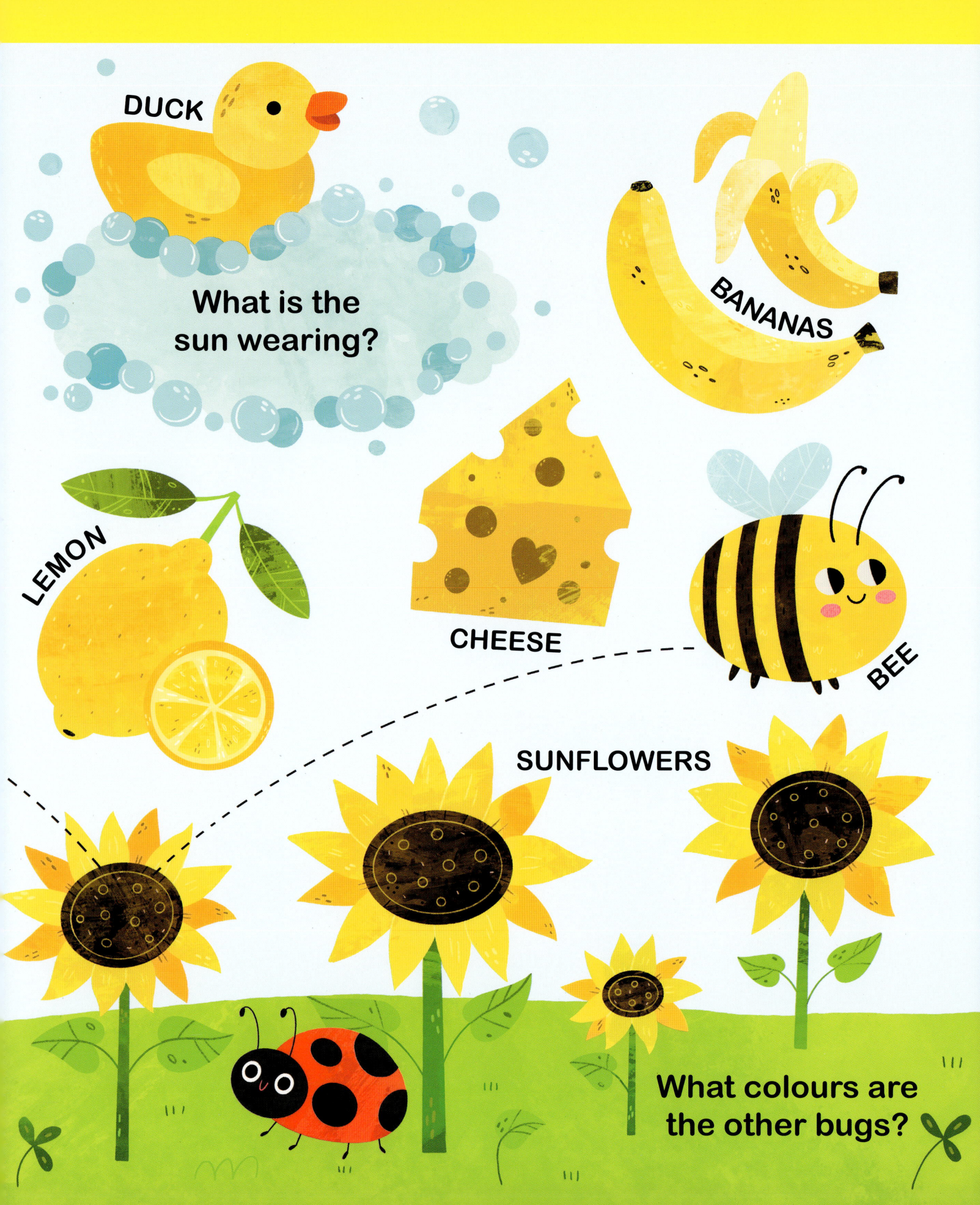

What's Orange?

ORANGE

BALLOON

How many legs does an octopus have?

PUMPKIN

OCTOPUS

FOX

FIRE